MW00762632

Kontonqua

Cavern of the Lost

ENJOY THE ADVENTURE!

R. Zacun

For Linda, the love of my life...

and for my parents, who let me daydream

A

Publication

Cover illustration by Ron Zalme

Kontonqua

Cavern of the Lost

By Ron Zalme

A

Publication

Newton, NJ 07860

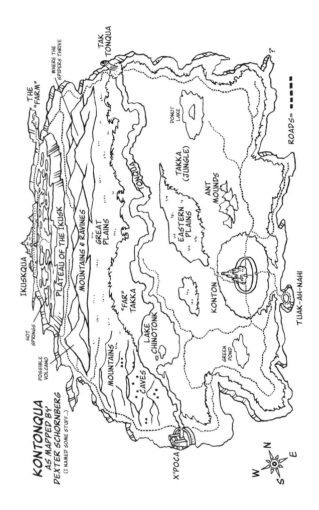

KONTONQUA
AS MAPPED BY
DEXTER SCHORNBERG
(I NAMED SOME STUFF...)

THE "FARM"

WHERE THE SPIDERS THRIVE

TAK TONQUA

IKUSKQUA

HOT SPRINGS

PLATEAU OF THE IKUSK

POSSIBLE VOLCANO

MOUNTAINS & RAVINES

GREAT PLAINS

TONQUA

DONUT LAKE

TAKKA (JUNGLE)

"FAR" TAKKA

EASTERN PLAINS

ANT MOUNDS

MOUNTAINS

LAKE CHINOTONK

KONTON

CAVES

GREEN POND

X'POCA

TUAK-AH-NAHI

ROADS = ▪▪▪▪

N
W   E
S

4

Contents

Prologue

Steven hadn't thought it was possible. To actually be *bored* in the Bahamas! But he sort of felt that way. Two months ago he couldn't wait for school to be over so he could accept his grandparent's invitation to join them for the summer. And for the first month or so, he just couldn't get enough of the beaches and the seemingly endless activities. But now, with still two weeks to go before returning stateside, he'd had just about as much sun and surf as any reasonable teenager could stand. And he was feeling just a little bit *lonely* too.

His grandparents had bought a little bungalow on the beach with their retirement savings, but they still needed to work part-time at a hotel down the beach, so they weren't always around. On top of that, there really weren't any kids his own age to hang around with. Most of the locals seemed to be working the resorts all the time... and the tourists were always leaving just as you got to know them. And though he hated to admit it, Steven was getting just a bit tired of the perpetually sunny clime. It was summer, and that meant it was continually unbearably *hot.* The big tourist season was in winter, when folks were escaping the frosty north to enjoy a few weeks in the sun. But at this time of year, it got pretty brutal in the Caribbean, and Steven was the color of a coconut to prove it. Yeah... perhaps it was time to go home... back to Jersey.

A big Gull landed with a squawk not ten feet away and Steven snapped out of his somber mood to look up at the little cove of turquoise water that gently lapped at the glowingly white sand of the isolated lagoon. The edges of the cove were densely covered with palms that partially hid the half-dozen cottages that surrounded this private paradise. A thrumming sound brought his attention out to sea where a motorboat came surging against the waves from around the promontory. A girl in a red bikini was water-skiing behind it and obviously having a terrific time, crisscrossing the wake of the boat just beyond the reef. He watched them as they crossed the horizon and disappeared around the opposite finger of land.

"What, am I *crazy?*" Steven thought aloud, "What a whiner! This place has got to be Heaven on Earth. And in three weeks I'm going to be sitting in class just kicking myself for not taking advantage of it!"

With that, Steven leaped up from his shady spot under a palm, (which sent the startled Gull catapulting into the air...), grabbed his snorkeling gear and ran headlong towards the water. The puffs of white sand his feet kicked up changed to sprays of water as he splashed into the rippling waves. When the water reached the bottom of his trunks and it became difficult to wade through, he stopped to put on his fins. They were much easier to put on when they were wet. Next, he straightened out the strap of the mask and rinsed the glass in the water while working up some saliva in his mouth. He poured out the remaining water and spit into the mask. It always made him chuckle to think how kinda gross this little routine was, but it kept the glass from fogging up. One of the boat skippers had showed him this particular trick and it nearly always worked. He spread the saliva around to a thin film and fitted the mask over his eyes and nose. He started moving forward again as he adjusted the snorkel under the strap at his temple, moving awkwardly with a duck's waddle because of the ungainly fins. When the water reached his waist he popped the rubber mouthpiece of the snorkel between his lips and lunged forward into the cool clear waves.

Liberated by buoyancy, Steven moved gracefully now, his large fins propelling him quickly and smoothly along the surface of the crystalline water. Arms at his side, his strong legs pumped in languidly rhythmic strokes as he breathed calmly through the flexible black tube which poked above the waves. As he swam into deeper water, he moved his head slowly from side to side and scanned the wonderland that lay beneath him. Scores of fish in outrageously bright colors surrounded the outcroppings of coral that dotted the bottom of the cove. Huge boulder-sized brain corals sprouted pinkish wisps from slender-fluted cylinders, and withdrew them with a sudden spasm if touched by a fish or Steven's outstretched hand. Great spreading fern-corals fanned out their branches like moose antlers, and plantlife of all varieties grew wherever a perch for their roots could be found.

Steven decided to explore the reef that extended near the promontory where he'd first seen the motorboat. It wasn't that far out and he knew he'd be relatively safe within the confines of the natural reef barrier. The reefs kept the water calm and kept out the boats, (not to mention the possibility of predatory fish... like *sharks!*). He hadn't explored this part of the reef yet and was hoping he'd find some "treasure", like last week when he'd found a perfectly good rod and reel, probably lost by some tourist too pressured to have a "fun-filled vacation" and couldn't take time out to search for it.

Steven got out to the reef and started his diving routine. He took in a lungful of air and bent his body downwards. With a kick and a splash of

9

his fins, he quickly descended the thirty or so feet to the bottom. Several multicolored fish innocently hovered in front of his mask and Steven not only completely forgot his previous feelings of boredom, but he quite nearly burst out laughing to see such curious fish, eye-balling this mysterious intruder. He swam along the bottom over the clumps of coral until his lungs ached and then sped back to the surface. He tilted his head back the moment he broke through and cleared the snorkel with a sudden exhale. He floated awhile on the surface, getting his breath back while surveying a new spot to dive to. This routine was generally repeated all afternoon, for he loved the water and there wasn't much better diving conditions than this to be had in all the world. But such wasn't to be the case today, for his routine was soon interrupted when he saw something glistening green just beyond a large coral outcropping. "Wow, treasure already," he thought, as he took another deep breath and dove once again.

He swam directly to the shiny object that was more than half-hidden under a branch of coral. As he got closer, he could see that it was fairly large and mostly covered with silt and algae. In places, coral was already beginning to sprout in an attempt to make the object forever a part of the reef. If he hadn't noticed the few shiny spots that were still poking through, it soon would have been lost to the world forever. He grabbed a branch of the coral that was partially covering it, to hold himself steady in the water, while he used his other hand to wipe away some of the muck that was spread all over its surface. Clouds of silt billowed into the water from his brushing, but not enough to obscure his view of this strange find. The "treasure" seemed to be a large jug. It was about as big as a beach ball, with handles at the sides and a wide mouth, more than a foot across, at the top. It did indeed shine in spots with a greenish shimmer like an old-fashioned Coke bottle, but it didn't seem to be made of glass. There were thick coarse ropes of some sort entwined around it and they were looped through the handles. He looked underneath the jug to see what they might possibly be attached to and saw a cluster of logs lashed together like a raft. Steven grabbed the jug by the encircling ropes and tugged at it. More silt billowed into the surrounding water but the jug didn't move. Steven was running out of breath, so he tried once more, this time shaking it violently to try and free it. Again, it didn't budge. It was either too heavy or lodged too firmly in the reef. He swam back up to the surface to contemplate his next move.

After he broke the surface and got his much needed air, Steven looked back towards his grandparent's cabin and thought about maybe swimming back to get some tools. How could he drag heavy tools back out to this spot, he thought. And to do what? Dig it out? Steven knew it was disastrous to coral to disturb it in any way. After all, it was alive and it took years to build a reef such as this one. Maybe he could just use a knife or...

"Wait a minute," he mumbled through the mouthpiece, "A knife! I can just cut through the ropes..." And then he had another idea that just might save him a trip.

Steven breathed deeply several times to give himself some extra time on the bottom and dove once again. He swam to the general area where the jug was and began to scan the sand and soon found what he was looking for... a wedge of coral that had fallen off the reef. The coral was often quite sharp and he'd scratched himself on it several times this summer. He swam back over to the jug and began sawing at the ropes with the wedge of coral. Yes. He could see that it *was* working. It might take him a few trips up and down for air, but he could see that he wouldn't need to swim all the way back to the house for a knife.

After the third trip down to work at the ropes, or whatever they were for they seemed to unravel rather than cut, Steven finally managed to free the jug. He grabbed it by the side-handles and gave it another tug. This time it pulled free of the crusty coral and began to float on its own, making its way slowly to the surface. This surprised Steven, for he'd thought he was going to have to somehow carry the thing up himself. The fact that it floated meant there was still air trapped inside. Perhaps there was something of interest contained within that hadn't yet been ruined by seawater. It floated very slowly upwards and Steven kept pace with it for a while until forced to speed ahead to get some air. The large jug bobbed to the surface beside him just moments later and Steven grabbed it by the handles. He held it out at arms length in front of him, like a paddleboard, as the propelling strokes of his fins pushed him slowly shoreward.

As Steven reached the beach, he stood in the shallow surf and lifted the mask away from his eyes and pushed it up on his head. He watched the large jug rocking in the gentle waves.

"Jeez," he murmured, as he spat out the snorkel tube, "What the heck *is* this thing?"

He reached down and removed his fins one at a time and threw them on the beach, near where he'd been sitting an hour before. He bent and once again grabbed the jug by its handles and hefted it. It was pretty heavy, maybe forty pounds, but Steven was in pretty good shape and had no problem toting it up the beach and depositing it in the shady spot by the palm. This was his favorite spot to relax in, and Steven could take his time here to fully examine his newfound treasure.

Steven squatted by the jug and began to rub some of the crust away from its surface. The large jug was an iridescent green all over with no apparent designs or markings. He figured a label would've washed off after being submerged, but he knew that bottle manufacturers usually stamped their names on the bottom, so he turned it over to have a look. Something shifted inside as he tilted it over and his excitement rose as he realized that there was indeed something contained within the vessel.

"Hmphh," he said as he voiced his thoughts, "There's not a mark of any kind on the bottom. No names, dates, countries... nuthin'."

He righted the jug and examined the top. It had a very short neck and the wide mouth seemed to be stoppered with a plug of wood that was sealed shut with a very waxy substance. He couldn't wait to open it!

Driven by uncontrollable curiosity, Steven grabbed at the stopper and twisted with all his might... no luck. The "cork" was wedged in tight. He ran to the bungalow and came out moments later with a sturdy kitchen knife, some rags, and a flashlight. He sat down with his back against the palm tree, wrapped his legs around the jug to steady it, and began working at the wax seal with the knife. All told, it took about 15 minutes to chip away the wax that held the plug firm. He was just about to wedge the knife into the seam to pry loose the wooden stopper itself when a sudden horrific thought occurred to him...

"What if there's something horrible inside?" he wondered. "What if it's smelly, or like a dangerous chemical? What if it's something alive…? Or worse… what if it's dead?!"

Steven rose to his feet and looked around. The cove was quiet and no one would be coming home for another couple of hours. He shook off his doubts and said, "This is ridiculous! This thing's been down there for a while. There can't be anything in there I can't handle. If it looks questionable, I'll just wait for Grandpa."

So, Steven picked up the kitchen knife once more and, standing *over* the jug this time, ready to back away if need be, inserted it into the circular seam. He rocked the knife back and forth to work it deeper into the groove… suddenly there was a hissing sound that startled him and he jumped back!

"Idiot," he thought, "That's just air escaping from the inside..."

Holding the wooden plug in one hand and the knife in the other, Steven pried the plug loose with an audible "pop", and jumped back once more just in case. The jug just sat there. He examined the stopper in his hand and even sniffed at it. There was nothing special about it, so he tossed it onto the sand by his other stuff. Slowly, he approached the jug. He thought he would have to use the flashlight to peer into the mouth of the jug, but as he got closer, he could see that it was already quite bright inside. He walked cautiously over to it and hovered over the opening, looking straight down into the strange vessel. Although he hadn't been able to look through the walls of the jug earlier, they seemed to allow the light to filter through without difficulty. In the center of the jug, bathed in the greenish glow of the diffused Caribbean sun, was… a book?

Steven squatted before the jug once again and gingerly reached inside for the strange contents. The air within the jug smelled a bit musty and he didn't want to keep his nose over the opening too long. He got his hand around the object within and carefully withdrew it from its prison. It was pretty big. About a foot-and-half tall, a foot wide, and maybe four inches thick, which accounted for its hefty weight. Steven held the book before him with both hands. It seemed to be homemade. It was tied all around with a kind of vine-rope; similar to the type of rope he had earlier sawed through to separate the jug from the sunken raft. The covers were thick and rigid, with holes punched through them on the binding side where more vine-rope had been used to bind the covers and pages together. The covers were of a strange material. Glossy black and rough textured with tiny bumps. The pages themselves were somewhat ragged at the edges and brownish in color. They appeared to be kind of leathery but thin.

Steven glanced into the jug again to make certain that it was empty, and indeed, the book seemed to have been its only cargo. He sat back against the palm tree with the crudely fashioned book in his lap and no longer noticed the beach, ocean, or passing sea gulls. This strange book now firmly held his attention and he slowly reached for the knot of cord that tied the book shut. It took him a short bit of time, for the rope was very stiff and somewhat brittle with age, but he got the knot undone and carefully unwound the coils of twine. Now free to open the book, Steven could hardly contain his excitement. He sat a bit more upright and took a deep breath, the better to delve into the mystery of its pages. He hunched over the large tome and delicately lifted the front cover. What he saw on the following page sent a chill up his back despite the warm Bahamian air that surrounded him. The book was handwritten in *English!* And the first page was dated at the top... May 16th? 1954. "1954! That was almost ten years ago!" Steven spoke aloud in surprise.

Neatly printed in the middle of the page was:

> *To Whoever May Receive*
> *This Book: The following is a true*
> *account of the accident, stranding,*
> *and subsequent adventures that*
> *befell us in a land deep beneath*
> *the surface of the earth. We are*
> *safe now, and mostly happy, but*
> *we wish not to be forgotten...and if*
> *possible, found! Please save us ...*

Below this introduction were the signatures of five people: Joshua (Buffalo) Brewster, Simon Tilton, Maxine Tilton, Dexter Schornberg, and Kwa-I-Anya. Beneath the names there was, what looked to be, the paw print of... a *dog?*

Steven gently grasped the first page and turned it...

My name is Dexter Schornberg, but I'm known to everyone as just plain "Dex". It has been over three years since we were first marooned and there has been no evidence of any attempt at a rescue.

Therefore, I have decided to record the events of our mishap, the strange adventures we have shared, and the horrific ordeals that the four of us, (and a dog), have endured. I have compiled the details of our incredible journey into the form of this narrative, (which you now hold before you), because it is not just a story about me. It is the combined tales of four Americans (and a dog!) and a fierce, but noble, lost tribe of Indians. All of us seemingly doomed to spend eternity in an undiscovered hostile jungle deep within the bowels of Mother Earth. And, of course, there are the insects... but first let me begin the tale...

Chapter 1
"Skipping on Ice"

December 1951 was going to be unforgettable. That had already been agreed to by all. Dexter Schornberg sat by the window next to a bunch of lumpy duffel bags and looked out over the wing of the C-47 cargo plane, that is… as much of it as he could possibly see, for the snow outside whipped quickly past the aircraft and obscured much of his view with milky whiteness. Ahead of him, bundled in with more supplies, sat Simon and Maxine (Max) Tilton. They were brother and sister and Dexter's best friends. They were also the reason he was here at all.

Simon and Max were also Dexter's neighbors, and all three had grown up together, attending the same schools, playing together, and generally spending as much time together as humanly possible. They were each a year apart, with Simon being the oldest at sixteen, and Dexter the youngest. Simon was a well-built athletic type that seemed to excel in every sport he ever attempted. He was a serious, if somewhat average, student with a high metabolism and a quick wit. Simon and Max were both blonde and blue-eyed and could easily have been mistaken for twins, but Max was obviously the prettier of the two!

Maxine had been dubbed "Max" by her father, probably because she'd been rather a tomboy when she was younger. But she had needed to be, for she'd competed with the boys since being a toddler. Now, she was considered to be one of the cutest girls in school and probably one of the most popular, though she didn't have to work at it, she was just extremely likable. She worked hard in all she did; her grades were above average, and she participated in most school activities... especially sports. Like her brother, she was athletically inclined, though not *quite* as gifted, having a tendency to be a bit clumsy. She offset any shortfalls though with her humor and perseverance. Although she was a year younger than Simon, she was a bit taller, which was accentuated by the tussled ponytail that she always wore to keep her hair out of her eyes whenever she was active... which was almost always.

Their father was a nuclear scientist that did research for the government. He was often away for several months at a time. Being a widower, he would hire a governess to come and stay at their house to watch over Simon and Max until he returned. Right now, he was stationed at an Arctic camp, and that was why the three of them were huddled together, amongst supplies and provisions, in the chilly passenger compartment of a very used WWII C-47.

The C-47 Skytrain was the military version of the famous Douglas DC-3 propeller-driven passenger plane of the 30's and 40's. This one had probably seen its fair share of action somewhere in wartorn Europe and had probably been bought after the war as surplus. Now it was just a poorly refurbished cargo plane with dim lighting and very few comforts. There were a dozen seats in the forward cabin and only three were in use by the kids. Everything else was piled high with their gear or provisions for the camp. A sturdy bulkhead had been installed behind them to create a place to hold the more serious and dangerous supplies and the kids weren't allowed back there. But the kids didn't really mind their discomforts at all... this was the adventure of a lifetime!

Professor Tilton had, a week earlier, radioed an invitation to his children to join him for the Christmas holiday. There was a transport bringing up supplies and they could be on it. Simon and Max had immediately asked if Dexter could join them as well, and after some hesitation, their Dad had agreed. He knew they were practically inseparable.

It had taken quite a bit more convincing though, to get Dexter's parents to allow it. After all, being Jewish, they didn't even celebrate Christmas! But they were often guilty of being over-protective parents, and they knew it - - Dexter was their only child. On the other hand, they also felt that Dexter had earned the vacation and the chance for adventure. He was a straight "A" student with high honors and always had been. From the outside, Dexter looked like quite a normal fourteen-year-old with dark tussled hair and glasses, though a bit short for his age. On the inside, Dexter had a mind that always seemed to think three steps ahead. His curiosity was unquenchable. He loved reading and spent most of his spare time exploring the stacks at the local library. Science was one of his keen interests and although Professor Tilton was Max and Simon's father, in many ways he was Dexter's hero and surrogate father too.

The plane bumped violently and the three friends shared a worried glance, then laughed a bit to ease the tension. The ride had initially gone well even though they felt like baggage in the cramped makeshift compartment. But the flight was getting more and more turbulent the farther north they flew. Dexter figured they were probably somewhere over the frozen tundra of northern Canada. The plane jolted again in the buffeting winds and the three let loose a "Whoa..." almost simultaneously.

A dog, (the pilot had said his name was "Jeep"), walked into the cabin from the curtained cockpit ahead and looked at them as if to check that they were all right.

"Hey, boy..." said Dexter. He'd always wanted a dog, and always made every effort to make friends with every dog he'd ever met. Jeep was a rust-colored Airedale with a big heart and a sloppy tongue! He was muscular and fast, Dex had seen him run earlier that day. Always starved for affection, the wooly-haired canine came right over to Dex to claim a scritch on the head. Max joined in and said, "You're a friendly one, aren't you?"

Suddenly they heard the pilot on his radio speaking loudly but calmly. They couldn't make out everything he was saying, but they could hear the urgency in his voice and distinctly heard "Mayday!" The universal distress call!

The plane bumped some more and the three pressed their faces to the tiny windows. They could see ice building up on the props and wings!

"Ice..." exclaimed Simon, "Is that why we're in trouble?"

Dexter ran to the other side of the plane and peered out that window. "Uh, no..." he said, "I think it's more serious than that."

The other two joined him at the portal and saw black smoke billowing from the engine. And the propeller didn't seem to be spinning on its own!

They heard some muffled swearing and then a booming voice yelled from the cockpit as the pilot commanded, "We're havin' trouble guys and I'm gonna hafta put 'er down somewhere. I want you kids to stay in your seats no matter what. Put the belts on tight and pack a bunch o' them duffel bags around yourselves!"

They didn't hesitate to follow the pilot's orders...

Up front, "Buffalo", the burly pilot, was struggling with the controls. As he brought the wounded plane lower on just one engine, he decided to give the radio one more go.

"Mayday! Mayday!" he repeated, and paused... No reply. He decided to radio their position one last time, repeated "Mayday!" a few more times, and then gave up on the radio to concentrate on flying the plane.

"Buffalo" Brewster was a huge Samson of a man. Large and rugged, he looked like a Viking or a

Mountain Man. He stood 6'3" and easily weighed in at 240lbs, and it was all muscle. He sported a full beard that was just as wiry as the coat on Jeep's back and just about the same color, too. His dark eyes became black as coal when he was serious or angry, and the foreboding menace in them had caused many a tough-guy to back down and seek shelter. Those that didn't, soon wished they had. However, the kids had noticed a twinkle in those same eyes that had revealed a deeply hidden humor and gentleness. Despite his gruffness, they had taken an instant liking to him.

Buffalo fought the controls to bring the limping bird down to where he could get a better view of exactly where they were. And that wasn't easy, what with the swirling snow and the ice building up on the wings. The flight yoke shook violently in his grasp and it was only due to his great strength that he was able to hold the plane steady at all. He knew they were miles from civilization and their only hope lay in finding a smooth enough spot to attempt an emergency landing and, if they didn't all get killed in the process, wait for a rescue team. He watched the altimeter closely as he circled and descended. In the whiteness, he couldn't afford to drop so rapidly that he would meet the ground before he could see it! He was just starting to worry that maybe the ground wasn't where it was supposed to be when he saw the gray shadows of ice cliffs below him. Buffalo had been over this terrain before, so he knew a little of what to expect. This particular area of Canada consisted of somewhat flat icy plains dotted with craggy ice cliffs. He wanted to try landing on the former and avoiding the latter! He brought the plane a bit lower and wheeled around for another pass to look for a suitable spot to set it down.

Buffalo was an expert pilot. He had been a fighter pilot in WWII from the opening days of the war. The fact that he had survived the *entire* war attested to his considerable flying skills and ferociousness in combat. His real name was Joshua Brewster, but because the first fighter plane he'd been assigned to was the *Brewster Buffalo*, a stubborn beast of a plane to fly, his fellow pilots had transferred the plane's name to him. What with his great size and slight resemblance to Buffalo Bill Cody... *and* his tendency for being a stubborn beast himself, the nickname just stuck.

As Buffalo circled back, he could now vaguely see that he was over a flat snowy plain that stretched for several hundred yards before ending in a vertical cliff-face of ice. He looked to either side and saw that the walls of these cliffs extended in a sort of horseshoe shape around them. He fought to bring the craft a little higher so as not to slam into the rapidly nearing cliff and hissed through his teeth as the plane just cleared the edge of the plateau. He didn't like the looks of this ice canyon and had just decided to look a bit further when a second engine lamp on the instrument panel began to blink. He looked out at the port engine to see that it too was smoking. He no longer had a choice, and didn't know how much longer he'd continue to have power, so he banked the plane sharply and headed back for a final approach. He hoped it wouldn't be *too* final.

As Buffalo lined up the plane with the ice field, he yelled back to the kids to brace for impact and began the descent. He didn't put down the landing gear because he felt that a belly landing would actually be safer. The wheels could suddenly dig into the snow and snap... or worse, flip the plane! This way, the plane would have less inclination to start "cartwheeling" and might just stop quick enough to avoid the looming wall of ice at the end of the valley. He lowered the flaps and kept the nose of the struggling plane up higher than he would've on a normal landing, and held it there as long as he could. His last official act of piloting was to cut the throttles and switch off the engines just before impact. After that, it was just a matter of hanging on tight and letting Lady Luck guide their fate.

For a heartbeat, the plane seemed to float noiselessly. Then suddenly, the tail bit into the ground with a sickening rending sound of tortured metal. The plane lurched violently as its speed was drastically reduced and then the belly of the plane slammed down into the ice field, sending all of its contents, cargo and kids, bouncing into the air. The shattered plane skidded and bumped along uncontrollably, careening wildly through the drifted snow. Buffalo saw the huge wall of ice looming ahead and prayed that the C-47 would be dragged to a halt before impacting head-on. His gaze was fixed on the shear face of the approaching cliff until the spraying snow and ice clotted the windshield, and his view was cut off, leaving him sightless in the darkened cockpit.

After what seemed an eternity of bumping along, the hulking transport finally came to a shuddering halt with a last vibrating groan. All was suddenly eerily quiet and Buffalo let out a sigh of relief that he wasn't splattered on the face of the wall of ice. He undid his belts and made his way to the cockpit door and pushed the curtain to the side. Looking into the next compartment, all he saw was jumbled bags and boxes! Then Jeep barked and leaped up from the back of the cabin and gingerly began making his way over the top of the mess that was now starting to undulate and heave as three groaning kids pushed aside the tumbled baggage that had buried them.

"You kids okay?" he asked.

"Y-yeah. I guess so," they all mumbled in confusion.

"Well, you better find your gear and put on your parkas. Without power, we ain't got heat. An' without heat, you're not gonna stay cozy in here for long. I'm gonna step outside an' see what this ol' bird's gotten herself into..." And with that, he reached into a side closet, pulled out a bag and parka of his own, and approached the side hatch. The jarring of the plane had misaligned the door frame and Buffalo had to put his shoulder to the door to force it open, but it didn't resist for long... not with *his* strength! It buckled with a squeal and suddenly he was met with a blast of crisp chill air and snowflakes. Buffalo stood in the doorway for a brief moment to look around and listen. To his left was the ravaged wing of the plane, black tendrils of smoke still curling up from the mangled engine... rising slowly to mix with the gently falling snow. How much more blizzard-like it had seemed when the plane was traveling at speed! The blades of the propeller were bent back around the engine cowling and hot metal ticked loudly as it was forced to rapidly cool. Beyond the wing, he could see the left wall of the canyon, about a hundred yards distant. To his right, was an enormous sheer wall of ice.

Buffalo jumped down the couple of feet to the ground and looked toward the nose of the plane. He walked slowly forward, his boots crunching in the crisp fresh snow and his breath a frosty vapor before him. He reached the tip of the plane and let out a whistle. There was his snow-covered cockpit... and there was the towering wall of glacial ice... just inches from the rounded nose of the plane! He looked up and the ice cliff rose from view to be lost in the grayness of the swirling snow. He chuckled at his good fortune and shook his head as he turned back to make a walk-around inspection of the wrecked aircraft.

He stepped right up onto the ground-level wing when he got to it, and made his way across it to the rear section. He was just about to step off the other side when he noticed the spreading green ooze that was seeping out from underneath the twisted fuselage. The plane had been carrying liquid and powdered chemicals in its aft cargo compartment for delivery to the arctic station to be used in Professor Tilton's experiments. The severe buffeting the old plane had endured in its landing had rattled the cargo bay and ruptured the fuel tanks. The chemicals were now mixing with each other... *and* the spilled aviation fuel! Buffalo watched the evil-looking mixture begin to boil and fizz and "pop" as it spread into the newly fallen snow. He didn't like the looks of this at all!

He turned back to head for the door and saw Simon hopping down from the open hatchway.

"Everybody out!" he yelled, startling Simon, who twisted his head quickly to gape open-mouthed at the vision of this bellowing bearded giant scrambling across the crumpled wing...

"Grab yer gear and run!" he shouted. He almost bowled Simon over as he leapt back up through the door of the stricken craft. Like a wild berserker, Buffalo began tossing kids and baggage through the open doorway. Even Jeep was rudely flung into the snow. He then scrambled back into the cockpit and stuffed as much survival gear as he could manage into his flight bag. Maps, matches, an array of snacks, flashlight... anything he thought might help.

Outside, the kids were picking themselves up and gathering their gear together and anything else they could carry. Jeep was running in circles in the snow, barking and wagging the little stump that passed for his tail. He was obviously very happy to be both back on the ground *and* in new fallen snow. The huge figure of Buffalo suddenly appeared and loomed in the plane's doorway.

"What's the matter?" asked Dex.

"What's wrong?" chimed Max.

"Don't you kids listen? I said RUN!" bellowed the giant.

Buffalo leapt from the door of the plane and everyone began to jog as best they could through the slippery foot-deep snow, doing their level best to put some distance between themselves and the twisted hulk of wreckage. Jeep enthusiastically led the way, snow puffs spraying to all sides with each pounce of his leaping gait. Huffing and panting, the kids shouldered their loads and plodded along, clueless as to why they'd had to leave the relative safety of the plane's cabin.

Dex decided to try again. "Why are we running... and from what?" he panted between breaths.

"Dunno exactly," Buffalo replied. "Some o' those chemicals and things in the back musta broke up in the landing. They're leakin' outta the bottom of the plane and mixin' with gas from the fuel tanks. It looked real bad and smelled even worse. I don't know if or what it'll do, I just know I don't wanna be near it when it does!"

Dexter looked back over his shoulder and indeed, there were now volumes of thick greenish smoke issuing from the ruptured seals around the rear cargo doors. Buffalo slowed and then stopped and everyone caught a much-needed breath, their throats achy from the frosty crispness of the air.

"Where are we going?" asked Max. "We won't last long out here in the open. Especially after nightfall."

"Well," said Buffalo offhandedly, as he scanned the walls of the cliffs before him, "I'm hopin' we won't hafta be out here too long. I radioed our position before we went down. And if that didn't get through, I'm sure we'll be missed soon. We were due to land in about two hours. They've got another plane up there and they're sure to backtrack in the morning. We just gotta find ourselves a cozy nest for the night." He paused and added, "...And I think it's right up there."

Everyone gazed along Buffalo's pointing finger and noticed a dark crevice in the face of the glacial wall in front of them. This cliff was not quite as sheer as the one where the cargo plane had stopped and the open crack, or cave, that Buffalo was pointing to was perched on an accessible ledge about a quarter of the way up the cliff facade.

"Well, let's go," chirped Simon, always ready for adventure and not the least winded by his load.

"Ugh... you would," groaned Dex, raising his pack once again to his shoulder and wiping snow from his fogged glasses.

It didn't take long for the little band to cover the hundred yards or so to the bottom of the canyon wall. Once there, they followed single file as Buffalo picked his way upward from ledge to ledge, blazing a path to their intended shelter. They slowly climbed closer and had gotten directly beneath the cave entrance ledge when Buffalo motioned them to halt. This last ledge was about four feet over their heads and there didn't seem to be a good handhold in the icy wall.

"I'll climb up first," said Buffalo, "and then haul each of you up."

Dexter spoke up suddenly. "I just thought about something," he said nervously. "What about polar bears? Don't they live in caves?"

This statement brought a quick gasp from both Simon and Max.

"I thought about that, too" replied Buffalo. "But first off, with all the noise we've been makin', I reckon a bear would be real interested to check us out first... and I ain't seen one yet. And second, and even more trustworthy, is ol' Jeep. He's got a good nose. If there were bears around, he'd let me know!"

With that, Buffalo threw his pack up onto the ledge and leapt up for a handhold. As easily as doing a chin-up, Buffalo raised himself to the edge and pulled himself onto the doorstep of their new home. He stood and briefly scanned the interior of the ice cave. "It'll do..." he murmured. He turned and gazed out over the valley floor, back to where they had started their journey. "Look at that," he said while pointing, and drew everyone's attention back towards the wrecked plane. Thick smoke was still pouring forth out of the damaged bird and lazily twisting high into the sky. "If she keeps that up, I don't see how a search party can miss it. I couldn't have made a better beacon. We might even be found before nightfall."

One by one the kids threw their bags up into Buffalo's waiting hands. Then Simon got the job of handing a squirming Jeep up to Buffalo. Jeep was a lot heavier than he looked and not very thrilled with being hoisted. He stifled a growl as Simon struggled to get the uncooperative beast within Buffalo's grasp. With a last minute shove from Max, Buffalo's waiting hand closed around Jeep's collar and he was assisted onto the ledge in an instant, shaking himself and eager for more adventure. Then each in turn, Simon, Max, and Dexter jumped with arms stretched skyward, to be snagged by Buffalo's huge paws. As easily as if they were toddlers, Buffalo lifted them up and over the ledge and deposited them, standing, in front of the cave entrance.

The fissure before them was indeed a cave with a narrow opening and seemed to extend quite deeply into the glacial wall. At least the inky darkness at its rear seemed to indicate that it did. Buffalo had taken a flashlight from his pack and shouldering the bag once more, said, "Let's check out our new headquarters."

No sooner had the group crowded into the entrance of the cave than a tremendous explosion erupted behind them! All whirled around in their tracks just in time to witness the remains of their wrecked plane being catapulted skyward in a fiery burst of twisted metal and glowing ash. A huge greasy black ball of smoke and flame billowed from the newly formed crater where the plane had rested only moments before. The deafening "BOOM" of the explosion followed and reverberated in echoes back and forth across the canyon as shredded chunks of plane fell back to earth, imbedding themselves into the freshly fallen snow. Suddenly, there began a very deep and low rumbling sound and the ground beneath their feet began to tremble. Everyone gasped in unison as they saw the entire wall of ice that had towered over the plane begin to separate from the mountain behind it! As though it were in slow motion, but with a thunderous roar, they watched in horror as the colossal peak split apart and tumbled down upon the smoldering remains of their doomed aircraft, completely smothering the smoke and flame, and effectively burying the wreckage from view. As the clouds of displaced snow began to settle, Buffalo muttered, "Well, there goes our smoke signal." The frozen plain before them was now strewn with snowdrifts and ice boulders. The snowy rubble gave no hint of the events of their crash or their whereabouts and effectively concealed all evidence of their ever having been there.

As they stared, awestruck, they again felt the ledge beneath their feet begin to tremble, but much stronger this time. Chunks of snow and ice began falling about them!

"Avalanche!" yelled Buffalo as he herded the kids into the mouth of the cave. "Run for the back!

They ran pell-mell, in fear for their lives towards the sheltering recesses of the cave just as tons of snow and ice came crushing down on the ledge where they had just been standing. The roar of the cascading ice drowned out their shouts and screams as they ran single file down the narrow darkening fissure. Suddenly, as if someone had flipped a light switch, they were running in total blackness as the falling mountain of ice behind them completely blocked the cave's entrance.

Dexter was in the lead when the lights went out, and in his blindness he managed about three more steps when, quite unexpectedly, his next footfall met with empty air! He quickly grabbed for the sides of the tunnel, but the ice was too slick. Realizing he couldn't stop himself from falling forward, he splayed his arms out before him, fully expecting to land spread-eagled on the floor of the cave. He didn't. He let out a scream as he now fell, tumbling end-over-end, in inky darkness, into a vast and bottomless pit!

Racing for their lives and unhearing because of the din of the avalanche and unseeing because of the sudden absence of light, Simon, Max, and Buffalo Brewster tumbled into the open void, one by one, right behind Dex. Only Jeep, with his heightened canine senses, managed to stop in time to save himself from following his Master's fate into the unknown depths.

Chapter 2
<u>"Adrift!"</u>

With the deafening roar of the echoing avalanche still drowning out his screams, Dexter plummeted through the darkness, tumbling end-over-end. Then suddenly, his fall and scream were cut off quite abruptly when, in the next instant, he felt his body splash into frigid water! He hadn't had any warning! He hadn't had time to take a breath! He felt himself being whooshed along in a very fast current as he kicked frantically to regain the surface. He struggled against the sodden weight of the thick winter parka that had cushioned and protected him as he'd hit the water. Still, his side stung with the force of the impact even *with* the parka. Dexter's lungs ached as he swam, (was he even swimming in the right direction?), and very soon he knew, the automatic and unstoppable impulse to breathe would fill his lungs with icy water and drown him! Just as he thought for sure that his end had come, he felt his face break the surface! Gasping and choking, Dexter paddled furiously as he fought to keep his head above water while he sucked in the life-sustaining fresh air.

He was bobbing and bumping along at great speed as he worked to refill his exhausted lungs. The roar of the avalanche was fading into the distance and being replaced by the loud echoing gurgling of rushing water. Often, he would be bumped against slimy smooth water-worn walls in the darkness and the realization came to him that he must be floating in an underground stream! Dexter's lips trembled as the shock of the events and the cold gripped him. His keen mind began to assess the situation as he continued his struggles to remain afloat in the wildly twisting current. The air was sweet smelling, not stagnant. The water was cold, but not freezing. This puzzled him since they were somewhere in the north of Canada in December. He hesitantly licked at his lips with his tongue... and then dipped them into the torrent and took a quick sip. It was fresh and clean tasting... well, at least he wouldn't die of thirst!

Suddenly, over the tumult of the rapids, he heard something else. His name. He heard his name being called!

"Dexter!? Dexter!? Are you there?" The calls echoed along with the loud burbling of the stream.

It was Max! She was alive and somewhere behind him! "Max!" he shouted, as best he could between breaths. "Are you okay?"

"Yes!" she yelled back in the darkness. "I'm okay... and Simon is too! He's behind me somewhere."

"Hi-ho, Dex!" he heard Simon's voice call out, much fainter, from somewhere further beyond Maxine.

Dexter managed a smile. He didn't feel as lost and alone now, adrift in the darkness. But, yipes! All three of them were stuck in this predicament! What were they going to do? Who could save them? What had become of the bearded giant that had been piloting their plane... their new friend and protector?

"What about you, Dex?" hollered Max, "Are *you* okay?"

Max's inquiry brought him back to the reality of the moment. "Yeah, if I don't drown, or freeze, or smack into something!

"Blow air into your parka! It helps!"

34

That's right! Dexter remembered now. The three friends had taken some water safety classes together and "inflating" their clothes was one of the tricks they'd been taught by the instructor, to allow them to tread water for hours! He grabbed the neck of his parka and began to puff air into it with each exhale. The sleeves began to expand and when he felt himself bobbing like a cork, he zipped it tight and pulled the drawstrings. It wouldn't last long, but it would allow him to conserve his energy and relax a bit until he needed to re-inflate it.

Because his eyes had tried, in vain, to become used to the impenetrable darkness, he was almost blinded when he was suddenly caught in a beam of light from a bright circle floating far away in the distance! But at least he could see! Dexter put his hand up to his face… his glasses! They were still in place! It hadn't occurred to him in the darkness, but miraculously, he hadn't lost them in the fall. He wiped the lenses to clear the water spots and glanced back at the source of light. It wouldn't stay very still because the stream twisted and undulated wildly, but it revealed to him his surroundings at last.

As he had guessed, he was hurtling through an underground tunnel that seemed to be about fifteen feet across and almost perfectly cylindrical. The light was very dim where he was, but it showed smooth damp reddish walls as he looked upstream. From Dexter's point of view, it looked like he was being swallowed through a huge esophagus! The speed at which he and the others were traveling was also incredible. The gushing torrent of water was angled steeply downward and there wasn't so much as a handhold in the slick walls to slow their progress, though trying to do so at these speeds would probably have proven disastrous. He noticed the silhouettes of Max and Simon's heads bobbing and weaving helplessly in the current behind him as they careened off the walls of the winding tunnel. All these observations passed through Dexter's mind in an instant, for his main question was the light itself… Where did it come from?

He no sooner posed the question to himself than it was answered - - by a familiar booming voice upstream… heard even over the roar of the rapids.

"You kids okay?" hollered Buffalo. "Everybody accounted for?"

The familiar voice must have been as much of a surprise to Max and Simon too, for there was suddenly a chorus of cheering and whooping as the three friends responded to Buffalo's inquiry. They were not alone! As terrible as their situation was, as hopeless their fate, they somehow felt relief… safer and calmer, knowing that they were all still together. The only one missing was Buffalo's dog.

Their thoughts must have been similar, for Simon then blurted out, "What about your dog? What happened to him?"

Buffalo answered back, "Jeep? He was right next to me 'til we fell. But he was smarter than *we* were! He must've sensed the pit and stopped before falling in. He always was a smart one…" Buffalo's voice got quieter and trailed off. Buffalo and Jeep had been inseparable since he found him as a pup. They always flew together. In fact, they did just about everything together.

The kids felt the loss in Buffalo's tone and felt badly about his losing the playful hound. Understandably though, their worry and confusion soon overcame their sadness and they piped up once more.

"Where are we?" shouted Max. "Where are we going?

"What should we do?" added Simon.

"How do we get out of this?" chimed in Dexter.

Buffalo had no idea and he told them so.

After several silent minutes, pondering their fate while they rushed along through the narrow confines of the tunnel, Buffalo spoke out once more.

"Listen up," echoed Buffalo's deep voice, "I'm not sure how long this flashlight is gonna last. I think it'll be best if I turn it on and off as needed. Maybe every ten minutes to check our situation. In the meantime, I'm gonna try and close the gap between us by swimming with the current."

The kids reluctantly agreed that it sounded like a good idea, though they didn't relish the thought of being plunged into darkness once again. But the light then snapped off as suddenly as it had appeared and their only comfort was to keep talking to one another... to keep fear of the unknown from overwhelming them.

Buffalo, with one arm crooked over the waterproof flight bag, swam sidestroke style as best he could manage... with the flashlight clasped between his teeth. He silently counted the minutes and paused to switch on the flashlight again after only six minutes because the creepiness of swimming blindly in the dark was overwhelming. Everyone welcomed the relief from their sightlessness and took quick inventory of their surroundings. Same walls, same tunnel, and same water. Buffalo did notice though that he had closed the distance between himself and Simon by about half. After checking everybody's status, Buffalo informed them that he would once again switch off the light and did so. Immediately, he renewed his efforts to reach Simon. He tried to home in on Simon's voice and encouraged Simon to keep talking. After several more minutes of swimming, he judged that he was very near. Buffalo stopped and switched on the light. There was Simon just opposite him!

"Mr. Brewster!" cried Simon, blinking his eyes in response to the sudden brightness next to him.

"Please, kid," Buffalo muttered, "Nobody's called me that since my boot-camp drill sergeant. Call me Buffalo."

"Okay..." smiled Simon, "If you'll call me Simon, and not 'kid'!" Buffalo reached out his great paw and they shook hands, after which Buffalo dragged Simon closer so he could clutch onto the straps of the flight bag. "That's my sister, Max, up ahead. Can we get to her too? And then Dex?"

"We'll try," said Buffalo, and hollered his intentions to the two up ahead. Max was greatly relieved that Simon was okay and was looking forward to being in his company again. He was, after all, her "big" brother and whatever befell them, she wanted to be with him when it did.

Buffalo and Simon now swam together and after three "flashlight" stops finally came within reach of Maxine. She threw her arms around Simon when he came within reach and in her happiness nearly pushed him under. "Oh, Simon," she sniffed, "What are we going to do? What's Daddy going to think when we don't turn up? What if he thinks we're... dead? What if we... soon *will* be? What if we hit something... or this stream just goes on forever until we get too tired to hold our heads above water?"

Simon looked to Buffalo and they both looked back to Max. There were no answers. They had been careening helplessly along in the current now for almost an hour. The steep angle of decline never ceased and kept them moving at great speed, like some wild rollercoaster. Buffalo estimated that they must have traveled many miles since their plunge and would be very deep beneath the surface of the earth by now. All they could do was take heart in the fact that they were still alive at all… and together. They checked in with Dexter, who was still floating in the lead, about twenty yards distant, and began pulling together to make their way to him.

They had gotten used to Buffalo turning on the light every ten minutes or so, so they were quite surprised when he flicked it on again after only about five minutes. He had stopped swimming and was staring very seriously into the tunnel ahead.

"What's the matter?" asked Max.

"It's leveled out… and it's not twisting anymore!" observed Simon excitedly.

"Yeah," mused Buffalo, "But I've got a bad feeling about it…"

The flashlight beam, aimed directly down the tunnel that now ran straight as an arrow, completely faded into the distance. Dex must have sensed the change too, for he now yelled back, "What's happening?"

They next became aware of a familiar type of sound welling up over the din of the rapids. A dull roaring that was getting louder as they rushed along. Following the beam of light into the darkness, they now began to notice a faint circular reddish reflection… that was quickly getting brighter! "Oh, no…" groaned Buffalo. "What?" asked Simon and Max. "What is it?"

"I think it's the end of the tunnel..." he quietly replied.

Their attention was riveted now along the path of light. The flashlight beam revealed what was certainly a solid wall of rock in the distance! As they rushed forward to their destiny, helpless in the seething current, they saw what appeared to be the magnified shadow of Dexter's bobbing head projected upon the approaching barrier. More rapidly than their thoughts could grasp the importance of, the roaring noise became almost deafening, the wall of stone became intensely brighter, and Dexter's shadow got smaller and smaller at an alarming rate! The shadow was almost exactly the size of Dexter's head... when it suddenly disappeared! Because so did Dexter!

The remaining castaways were doomed by the current to follow Dexter and share his fate. Buffalo barely had time to shout out, "Waterfall!" before he and everyone else were drawn over the edge to find themselves, once again, tumbling downward.

Chapter 3
"Lake Placid?"

Luckily for all, the falls was not a long one. At least not as long as their first drop into the underground stream! Buffalo's brief warning had allowed Max and Simon to get a breath this time and, after being plunged into unknown depths by the falls, each one was able to work their way back to the surface with a few frantic kicks. Spluttering and gagging as their faces broke through the churning foam and bubbles, they began to tread water in the semidarkness and rapidly became aware of many things at once. First of all, they could still see... sort of. A dim light was approaching from below and illuminating them through the murky roiling water. Next, the water was no longer moving at such a pace as before. It wasn't a torrent anymore. They were slowly drifting away from the noise and frothing of the nearby falls. And it was getting warmer! The water here was much warmer than the cold rapids of the tunnel... but the air was warmer still! Quite warm, misty, and humid... almost tropical!

In the next instant, they heard Dexter's voice shout, "Guys?" Much relieved to hear their friend's voice, they had barely returned his inquiry with an enthusiastic, "Over here!" when Buffalo's flight bag bobbed to the surface beside them. The light beneath them quickly made it's way upward towards them, and then Buffalo, still holding the flashlight, burst to the surface and gasped for air.

Still breathing heavily, he shook the water from his face and beard and looked towards them. "Well, that was dandy. You kids okay?" Simon and Max nodded assent. "Let's see if we can find out

41

just where we are," he continued, "and what happened to your friend."

"He's…" started Max.

As if to finish her sentence, Dexter, who had been homing in on the beam of light, swam up to them from the other side of the falls. "Right here!" he chimed.

Rejoined at last! Despite the hopelessness of their situation, smiles and laughter lifted their spirits as they gathered around the floating flight bag, tread water, and quickly swapped thoughts and feelings… united again for the first time since the fall from the ice cave.

While the kids were excitedly chatting, Buffalo scanned all around them with the thankfully waterproof flashlight. Its beam searched out their surroundings and revealed a small cavern. The ceiling was jagged with stalactites and roughly forty feet over their heads. The walls were steep and smooth and near the water's edge appeared to be slimy with algae. The light's beam also illuminated the wall nearest them, the one from which the water of the underground stream was furiously pouring forth from a large hole twenty feet up its sheer face. "Jeez," thought Buffalo, "this pond must be awful deep to not fill up with all that water pouring into it!" As he gazed around he noticed that there was no place to beach themselves. The walls were all too steep. On the wall opposite the falls, there was a very dark oblong shape that puzzled him at first. It rose above the water's edge about two feet and the current seemed to be drawing them towards it. His observations were halted when he became aware that the chattering of the kids had stopped. He looked their way and saw that all three were looking silently, inquisitively, at him.

Max was the first to speak up. "Well... we made it this far. What are we going to do now?

"Don't ask me," retorted Buffalo. "I'm a pilot, not Esther Williams."

The kids smirked at his flippant reference to the famous Olympic swimmer and Hollywood starlet. "No, really," tried Dexter, "What's our next move?"

"Alright," sighed Buffalo after a moment, "I guess we might as well pretend there's actually some way outta this..." He noticed the hopefulness on their faces suddenly turn to sadness and quickly added, "And...and there probably is. Who knows? These underground rivers could lead just about anywhere..."

Buffalo searched around with the light again and saw that they were much closer to the dark oblong shape that now revealed itself to be an opening in the wall. "Okay, look," he continued, "there's nothing in this cavern that will sustain us. The sides are too steep to climb and there's nowhere to rest. We're gonna need some sleep sooner or later or risk slipping off into the water and drowning. We can't go back the way we came, so it looks like we've gotta go that way." And he pointed to the black hole towards which they were floating.

As they neared the oblong hole, they realized it wasn't really a tunnel but merely a passageway. The current drew them in quickly and they floated beneath its low roof and shortly emerged into a *huge* cavern. So large in fact, that Buffalo's light could barely reach across it. "Wow!" they gasped as one. The water was even warmer here and very calm. None of the waterfall-churned waves here! It was smooth and still. "An underground lake," whispered Dex. "Yeah," acknowledged Simon and Max. It was eerily quiet now that the thick stone walls insulated against the roar of the falls behind them.

Buffalo once again scanned their position with the light and they saw that the lake was longer than it was wide. The beam of light was dimly able to pick out some dark shapes on the wall opposite them, but it was lost *completely* into impenetrable darkness to either side. The ceiling as well was apparently beyond the reach of the faithful bulb, for scanning in that direction revealed no secrets either. Looking back, they saw that the walls nearest them were just as steep and inhospitable as the ones they'd just left behind in the smaller cavern, again leaving them nowhere to beach.

"I'd suggest we go looking over there," spoke Buffalo quietly and he nodded towards the far wall. Something about the awesome stillness and size of the cavern humbled them…like being in a huge cathedral. They swam together quietly and deliberately, huddled around and clinging to the flight bag like a life preserver. When they reached about halfway across the lake, Buffalo paused to again use the flashlight to check out the far side of the immense chamber. To their uneasiness, they saw that one of the dark shapes they had noticed was apparently the mouth of a tunnel like the one that had brought them here! Water was being drawn into its aperture in great volumes and they once again heard the all too familiar sound of rapids.

"We don't want to go in there again… do we?" asked the kids nervously.

"Not if we can avoid it," replied Buffalo decidedly. "Let's go further that way," and he nodded to the right where many shadows seemed to indicate outcroppings of some sort. "Maybe we can find a place to rest."

"Hey, quit it," said Dexter suddenly. "Not now... it's not funny."

"Quit what?" replied a startled Simon next to him.

"Pinching my leg, that's what! I'm creeped out enough in this spooky place."

"I'm not doing anything," said Simon.

"Me neither," added Max.

"Then what...?" said Dex nervously, and he gave a quick violent kick with his legs!

With the sudden disturbance, the water beside them erupted and a large colorless fish, almost two feet long, leapt up into the air! It's skin was translucent and they could see its pink flesh through its sides. But the feature they noticed most, was its lack of eyes! There were only silvery sunken hollows where its eyes should have been. The creature fell back to the surface with a resounding smack and disappeared back into the depths. Buffalo, Max, and Simon, unable to contain their amusement, burst out laughing. Dex was still a little nervous at being considered fish food, but the laughter was contagious and he soon found himself joining in.

When the giggles subsided, and Dex got his composure back, he redeemed himself by explaining that their recent visitor was a blind cavefish. Since there was no light down here the fish didn't need eyes, so they either never developed them, or lost them through evolution. Buffalo added a more practical note... he suggested that if they had to stay here a while, they might be able to catch such a fish and not go hungry.

They were just about to continue on towards the shadowy shoreline, when suddenly, and quite unexpectedly, a loud bark shattered the stillness of the huge cavern! It issued from the direction of the falls chamber they had just quit and reverberated off the walls of the enormous catacomb. Buffalo quickly swung his light back towards the low oblong passage they had just passed under... and to everyone's amazement, they saw Jeep! Swimming in true dog-paddle fashion, his head barely visible and obviously exhausted, he was gallantly trying to catch up to them!

"Jeep! You ol' dog!" yelled Buffalo. His demeanor changed abruptly into what could easily be termed as "the happiest man on Earth"! Jeep barked again in enthusiastic reply, and if he'd had much of a tail, he would have been wagging it then!

"He must've fallen down the hole too!" said Simon.

"Oh, I know Jeep," remarked Buffalo with an ear-to-ear grin, "He didn't fall... he jumped! That's why he was so much further behind us. He didn't wanna be left behind. What a pal! Look at him... poor ol' dog's nearly half drowned..." And with that, he pushed off from the group and began swimming strongly back the way they had drifted, flashlight once again clenched between his teeth, to save his old friend.

All eyes were on Buffalo as he swam within reach of his canine buddy. Jeep began yipping and wildly licking Buffalo's face as soon as he drew near, his happiness eclipsing his exhaustion. The rescue nearly complete, Buffalo wrapped a huge comforting arm around his friend and supported Jeep's weary body on his hip while he side-stroked back to the kids.

While everyone waited for Buffalo to close the gap that separated them, Dexter suddenly became aware of a hissing sound to his left. At the same instant, he heard Jeep begin a low growl. "What's tha..." he began, and Max and Simon turned their attention towards his gaze. At the edge of the darkness, about fifty yards away, they saw a pale serpent's head begin to rise up out of the water, swaying menacingly upon a long slender snake-like neck! It had but tiny slits for eyes, but the mouth of the beast was enormous and bristled with many rows of sharp thorn-like teeth. Water dripped noisily from its hissing, snapping, reptilian snout as it elevated its head fully twelve feet or more above the surface of the lake! Its skin was, like the fish, pale and colorless. Throbbing red and blue veins stood out clearly against the milky semitransparent flesh of the undulating neck which slid effortlessly through the water... followed by a huge glistening hump of a back. For all its size and menace, the creature swam gracefully and silently, gliding through the fathomless blackness of the subterranean pool with nary a ripple. Dexter immediately recognized the creature for what it was... "A Plesiosaur!" he shouted.

Max screamed. Buffalo hadn't seen or heard the hissing of the beast, but he heard Max! He turned his head and saw the ancient Saurian for the first time and he gasped and cursed at the same time. Thinking quickly, he shouted instructions to the kids and told them to swim for the tunnel - - the one that the lake was emptying into - - the one they had tried so desperately to *avoid!* Now it was their only chance! He redoubled his own efforts to join them, for the creature was closing the distance quickly and was likely to cut him off from the kids before he could cross the pool.

Simon, Dexter, and Max swam for their lives. They kicked and paddled furiously to move themselves and the inflated flight bag towards the black opening of the tunnel's mouth. Just as they thought for sure that they would be unable to outrun the slavering jaws of their pursuer, they caught the brisk flow of water that was pouring into the dark hole. With the aid of the rapid current, their speed increased greatly until suddenly, they were rushed so swiftly towards the aperture that they were almost sucked in! But, they had no intention of leaving Buffalo and Jeep behind, even to save themselves! Simon, being in the lead, managed to grab a handhold on the right side edge of the tunnel. Being anchored on the one side, the current swung the large inflated bag, along with Dex and Max, across the opening where Dex succeeded in grappling the left side. There the three of them were… stretched across the opening of the tunnel and against the current of the underground stream, as if suspended in the mouth of a large drain!

As the three struggled to maintain their grasp on the entrance, they faced full witness to the horror of the scene that began to play itself before them. Buffalo had made considerable progress in his efforts to cross the pool with Jeep in tow, but it was obvious that the Plesiosaur would easily overtake him before he ever reached the safety of the tunnel! Buffalo was still about twenty yards away when the giant leviathan swam within striking distance! With dripping jaws agape, the creature swayed its head backward in preparation for a stabbing forward lunge. Just as it did so, Buffalo twisted in mid-stroke and grabbing the flashlight from between his teeth, leveled the bright beam of the light directly into the slits of the Saurian's cave-blind eyes! The animal let out a horrible high-pitched screech and shook its head and neck violently. It paused, hissing loudly and blinked its narrow slit eyes, then once again it sought out its helpless prey. But Buffalo had used the opportunity to swim into the stronger current. He and Jeep were quickly swept into the mouth of the tunnel... right into the middle of the bag being stretched across its opening! Buffalo threw Jeep on top of the bag and the added weight of the two of them in the rushing current was enough to cause Dex and Simon to lose their grip. They were drawn in behind Buffalo, Max, and Jeep as the group began floating once again into the dark unknown. But they were barely clear of the entrance when they heard a loud snap and Simon seemed held fast! The current swung Dex downstream until he was once again in the lead and then... they seemed to be slowly heading *against* the current!

Buffalo was now the closest to Simon. He looked back upstream from his perch on the flight bag and with the beam from his flashlight saw the cause of their trouble over Simon's shoulder. The Plesiosaur, having quickly recovered from the blinding light, and seeing its prey disappear into the tunnel's mouth, had lunged forward and thrust its long neck into the opening! Its body was too large to fit into the small tunnel but its razor-filled jaws had managed to capture the hood of Simon's parka and now it was slowly, but successfully, hauling its prize back to the lake!

"Whatever you do Simon," yelled Buffalo, "don't let go of the bag!"

Simon's face was just a strained grimace as he fought to retain his grip, torn between the strong current and the pressure of the creature's dragging hold, but he managed to nod. He could feel the hot snorting from the reptilian's nostrils on the back of his neck as the animal strained to reel them in against the rapids. Buffalo was reaching down into the water and fumbling with something. Suddenly, his hand emerged brandishing a sleek hunting knife! He handed off the flashlight to Max and then put the *knife* between his teeth. Hand over hand he quickly climbed from the bag to Simon and then continued up Simon's arms until he reached his head. With one arm around Simon's chest, Buffalo peered over Simon's shoulder and found himself looking directly into the slitted evil eyes of the beast! It looked angry. The creature saw Buffalo too, and sensing the threat from this odd intruder, rumbled a warning with a terrible gurgling hiss. They were almost dragged clear of the tunnel now, but Buffalo had no intention of letting himself or Simon be dinner! On the other hand, he had no desire to get anywhere near those frightful dagger-like teeth either, so instead of attacking the creature outright, he began sawing at the hood of the parka with the keen blade of his hunting knife.

With a few deft hacks and slices, the hood suddenly parted from the coat with a crisp rending sound. They were free! Buffalo, Jeep, and the kids were quickly sucked back into the safety of the tunnel by the current and the angry Plesiosaur was left behind holding a useless scrap of cloth! They heard it bellow its frustration and defiance one last time as they continued their forced journey into unknown darkness.

Chapter 4
"Tunnel's End"

Once again, the castaways found themselves adrift in a seemingly endless subterranean tunnel. They were elated and thankful for having escaped the hungry jaws of the Plesiosaur, but they were also overwhelmed by feelings of impending doom, brought on by a combination of helplessness and hopelessness. Gloom engulfed them as they were swept along in the dark like so much driftwood - - held captive by the imprisoning flow of yet another meandering underground river.

But, on the bright side, some things had changed to improve their situation. For one thing, they were all finally together again... now that Jeep had rejoined the crew! And for another, the air and water of this particular tunnel was *much* warmer than the almost unbearable cold of their previous captor. As they talked excitedly about their encounter with the ancient dinosaur, they nervously took in the surrounding characteristics of their new confinement... revealed to them by the light that Buffalo was still holding. This passage was larger than the other tunnel, but its walls were just as smooth and now of a grayish color. The current wasn't nearly as wild either, or the tunnel as twisting, so they were being swept along at a somewhat less reckless pace - - though it could hardly be termed a "lazy" river!

Confounded by the uncertainty of their new predicament, and jittery from their recent escape, Buffalo and the kids were reluctant to immerse themselves into the total darkness they knew would surround them the moment they switched off the light. But, after drifting rapidly along for about a half-hour, that decision was made for them… by the limited life of flashlight batteries. The trusty light began to slowly fade until it was just a dim ember behind the waterproof shield of the lens. There seemed to be little sense in trying to conserve it now... after a few more minutes, it finally gave up. Plunged again into sightlessness once more, the weary band floated along, taking their only comfort from the company and conversation.

As the hours passed, the rigors, fears, and excitements of the underground journey began to take their toll. Hunger and exhaustion were beginning to become a real threat to their very survival. There was, of course, some food and snacks in the flight bag they were clinging to, but to retrieve them would mean opening the bag and letting out the precious air that kept their little "life raft" afloat. And in the unpredictable current they might risk dumping out the contents of the bag entirely! Vital stuff that could come in handy if they ever found a place to rest. They unanimously decided to hold out a while longer, and made do, by sharing a soggy chocolate bar Dexter found in his pocket and a bag of salted peanuts that Max had in hers. Also, between the four of them, they assembled no less than nine packs of chewing gum… mostly thanks to Buffalo, (because he loved the stuff and always carried extra sticks in his flight jacket for long trips).

They had temporarily solved the problem of their hunger, (though not very satisfactorily), but the greater problem of exhaustion was still slowly creeping in upon them. They knew it was their greatest immediate danger, for there was no way to avoid sleep forever. The air in the tunnel became increasingly warm and pleasant and their travel through the darkness was actually very soothing, what with the constant burbling of the stream and the strong but gentle current wafting them along. They all tried desperately to keep each other awake through talk and simple games, even singing, but eventually they succumbed to their need for slumber. Simon was the first to snooze as the bobbing current lulled him to sleep. He nodded off and slipped from the bag just enough to dip his nostrils into the water, which startling him awake with much gasping and snorting to clear his nose of the suffocating fluid. The sudden outburst brought the others out of their own drowsy stupor with a start and Max found herself looking at Dexter. She felt confused by her sleepiness and her mind was hazy, but there was something wrong here... she was looking at a faint image of Dexter and he was sleepily looking back. Was she dreaming? She could *see* him!

Shocked to sudden wakefulness, she actually screamed, "Dex! I can see you!"

It was true! The light was extremely dim at first but it seemed to get increasingly brighter as they drifted downstream. They were all now momentarily alert again, groggy... but stimulated by this new phenomenon. At first their hopes were focused on the possibility of daylight somehow seeping into the tunnel. But they knew from their daylong downward journey that they had to be very deep within the bowels of the earth. Closer observation seemed to indicate that the light was actually coming from the walls themselves! They were no longer the dull stone gray that the flashlight had earlier revealed... now they had texture and were more of a yellowish white... and definitely getting brighter! Buffalo and the kids marveled and wondered aloud at this new curiosity that afforded them the luxury and comfort of sight. Dexter wished he could get a closer view of the walls, to try to locate the source of the glow, but the current kept them frustratingly in the middle of the stream. For the moment, all they could do was be thankful for their good fortune, as their prospects seemed to brighten.

They hadn't traveled for very long however before they realized that they might be in for too much of a good thing! The light had been becoming increasingly brighter with each new mile of their travels. For awhile, it had been like being in a well lit room. Then later, it seemed like daylight, but it got even brighter than that… so much so, that soon, the group found themselves starting to squint at the intensity! Their eyes were beginning to actually tear from the brightness. Yet, curiously, there didn't seem to be any heat involved. They had at first feared that they might begin to "cook" in the intense light, but the air was only slightly warmer than it had been before, moist and tropical. Whereas they had earlier been trapped within total darkness, they were now in just the opposite trouble. The light was now so brilliant, that it washed out all detail to whiteness! They could barely see each other… it was like staring into a floodlight! Then, just as they began to think that they would surely be blinded forever, their fears were diverted to a new threat as they heard an all too familiar rushing sound... and without further warning, the steadily moving stream tilted severely downward! For one dizzying moment, they paused at the crest of the cataract, caught in the swirling eddying current, then suddenly over and down they went… cascading in a torrent of water as though they'd been drawn over a dam! The water rushed at terrific speed downhill and they all screamed and wailed as if they were on a Coney Island rollercoaster! Then just as suddenly, the watercourse leveled out and then up like a waterslide, and "WHOOSH!" - - they had time for just one more brief scream as they realized they were air-borne and once again falling!

Dazzled by the blinding light, they had no idea what their new predicament was, but with five resounding splashes, they found themselves again in water and spluttering for breath in frothy waves! All five heads bobbed back to the surface, blinking their weary eyes in the light of their new surroundings. Their vision was still adjusting as they slowly floated away from the gushing waterspout, but their ears revealed to them that they were finally out of the echoing tunnels and into a vast open area!

"This way!" directed Buffalo. And the group, including Jeep, swam towards what appeared to be a shore! Their eyesight was improving now, quickly adjusting to the new environment, and as they swam they began to comprehend the mystery of their surroundings… and what they saw entirely astounded them! They were floating in the midst of a wide river that meandered calmly away through a dense green tropical jungle! Incredibly huge trees and broad-leafed plants flanked the river on both sides so thickly that their leaves and roots hung over and into the gently flowing waters. They could see that the river downstream was "soupy" with bright green algae that flocked the surface of the water. As they looked on, a fish of some sort leapt from the water and splashed back down, leaving only ever widening rings to mark the spot where it had disappeared.

Behind them, the churning waters of the tunnel from which they had just emerged gushed mightily from a bright hole that seemed to "hang" in mid-air some twenty feet above the river! Although they had already floated some thirty yards from the spot where they had been so rudely dumped into the river, it was very difficult to look back and see exactly what sort of hole it was, or why it should have such a curious appearance, "hanging" in the sky that way. The light in that direction was very bright and they needed to squint just to glance at it. Any additional details they might have discerned was further obscured by a thick mist that enshrouded the falls and hung in the air in great roiling white clouds that further blended into the brightness of the sky.

In fact, the sky itself was just as peculiar as the odd waterfall. For although they could see no sun, the sky was so bright that they could not bring themselves to gaze at it for long. There was no blue color or clouds, just brightness, and the brightness extended evenly in all directions as far as the eye could see... even down past the treetops! Turning their attention back towards the jungle, they noticed a few dark shapes flying through the air in the distance and far overhead, but no one recognized them as any particular kind of bird. Everything seemed so still and peaceful, but yet it had an unnatural feel to it. The air was tropically warm and humid, but there was no breeze at all. Not a hint of wind to stir the leaves of the dense jungle foliage. And for a jungle, it was eerily quiet. Other than the splashing din of the falls, there was no squawking or singing of birds, no incessant buzzing of insects, just an occasional distant whirring or humming sound.

The exhausted and bedraggled castaways headed for shore as quickly as they could manage. They had fully had enough of swimming for quite awhile! They also had no idea what they were up against and wanted to take stock of their situation as quickly as possible. Had they emerged back onto the surface somehow? If so, what jungle could this be? What dangers from the river or the jungle could they expect? Piranha? Crocodiles? Jaguars? They knew they had floated in the tunnels for about twenty-eight hours, according to Buffalo's aviation watch, but they couldn't have reached the Amazon or Africa in that time! It wasn't possible. It was also too warm to be in any known geographical region that they *could* have reached from northern Canada in that amount of time. So, if they weren't on the surface, where were they? If they were still underground, where did the bright light come from? And could a jungle exist other than on the surface of Mother Earth? What new and unknown dangers might they now be facing? And even more importantly, how would they get home?

As the weary group drew near to the shore, they felt their feet make contact at last with the slippery bottom ooze of the river. Their relief was mixed, for although their spirits were delighted with the idea of emerging from the water at long last, the loss of buoyancy and reapplication of gravity was quick to remind them how tired and strained their aching muscles were! With shaking legs, and much groaning and grumbling, they managed to drag themselves through the weeds and lily pads that grew near the shore. Reaching the final obstacle, a short embankment, Buffalo tossed their precious flight bag life-preserver onto the shore where there appeared to be a grassy clearing. Then he had everyone remove the waterlogged parkas they wore and threw them up after the bag as well. Standing in chest high water, they would surely never have been able to climb out of the river under the enormous weight of the sodden winterwear! Buffalo then lifted an anxious and whimpering Jeep out of the water - - and he couldn't have been happier to be the first deposited on shore! He shook the water off vigorously and then ran around in circles... then back and forth between the shore and the clearing, as though to continually check the castaway's progress. Buffalo assisted each water-weary kid up the embankment - - his strength was simply amazing! He had to be at least as tired as the rest of them and yet he still had the power and stamina to thrust Max, Dex, and Simon, in their waterlogged clothing, up the mossy riverbank to safety. Without his help, they might have perished in the water after all... right on that spot... too tired to lift themselves up the short hillside and out of their liquid prison. Lastly, Buffalo dragged his own beleaguered body up the slope with the last of the strength that he could muster... crawling through the damp weeds and using handfuls of grass to hoist himself out of the muck.

Standing at long last, the crew of four slowly and agonizingly forced their aching quivering legs to wander towards the clearing where Jeep had already staked out a clump of grass he had trampled into a nest. He was already dozing off as the kids and Buffalo fell groaning to their knees in the midst of the clearing, surrounded by low bushes on one side and tall woody giants on the other. Each one fell forward onto their stomachs where they knelt, as waves of exhaustion swept over them. With some final moans and whimpers, the kids curled into tucked sleeping positions and quickly drifted off. Buffalo rolled over onto his back and breathed in deeply, glad that they were finally out of those damnable tunnels... and alive! He felt that he should somehow find the energy to secure their "camp"... instead, he felt himself rapidly getting so drowsy with fatigue that he knew he wouldn't be able to remain awake long enough to manage it. The rhythmic snoring of the sprawled kids was having its effect and lulling him to sleep. He had no energy left to get up and check out their new environment. He had no idea where they were or what dangers they faced. He didn't know what to do next or how to go about getting home...but he was soon too tired to care. It could wait until later, couldn't it? Jeep was comfy, why shouldn't he be? As he surrendered to the beckoning peace of slumber, he briefly thought, "Probably gonna get eaten alive by mosquitoes though..." And then, "That's funny... actually haven't seen so much as a gnat yet..." And he was out.

Chapter 5
"Strangers in Paradise?"

Buffalo Brewster opened his eyes into the darkness of night. He was rolled onto his stomach now and his cheek was pressed into the damp sweet-smelling grass, several blades of which tickled his nose. He blinked his eyes several times and stiffly craned his neck upwards. It seemed like a typical moonlit night. The trees and fronds of the jungle were highlighted in a glowing blue-white light that appeared quite bright against the darker deep purple and black of the dense shadows. Buffalo heard noises now too, more than he'd heard earlier. He could still hear the cascading of the falls of course, but he heard strange and distant wailing noises as well. Also buzzing and whirring noises. And croaking, chirruping, and clicking noises. But none of them seemed near enough to be concerned about. In fact, the loudest noise he heard was the rhythmic breathing and snoring of the three kids and his dog!

Reminded of their presence, he picked out each dim shape huddled in the darkness and made a quick head count. Every exhausted one of them lay where they had fallen, finally getting a well-deserved rest after their horrific ordeal. Having satisfied himself that all was well, Buffalo rolled over onto his back again with a groan, forcing his sore and complaining muscles to oblige him. As he settled into the most comfortable position he could manage, he gazed up at the sky and was surprised to see no moon at all. Instead, the night sky was dotted randomly with clusters of very bright stars. In confusion, Buffalo's eyes darted back and forth across the vastness, searching the heavens for a pattern of stars he could recognize. Some stars stood isolated or loosely bunched into oddly configured groups while others joined together to run in great ragged splotches of glowing brightness across the night sky. As a pilot, Buffalo had been trained to be familiar with all the major constellations of both hemispheres. He had depended on them more than once to get his bearings when instruments could not be trusted. But looking up at this haphazard riot of stars, Buffalo could recognize nothing that looked even vaguely reminiscent of the star charts he had memorized.

As Buffalo pondered this oddity of the night, and the greater question of just where on earth the band of castaways could possibly have wound up, his bone-tired body increasingly forced its craving for sleep upon his brain once more... and away he drifted again into a fitful slumber.

*   *   *   *   *   *   *   *

Buffalo awoke with a start as a giant slobbery pink thing was attacking his face with a sloppy wet slurping motion. "Jeep! Cut it out!" he yelled. Jeep was standing over him, licking his face and threatening to wag his little stump of a tail right off his backside. Somebody let out a giggle and Buffalo sat bolt upright to see Dex, sitting in the grass nearby, and obviously amused by Jeep's antics. Max and Simon were still out, but small stirrings warned that they too would soon be up and about. Buffalo scratched his curly reddish beard and grinned at Dex. "Mornin, ...I guess" he offered. It was light again now, but remembering the odd star arrangements of the night, he looked skyward with curiosity. It was another bright and balmy tropic day, but there was no sun to be seen in the sky anywhere... and no clouds either. This wasn't the typical blue-sky he'd known all his life and flown through so often. Just a yellowish-white bright glow that extended from horizon to horizon.

The temperature was exactly as it had been the day before, warm and humid, and Buffalo thought it odd that although he was sitting in the open of the small clearing, he felt no sunlight upon him. He looked around and examined their surroundings with greater interest now that he was rested. The jungle looked familiar and yet odd at the same time. The jumbo-sized plants and trees were lush and exotic all right, but they didn't quite resemble any type of jungle vegetation that he'd ever seen before. And they were as motionless as indoor houseplants. There was absolutely no breeze whatsoever to stir them.

"Weird, isn't it?" said Dex, reading Buffalo's expression as he stood up. "And look… there's hardly any shadow to speak of!"

Buffalo arose as well with a few grunts and groans and looked down at his feet. "Well, I'll be…" He then lifted his foot a bit. "There's a shadow when something's very close to the ground, but not when it's farther away. It's like the light is coming from... everywhere at once."

"And there aren't any bugs," added Dex.

"That's right!" Buffalo hearkened back to the last thoughts he'd had before drifting off to sleep yesterday - - about mosquitoes. He hadn't gotten a single bite that he knew of. And there were still no flies, gnats, or annoying insects of any kind to be seen... even this near the water. "I don't miss *that*!" he confided to Dex.

The two of them ambled over to the spot where they'd hauled themselves from the river. Buffalo gazed to his right and saw the river winding its way around a bend and back to the falls, which he could hear but not see. Somewhere, behind the tall brush, the waterfall that had delivered them here was still pouring forth and not at too great a distance. But it was rather difficult to see exactly what was going on back there because the light was brighter in that direction than in any other. The river itself was fairly wide and seemed to absorb the constant flow of the waterfall easily, for although it was somewhat turbulent upstream, it appeared nearly stagnant and choked with algae as it meandered downstream. Buffalo figured that the river was probably very deep and absorbed the influx very easily. Bushes, ferns, and low scrub seemed to predominate on both sides of the river here at its source, nearest the falls, but they were replaced by numerous taller trees and palms as the river flowed downstream. In fact, further downstream the jungle trees took on immense proportions and grew in such extreme profusion that they wove together into a seemingly impenetrable tangle of green. It was as if the green algae-encrusted river was swallowed by an even darker green mist-enshrouded tunnel of leaves, vines, and creepers. And, but for the oozing flow of the river, the thick jungle was forebodingly still, its only motion being the rhythmic waggling of leaves and vines that actually hung directly into the flowing waters.

Buffalo looked at the lily pads they had waded through and saw that further down, they too grew to very large proportions - - huge plate-shaped disks of six to eight feet across and dotted here and there with lacy pink flowers. Then he noticed for the first time, some ripples of movement beneath the carpet of algae that seemed to indicate the presence of something swimming. Fish perhaps? He caught a flash of movement to his left and something splashed into the river and disappeared under the green mat. He couldn't be certain, but he thought he'd seen the familiar form of a large frog leap through the air from the riverbank.

But what should have been a familiar scene was somehow... unfamiliar at the same time. This river and the surrounding jungle were strangely unnatural and alien. Similar to all the dense jungles of the tropics that Buffalo was familiar with... but quite different as well. Things weren't quite right. Where was the sun? And the oppressive heat of such an equatorial setting? Why was the light so all-pervasive, and the shadows so oddly absent? Where was the wind and the typical forest noises? And where were the jungle animals and birds? And bugs! Especially bugs! The scene before him should be teeming with mosquitoes and gnats, dragonflies and moths! Swarms of flies should be working the river's mists while water-striders skimmed erratically upon its surface. Not that Buffalo missed their company, but there wasn't so much as a butterfly to be seen. What kind of tropical paradise *was* this?

Buffalo turned to head back and almost stumbled over Dex who was in the grass on all fours. "What the heck are you *doing*, Dex?" he asked, somewhat annoyed at having almost fallen over him.

"Looking for bugs. I can't seem to find so much as an ant!"

"Yeah. I was just wonderin' about the lack of pesky bugs myself..."

"That's not all I've noticed! The more I look around, the weirder this place gets. The plants and trees should be familiar, but they're... different... alien somehow. And this jungle is just unbelievably huge and dense. It's not like anything I've ever seen, read, or heard about!"

"Ya got *that* right." Buffalo agreed, and the two of them returned to the clearing in time to find Max and Simon excitedly comparing their own notes and perceptions about the strangeness of their jungle sanctuary. They jumped to their feet as they saw Buffalo and Dex approach and bombarded them with many of the same questions and observations that *they* had already noticed and pondered... and quite a few new ones as well. Buffalo expanded the mystery by telling them all about the puzzle of the stars in the night sky and how he had failed to recognize anything familiar with which to attempt to locate their position.

While Buffalo had the kid's attention, it seemed like a good time to assess their situation. So, in order to try to make sense of their predicament, he went over the events since the plane crash to try to determine their best course of action.

"As I see it," he began, "We drifted very quickly in those tunnels for over a day and very well could've traveled hundreds of miles. But this jungle surrounding us is more like something from the tropic zones... like the Amazon... or Borneo. Those are *thousands* of miles from where we crashed. There's no way we could've drifted that far, or changed climates that dramatically. And I don't exactly *understand* this jungle either. I spent a couple of years island hoppin' the South Pacific after the war and got kinda familiar with that kinda turf. This place is kinda similar to those other jungles I've seen, but it's *different* - - for a lot of the same reasons you've already noticed... and then some. It's weird and unnatural. Sort of primitive, like something you'd see in a museum behind a display of dinosaurs."

Buffalo paused for a moment, as though to consider how to broach his next subject, and then continued on a different note. "We might as well be realistic. I'll level with ya and I won't pull punches... that's just me. I'm afraid we drifted too far for any search party to ever find us. As you saw, the plane was completely wiped from view by the avalanche. I'm pretty sure it also covered our tracks too. So... we can't just figure on being rescued... and we obviously can't go back the way we came. Wherever we are, we'll hafta work together and get ourselves out of this on our own. My best suggestion is that we grab a bite to eat and then scout around a bit to find out just what we've gotten ourselves into. Maybe then we can figure out what our next move should be."

Everyone agreed it was the most sensible course of action and the rumblings from their stomachs cast the final vote. Buffalo grabbed the waterproof flight bag that had, until recently, been their life raft and tossed it into the center of the clearing. Then squatting next to it, he unzipped it and began rummaging through its contents. Simon, Max, and Dex formed a circle around the bag and sat cross-legged, eagerly anticipating their long overdue breakfast. A hungry Jeep wandered over also and lay panting in the grass next to Buffalo. Dipping into the bag, Buffalo produced a few handfuls of "survival rations" - - a can of Spam, a box of Oreo Creme sandwiches, two bottles of root beer, a package of Cracker Jacks, more gum, and some dog biscuits. The kids all stared open-mouthed at the odd assortment of snacks.

"What?" asked Buffalo defensively.

"That's it?" asked Max, somewhat incredulously. "Those are our *survival* rations?"

"It's my stuff," explained Buffalo as he doled out the meal. "I just bring enough food to keep me an' Jeep from gettin' hungry on the flight. Plus a few tools, some personal stuff, a knife, and a flashlight"

Actually, the group was so hungry by now that the miserable collection of junk food tasted like dinner at the Waldorf anyway. They shared everything and were soon busily munching and cramming the sugary snacks into their very empty bellies. Of course Jeep got the dog biscuits all to himself and was happily enjoying every morsel. After the initial pangs of hunger subsided, Buffalo went on with his speech while the kids continued to finish their repast.

"Ya know, I really wasn't much prepared for this…" The kids shot him a sarcastic glance as if to say "Who would be?" So, he held up his hands and began again. "What I mean is, I only signed on to pilot that cargo hopper. It was supposed to be a quick gig. In and out. Drop off some scientific junk at the arctic camp and get back home in time for Christmas. There weren't supposed to be passengers involved, let alone… you guys."

Max looked hurt, "You mean, *kids*?"

"Well, I felt that way at first, but you guys have really held up pretty good. Ya see, I never worry about myself - - I just roll with the punches. But I've never had to look out for nobody *else* before... 'cept Jeep. Back at the plane, I was afraid I was going to be playin' scoutmaster to three namby-pamby kids. But after all that we've been through, you've been okay. Better'n okay. You've shown the kind of courage and smarts that would put a lot of grown men I've known to shame. I don't know what we're in for, here in this place, but if you guys keep it up, it's a fair bet we'll all get through this somehow and find our way home."

Everyone ate rather quickly, both because they were so terribly hungry and because, despite their sore muscles and weary bodies, they were very eager to go exploring and learn more about this strange land they had found. They first decided that the clearing they had slept in would make a pretty good temporary camp - - it was close to fresh water and the thick jungle surrounding it seemed to make a natural wall of defense. They gathered their "breakfast" litter and buried it using sticks to dig with. They hoped that would get rid of any food smells that might attract predators.

Next, because of the clammy heat, they needed to get rid of some of the extra clothing they were still wearing. Much of it was still damp from their time in the water and they were happy to discard their sweaters and sweatshirts and roll up their shirtsleeves. Luckily, everyone, including tomboy Maxine, was wearing jeans and sturdy sneakers or boots that would now prove quite useful in this jungle terrain. Simon decided to just wear his plain white T-shirt, in which he was always most comfortable anyway, and removed the plaid flannel shirt he'd been sweltering in, tying it around his waist in case he might need it later. Buffalo stepped behind some bushes and within a few moments, came back with a bundle of thermal long-johns he'd been wearing under his clothes the whole time! He then began rummaging around in his flight bag again and produced a light blue cotton work shirt and a rather large bone-handled Bowie hunting knife in a leather sheath. It had a fastener for attaching to his belt and he did so. He then went down on one knee and rolled up his right pants leg a bit. There, in another sheath tucked inside his tall leather work boot was a second knife only slightly smaller. He took it out and examined it closely. It was the knife he'd used to separate Simon from his parka hood thereby depriving one Plesiosaur of it's lunch. Buffalo wiped the blade on his thigh and then replaced it, rolled his pants back down and stood. He turned then to see all three kids staring at him. Simon spoke up and said, "I was going to mention that I had a pocket knife, but I guess it's a little out classed..." Buffalo grinned and Max and Dex chuckled at Simon's sarcasm. Feeling refreshed and significantly lightened, the little band was ready to begin their exploration.

Buffalo confided that the first thing he wanted to check out was the tunnel they had emerged from because its appearance had been so confusing. They all agreed, eager to solve the mystery of the curious "floating" waterfall. To get there they would only have to follow the river about a hundred yards or so upstream... but that wasn't necessarily easy. The jungle growth was still very thick in that direction, though it lacked the great trees and palms that grew in such profusion in the rest of the jungle. Buffalo did the best he could to clear a path with his Bowie knife, but they really could have used a machete to hack through such dense foliage. It was slow going for the first thirty yards or so of tangled brush and vines and then the plantlife began to thin out. It was also getting increasingly brighter around them as they proceeded. They followed the noise of the waterfall and the next twenty yards went fairly smoothly. They knew they were getting close, for the air was getting more humid with mist and the plant leaves were wetter. Then the tall plants that blocked their view suddenly gave way to low bushes and scrub that only grew about knee-high. As they burst forth from the veil of exotic flora that had obscured their vision, they found themselves in full view of the tunnel that had entrapped them... and the waterfall that had so rudely deposited them here.

Just ahead, pale green water gushed furiously from a glowing hole about twenty feet in diameter that seemed to "hover" several yards above the river. The cascading waters of the falls churned up a fine mist that filled the air and coated all the vegetation growing near or along the riverbanks. The cooling spray felt refreshing on the faces of the intrepid explorers, but the white mist blended so seamlessly with the background of white light, that almost all detail of the hole was obscured from view. The brighter hole seemed fixed in the midst of an all pervasive white light that arched upward in every direction to become the sky!

The brightness of the "sky "hurt their eyes and they were forced to avert them. They gazed instead into the river and watched the roaring water of the cataract churn the roiling waters to foam. Behind the falls, wavelets lapped at a glistening gray rock wall that was drenched by the constant turbulent splashing of the falls. And somehow, as the wall rose upwards, the angular rock seemed to just blend right into the uniform white light of the dazzling sky! But getting even that much visual information was blinding and they found themselves soon squinting through teary eyes. Jeep whimpered a bit and turned to head back into the protective wall of vegetation.

"C'mon," said Buffalo, "Jeep's probably got the right idea, but I think we may get some answers to this puzzle if we can get a little closer and away from the mist."

Wordlessly, and with heads lowered to protect their eyes, the group followed Buffalo as he moved forward and more to the right, away from the river. Their progress was easier now for the taller plantlife had not only ended in the virtual "wall" of foliage they had broken through, but the scrub growth and bushes diminished to just grass with each step they took towards the ever increasing brightness. Very soon however, as they drew just about even with the erupting falls, they were forced to a halt. Here the light was so intense they could barely see where they were going. The plants and grasses on the ground were brown and withered and stopped growing in an almost perfect line several feet in front of them. Bare soil and rock extended from that line directly into the brilliant whiteness!

"Turn around, go back!" commanded Buffalo, "Turn your backs to it and don't look at the light… it's too bright! I've gotta try one more thing though…" And with that, he clapped one hand over his tightly shut eyes and with his free hand extended rigidly before him, he faced the brightness and slowly walked forward, counting the paces aloud. He had just gotten to twenty-one when his hand contacted a solid barrier before him! It was moist and spongy but firm! He felt what seemed to be something organic, like leaves or moss! The light here was so intense that he could "see" the bright pinkness of his own blood through his hand and eyelids! And yet there was no heat to accompany the light. It was as temperate here as in the rest of the jungle. Buffalo's suspicions were confirmed and he carefully turned around again. He then retraced his steps, counting again to twenty-one before removing the protecting shield of his hand.

With a muttered, "Let's go," he continued on past the kids who were waiting by the copse of taller vegetation and only too glad to fall in behind him and get away from the blinding wall of light. When they reached the spot by the waterfall where they had moments before emerged from the forest, they found the path they had hacked from the woods and quickly reentered the sheltering shadows of the stumpy broad-leafed trees and ferns. They collectively sighed with relief, for the darker shade was very soothing to their bleary eyes. They stopped a little further on where they found Jeep waiting with waggling stump in the path before them.

Glancing down, Max suddenly gasped and exclaimed, "Mr. Brews... Buffalo! Look at your hand!"

Everyone stared in disbelief as Buffalo raised his hand to inspect it. It was glowing brightly! "Well, I'll be..." he remarked. Buffalo clapped and swished his hands together to clear them of what appeared to be a glowing dust. Now both his hands were glowing! He slapped his hands against his pants legs and the glowing spread to his thighs and filled the air like powder! Then the glow slowly faded away and his hands and pants legs returned to normalcy. "Well, anyway, it comes off... sort of... no harm done... I think." By way of explanation, he then told them of his encounter with the solid wall of light.

"What does it all mean?" asked Simon. "What is it?"

"I think it's *plants*," answered Dex. "I scooped these off the ground while Buffalo was exploring the wall." All heads turned to see what Dexter had to display. In his outstretched hand was a clump of tiny dry brown leafy shapes that looked like confetti. "The ground was littered with them. I think it's some kind of moss or lichen that glows in the dark! Kind of like a lightning bug or those deep-sea fish we learned about in Mr. Benning's science class last year."

Here Buffalo broke in, " Apparently, they completely cover the walls... they grow together in a thick wet tangled mat. I felt it. It was spongy and damp."

"Yes," continued Dex, "And when they're glowing all together, it makes a light bright enough to seem like daylight. They were probably growing in the tunnel that brought us here, too... spreading back inside from the mouth of the waterfall. Farther back in the tunnel, farther away from here, the plants would start to diminish... and the thinner growth at the edges of their range made the light appear very dim to us at first. That's why the light got so much brighter the closer we got to... here."

"Yeah, but where is *'here'*?" interrupted Simon. "Plants have to grow on *something!* In the tunnel they were on the walls and ceiling, but we spilled out of that tunnel and now we're in a *jungle!* If these glowing veggies are making all this light and they need to cling to walls or something to grow, then that would mean..." and it slowly dawned on him, "that... we're not outside at all... and we're still...in a..."

"...Cave," finished Buffalo.

They all lifted their faces to stare at the endless false "sky" above them. "It must be *huge!*"

observed Max, voicing everyone's thoughts aloud. "It's got to be *miles* across! The biggest cavern *ever*! And it's whole ceiling is totally covered with this glowing moss? So... they must make enough light to even support the growth of all these tropical plants and trees! The light they create feeds all the plantlife in the jungle all around us! Through... what did Mr. Benning call it? Photo.. photo..."

"Photosynthesis..." said Dex, completing her thought.

"What about heat... and water?" wondered Simon, "Jungle plants need lots of warmth and moisture to grow *this* well. It didn't feel any hotter where we were, near the wall."

"No," answered Buffalo, " It wasn't hot at all, but it *was* very wet. I suspect the heat comes from elsewhere within the cavern. We drifted for a long way in that tunnel and we're probably very deep underground. Perhaps deep enough to feel the heat generated by the core of good ol' Mother Earth."

Dex jumped in to add some thoughts that jibed with Buffalo's, "Maybe there are hot springs, or tar pits, or maybe even a lava flow somewhere in here. Being a sealed cavern, it would trap the heat and hold it pretty well. Like a huge terrarium. As for the water, well there's the river of course... I'm not certain about the whole mechanism yet, but I have my suspicions."

They stood quietly in a tight group, again searching the "sky" above for more answers to the mysteries of this strange jungle world entombed far below the surface of the Earth. Now that the true identity of the cavern had been revealed, it brought to light answers for so much of the weird phenomena they had observed since their arrival. It was also very disquieting to realize that their newly discovered sanctuary, could also be a new prison. Where could they go from here? Was there a way out... back to the surface? Back home? Absorbing all this information and pondering the enormity of their situation made them feel quite small and helpless, lost in the vastness of this undiscovered land.

Their moment of reflection was suddenly broken however, when the unexpected happened. Something that none of them were prepared for. It had been, up to this moment, and with their present sense of isolation, the farthest thought from their minds. They heard a scream. A distant scream that filtered through the leaves and fronds of the jungle. The frantic screams of a woman in danger!

Chapter 6
"Beetle Battle"

For the briefest moment, time itself seemed to stop. The jungle became even quieter than before, if that were at all possible. All heads turned towards the direction from which the screams had been heard. Hearts stopped beating and breath was held for that one instant of disbelief that gripped them all. Then another scream rang out and Jeep took off with a bound into the dense jungle foliage! Just as quickly, and without a second thought to consider the possible dangers that might befall them, all four castaways turned as one and lunged after him, back down the crude path that Buffalo had earlier hacked through the impenetrable wall of growth.

They raced as fast as the vines and creepers would allow and reached their little campsite clearing just in time to see Jeep's rump disappear through the tangle of greenery on its opposite side. Buffalo took the lead and plowed into the thick wall of woven vines and stems like a bulldozer! Tearing and hacking like a wildman at the incredibly dense foliage with his Bowie knife, he sometimes ripped the stems and fronds off the plants or pulled the woody vines down from the trees with his bare hands! They were making considerable headway, but they feared their progress was much too slow. They wondered also if they had mistaken their direction. Then everyone froze for an instant as another scream suddenly pierced the forest. It was much closer this time!

With renewed vigor, Buffalo heaved his huge torso into the impenetrable wall of plantlife with an audible growl, and to everyone's surprise, they broke through the foliage and onto a wide trail!

It was as wide as a cart-path and ran reasonably straight in both directions. They heard Jeep barking off to their right and looked to see him standing in the weed-covered trail, about three city-blocks away. Now they launched into a full run, for the low grasses of the trail was akin to a sidewalk compared to the thick matted tangle they had just left. As they approached Jeep, he turned and darted off again to the left... into the dense green growth of the tropical jungle! They thought they were going to have to plow into the impenetrable snarl of leaves and stems again, but as they reached the exact spot where Jeep had been standing, they saw that he had actually dashed off down a much smaller path that was almost hidden from view by the large palm fronds that overgrew it. Without hesitation, they wheeled and raced into the path in single file, the leaves and branches whipping at their faces and bodies as they recklessly bounded along the unevenness of the root-covered ground. Buffalo was still in the lead, followed closely by Simon and Max. Dexter, who tripped once and almost lost his glasses, brought up the rear. They ran as fast as they dared through the curtain of fronds and then, quite suddenly, they spilled out into a small clearing, almost stumbling over Jeep! He was standing right in front of them at the path's end, his bristling back toward them and growling menacingly at something like a wolf at bay!

Astonishment and surprise turned to horror and fright as their eyes lifted to see what Jeep was snarling at. It was an insect. But, *what* an insect! It was easily the size of a small car! Their gasps caught in their throats as their minds raced to cope with, and make sense of, what their eyes were witnessing! Before them, in this leaf-cluttered clearing, stood a tremendous orange and black striped beetle - - bigger than any bug any of them had ever imagined possible! It had its back turned to them and was apparently as yet unaware of their presence, allowing them a full view of its broad glossy back and rhythmically throbbing hairy abdomen. In fact, at this size, it was quite a revelation to see just how "hairy" an insect could be, for the beast's legs and underbelly were covered with thick black bristles… some as thick as a human thumb! Its six legs were bright orange and appeared stout, yet it moved upon them very nimbly as it quickly and lightly scurried from side to side in small rapid movements. They couldn't see its head, which was hidden by the bulk of its body, but they could see a feathery pair of sooty-black colored antennae that stretched out to either side like a bizarre rack of antlers.

The giant seemed to be very much interested in something immediately in front of it across the clearing. They looked closer in that direction and noticed for the first time that there seemed to be a netting of thick ropes or vines amongst the leaf litter… with something moving and twisting beneath it as though trapped in a spider's web! It was this unknown helpless victim that the monster was obviously intent on attacking.

All of these thoughts and observations took but a moment to flash through to their stunned senses as they stood transfixed in disbelief. They had been caught entirely by surprise and were frozen with uncertainty - - totally unprepared as they were, for the shock of these discoveries about the land they were marooned in. But, when once again that voice cried out in desperation, the terrified scream of a woman in mortal danger, *and* from directly in the path of the shuffling beast before them, the castaways exploded into action as though their plans were carefully rehearsed! Buffalo Brewster lunged forward, Bowie knife in hand, and leaped upon the creature's shiny striped back! Its hard armored wing-covers were slippery as well as glossy, like a newly waxed floor, and Buffalo almost tumbled right off the beast! But instead, he dropped quickly to his knees and used his forward momentum to slide right up to the monster's neck and head where he grabbed hold of the neck carapace and tried to find a soft spot where he could insert the razor-sharp point of his blade!

The kids meanwhile, grabbed sticks and stones from the path and charged the animal from all sides. They spread out until they had encircled the behemoth bug and began darting in and out, alternately beating about its legs with the sticks and pelting it with stones to harry it, all the while screaming like banshees! The enraged and confused insect didn't know what to make of this sudden new threat. It danced and spun wildly, trying to shake off the rider who continually stung its neck. Its small orange head had large brown expressionless compound eyes that glittered in the dappled forest light as it wobbled from side to side, trying to focus on the intruders. Dripping with thick milky-colored drool, its large vise-like mandibles snapped and pinched at the air in anticipation of battle. It tried to lunge after the three who surrounded it, but each time it singled out one attacker for revenge, the other two would redouble their efforts and distract the beast from its purpose. Jeep too, did his best to worry the giant insect by leaping and circling around it, barking and growling as he did so.

Suddenly, the huge insect seemed to make up its mind to deal with its attackers one by one! It darted straight for Dexter and nothing Simon or Max could do would deter it! Dexter had to backpedal furiously to evade the snapping slathering jaws and fell backwards to the ground as he tripped over another tree root! Jeep bounded to his side instantly and stood growling and baring his teeth menacingly at the charging beetle. Confronted by this new unfamiliar threat, the creature momentarily stopped in its tracks.

Buffalo knew the bug would not be diverted from its target for long, and that Jeep was really no match for those fearsome mandibles! Frustrated by his futile attempt to inflict any damage on the armored creature with his knife, Buffalo suddenly changed tactics and reached forward and grabbed one of its feathery antennae, and then began twisting it with both hands! That was when the giant insect decided it'd had enough! Its smooth broad back suddenly parted in the middle and the two orange and black striped shields swung up and out to either side. Great greenish transparent wings followed suit and became a sudden blur as with a thunderous roar and a mighty gust of wind the behemoth became airborne as effortlessly as its inch-long "cousins" of the surface world! Buffalo barely had time to slide from its back as it lifted off, or he would have been borne away by the beast!

The wind subsided. The dust and leaves settled... and the creature was gone. Even its buzzing disappeared over the treetops, quickly receding into the distance. The rescuers dusted themselves off, gathered together, and slowly approached the rope netting to see what exactly it was that they had rescued.

Chapter 7
"A Friend Found"

The crew of four moved in closer around the large square net in the midst of the clearing and stood for a moment with their mouths hanging slack. For there, trapped beneath the webbing of cords was a girl of no more than nineteen or twenty! A girl in primitive trappings with tussled jet-black hair and smooth reddish-brown skin. Large dark eyes blazed out from beneath the long strands of dusky hair that fell across her face and she gazed unwaveringly at them with a defiant and menacing gleam that betrayed the fear and anger she felt. Her eyes never left them as she awkwardly backed away in the crouched position that was all that the weight of the netting would allow her. She reminded Simon of a sleek Black Panther at bay, confused and enraged in its confinement, and ready to pounce on any unwary captors. She seemed to pay particular attention to Buffalo's movements and sought to keep as much distance from him as possible.

Buffalo broke the spell of silent wonderment, as he spoke softly and gently so as not to further frighten the ensnared girl. He suggested they spread out and attempt to lift the trap from the ground. The soothing sound of his soft deep voice seemed to effect a subtle change in the girl, for she seemed to become a little less rigid. As they gathered around the edges of the netting, they noticed for the first time how cleverly the trap had been constructed. It was basically a large square net of woven creepers about thirty feet across in size and attached to a frame of strong but flexible saplings. These in turn were attached to a larger thicker beam of wood that lay flat on the forest floor and disappeared into the tangled jungle. It was really somewhat like a giant flyswatter in design, but the netting was much looser so as to trap its victim rather than squash it. It was probably intended to snare the kind of prey that they had just battled with and not the human kind it now mistakenly contained.

Spread out evenly along the trap's perimeter, they grabbed hold of the frame and struggled in vain to lift it. Even with Buffalo's great strength, the "swatter" resisted their efforts to budge it. It was either a lot heavier than it looked or something was holding it down. Buffalo pondered for a moment and decided he would have to begin cutting through the vines themselves to free the girl... a considerable task given the thickness of the tough fibers. Just then, Dexter called to him from the edge of the clearing, where the main beam extended into the jungle, and he went over to investigate. He spoke with Dexter and then slipped into the woods for a moment, only to return once more to caution them all to stand clear of the trap.

The kids moved to the edge of the clearing and Max knelt down to hold Jeep back - - his curiosity would easily have him wandering onto the netting! His little stump was wagging overtime and the overly-friendly dog seemed very anxious to introduce himself to the newly discovered human. Suddenly, there was a terrific snapping and crashing in the jungle and all heads turned to see a huge boulder trussed with rope descend from a tall tree! The trap frame beside them lifted about a foot off the ground and bounced once, sending up a cloud of leaves and forest litter. Then it rapidly tilted into the air to swing back into its original position amongst the jungle trees, where it stood hidden from sight to await another victim.

Buffalo leaped from the forest with a big smile because of his achievement and then stopped in his tracks. Everyone turned to look in the direction he was gazing... towards the hapless girl captive. For the second time today they had their breath taken away as they stared in awe.

Slowly and cautiously, with a proud and defiant gleam in her coal-black eyes that carefully scanned the strangers for any sign of aggression, the raven-haired girl stood to face them. Her foot was still tightly encircled with a loop of rope that had probably first triggered the trap to spring. Knowing that she could not run, she bravely faced her strangely dressed alien captors. Her chest heaved with long slow deliberate breaths as she drew herself to her full height. A visible nervous tremble ran through her slim athletic frame as her hand came up to brush back the long tussled strands of ebony hair that effectively hid her features. As she tucked the loose strands behind her ear, they glimpsed for the first time, the soft oriental-like contours of a delicate but determined girlish face. Her smooth bronze skin and long sleek dusky hair further endorsed the impression that this elfin-faced beauty was likely of Asian, or perhaps American Indian descent... yet her primitive costume reminded them more of ancient warrior tribes, like Vikings, Egyptians, or even Aztecs.

"Whoaaa..." observed Dex, "She looks like she stepped right out of a Tarzan book!"

The others all nodded in silent agreement. The total charm of her radiant and savage beauty was absolutely breathtaking in its combination of feminine prowess and barbaric ferocity. Her strong lithesome figure was clad in a primitive but elaborate tunic that covered her torso much like a swimsuit and left her shoulders covered only by her long dark hair. It was a pliable garment, fashioned of some sort of strange shiny brown leather, and trimmed with pewter colored metals inlaid with tiny colorful patterns of coral red and indigo blue. The bottom of the tunic was fringed into a *very* abbreviated skirt and around her hips she wore a thick metal inlaid belt from which hung an empty jeweled scabbard, probably intended for a dagger or short knife. Her fine athletic legs were bare and she wore thin but sturdy looking sandals to protect her feet. A delicate silver bangle with tiny tinkling bells was wrapped around one slender ankle. But that was not the extent of her jeweled adornment! She also wore several bracelets on each wrist, a thin metal collar with charms of gold and lapis lazuli around her neck, and she even had a silver armband around her left upper arm with an embossed serpent motif. She wore no earrings though, or facial makeup either, for that matter. That face, those eyes, needed nothing more to enhance the beauty of her features!

Her body stood tensely rigid for action, and though she must've been inwardly frightened by the strange appearance of the fair-skinned "alien" beings that surrounded her, her mouth opened and a soft firm voice spoke to them in a language like nothing the little band had ever heard before. It was a guttural sounding language with many harsh syllables and uneven syncopation, yet her lilting inflection and gentle timbre made it sound almost lyrical to their ears. The several brief phrases she spoke ended with a questioning upward modulation, and although they didn't understand the words themselves, they could imagine the general intent of their meaning. They probably would've roughly translated into something like: "Who are you and where are you from?" or "What do you want and what are you going to do with me?"

Buffalo cleared his throat and spoke up for the group in a gentle and soothing voice, "We mean you no harm," he began, "We are friends..." and with that, he took a step forward. Immediately, the warrior spirit in the girl took over and she recoiled into a crouched defensive position, instinctively reaching for the knife that should have been in the scabbard by her side. Buffalo's eyes went wide and he stopped short and threw up his hands in submission. "Whoaa... take it easy..." he soothed as he took a step back. A huge grin spread irrepressibly across his face. Many toughs and rugged men had stepped aside with a shudder when Buffalo approached. To see this dusty, exhausted and disheveled, girl-savage ready to battle him at such disadvantage, presented him with a show of spunk he'd never really encountered before. He'd already been charmed by her exotic and primal beauty, but this display of feisty temperament and warlike posture was enough to warm his heart through and through. Her feminine ferocity seemed adorable to him and he suddenly felt so lighthearted that he broke out laughing! Buffalo didn't know it yet, but he was a man enchanted.

Buffalo's booming laughter broke the tension of the moment and Jeep took the opportunity to run forward, with his stump wagging, to greet the newfound friend. The girl, meanwhile, straightened up slowly and her brow furrowed as she stared intently at Buffalo, then across to the kids (who didn't know what to make of the situation), and then to Jeep who now sat at her feet waiting for a friendly pat on the head. She seemed genuinely concerned and worried that Jeep should take an interest in her, as though she'd never seen a dog before. She looked back at the form of the huge bearded giant she'd heard the young ones call "Buff-a-loo" and he was still chuckling, obviously unimpressed with her pitiful attempt to defend herself.

She was greatly puzzled by the strange appearance and costume of these unusual beings. She had never encountered, or heard of, any such tribe as these in all of Kontonqua, and knew not if they were friend or foe. She was wary by nature, all her people were... but something about these foreign strangers and their actions seemed reassuring and friendly, so she relaxed her guard a moment to stop and reconsider the whole situation. "Who were these odd-looking pale folk that dressed in such brightly colored blankets and spoke gibberish? And how is it that they traveled with one of the ancient Wolf-Friends that were known only through the tales of The Beginning? Did they mean her harm? It was true that they did rescue her from the Clekweg that was about to make a meal of her. And they freed her from the hunter's trap that had snared her as well... even though they had her at a disadvantage. And they were certainly not Ikusk... so perhaps they were not an enemy. There was something gentle and friendly in the manner of the strong giant warrior with the jolly laughter... he who could battle Clekweg almost barehanded with nothing but a blade... and backed by a party of children at his side! They were most courageous... perhaps foolish... but they didn't seem at all threatening..."

At that moment, Max decided to take action and stepped forward to try *her* hand at winning over the captive girl... speaking softly as she approached. When the savage warrioress saw the kind smile and the genuine sparkle of friendship in the eyes of the fair-skinned blonde-haired girl, she realized just how badly she needed the help of these strangers... she needed friends now more than ever. Despite their odd appearance and weird behavior, she had made up her mind to give in and succumb to her intuitions. She relaxed her hostile stance, drew a long calming breath, and with a final exhausted shudder, she shook the hair back away from her face... and smiled broadly in return.

Chapter 8
"The Wisest Path"

That warm pretty smile gave Max some reassurance, so she cautiously continued her approach towards the savage-looking jungle girl, not knowing quite what to do, or say... or what to expect in return. Max was fairly tall for her age and as she drew close to the rather petite, though athletically muscular cavern-dweller, she realized that she was almost eye to eye with her. This was somewhat unnerving, for those large coal-black eyes, heavy-lidded and long lashed, never wavered their gaze as the warrioress kept her stare fixed directly on Max alone. Max continued forward bravely and Simon and Dex slowly followed in her wake. Buffalo thought it best to stay back and let the kids make the introductions. Perhaps they'd be perceived as a little less threatening to this distraught and confused girl that moments ago was about to be devoured by a bug and was now confronted by "extraterrestrials". Everyone smiled and kept their movements slow and obvious so as not to further frighten her.

But, when Max got within a few feet of her, the girl suddenly reached out with her right arm extended stiffly and gripped Max by the shoulder. Max fairly jumped at the sudden contact and let out a tiny yelp! But a quick look into the jungle girl's eyes assured her that no threat was meant. She looked at the girl's outstretched arm that next gave her shoulder a gentle squeeze and she understood the meaning of the simple gesture. Max raised her own right hand and, with only a moment's hesitation, gripped the girl's left shoulder in return.

Immediately, a change came over the warrior-girl. A larger winsome smile flashed across her face and she loosed an obvious sigh of relief. She then began speaking and gesturing quite rapidly, as though they'd all been the best of friends for years! Her lovely features became fully animated as her dark eyes danced to the events and emotions contained within the story she was telling. Her expressive eyes would widen and flash, or suddenly narrow and glance sidelong, as they played accompaniment to the primitive words she spoke in her soft melodic voice. She gestured wildly with her hands and body as she talked, and it became apparent from her actions, that she was attempting to relate her recent adventures to the foreigners. Buffalo couldn't help but chuckle at the sudden and delightfully girlish change in the fierce jungle warrior. She stopped abruptly at the sound and tilted her head to see past Max... and looked directly at him with a slight scowl and a bit of a pout. Perhaps his amusement had been ill timed. It seemed as though she had taken his chortle to be a comment on something that she'd been explaining in her story. Her brow furrowed and she pursed her lips. Then with all the poise of a prima ballerina, she tossed back her head, placed her hands on her hips, and extended her shapely leg, her sandaled foot delicately held aloft with toes pointed, to display the rope which still held her bound. She directed her limb, and a stern gaze, at Buffalo as though to say, "Well, what are you waiting for?" And then she wiggled her foot as though to add urgency to the demand.

Buffalo took the hint and quietly approached the girl. She inspected all his actions with great interest as he knelt down and cut the thick restraining vine from her slender brown ankle. Her eyes widened in wonder at the sight of the bright shiny steel blade of the Bowie knife that so effortlessly sliced through the woody strands. She found herself suppressing a small thrill of excitement as she felt the big man's hands grasp her foot and ankle. And there was an impish gleam of approval in her eyes as she noticed the bulky muscles of his arms and back rippling beneath the strange fabric of his shirt. Yet, she hid her observations and feelings well, for when Buffalo was through and looked upward for approval, he was met only with cool disdain and a bit of a smirk.

With a sudden intake of breath and a quick turn on her heel, the girl dismissed Buffalo and turned her attention back towards the kids and resumed her story, presumably where she'd left off, as though there'd been no interruption at all. They listened to the girl's tale with riveted interest, though they understood not a word. There was just something refreshing and fascinating about the jungle-girl's narrative style. Done in that pleasant and melodic tone that added such nuance to a foreign language at once so primitive and yet vaguely familiar.

When the girl finished her story, she looked around at the group as though expecting some sort of reaction to her tale, or perhaps questions. The kids stood smiling and nodding as though they'd understood every word, but she soon sensed from their silent and grinning faces that they were merely pretending to. After a momentary awkward silence, she gave a nervous chuckle and shrugged her shoulders… obviously at a loss as to what to do next. Max again took the initiative and stepped forward to get the girl's attention. She then placed her index finger upon her own chest and spoke her name slowly and clearly in an unmistakable gesture of self-identification. Then, pointing, she proceeded to name each member of the castaway troop in the same manner. Even Jeep.

The jungle girl caught on immediately. She knew exactly what Max was up to and with a broad smile she pointed to herself and announced, "Kwa-I-Anya". It was a pretty name. Especially, the way she said it. And they all practiced to say it precisely the way she did, (except for Buffalo, who insisted on calling her just "Anya". This seemed to ire her even more at the time, though no one knew why. Soon, however, they were all calling her "Anya" and she was eventually comfortable with that.). She learned their names quickly and it made them all beam with delight to hear their names spoken by this beautiful barbarian girl with the soft sweet voice, but uttered with the strange accent derived from her primitive and mysterious native tongue.

"Moks... Tsigh-Moon... Deks-toor... Buf'Alow... en **Cheep**!" she repeated as she pointed to each of them.

Jeep had been wandering around sniffing out this strange new place, but at the mention of his name, he perked up immediately and saw his chance to make his acquaintance at last. So, with great loping strides, he bounded across the clearing and right up to the startled girl, where he stood and placed his paws squarely on her shoulders, almost knocking her over! The bewildered girl was caught entirely by surprise, and though she took a quick step backward, she was not fast enough to avoid a great sloppy kiss from the over-affectionate hound! She was completely taken aback and stood spluttering and wiping her mouth for a moment.

Then, with hands on hips and a fearsome scowl, she glared down at the innocent curly-haired pooch that now sat at her feet with a wistfully tilted head and vigorously wagging stump.   Her anger melted away... dissolved by Jeep's cuddliness and friendly optimism. She smiled once again and, giving in to her curiosity, she haltingly extended a hand to give Jeep a tentative pat on the head. He licked at her hand, but undaunted, she bravely continued on to touch the soft curly hair on his head. When she felt the warm tickly softness of his kinked fur, she giggled and looked to the others for approval.

Max suddenly realized, from the girl's behavior, that she probably had no experience with dogs. So, she knelt down beside Jeep and gave him a big hug, to show her that it was all right to return the animal's affection. Anya, reassured, knelt down and gave Jeep the biggest hug he'd had in weeks! Everyone laughed, and suddenly it was as though they'd all known each other for years. A "forever" bond of friendship had been struck at that moment, forged as it often is, through the mediation of unselfish affection displayed by a loyal pup.

Buffalo led the way back out of the booby-trapped clearing by retracing their steps along the narrow path.   The girl walked along with the castaways without complaint until they reached the larger wide jungle trail that led back to their makeshift camp. At that point, she seemed confused as to why they would want to go in that particular direction. With a determined shake of her head and a few imploring words she pointed the other way... down the unexplored part of the trail. They could not, at first, make her follow them. She stubbornly refused to head in that direction, so Simon ran down the trail to the spot where they had earlier burst though the thick vegetation and pointed into the jungle. Still, she adamantly insisted on going the other way. Buffalo was considering whether to leave her behind or put her over his shoulder, when Simon disappeared into the jungle for a few moments and returned waving Buffalo's flight bag. It was then that the jungle girl understood that there was something there that they needed or wished her to see, so she relented and cautiously followed them back down the wide trail and through the rough-hewn path until they reached the clearing by the river.

The girl, Anya, was obviously very uncomfortable about being out in the open in the clearing that passed for their camp. She kept looking around and upward, nervously scanning the "sky" and jumping at any sudden noise. (It was only much later, when they'd learned more about their adopted home, that they'd realized just how incredibly lucky they had been to move about and even sleep out in the open, without an attack by one of the many gigantic insect predators that patrolled the air above!)

Before gathering their belongings, Buffalo decided, out of curiosity, to lead the girl to the spot where they could get a good view of the "floating hole" and the accompanying erupting gush of water from the underground stream. The girl appeared especially uneasy to proceed in that direction and as soon as they emerged from the trail and were in sight of the falls, she unexpectedly fell to her knees with bowed head and arms extended stiffly! She then shouted a short phrase three times in succession above the din of the rushing torrent. The castaways looked at each other with momentary chagrin, uncertain of the meaning of the girl's obeisance, but she just as suddenly popped back up and acted as though nothing had happened. In fact, she appeared to be more at ease than before.

Buffalo cleared his throat and pointed at the tunnel's opening and said, "Home." He then pointed to himself and the kids and repeated the single word and the gesture several times. Anya looked at him quizzically, with furrowed brow, trying to understand the significance of his motioning. She then brightened as though the message had gotten through, but she instantly brought her hand to her mouth, averted her eyes, and began to giggle! As though she'd just been told a joke! She could hardly contain herself, and seemed to blush, as she looked back and forth from Buffalo to the tunnel. Then she quickly turned and walked back down the path, shaking her head and chuckling. If she had correctly understood their attempt to reveal their origins, then she didn't believe it for a minute!

When Buffalo and the kids returned to the makeshift camp, they found Anya smiling and awaiting them by the rough pathway back to the wide trail... decidedly ready to leave. Buffalo drew the kids aside for an impromptu meeting.

"Look," he began, "We've been through a lot the last coupl'a days, but we shouldn't just go runnin' off without thinkin'. We've got some big decisions to make and we're all in this together, so we'd better make sure we're all agreed." There was a general nodding of heads, so Buffalo continued, "First of all, like we discussed before, there's little likelihood of us being found or rescued. And it's for darn sure we can't go back the way we came, so we've gotta find another way outta here. But... after that insect we've just come across, I'm not sure we'd be able to *survive* long enough to find it. This jungle-girl seems to know her way around and can possibly help us, but we really don't know a thing about her."

"That's true," interjected Simon, "But, do we really have a choice? The Amazon and the Congo are bad enough... we'd never survive against the leopards, lions, or crocodiles... or even the snakes of those jungles. But *this* place has got bugs the size of *Oldsmobiles!* How will we deal with the next one we find... or that finds us? How will we know where to look for a way out? How will we know what we can eat and what's poison? Even the plants here are different from anything we've ever seen."

Dexter broke in, "It seems to me that Anya is our best bet. She lives here and probably knows how to survive in this jungle. It's apparent from her manners, language, and garments that she is part of a larger probably successful civilization, primitive though it might be. If we could accompany her to her village, perhaps they would give us sustenance and lend us assistance..."

"Dex!" interrupted Maxine, "Stop talking like an encyclopedia! I mean, I agree with all of you, but what about Anya... the *person.* What about the fact that we just rescued her and made friends? I trust her. I don't think she would intentionally harm us. And like Simon just said... 'What choice do we really have anyway?'"

"Well," rejoined Buffalo, "You've all got good points, but just because she seems to be a friend of sorts, doesn't mean her people will be. What if her tribe, or whatever they are, doesn't *like* strangers in their territory? They could be headhunters for all we know. Look, all I'm sayin' is just let's not rush off blindly just 'cause she wants us to. Let's get out of this clearing and under the safety of the trees and then see where she wants to go. We can travel along with her as long as it suits us, find out just how trustworthy she is, and maybe learn a few things along the way."

That seemed to sit well with everyone, so they went about their business to prepare to leave. The kids chose what they wished to keep from the clothing they had earlier discarded and stuffed it all into Buffalo's flight bag. Dexter found an empty Army canteen in there and Buffalo brought it down to the river to fill it.

Buffalo's thoughts were heavy and his worries seemed to multiply by the minute. His life had always been a rather simple one, and rather predictable too. But from the moment that these kids had boarded his plane, things had not only gone terribly wrong, they had gone so completely out of his control as well. Buffalo was a man that liked to stay in charge of a situation. Even in the war, he felt that he'd always been somewhat in control... ever on the offensive and guiding his own destiny from the cockpit of his fighter. But now, in this hostile miserable jungle, he was entirely out of his element and still being "swept" along with no more options than he'd had in the underground stream! Events were controlling *him* rather than the way he liked it, the other way around.

As he squatted by the river's edge, filling the canteen, Buffalo was too absorbed in his thoughts to notice the undulating ripples in the thick blanket of bright green algae that covered its surface. Something was moving beneath the matted ooze and swimming directly towards his perch on the riverbank. Something big... and then it disappeared.

As the last of the air-bubbles gurgled out of the mouth of the canteen, Buffalo knelt to replace the cap. Just as his hand cleared the water, a huge gaping mouth with hairy mandibles rushed from the depths and snapped shut right where his hand had been! The creature was an immense Water Beetle... and its large paddle-shaped legs furiously beat the water to foam as it tried to lift its glossy black bulk above the water's surface to get another try at its elusive prey! But despite its efforts, its weight worked against it and dragged the beast back below the river's surface.

Buffalo watched as the hideous head sank backwards into the murk of the depths and was held transfixed by the cold menace of the lifeless black eyes that had briefly stared back into his. He knew at that moment that any further delay would mean certain death! Buffalo spun and scrambled back on all fours up the riverbank, racing for the safety of the grass and bushes. As he fled, the behemoth burst forth from the water once more, its gathered momentum now being enough to launch it almost completely airborne! Instinctively, Buffalo rolled to his back and landed a well-placed kick, with the heel of his boot on the monster's "chin" that sent it tumbling... careening backwards to land upside-down in the river on its armored carapace with a tremendous splash!

Everyone must have heard the commotion, for when Buffalo reentered the clearing, they were all looking directly at him. He tried to hide his disquietude, but they could see he was a bit shaken.

"What happened?" they all wanted to know.

"Nothing much," he replied, "C'mon. We're going with Anya."

Chapter 9
"Jungle Journey"

For the remainder of the day, an odd little safari - - four bedraggled castaways, a primitive native beauty, and a wooly hound - - traversed the jungle trails of a strange, mysterious, and forgotten world deep within the strata of the Earth. A primeval savage land of deadly flora and fauna; enormous bloodthirsty insects locked in constant battle between predator and prey. An environment hidden for centuries from, and oblivious to, the comforting glow of sun, moon, and stars so familiar to the displaced surface-dwellers.

The little band, led by Anya, traveled along carefully and quietly in single file, winding their way beneath the thick forest canopy that shielded them from the carnivorous eyes of the gruesome insect giants that patrolled the skies above. The breathtaking and exotic beauty of the locked-away landscape was a constant marvel to the strangers from the surface-world and they were awestruck by the humid windless stillness, the solitude, and the prolific diversity of this undiscovered Antediluvian garden of giants.

Huge fernlike trees spread their fronds like great green umbrellas, barely allowing the lichen-generated light from the cavern ceiling high above to filter in. Here and there, a chink in the botanical armor overhead would permit a bright-white shaft of light to extend through to the forest floor, its path revealing the haze of dust and pollen that permeated the atmosphere. The milky columns of light created the odd illusion that the shafts supported the canopy of green leaves like great glowing pillars. The dimly lit forest was far from gloomy however, for though the broad flat leaves of the giant trees and palms intertwined thickly, they were of a semitransparent nature which still allowed *filtered* light to penetrate. The resulting wash of emerald radiance bathed all the wonders beneath with a glowing tint of green. Overhead, delicate web-like veins stood out darkly against the brightly backlit greens of the gigantic leaves and made a wonderful mosaic pattern. The overall effect was not unlike being under an enormous green stained-glass window.

This curious phenomenon did not seem to hinder growth below it at all, for life on the forest floor flourished without parallel. An enormous variety of plantlife sprouted, crawled, twisted, hung, clung, or otherwise struggled upwards from the rich black humus in a relentless battle for space, water, and light. Vines and creepers draped from the towering trees in great cascades of gnarled tendrils and everything that grew - - vines, shrubs, and trees alike, were covered with clumps of mosses, fungi, and flowers that dotted the scenery with riotous splashes of the most surprising colors and patterns!

And by Mother Nature's design, all of this wildly intertwining vegetation served a special purpose that was absolutely essential to the survival of all the inhabitants of this hidden cavernous Eden. The thickly tangled flora acted as a "lid" to hold in the heat and moisture for all *other* life to thrive on. And the system worked so well, that a constant fine mist hovered over the ground and spread precious water to every living thing in the jungle. Fueled by the process of photosynthesis and the evaporation of the slowly meandering river that wound capriciously through the center of the cavern, the mist kept everything continually damp. As a result, water droplets collected on every leaf and stem and continued to swell until, eventually, they rolled off to fall, pattering like rain, onto the leaves below. There, they would collect and fall to the next group of leaves, and so on, until finally trickling to the spongy forest floor itself.

The incessant dripping left the impression that there had recently been a torrential downpour, but in this enclosed subterranean tropic world, it never rained for there were no clouds in the "sky" above to provide it. Just the constant turnover of humidity as the heat, generated from the Earth itself, evaporated water from the soil and river and cycled it over and over beneath the protective fronds of the great fern trees.

The unusual smells and odors were not lost on the travelers either for the circulating heat and humidity efficiently wafted both the effluvium of the decaying vegetation and leaf mould, along with the pungent aromas of fragrant exotic flowers. So, while the musty sweet smell of the forest floor assailed their nostrils like a freshly opened bag of potting-soil, the delicate perfume of jungle-blossoms delighted their senses with sensations akin to being in a flower shop. In fact, the entire alien jungle environment, for all its exotic foreign splendor, reminded the castaways very much of a gardener's greenhouse after its daily watering.

A very unwelcome effect of the oppressive heat and dripping humidity however, was that the clothing of the marooned crew of four was soon sodden and most uncomfortable. Their clothes clung wetly to them, as though they'd been swimming in them, and hampered their every movement. Their hair hung limp with sweat and they inwardly envied the lightly clad jungle-girl who led the way and seemed to be totally unaffected by the clamminess of the tropical surroundings. Her bronzed skin glistened with a film of moisture, but her hair and garments stayed dry somehow. She looked perfectly at ease and blended as one with the primeval world she was moving through.

Simon was the first to rebel and he startled everyone when he suddenly exclaimed, "This is ridiculous!" and began to shed any further unwanted clothing, tossing his flannel shirt and any other offending wet apparel into the jungle. The others laughed initially, and then they too saw the wisdom of his actions and soon joined him. When they were all down to plain T-shirts and trousers, Max had an idea of her own. She disappeared behind a large tree for a moment shouting, "Stay there!" as she disappeared behind the huge bole. They heard the sound of rending and tearing and then Max emerged wearing a crudely done but perfectly sensible pair of "cut-off" shorts, fashioned from her soggy bluejeans. The idea was an immediate hit, and the boys dashed off behind the tree to do their own tailoring!

Buffalo however, content to remain in his rugged cargo-style flight-pants, decided to just discard his cotton work-shirt and keep his sleeveless undershirt on. Anya, who was at first confused by Simon's sudden outburst, stood by and watched with curiosity, obviously amused by their antics and nodding with approval at their change of fashion. She hadn't understood from the beginning why these strangers were so overdressed in the first place. When she caught sight of Buffalo in his tightly knit singlet however, her eyes widened and she caught her breath. The man had muscles like she'd never seen before! For Buffalo, his physique was the result of hardy genetics, the constant exercise that was part of his job, and a little weight-training on the

101

side. For Anya, it was astounding. None of her people had ever attained such strength and form… if it were even genetically possible. For in truth, she wasn't aware of any men of her race that quite approached his height or bulk either. She found herself suddenly flustered by her thoughts and felt exceedingly warm. She turned away quickly, afraid that he might notice her sudden embarrassment. She couldn't understand it. She'd seen many strong and brave warriors practically naked in ceremonies, but the sight of this foreigner's powerful physique brought a blush to her cheeks.

Ready to once again get underway, the greatly less encumbered group began to thread their way once more through the tangle of growth. Anya led the way with a certainty and confidence gained through total familiarity with her native jungle environs. She walked with the kind of smooth effortless stride that, only now and then, allowed the slender metal bracelets on her wrists and ankle to tinkle like far-away wind chimes. Her manner was like that of a panther on the prowl, noiselessly slinking along the overgrown path and carefully negotiating her way with all her senses on the alert. She would scan the foliage in all directions as she forged ahead, seeking out hidden dangers with a keen and practiced eye.

She depended heavily on her hearing as well and would often motion everyone to a halt as she stopped to listen, permitting the jungle sounds to relate the story of what was transpiring beyond the encircling trees. The chattering and rasping and buzzing of some hidden insect behemoth could often be heard an unnervingly short distance away, but like the chirping of a house cricket, it would always ominously stop as they drew near and then chillingly resume after they'd passed.

Sometimes, the whirring and droning of mighty wings would filter down through the dense leaves whenever some insect titan flew through the skies directly overhead. And sometimes, the flying behemoths were even close enough to set the leaves and branches fluttering and swaying from the breeze of their passing flight, unintentionally drenching the group in the resulting downpour of water droplets shaken loose from the great fern fronds above. A couple of times, their aerial maneuvers caused Anya enough concern that she abruptly halted and motioned for everyone to be silent and to scatter off the trail. Then, she would stand stock-still, hunkered beneath a protective frond and gaze upwards for long anxious moments, apparently awaiting some sort of deadly attack from above. Each time, however, the danger would pass as quickly as it had come and the troop would resume its march.

Despite the presence of insect carnivores all around them, the group's progress was actually made more treacherous by the vegetation; the thick tangle of plants and vines and roots threatened to strangle the narrow paths they were attempting to traverse and were slippery and clutching.

Anya had left the easier-to-travel "wide" trail soon after they'd quitted the clearing where the castaways had spent their first night. This had bothered Buffalo somewhat for he knew that he personally would have instinctively chosen the wider well-traveled trail… in hopes of meeting the humans who'd made it. Anya though, had appeared nervous on the big trail and that bothered him even more. After the fearlessness this primitive girl had shown in all her recent adventures, Buffalo couldn't fathom what it was that she was apparently terrified of. So, when she indicated her desire to depart from the trail and march off into the jungle on this almost invisible narrow footpath, Buffalo, unwilling to face what might've made Anya afraid, had reluctantly nodded consent.

He had known he was taking an awful risk, but there were so many things about the girl that suggested confidence, sincerity, and trustworthiness ... her mannerisms, her voice …her eyes. (Or had he just fallen *prey* to those seductively dark eyes?) Buffalo had felt suddenly annoyed with himself at the time and gazed for a moment up and down the wide trail to clear his thoughts. But he knew he was forced to trust the girl. So, with a furrowed brow, he had quickly ushered the kids in behind Anya, who had already begun to forge ahead through the tangle, and he took up a position at the rear of the little column.

But, whether that was to protect against attack from behind or just to keep his distance from the wiles of the alluring jungle girl, he wasn't sure… and hadn't cared to dwell upon. What *did* concern him was her avoidance of that big easy trail. What had she been afraid of? Against his instincts, Buffalo had caved in and allowed this newcomer... this delightfully precocious native girl... to lead the way. Somehow, despite having known her for but a few hours, he trusted her with their very lives. He felt that he would eventually find out what it was that had troubled her. But, for now, for the first time in his life... Buffalo the pilot, the fighter, the big man... experienced an unusual comfort in acknowledging someone else's leadership and guidance and willingly became a follower... for the time being.

Moving gruelingly onward, the concealing cloak of foliage surrounded and engulfed the makeshift safari almost *too* effectively... and the castaways toiled for many hours that first day to make little headway. The pace was slow and lazy for Anya, who in fact, had purposely slowed her normal stride to match what she felt the young foreign teens might handle. But the unrelenting heat, humidity, and the constant struggle against the unyielding barrier of plant-growth quickly exhausted the newcomers anyway. The soft loamy earth itself dragged at their feet, for it was much like walking on sticky marshmallow. It was a thick wet mat of decayed vegetation and would often trip them up - - a foot might suddenly stick fast in the slimy goo of a recently deceased frond, or perhaps tangle in the iron-hard grasp of a desiccated creeper - - and when it did, there would be a sudden gasp, yelp, or squeal, and someone would disappear beneath a rustle of fronds, only to reappear momentarily... covered in muddy greenish ooze.

When Anya realized her charges were beginning to lag farther and farther behind in an ever-lengthening column of sweating, swearing, and bedraggled stragglers, she decided a rest-stop was in order. As she turned and waited at the top of a small crest for them to catch up, she observed their labors and struggles. It was plain to her that these strangers were not only unusual in appearance and habits, but they were obviously ill at ease in the depths of the jungle; the heart of Kontonqua. This really confused her for Kontonqua was the only real world that Anya and her kind had ever known. Until now, she'd assumed that the strangers were perhaps from some distant corner of Kontonqua, hitherto undiscovered by her people. But, she was beginning to have doubts...

Her first fear of course, had been that they were Ikusks, "The Unclean Ones", but she'd quickly discarded that idea when she'd gotten a better look at them after they had rescued her from the Konksihautl trap. How stupid it had been for her to run so recklessly when she first heard the commotion of their foreign voices! Her people regularly hunted and trapped the Konksihautl in these territories and she should have been on the lookout for snares as she ran. How foolish to fall prey to the trap! Even if the Clekweg hadn't eaten her, the Ikusks might've recaptured her!

So... her initial fear had turned to confusion. If these strangers weren't Ikuskquan or Kontonquan, who were they? After they had begun to communicate with her, she had tried vainly several times to ask where they had come from, but they refused to speak Kontonquan and only continued to babble in their odd croaky tones. Despite the language barrier, she had fully understood what the huge male had been trying to convey to her at the falls, but assumed that he had been trying to joke with her. Imagine trying to convince her that they, or anyone, could have been spewed forth from the mouth of Tak-Kwa-Tonqua, "The Life Fountain", the mother of the river!

And yet, as she watched them struggle their way through the thick tangle, it became clear to her that *her* home was not *theirs...* and they were quite unfamiliar with jungle woodcraft. They marveled in wonderment at simple things that Anya found most commonplace. And they fought and strained against Takka, the mother, the forest, instead of threading their way quickly and smoothly through the

106

embracing foliage, safe and secure beneath the protective canopy of her arms. What if the great bearded one, Buff-aloo, had been telling the truth? If they had indeed come from the lips of the Life Fountain, might they be Gods?

At the very thought, Anya's eyes widened and she gave a slight tremble as she waited stiffly for them to approach. If they were Gods, she had been acting inappropriately and was sure to be punished! But at that moment, Dexter Schornberg, who was next in the line and now closest to Anya, caught his foot in a fern root and fell headlong into a soggy pool of muck that smelled like mashed bananas! "Ewww, gross!" he spluttered as he struggled to sit upright. Jeep ran up with his perpetually wagging stump and began to lick the goop off his glasses. As Simon, Max, and Buffalo caught up to Dex, they laughed and poked a little mild fun at him while they helped him back to his feet. Anya couldn't help but giggle at the sight of him as well and instantly relaxed.

"No," she thought, "These people aren't Gods, but they are certainly unusual... and now that they are my friends, they are going to need a lot of looking after. Perhaps they do come from a place other than Kontonqua... but, what a silly thought... what other place could there be? Perhaps better to let others deal with that question and for now stay focused on getting home without further mishap!"

Once they were all gathered, Anya stepped off the thin trail and through a seemingly impenetrable wall of vegetation. For a moment, the castaway group looked at each other, uncertain about her intentions, but upon hearing her call, they followed her lead as best they could. They'd walked only a few yards however when they suddenly emerged into a *dry* grassy clearing! The entire clearing was only about twenty yards across and ringed with foliage as thick as that through which they'd just passed, very effectively hiding it from view. Not one of the wayward foreigners would ever have suspected its existence had not Anya revealed it to them. The kids were extremely happy, perhaps Dex most of all at the moment, to find a dry spot on which to sit. Even Jeep took the opportunity to stretch out on his back and roll in the short leathery blades of grass.

Buffalo was the last to enter the clearing and, looking around with a satisfied grin and a nod of approval, settled himself down with a bone-weary groan. He automatically reached out and began to scratch Jeep's tummy with one hand, while he rooted around in the flight bag with the other. "Voila!" he exclaimed as his hand emerged cradling a box of chocolate Moon Pies, "I deliberately held these back... you didn't notice *these* before, did you?"

"All right!" the kids cheered as one.

And when next Buffalo tossed the box into their midst, they fell upon it and greedily tore at the battered cardboard box to expose the familiar cellophane envelopes within. However, they still maintained enough composure and dignity to at least offer the first little pouch to him. "No, it's okay," he said, "Enjoy..." And he reached into the bag and pulled out another box! "Never leave home without 'em," he quipped, "But I'm afraid that's the last of my surprises... unless you're interested in a few dog biscuits." Which he then summarily extracted from his bag and offered to the eagerly awaiting hound.

As Buffalo tore the lid from the second box, he looked around to offer one to Anya and discovered that she was gone. "Now where'd she get off to..." he wondered aloud. And just as he was about to rise and search for her, there was a rustling in the wall of palm fronds and Anya reappeared with an armload of violet hairy-skinned oblongs about the size of short squat cucumbers. Her beaming smile of triumph quickly changed to an expression of wide-eyed wonder as she noticed the glint of the transparent wrappers the kids were eating out of. She gracefully kneeled down and allowed her armload to gently tumble to the ground in a pile in the middle of the group, but she never took her eyes off the chocolate marshmallow treats that were being consumed. Her eyes were filled with intense curiosity as she tucked her beautiful long black hair back behind her ear with one hand and reached slowly forward with the other towards Simon's snack. Simon held out his cookie and said, "Here, have some. We don't have any RC Cola to go with it... but they're still great. You'll love..." But his voice trailed off as he realized that it wasn't the snack that Anya was interested in. The girl moved her hand right past the offered pastry and reached for the shiny wrapper instead! She brought the clear sleeve in closer for examination and rolled it between her fingers while she marveled at its thinness, transparency, and flexibility.

"Here ya go," said Buffalo while extending an unopened package in her direction, "A whole one all to yourself." Anya accepted the little see-through pouch gleefully and turned it over and over in her hands. "No. Like this," instructed Buffalo, and he demonstrated the classic "pinch & pull" technique so popular with surface-world snack lovers. Anya was a quick learner and after successfully opening her own little package, she closely inspected the contents and tentatively sniffed at the round brown cookie within. She pulled it out and warily nibbled a bit of the chocolatey marshmallow treat. Her eyes widened in surprise and she broke into a broad grin as she approvingly lilted, "Hmmm!" She then settled back more comfortably into a cross-legged sitting position and concentrated on devouring the snack without missing a crumb, lingering over every bite of the cocoa-covered tart so as to fully appreciate the new taste sensation.

As she munched happily, she suddenly noticed Dexter examining one of the purple hairy fruits and realized that she had entirely forgotten about her own contribution to their impromptu picnic. Dexter was turning the strange object end over end and wondering what to do with it. Anya carefully put the remainder of her Moon Pie back in its wrapper and tucked it into a small pouch at her belt. She then picked up one of the other soft hairy oblongs from the grass and held it upright on its end between her extended fingers. "No. Like this," she mimicked Buffalo, instantly surprising everyone! Their eyebrows flew up and they grinned from ear to ear at her excellent attempt at English, and her proper timing of the phrase.

While they watched carefully, Anya reached up with her free hand and grasped the small stem at the top of the fruit and gave it a twist. The stem popped off and for a moment nothing happened. Then, like magic, the hairy violet skin began to separate and slide down the sides of the plump little fruit until it hung limply, inside out, over Anya's hand! The fruit inside was golden-colored and wiggled like Jell-O! It was even somewhat transparent like Jell-O and they could see rows of tiny black seeds in the middle of the quivering column. Carefully balancing the wiggling blob,

Anya brought the golden fruit to chest level and took a bite of it from above. She then looked up with a big smile, licked her lips, and made another "Yumm" sound while she gestured for the others to help themselves.

Simon quickly picked up one of the purple fruits and balanced it on his fingertips as Anya had done. "Oh, you mean like this?" he affirmed as he pinched the stem between his thumb and forefinger. He gave it a twist and the sides began to droop, but he must have been squeezing the base of the fruit too tightly because the golden center suddenly shot out the top of the peel! He then made his second mistake by trying to catch it in midair! The delicate wiggly fruit burst in his hand and covered him with sticky sweet golden goo! He just sat in amazement, staring at the empty skin in one hand and the puddle of glop in the other. Everyone burst out laughing, including Anya, who had to quickly clap a hand over her mouth to prevent herself from spitting her own mouthful of golden goo across the clearing!

When the fit of laughter finally subsided, Simon shrugged and tasted the pool in his hand with the tip of his tongue and suddenly wished he hadn't spilled a drop! The taste was indescribably good! Like lemon and honey and cantaloupe all mixed together! He tried briefly to explain the taste to the others, but his delight was obvious and more than enough evidence to convince them to eagerly tackle the tricky fruits for themselves. Jeep was happy just to be licking the splattered goop from Simon's arm.

Dexter was the next casualty. He had no trouble getting it peeled, but he couldn't balance it to control the wiggling! Every time he tried to take a bite, the quivering mass would lean over and slip from the peel at the last possible second and burst in his hand or his lap! If Anya hadn't peeled one and held it for him, he might not have tasted one of the delicious golden jungle-treats at all! Max got the hang of it on the very first try and Buffalo met with success on his second attempt. Jeep got the best of it though, for he had more than he could handle just mopping up the remains of the failed efforts!

The wonderful taste of these jungle-gelatins was like nothing the castaways had ever experienced in the outer-world and would long remain a special favorite on their preferred snack list! However, what they didn't realize at the time, but were soon to find out, was that the gooey goodies packed a wallop of energy too! Within moments of downing the golden fruits, they began to become more alert and strengthened, feeling as refreshed as though they'd had a long nap. Then, as they finished off the last of the pastries and hairy fruits, they discovered one *unfortunate* side-effect of their newfound jungle treats. Despite how pleased they felt *inwardly*, outwardly, they were now in worse shape than they were before... because the dried goo became incredibly sticky!

They had first sat in the welcome grassy clearing with just sweat-dampened hair and skin and clothing covered with jungle-muck and burrs. Now, on top of that, they were covered head to foot with golden sticky syrup imbedded with pastry crumbs and itchy purple hairs, shed from the discarded peels of the fruits! Wiping at the sticky goo only made it *dirty* sticky goo and didn't improve the situation at all. Anya giggled at their frustration and with a gesture that they should wait a moment, she arose and began slowing circling the edge of the clearing, keenly peering beneath the large frilly leaves of low-growing ferns. Apparently, she soon found what she was searching for, because she suddenly knelt down and began digging at something under the shadows of the broad fronds. The kids, their curiosity aroused, were about to get up and see exactly what it was that she was up to, when she suddenly turned with triumph to hold aloft an entire plant, roots and all, that she had dug from the earth.

It was actually a rather small plant, compared to all the other enormous ferns and palms that abounded in this jungle cavern, and its leaves were no larger than a dinner plate... being flat with frilly edges, of a bluish color, and fuzzy. But, what was most astounding about this particular plant was its overly large central root, which hung like a large football beneath the stem that Anya held with both hands, for it was apparently also quite heavy. She returned to where she'd been sitting and placed the plant upside down between her knees. She then turned to Buffalo and indicated that she would now need the large Bowie knife that hung in its sheath at his side. He had an inkling of what she might be up to and handed over his prized "Woodsman's Pal" without hesitation.

Everyone watched anxiously, as she skillfully worked the big knife like a drill, making a hole in the bottom of the root, which seemed to have a shell rather like that of a coconut. When her work was complete, she handed the knife back to Buffalo and reached down to rip off one of the fuzzy flat leaves. She held the leaf near the base of the tuber and tilted it slightly until a trickle of clear syrupy fluid ran out of the hole and onto the flat part of the leaf. She then scrubbed the leaf up and down the length of her arm and the accumulated dirt and stickiness disappeared as quickly and easily as any modern-day miracle soap might have done! She passed the leaf to Simon and tore off additional leaves and wetted them down for the others. The grimy crew wasted no time in washing away the built up sweat and dirt of the day's journey and felt a welcome surge of renewed strength and vigor as they did so, for the peculiar aroma of the plant's sap seemed to have a refreshing stimulating effect on their senses.

When they were done washing, they began to clean up their things to prepare to take up their journey once more. Anya was busy collecting all the empty pastry wrappers and to the amazement of everyone, was very carefully folding them into a tiny bundle, which she then tucked away into the slender pouch on her belt. She glanced over and noticed Dexter, the inquisitive one, inspecting the insides of the now empty root of the "cleansing plant" and she realized that a perfect opportunity was at hand to begin educating the strangers. She stepped over to his side and pointed at the hollow rind and said very slowly and deliberately, "Tikquan." Dexter looked up at her questioningly and she repeated the single word with emphasis, "Tikquan."

"Teek-wan," Dexter mimicked, and in turn pointed at the bulbous tuber and said, "Root." Anya smiled broadly and returned the word perfectly. The others, hearing what was going on, joined in immediately and they all had to take a turn repeating the newly discovered word: "Tikquan".

Anya then picked up a limp purple peel of the golden fruit they'd just enjoyed and said, "Amak!" Again, everyone willingly repeated the name and tried to return an equivalent meaning in English for her to learn.

Thus began the mutual education of the jungle-travelers. From that moment on, and in the weeks to come, as they trod the jungle paths, they would point out the curious and the commonplace things they passed and strive to learn the name and function of each. Whenever they stopped to rest, they would review the words they'd learned and then expand their usage to include verbs and adjectives. It became a game and they caught on quickly. By the end of the first week, they could roughly communicate... though it wasn't brilliant conversation, just a crude discussion of the things they'd encountered on each day's journey. Each night, before bedding down, they would try to broaden their knowledge of each other's language by speaking more of concepts... like their experiences and thoughts. And soon, they began to gain a genuine understanding of each other's ideas, customs, and habits as well.

But for now, on this first day, they were delighted in the prospect of communication alone. Thirsty for knowledge, they were eager to delve into the mysteries of each other's situation, history, and civilization. But that would come later, with acquired fluency in their new native tongue. At the moment, the castaways were just thrilled to feel like they "fit in"... to understand their place in the nature of the jungle home they were forced to adopt as their own.

Chapter 10
"Stampede!"

Once more, the unusual assortment of travelers took up their march, but this time with renewed strength and vigor. With their bellies full, and bolstered by the combined rejuvenating effects of the Amak and Tikquan, they hiked along happily... and with much greater efficiency than earlier. They eagerly learned as they traveled and Anya pointed out many wondrous sights of flora and fauna, calling each by name as they threaded their way through the primeval forest. Also, they were becoming handily more aware of the kinds of traps and pitfalls that were an expected part of jungle wayfaring in this dangerous land. With Anya's expert guidance, they negotiated the narrow and sometimes treacherous trails with a newfound confidence and savvy. They'd have done any surface-world safari proud, for they managed a fair bit of distance after all, clambering through the dank riotous tangle of roots and plant fronds all day. But eventually the stimulating effects of their meal wore off. The accumulated excitement and anxiety of their misfortunes, the physical stress of their adventures, and the rather long underground "day" were beginning to take their toll on the castaway crew.

The concept of a "day", in relation to the underground cavern-world, hidden as it was from the sun and its role as celestial timekeeper, was hardly inappropriate. The glowing lichens that completely covered the walls and ceiling of the enormous cave did not glow constantly. As with all plants, the lichens needed a regular period of respiration to consume oxygen and produce carbon dioxide and water. When they did so, they ceased to glow during that time. Through evolution, these tiny wondrous plants had somehow coordinated their phases so that the vast majority of them were all glowing at the same time, simulating "daylight" conditions. However, a small portion of the plants were apparently defying the system or perhaps not yet evolved enough to be in sync, for they were not attuned to the same cycle and did *their* glowing while all the others were darkened. It was these splotches of "rebels" that Buffalo had seen and mistaken for stars last "night"; when he had awoken in the middle of the dark-time.

The blessing was that the streaks and spots of luminance in the "night" were enough to create a subtle effect similar to "moonlight" and prevent total darkness in the enclosed cavern. To the relief of the castaways, the rhythmic exchange of light and dark, as dictated by the two cycles of the glowing lichens, was of exactly equal duration and somewhat mimicked the day/night phases of the earth's rotation on the outer-world. This effect at least gave them a sense of time familiarity with their adopted home. Unfortunately, the frequency of the cycle was based on a twenty-*eight* hour "day", not twenty-four. This greatly annoyed Buffalo, for it rendered his rugged military watch almost useless, devised as it was to count the hours as a duration of twenty-four... not twenty-eight.

It was however, still the very first full day that the marooned ones had spent in the cavern and they were as yet unaware of this peculiar diurnal arrangement. They'd spent most of their first day on an exceedingly strenuous march through seemingly endless jungle without any idea of *when* it would end! Their bodies told them the day was nearing a close, but the light remained unchanged. The wayward band of four were beginning to reach the limits of their endurance and were badly in need of a good night's rest... even Buffalo. Anya saw it, but for reasons of her own, wished to put all possible distance between herself and the clearing of the Konksihautl trap where they'd found and rescued her. She alone knew that night would soon befall them and she also knew all too well of the dangers that the night could bring. So, she urged the weary bunch to make as much speed and progress as they could muster while the light still held.

Just as the kids were certain they would drop in their tracks from drowsiness, Anya signaled them to a halt and disappeared from the trail ahead. They gathered to see where she'd gone this time, and peering between the interlaced leaves of some gigantic Bromeliads, they spotted her a short distance away, motioning for them to follow. They quitted the narrow path and plodded ahead in her footsteps through the snarled blades and stems. They were hoping for another of the mysterious little clearings, like where they'd had their snack, so as to relax and nap awhile. What they happened upon next however, was quite different... and Anya stood in the middle of it with a broad grin on her face, obviously pleased with her discovery. The tangle of jungle growth had abruptly subsided. But, instead of a pleasant dry clearing, they were in the midst of an acre-sized patch of great broadleaf circular plants that looked, for all the world, like immense skunk cabbages!

All the other jungle plants they'd recently become so familiar with were conspicuously absent. No palms and ferns or vines and creepers grew here. Just gigantic cabbages sprouting from the spongy black loam. It was noticeably darker here than beneath the green-tinted glow of the normal jungle for the large flat leaves of the tall stalks blotted out much of the available light... and if possible, it was wetter, too. The only seeming advantage of this place was the welcome relief from the closeness of the confining jungle. Here, they could move about freely between the giant dark-green shoots because of the total absence of ground cover. But, this certainly didn't look like a comfy spot for a rest.

They looked quizzically at Anya, uncertain as to what she expected of them. She looked thrilled with her find, but they didn't know why. Were they to attempt to sit and relax in the thick wet black muck that passed for soil? Or was there something here that they were supposed to eat? If so, the odor of the cabbages, while not exactly repellent, was still rather unappetizing. Anya noticed their confusion and made a gesture of putting her head on her folded hands, closing her eyes, and softly snoring. She opened her eyes again to see their curled lips and expressions of disgust as they surveyed the muddy ooze at their feet. Sleep? Here?! There wasn't a dry spot big enough for Jeep to curl up on! But after all that they'd been through, and forced to deal with in this weird cavern-world, these particular wayfarers were ready to accept just about anything. They were now so utterly exhausted that one more indignity hardly seemed an obstacle. If any objections were to be raised, it would have to be done soon, for the light was finally beginning to fade into night. It was already conspicuously darker than when they'd entered this dreary spot.. but not one of them had energy left with which to argue.

Reluctantly, they began to mill about searching the ground for an area that looked somewhat drier than the rest. When Anya saw that they had misread her intentions and were getting ready to bed down on the wet ground, she gave a little squeal of horror and shook her head violently shouting, "Na! Na!." Startled, they all stopped to look at her.

"Na?" inquired Dexter.

"Na!" she repeated emphatically. Anya raised her hands over her head, one in a fist and the other held open above it with her fingers wiggling, while she began to make loud buzzing noises. She stopped and pointed upwards and then continued the pantomime.

"Bugs… insects!" called out Max as she caught on, (Charades was always one of her favorite games).

"Ixtl," said Anya nodding. She then made the flying-bug-gesture again while she exaggeratedly looked all around the clearing. She stopped and looked at her gathered charges and shook her head slowly while making that "tsk, tsk," tongue-clicking noise that has come to mean "What a pity…" to those of the surface-world. Apparently, it meant pretty much the same to the inhabitants of the cavern! Anya then made the bug-gesture again while sniffing the air around her. She stopped wide-eyed, staring at them again, and shook her head slowly using the same tongue-clicking sound.

"I think she's afraid we'll be discovered by our buggy friends above," said Buffalo, "that they might see us or smell us. Okay, but what are we going to do about it? How can we prevent it? We'd be sittin' ducks right here where the ground is clear."

It was getting quite dark now. Clearly, when night descended on this tropic underground world, it did so with alarming speed and without the ceremony of "sunset"! Anya, sensing Buffalo's concern and pressed to haste by the failing light, ran over to one of the great cabbage-like plants. She leaped up and snagged one of the tall broad leaves and kicked herself away from the central cluster of stalks. The huge leaf bent to her weight quite easily and she pulled it all the way to the ground until it lay flat upon the dark soil. She then stepped onto the flat leaf and walked to its frilly tip. Once there, she promptly lied down, grabbed the leaf-tip with both hands, and began to loosely roll herself up inside! When she'd finished rolling, she was a neatly wrapped bundle at the base of the giant plant... like a Chinese Egg Roll! The strangers stood and gawked in amazement and then began giggling when they suddenly heard loud raspy snoring coming from inside the roll. Anya was trying to let them know that the rolled leaves were intended to be their sleeping quarters for the night, but the sound of the graceful jungle-girl snoring like a grizzly bear was hilarious!

"Well, I'll be..." said Buffalo, "Stuffed cabbage!" The castaways burst out laughing at this new observation and Anya unrolled herself to find the entire bunch in stitches. Her first reaction was one of indignation and annoyance, for she thought they were laughing at her. But the kids' uncontrolled giggling was infectious and she soon found herself joining in and chuckling with the rest.

While they were enjoying Buffalo's joke, a humming sound began to well up overhead, unnoticed by all except Jeep who started to whine as the droning sound became louder. Anya suddenly heard it too, and immediately stopped laughing and exhibited great concern. They'd been very foolish to waste time and act so recklessly at nightfall! She leapt to her feet and frantically waved her arms to get everyone's attention and motioned them to silence. The merriment quickly subsided as the rest of the group caught the threatening noise from above. They now understood the need for urgency and proceeded into action like a well-drilled squad of soldiers. Buffalo and Anya hurried to the base of the nearest skunk-cabbage and pulled down leaves for the kids to wrap up into. Following Anya's example, all three were momentarily rolled into identical bundles around the base of the same plant. After affirming their status as "comfortable", Buffalo and Anya sought their own leafy accommodations.

Buffalo wanted to see that Anya was safely wrapped up as well, but she was insistent that he roll up first. And it was well that she was, for he needed to take Jeep into his roll with him, and although Jeep was an exceedingly well-behaved dog, he wasn't at all thrilled by the prospect of being confined in a vegetable Burrito! With Anya's help however, the two of them got Jeep settled down enough to get Buffalo's roll completed and Buffalo wound up lying on his back with Jeep neatly tucked at his side. He could hear Anya's efforts as she quickly rolled herself into a leaf very close to his as the droning buzz from above continued to get louder.

The cabbage roll wasn't nearly as uncomfortable or confining as Buffalo had expected it to be. It was clean, cool, and sweeter-smelling inside than out. And since all the bugs of the cavern-world were oversized, there were no troublesome tiny flies and gnats, or little creepy-crawlies to annoy the occupant. The large thick leaf was loosely rolled and tube-shaped with plenty of room to shift position within. It's rolled layers were soft and spongy, like a foam mattress, and the open ends of the roll, which extended several feet beyond Buffalo's 6'3" frame, allowed air to circulate freely.

Anya had chosen their sleeping arrangements with more than comfort in mind though. These particular cabbage-like pitcher plants were avoided by the huge insect denizens of Kontonqua. The pungent aroma of the plant was repellent to the behemoths and therefore thoroughly protected the human occupants from detection. The insects were gigantic, but not terribly bright. The two main senses employed by the predatory insects to track and hunt their quarry were sight and scent. If they couldn't directly see their prey or smell it, they were pretty much oblivious to it.

Buffalo and the kids were uncomfortably unaware of the peculiar attributes of their bedrolls however, as they listened to the ever-increasing buzzing noise of descending whirring wings. Something big... *very* big, landed in the clear space between the cabbage plants where the group lay divided and then the deafening buzzing suddenly stopped. The ensuing silence was almost maddening. They lay trapped within their leafy green rolls, the hum of the wings still ringing in their ears, while some hideous six-legged monster was preparing to make a meal out of them! Jeep, who'd always shown the utmost bravery, and usually began growling at the slightest provocation, this time began to softly whimper instead. Either because of his confinement, or the nature of the predatory beast outside, Jeep was considerably agitated and Buffalo did his best to keep him quiet and comforted.

Buffalo was certain that it would be mere moments before he would feel the piercing jaws of a giant insect butcher stab through the walls of his vegetable coffin to lift him and Jeep, plant roll and all, into the air to be borne away to a horrible death. Suddenly, something bumped the side of the leaf-roll, causing it to rock back and forth unnervingly. Buffalo was not the kind of man to hide inactive while danger threatened. He'd always been a man of action first and he felt a keen sense of duty to protect Anya... and especially the young teens that fate had thrust into his care. He was just about ready to crawl out the end of his roll and confront the beast as best he could when the mighty wings suddenly stirred once more with a deafening buzz. There was a loud rustling of leaves all around them and then the creature lifted off, the rapidly diminishing drone of its beating wings subsiding into stillness. Had the intruder left with one of the *others* in its slavering jaws?

"Everybody okay?" called out Buffalo.

One by one, the muffled jittery voices of the kids replied with an "Okay!" or "I'm here!" and then Buffalo heard the clear nearby voice of Anya mimic, "O-kay!" He tilted his head backward to see the silhouette of the resourceful jungle-girl's head framed upside-down in the opening of the tube, her hand restraining her long dark silky hair that would've hung to the ground, for she was bending over to peer into his bedroll. He saw the shadow of a finger point over to where the kids had been stashed and again she uttered softly, "O-kay." Even in the darkness, he saw the flash of her bright smile and the twinkle in her eye. Dear girl, she had unrolled herself to check on everyone like a mother hen. Buffalo smiled back and said "Goodnight, Anya" and she seemed to understand, for she said something softly and sweetly in her own language and moved off to re-roll herself for the night.

Jeep had now settled down comfortably and was his old self again, soon to be fast asleep, as dogs seem to have an uncanny ability to do at a moment's notice. Buffalo could hear the kids whispering to each other like excited campers on a sleepover. But everyone was much too tired to carry on for long and he soon heard the soft rhythmic snoring that told him that everyone had found respite and relief in welcome slumber. He then heard a much louder snoring that startled him at first, until he realized briefly that it was his own... and he was out too.

*   *   *   *   *   *   *   *   *

When Buffalo awoke, he opened his eyes and saw nothing but green... bright green surrounding him! Then, as his eyes focused on the veined texture of the green, he remembered where he was... contained within the folds of an enormous rolled leaf! And then he was startled to realize that the leaf-roll was gently rocking.

"Buff-Alloh?" He heard Anya's muffled voice call softly from without and the rocking stopped. He looked to his side and noticed that Jeep was gone. "Buff-Alloh?" Anya repeated loudly, her head once again framed at the circular end of the rolled tube.

"Yah... comin'" grumbled Buffalo. He heaved his body to one side and then the other and the leaf began to unroll with a speed and springiness that made him dizzy. In fact, it's sudden brisk unfurling almost sent him spilling into the black muck of the surrounding soil! He sat up at the leaf's tip, blinking in the bright light of day, and had to rub his eyes when he saw Anya standing over him stifling a giggle. The primitive jungle-girl looked fresh and spirited after the long night's rest and he was again struck by her incredible beauty. The long dusky hair, the soft friendly almost "oriental" features with those dark almond-shaped eyes, the golden glow of her smooth skin, and her strong athletic and lithesome figure... all set in stark contrast to the strange and savage costume that barely covered her body.

The harness and accouterments that adorned her were those of a fierce female barbarian warrior. She *looked* seductively innocent, but he had no doubt that in a proper fight, she'd have no trouble matching the implied ferocity of her costume. And that just about made her the epitome of perfect womanhood as far as *he* was concerned. He suddenly realized that he'd been staring awkwardly up at her slack-jawed and gruffly mumbled a "G'mornin'" as he quickly averted his attention. Anya glanced sidelong with her sultry eyes at the amply-muscled giant with the sleep-tousled hair... she'd caught the admiration in his eye and a wide smile spread across her face. She moved off humming a pleasantly girlish tune and then began singing softly to herself in her native tongue.

Buffalo looked around to see Jeep's back-end sticking out of Max's bedroll with, of course, his stump of a tail wagging wildly. He was probably getting a good tummy-scritching from Max and judging from the occasional squeal, she was getting thanked with an occasional sloppy "kiss" from that long pink tongue! Buffalo and Anya set about unrolling the kids, controlling the big leaves so their rapid unfurling wouldn't fling them out into the clearing. Everyone spent a good deal of time yawning and stretching as they emerged from their vegetable cocoons. They had all been so tired, they'd slept through the entire fourteen-hour night without once awakening. The soothing aroma of the "cabbage" leaves was partly responsible... and had a favorable rejuvenating effect also!

Again, Anya disappeared, but they were fast becoming used to that sort of thing. Inspecting their camp, Simon found another Tikquan plant, uprooted and lying at the base of a nearby "cabbage". Anya had apparently left it for them. Now that its secrets had been revealed, they made use of it and spent their time freshening up and washing away the traces of their journey and the accumulated cobwebs of sleep as best they could. Anya returned shortly with a beaming smile and an armload of green round things the size of cantaloupes. The skins were smooth and leathery and she easily split them open to scoop out a pithy yellow pulp that tasted kind of like pasty oatmeal. They weren't nearly the treat they'd had the day before, the hairy purple Amak fruits, but they were palatable, filling, and at least *seemed* like breakfast! Anya called them "Dujong" and they would later turn out to be one of the staples of Kontonquan diet.

As they got up to prepare to leave their little campground, Dexter noticed the deep holes left in the soft ground by their nighttime visitor. He whistled softly at the size of the tracks and the spacing between them. He paced off the distance of one set left by the front legs to the rear set, while the rest of the group stood gawking in amazement. Anya merely glanced at them, shrugged, and went about her business. "Twenty-five feet, at least!" shouted Dex with amazement. Issuing a collective sigh for their narrow escape, the castaways gathered their stuff, fell in line in the same order as the day before, and off they trudged in single file to begin their second day's hike - - wading through the tropical mists of a dense sea of jungle.

The second day's hike was really much like the first. For that matter, so was the third, though things got much easier with experience. Generally, their routine of marching, eating, and sleeping followed the same daily pattern for almost three weeks. Yet, it was never really dull or boring. Each and every day, their astounding journey of adventure continued to amaze and enlighten them about the incredible diversity and unique order of life that was their new home. They learned much and became intrepid explorers and curious naturalists. Anya led the way boldly and did her best to protect them and provide for their every need. She gathered foodstuffs whenever possible, mostly the mealy Dujong, but she twice caught some sort of large rodent and once, even a snake, for dinner! This stunned the newcomers, for up to that point, they'd assumed the only animals to be found in this strange underworld were humans and insects of the "giant" variety. It came as quite a surprise to learn that some small mammals, reptiles, and even amphibians also called this cavern "home"... and that they, at least, were all mostly of a size comparable to their surface-dwelling counterparts! However, the realization that there were other denizens of the Kontonquan jungle scurrying or slithering beneath the canopy of green was a bit unsettling and they henceforward picked their way through the foliage with a little more care.

Anya taught them woodcraft and schooled the foreigners about the dangers that lurked in the tropical forest... many of which they might easily have fallen prey to but for her expert leadership. Her keen instinct and intuition guided them safely around many obstacles, traps, and beasts of all kinds. Once, they had come upon an open space in the trail with a large cone-shaped hole in it's midst. The sandy circular depression was at least thirty feet across and just as deep. It looked harmless enough at first glance but Anya pointed out the cruel jaws buried at the very bottom of the pit, lying in wait for some hapless victim to stumble over its edge and slide down the loose gravel to an unfortunate end below. Needless to say, they very carefully skirted the pit, hand-in-hand, until they had again picked up the trail on the other side.

As they worked their way "inland", away from the cavern's wall, the din of insect noises of all kinds became an almost constant companion to their travels. And of course, there was the threatening drone of wings overhead to continually remind them of the persistent danger of winged predators.

However, not all the insects were predacious, they actually saw a great many other giant bugs during their daily marches and became familiar with several types. Some occupied and worked the huge trees that towered over their passage while others foraged among the fronds of the forest floor. Anya eyed a few of them warily as they maneuvered past, yet others she just ignored completely as though they were merely cows in a field. The outlanders though, were enthralled with every one they encountered. The sizes, colors, and variety of the huge but agile multi-legged wonders was a source of constant fascination. Their tiny cousins of the surface-world were often overlooked and taken for granted, but the shear size of these behemoths commanded both respect and attention. What would normally require a microscope, was now revealed to them in every minute detail. The full purpose of anatomy, form, and function... every nuance of attitude and behavior... of these enormous beasts began to make itself apparent to the curious castaway band. They could clearly see, and study, the intricate structure of the enormous exoskeletal bodies: the glistening many-faceted compound eyes, the delicate probing antennae, the constantly laboring mouth-parts, and the slender multi-jointed legs that so nimbly supported the great armored organisms. A very different world of biology existed here. Insects, by size, variety, and numbers, held dominance over all the other forms of life.

Their journey to a place called Konton, (for that was indeed, as they had learned from Anya, their ultimate destination), was for the most part exhilarating and even fun. But three times, they witnessed horrific incidents that were both terrifying and astounding. If Anya heard the thrumming noise of certain *types* of wings overhead, she would quickly usher them to safety beneath the veil of fern-fronds... and they soon learned why.

On one occasion, there was a sudden rustling of the great leaves in the ceiling of green and a huge black and yellow Hornet descended from above! It swooped down with terrific speed and a deafening whirring of wings that set all the jungle's vegetation shivering and swaying... as though a great helicopter were attempting to land! There had been several large docile plant-eaters, Leafhoppers Dexter called them, grazing amongst the broadleaf ground cover, but they were now desperately leaping and careening in all directions, flying for their lives! But for one of them, escape was too late. The Hornet was upon him before he could leap to the safety of the thicker trees.

The Hornet had the Leafhopper pinned down with its forelegs as it struggled to get free. Then suddenly, the Hornet's abdomen bent double beneath its body and pierced its victim with one thrust of its deadly stinger. With an audible "crunch" the cruel spear defeated the protective armor of the Leafhopper's body and the hapless creature let out a chilling *scream* as the winged invader pumped its venom into the breach. That bloodcurdling cry of death raised the hairs on the necks of the castaways! They were used to normal insect sounds, but no one had expected them to voice fear and pain! The Leafhopper ceased its struggles in less than a minute and the Hornet used the time to groom itself, apparently tidying up after the kill. It flitted in place momentarily, looking from side to side, presumably to check for more victims, or perhaps it was wary of challengers to its meal. Then, without further hesitation, it firmly grasped the Leafhopper in its claws and lifted away into the sky above the treetops. In mere moments, after the marauder had passed, the remaining grazers returned to feed and the jungle seemed once again as peaceful as it had before.

On another occasion, they hid behind a massive old tree while witnessing a battle between two winged beetles! Following Anya's direction, they had barely gotten off the trail when there came overhead a tremendous crashing of leaves and branches. Leaf litter and great boughs rained down into a small clearing as two giant iridescent blue monsters, clutched in a grappling ball, fell to earth with an impact that shook the ground! Bright light poured through the rent opening of leaves to illuminate the battle like a spotlight, giving the clearing the appearance of an arena. The two combatants remained in a locked embrace as they rolled and tumbled in all directions, each one trying desperately to gain advantage over the other. The cowering band may not have been in danger of being eaten, but they were certainly in danger of being flattened! The thickly armored beasts were each the size of a dump truck and they wrestled haphazardly through the field of waist-high jungle palms, crushing all plantlife beneath them.

At one point, the scrapping pair of beetles rolled right for the hiding place of the captivated spectators. They hit the huge bole of the old wooded giant with such force that it ripped a sheet of bark from its side and the resulting vibration sent such shivers up the sinewy old trunk that it rained water, leaves, vines, branches... all sorts of debris, down on top of the castaways. The enormous brawlers continued their contest for several more moments, until one of them suddenly gained the upper hand by deftly snipping an antenna from the other! Immediately, the two separated, as though a referee had blown a whistle, and they stepped apart to shake themselves free of accumulated dirt and debris. Then, without further ado, their armored backs split apart and a blur of wings beat the air to lift the giants effortlessly up from the forest floor and, flying in a corkscrew pattern, they exited one after the other through the hole they'd just torn through the jungle canopy.

The third encounter with the immense insects was however, by far, the most dangerous for the relatively fragile humans. They were moving through an area that was a bit different than their usual day's trek. Instead of the usual broad leaves and waist-high fern-fronds, they were trudging through a wide channel of tall grasses. An open plain without tree cover that made Anya visibly nervous. Buffalo was the only one really tall enough to be able to just about see over the tops of the grass stems somewhat, though Anya seemed to know her way intuitively through the tangle just by woodcraft.

Suddenly, Anya stopped dead and motioned them all to silence. Buffalo and the kids listened intently but couldn't hear any of the insect noises that usually alerted them to danger. Buffalo stood on tiptoe and looked in all directions. He checked the tree line to either side, and the sea of grass in front and behind, but couldn't see any *visible* signs of a threat. It was then that he became aware of a vibration through his feet. The kids felt it too, and it was already increasing to more of a trembling sensation. Buffalo was certain they were experiencing an earthquake and said as much. Anya became greatly agitated and urged them to race for the tree line! He couldn't understand her urgent response to the threat. If they were having an earthquake, they would be much safer in the open, wouldn't they? He tried to argue the point with the frenzied jungle-girl, but her desperate pleading in broken English and the increased rumbling convinced him that perhaps he should follow her instructions post-haste. After all, she hadn't been wrong yet. His hesitation almost cost them their lives.

They ran for the safety of the nearby trees and prepared to take their usual hiding places amongst the boles, but this time Anya insisted they *climb* the trees! Though puzzled at first, they sensed her urgency for speed, so they did their best to follow her up one thick and twisted old fern-tree. Its moss-covered trunk was knotted and heavily veined and, combined with the multitude of creepers and lianas draped upon it, fairly easy to climb. While the rumbling tremors increased in volume to actual violent shaking, they struggled and shimmied upwards, against the danger of being rattled loose, until they reached a natural "platform" created by the branching of several great stems. Buffalo, encumbered by having to climb with Jeep draped over his shoulder, was the last to reach their spur-of-the-moment sanctuary. And not a moment too soon! The worried band clung precariously to each other and the protective limbs of the tree while a dull roar, accompanied by an ever increasing quaking, grew to disturbing intensity.

"Look!" shouted Dexter above the din. All eyes riveted themselves to where he pointed up the trail. Through a cloud of debris, what could only be described as a thunderous *herd* of Aphids, each the size of a Rhino, suddenly came stampeding into view! By the hundreds, thousands, they ran in blind panic, trampling the vegetation and everything in their path as they drove forward like a green tidal wave. The matte-green backs roiled and bounced in tightly packed confusion as the swarm of frenzied insects plowed their way through the dense grasses. Within seconds, the spearhead of the column had made its way to where the castaways had been standing only moments earlier and, by the time they'd passed by, the spreading mass of ensuing bodies completely filled the expanse between the tree lines! In their mad dash, the crazed animals collided with each other and bumped and banged the trees as they passed. The intense trembling of the ground made it already difficult for the little band to cling to their perch, but when a cluster of Aphids suddenly veered and careened directly into the trunk of the tree-fern harboring the fugitives, the huge bole shook with a tremendously violent shock! With a shriek, Maxine lost her handhold and tumbled backwards from the forked crux of branches! Buffalo lunged towards the plummeting girl and his huge paw encircled her tiny wrist just in time to prevent her from falling into the fringe of the raging herd. For one frightening instant, Max swung by one arm perilously close over the backs of the heaving throng below while Buffalo struggled to get a better hold on the slippery moss-covered bough he hung from. It seemed an eternity, but as soon as Buffalo gained a secure grip, he was able to easily haul the shaken teen back to the safety of their refuge.

As quickly as the rampaging beasts had descended upon them, their numbers dwindled and the thunderous roar faded into the distance down the plain they'd been crossing just moments before. In the space of just several minutes, the stampeding torrent had transformed the lush plain of tall grass into a wasteland of trampled pulp as the last few stragglers hurried past to catch up with the herd. After a few tense minutes of silent waiting, Anya let out a sigh of relief and started back down the tree. Buffalo, with Jeep across his shoulder again, followed and he and the kids dropped down one by one. They stopped and listened again when they'd collected themselves at the base of the large fern. Hearing nothing unusual and reasonably assured that the danger had passed, the intrepid little band ventured back out into the flattened avenue of grass. For the first time in days, they had an unobstructed view of their surroundings, for the wide swath, cut by the Aphid stampede, stretched on for quite a distance before winding out of sight. Already, the hardiest plants and grasses were beginning to spring back upright, but for the remainder of that day, they would make good time traversing the "highway" plowed by the Aphids and Anya urged them forward to take advantage of it.

As they traveled the ruined plain, they spotted several carcasses of fallen Aphids amongst the wreckage, trampled in the melee by their own kind. At one point, Anya borrowed Buffalo's Bowie knife and warily approached one of them. After making certain it was dead, she went to work on its underside with the sharp knife. The strangers watched intently from a short distance and wondered aloud what she was up to. In a moment, she was on her way back and carrying a bloated translucent bag of white liquid. She offered it to the kids first, but they had no idea what she intended until she made a gesture of drinking from the recently amputated bag! They were completely grossed out by the prospect of partaking of anything of insect origin and gagged and groaned at the suggestion! Anya giggled and shrugged and then hoisted the soft unwieldy bladder to her lips and, throwing back her head, took a long refreshing draught of the milky fluid within. When she'd done, she grinned broadly at the kids with a thick white milk "mustache" across her bronzed upper lip and said, "Yummm…!"

The teens had not had much more than plain water to drink ever since they'd left their doomed plane on the frozen ice field and this resourceful jungle girl had already surprised them with several strange and wonderful delicacies. So, their loathing gradually subsided and gave way to curiosity. Soon, brave Simon stepped forward with a grimace, tempted onward by the milky smile on Anya's face and the prospect of discovering a new treat. In fact, they were all feeling somewhat more adventurous than they ever thought they could and they all lined up for a sample. Cautiously, they each tasted the warm white liquid. They were not disappointed! It wasn't at all what they were expecting, warm cow's milk or yogurt or something, it had a peculiar sweet flavor that made it irresistible and to Anya's delight, they soon fought over the bag until the last drops were drained!

They resumed their journey with satisfied bellies and made good time crossing the flattened landscape. However, eventually the trampled grasslands gave way once more to sweltering impenetrable jungle and, despite the foreigner's fascination with all they encountered, the daily laborious drudgery of the march began to take its toll. It was to last for several more days and sometimes sleepless nights! Where were they going? It was only Anya's boundless enthusiasm and optimism that boosted their morale and kept them going through it all. The weary castaways had no idea their journey would become so tedious and seemingly endless! Just how big was this underground lost land anyway?

Just as they thought they could withstand it no longer, they noticed that the dense jungle growth was perceptibly beginning to thin. It was becoming easier to traverse the forest floor and the great trees were getting more sparse as left over stumps attested to their deliberate deforestation. This change seemed to elevate Anya's spirits even higher and she became more lighthearted than before... often singing softly to herself as she led. She assured them that their journey was soon to end and *that* bit of news lightened everyone's mood considerably.

Anya was in high spirits because she was now absolutely certain of where she was and knew she was very near to home. She pressed on even harder as she recognized familiar landmarks of her local territory and her excitement became infectious. At one point, they suddenly exited the narrow jungle trail and hit upon a wider well-traveled trail that Anya did not try to avoid and they guessed they were safely in Anya's home territory. The thrill of finally reaching the destination they had been striving for through all those many miles of hardship was exhilarating! Civilization! Anya's people. They didn't know quite what to expect, but they hoped they would be welcomed and assisted. Fate had driven their destiny up until now and had made all their decisions for them for the better part of three weeks. Now, they were eagerly looking forward to allowing someone else, or new events, to aid and determine their course and future.

As they walked the last few miles of open trail, leaving the hostile steamy jungle behind them, Anya's anticipation became electrifying. She hastened along with a bouncy girlish gait and spoke little. She alone knew what lay at their journey's end, but she told them nothing, eager to surprise the foreigners with the sight of her home.

The forest canopy became very thin now, the result of harvesting, and the trees here were smaller younger versions of the giants they had been laboring beneath for weeks. Without the overhead canopy of green, the cavern light was bright and cheerful. Yet, they were almost totally unprepared for actually completely *leaving* the jungle. Reaching its "edge" so to speak. So, they were caught quite by surprise when it just stopped, rather abruptly, and they found themselves emerging from a well-defined tree line and standing on a stone-paved road atop a grassy knoll overlooking a shallow valley. As one, they caught their breaths and stood gazing in silent awe.

For there, in the distance, across miles and miles of cultivated fields, and shrouded in tendrils of mist, rose an imposing architectural wonder. An elaborately wrought and ornamented vertical mound-fortress of immense proportions! It was taller than any New York skyscraper and much more massive in girth. Easily large enough to contain a *modern* city within its bleak ebony facade... but the many columns and towers of the imposing edifice brandished all the turrets and spires of some dark and sinister *medieval* castle.

"Konton!" exclaimed Anya proudly, extending a hand towards the impressive tower.

A low whistling exhale escaped the slack-hanging mouths of the mesmerized castaways as they stared at the ominous and intimidating structure. Jeep issued a soft rumbling growl and the concentration of the spellbound crew was broken long enough for them to pull their gaze away momentarily. They'd expected perhaps a village... instead they'd encountered a giant foreboding metropolis! They looked to each other for some assurance, but all they saw was the doubt and worry they each felt, mirrored in each other's faces.

Chapter 11
"The Fortress City Konton"

Anya stood tall with quiet dignity, tense with anticipation and obviously moved by the scene before her. Though a broad smile was fixed upon her face, she involuntarily shuddered with the sudden convulsive wrack of a sob brought on by a flood of emotions. She could feel tears of joy welling up in her eyes as she gazed at the massive walls of Konton, the city of her birth. The city of her people. The home that several weeks ago, she had been certain she would never live to see again.

The others stood by silently, shifting uncomfortably with anxiety and uncertainty. They'd become accustomed to seeing many strange and wonderful things in this most unusual land, but the things they'd previously seen seemed somehow... "natural". Much of what the strangers had observed or experienced bore a distinct resemblance to familiar jungle settings of the surface-world, while some of the more curious discoveries became almost predictable, once you accepted the new set of biological rules that governed the cavern. The jungle, river, trees, plants, animals, and even the *bugs*... seemed to just belong, to fit into a scheme so to speak. Sure, they were exotic, huge, peculiar, and sometimes just plain weird, but still they seemed to have their place in a natural order... a world wrought by Mother Nature, albeit along a different set of guidelines than they were used to.

Now though, they were faced with something unexpected and unpredictable. Across the fields and shrouded in mists, dark and almost obscured by the distance, stood a vision beyond their wildest imaginings. An ominous structure they couldn't have anticipated, for its existence departed from the natural realm entirely. This was no design of Nature alone. The ingenuity of Man was in evidence here! And yet, its architectural inventiveness went far beyond anything commonly found on Earth's surface, past or present. They had been expecting perhaps a village or at most a primitive town, but the civilization that had conceived, built, and managed what lay before them was unprecedented... and primitively advanced in ways and methods they couldn't yet comprehend.

On closer inspection, one could discern, upon its dark-brown façade, vague similarities reminiscent of known ancient cultures and exotic lands. Some if it's more prominent architectural features for instance called to mind images of the lost cities of the Orient, India, and Central America. The construction techniques employed in its massive stonework, were a dark and brooding blend of styles evocative of ancient Egyptian, Mayan, and Aztec civilizations as well. But the one unmistakable unifying "link" that bound together these otherwise discordant styles into the single gloomy and foreboding alien edifice that towered and twisted upwards through the curling mists in the distance, was... *insect!* The configuration of the enormous fortress-city gave the impression of an immense hive, a termite mound, an ant colony... but a bizarre construct of both human and insect manufacture!

Unnerved by the shock of seeing this mountainous brown monolithic-Metropolis looming ahead in wait for them, the wayward foreigners took a few moments to survey the surrounding landscape. The knoll, upon which they stood, afforded them an unobstructed view of the entire valley that was Anya's home. The path they'd been following had widened from a well-beaten dirt road to an "avenue" of crushed hard-packed stone and they could see that it was just one of many that radiated outwards from the tower-city like the spokes of a wheel. As mentioned, the land between was cultivated in a patchwork of carefully maintained fields and orchards. Looking more closely, they could see the sweat-glistening backs of many workers laboring amongst the colorful rows of fruits and vegetables. But the sight that amazed them even more, was that alongside the native farmers, were the unmistakable shapes of large black ants! They were easily the size of oxen and seemed to toil in the same capacity! They appeared to be harnessed with man-made trappings and while some were pulling plow-like devices, others were hitched to carts or crude sledges.

Like seeing a housefly out of the corner of your eye, a flurry of movement in the sky over the far away city suddenly caught their attention. A multitude of black dots were now whirling and circling in the air high above the dark spires of the fortress stronghold. Funny... they hadn't noticed them when they first laid eyes on the structure. As they watched, the dots seemed to quickly arrange themselves into formations and then a cluster of them suddenly broke away from the larger group and started flying in their direction with impressive speed! As they rapidly closed the distance, the castaways could see that the "black dots" were actually people astride winged ants even larger than those that they'd seen in the fields below! They began to shuffle backwards, for their first impulse was to turn and run back to the shielding safety of the jungle behind them. But Anya, who had been apparently expecting a reception committee, quickly indicated that she wanted them all to sit quietly on the ground. She alone would face the oncoming patrol with nothing more than outstretched arms in a "welcome" greeting!

Once again, because of their bond of trust, the castaways followed Anya's instructions and sat down in place to nervously watch the approach of the winged guard, for that was indeed what they were. As they drew nearer, it could be seen that the riders were armored soldiers, dressed in a rugged dark leather harness similar to Anya's, but more fully protected by iron mail and thick plating cleverly fashioned from insect parts. Upon their heads, were shining silver open-faced helmets capped with colorful plumes! And *these* warriors were not weaponless! In fact, they fairly bristled with cruel-looking spears, clubs, and what looked to be harpoons, as they flew in tight formation and rapidly closed the distance towards the helpless band of jungle refugees. Buffalo sat with one hand on Jeep's collar to restrain him, for Jeep was already focused with furrowed brow on the advancing troop and the fearless hound was beginning to rumble a low-throated growl. The sight of those soldiers and weapons gave Buffalo cause for concern and he hoped fervently that their trust in Anya hadn't been misplaced!

He saw that it was now too late, however, to change their minds, for the terrific speed at which the winged patrol sped towards them made running impossible. Even to attempt the short distance to the safety of the jungle behind them, with such fleet insects bearing down on them, would be like trying to outrun a fighter plane. Instead, he put his other arm around Jeep's middle, both to hold him close and to keep his hand on the reassuring hilt of his

Bowie knife where it couldn't, because of Jeep's intervening body, be seen by the riders.

They could hear the droning of the wings getting louder and something else... the echoing bellow of a deep horn. The field-workers heard it too, for they suddenly stopped their farming and ran to the nearby sledges to exchange tools for weapons and to gather in well-armed clusters, braced for any possible attack!

The flying-ant squadron was directly above them now and dove at them with spears and lances poised to impale! A sudden fierce battle cry arose from the throats of the charging berserkers that made one's hair stand on end, and for a single awful moment, the castaways were frozen with terror and certain that their struggles in this world would soon be over! However, Anya, who had been passively awaiting the arrival of the guard, confronted the sudden threat by leaping into the air from her standing position and then striking a pose with arms and legs fully outstretched in an "X" shape. She shouted something and shook her arms and a sudden look of recognition crossed the face of the leader of the squad, a more muscular sinewy warrior with a bright red plume affixed to his helm that flew in the lead of the attacking column. He immediately raised his spear and shouted commands to his followers as his other hand found and waved a bannered staff that had been fluttering from a holder on his saddle rig. Instantly, the whooping stopped and the weapons of the troop were upraised.

Unfortunately, it was too late to halt the speeding forward momentum of the squad of winged ants, for they were practically on top of the huddled strangers! So instead, the leader gave a quick signal and the diving column of warriors peeled off one by one, alternately left and right. So close did the great winged beasts pass overhead and to the sides that the grass all around them was flattened and the castaways were pressed to the ground as their hair and clothing whipped wildly in the tempest! The whirring of the mighty wings was almost deafening at such proximity and luckily, they instinctively shielded their faces and closed their eyes against the swiftly rising dust cloud stirred by the swooping insects. The tumult quickly subsided... and when the castaways ventured to open their eyes, they looked up to see the sinewy leader of the patrol sitting astride his great beast in the trail right before them! The rest of the mounted soldiers circled lazily, high in the air over their heads, in wide arching loops.

Their attention was drawn back to the grounded figure before them when, with a clatter of armor and gracefully waving plumes, he slid from the saddle of his glistening black flyer and made his way around the sturdy multi-jointed legs of the insect. His elation and excitement was obvious, yet he stopped for a moment at the creature's large triangular head, with its wide-set and bulbous shiny black eyes, and the beast suddenly ran its antennae over the warrior's face in a flurry of movement! Then, just as quickly, the insect's feelers withdrew and it stood silently waiting, almost motionless but for the rhythmic throbbing of it's abdomen and the occasional spastic flexing of its long transparent wings. The anxious soldier turned towards Anya.

"Kwa-I-Anya!" almost whispered the visibly shaken guard in a solemn but happy tone. The crimson-plumed warrior then fell to one knee and bowed his head in an obvious display of submission and respect. "We feared you lost forever, my Princess," he continued with eyes averted.

Not all the words were yet known to the wayward travelers, but they caught enough of the soldier's speech to understand the context and realize that they were in the presence of an extremely important personage! Namely, Anya! The beautiful bronze-skinned warrioress that they had rescued from death, befriended and faithfully followed through a jungle of hazards... and come to love as their own... was some sort of primitive "nobility"! The jungle-savvy barbarian girl had proven herself to be a natural leader, a hunter, a fighter, and a friend, but they never once suspected that all along they'd been in the presence of... *"Royalty"?* The four looked at one another with raised eyebrows as this new development sank in.

Anya composed herself and strode forward with a measured step and carried herself with regal decorum, though she could barely contain the happiness she felt at being home and amongst her people. She approached the kneeling guardsman and bade him rise. When he did so, they looked stoically at one another for a moment and then broke into wide grins and Anya threw her arms around the older man in an affectionate hug! The fierce-looking soldier looked a bit embarrassed, though happy, and endured the hug for several moments before breaking it off. Anya stepped back a pace and the two began speaking in low tones with much gesticulating. Several times during the conversation, the veteran guard looked past Anya to stare quizzically at the seated strangers and nodded. He then pointed back towards the city and said something that Anya found disagreeable, for she vehemently shook her head and again indicated the seated castaways. He continued to plead his case, again pointing to the far-off city, and must've finally won his argument, for momentarily Anya almost imperceptibly nodded her head, shrugged her shoulders, and sighed. She turned slowly with a pained expression on her face and strode back to Buffalo and the kids with her arms tightly folded. She squatted on her heals before them and spoke in sullen tones.

"I must go now," she began, "I have been too long from my people. You will be taken care of and brought to Konton. I… I do not know when I will see you again, but…" Here her voice broke and suppressed tears welled up in her eyes. "I want you to know that the past several weeks have been very happy for me… and I consider you all to be my very best friends. I thank you for… for rescuing me... for trusting me... and seeing me safely back home. But... there's more than that... I... I..." But her voice trailed off and she couldn't continue.

Instead, she stood, momentarily flustered, and turned to trot back to the waiting Captain of the Guard who was already mounted once again on the smooth back of the huge ebony insect. Jeep barked questioningly with his tail wagging, (which seemed to upset the Captain very much), and he strained at his collar in an attempt to follow after Anya. Buffalo rose and shouted for her to wait, but she only paused briefly and turned a tear-stained cheek in a quick parting glance before continuing on her way to the patiently waiting flyer.

Once again the antennae of the huge ant darted forward, this time over Anya's winsome face as she passed before the large head with the polished coal-black eyes. Eyes whose glossy depths hinted at a consciousness and intellect the stranded foreigners had not before suspected in... a bug. Anya appeared perfectly at ease as she grasped the proffered hand of the Captain of the Guard and deftly swung into the saddle behind him.

In the span of the few brief moments that it took for all this to transpire, a group of field workers had made their way to the knoll. They were extremely wary of the strangely clad castaways and even more so of Jeep, but upon seeing Anya, a great cheer of joy went up across their ranks! She waved in response to their exultation with a vigorous hand and a broad white smile as the Captain shouted some instructions to the nearest of the men in the gathering throng. Then, without warning, the mighty wings of the ant vibrated into a blur of motion almost too fast to see and the beast, with it's double load, lifted smoothly into the air - - spiraling upwards to join the loitering patrol above. The regrouped guard circled overhead twice and they could see the Captain shouting and signaling to his men. Then the squad suddenly turned as one and flew in a lazy sidling pattern off towards the distant mist-enshrouded city.

The cheering of the assembled crowd subsided as Anya and the mounted-guard disappeared from view and the jubilation was quickly replaced with an eerie stillness. Buffalo and the kids lowered their gaze from following Anya's vanishing escort to see that they were confronted by hard grim-faced laborers who stood woodenly with weapons at the ready. The wary farmers obviously distrusted them and stared menacingly at them with smoldering black eyes. The castaways didn't know what to do or how to proceed. The situation and the silence was both uncomfortable and unexpected. They'd lost the one friend that had carefully guided them through this dangerous world and now they were left to deal with a mob of coarse and hostile villagers whose intent was unknown!

Unfortunately, the castaways had no way of knowing at the time, that all of Anya's people were ordinarily wary of (and openly aggressive towards) *all* strangers... even their own kind. Anya had warmed up to them rather quickly, considering the strained nature of their first meeting, and they had no other native encounters for comparison. But strangers such as themselves were totally unheard of in the closed society of this hidden subterranean world. The situation was probably much like North American Indians discovering Europeans arriving on their shores for the first time... wonderment accompanied by fear and mistrust. The castaway's clothing, pale skin, blonde hair, Buffalo's size (and beard), Jeep... all these things and more, confused and troubled the suspicious and superstitious minds of the gathered peasant farmers.

Simon and Max smiled nervously and tried in vain to ease the tension by speaking words of friendship in the language they'd learnt from Anya. But the workers, both male and female remained stoic, silent, and impassive. The men were clothed (appropriately for the heat and humidity) in only a brief skirt, much like the ancient Egyptians had worn, and fastened it with a wide leathery belt similar to Anya's, only theirs featured loops and hangers which held small farming tools. They wore rough sandals and most kept a soft absorbent cloth twisted around their foreheads to keep their long loose hair out of their faces and to soak up sweat before it reached and irritated their eyes.

The women were costumed in simple short tunics gathered at the waist by woven fiber belts. They were a little more colorful than the men in that there were hints of colorful patterns and borders at the sleeves and hems of the mostly ivory-colored garments.   Unlike the men, the women were barefoot, braided their hair, and wore more ornaments of bronze, silver, and precious stones. Collectively, they were a proud and impressive looking people, though the fabric of their tunics was heavily soiled with the accumulated sweat and dirt of the day's toil.   They all shared the same ebony eyes and dusky hair, bronze-hued skin, and vaguely Asian/Indian features that Anya exhibited... though none came close to her class of beauty.

The largest of the group, a thickset burly man with a cudgel, the one to whom the Captain had given instructions, turned slowly without taking his eyes off Buffalo and gave a signal to someone at the rear. From behind came two men leading a large black ant pulling a crude wooden sledge with high walls of interwoven saplings.   As they drew up close, they turned the ant full-circle until the back of the sledge was facing the castaways, then one of the men loosed a restraint on either side and the back wall of the wooden enclosure fell open to the ground, like a ramp leading into a cage! Buffalo and the kids were horrified at the very idea of confinement, but suddenly they felt hands pushing them from behind! They hadn't even heard anyone come up behind them!

Buffalo was not about to be taken so easily and he spun to face his ambushers. But the three rugged-looking natives that faced him, armed with long cruel daggers of rough-cut obsidian, meant business and he knew he couldn't save himself *and* the kids if trouble started.   The odds weren't favorable and his options were minimal.   So, he forced himself to back down and told the kids to calmly head for the sledge. The three toughs behind them insisted on unnecessarily guiding them anyway. So, with some rough handling and prodding, they were scornfully herded into the straw-filled back of the waiting pen. The tailgate was raised and quickly locked and they were... prisoners! They looked at each other with sudden frantic concern and were about to voice a protest when the harnessed ant started forward. The resulting sudden lurch of the sledge, combined with the pitch of the sloped floor, sent them all sprawling backwards in a tangled heap of arms, legs, and straw!

The grim-faced laborers surrounding the sledge chuckled and ridiculed the foreigner's plight as Buffalo and the kids sorted out their limbs from the tangle and scooted along the floor to sit back against the latticework walls of the enclosure, nervously chuckling at one another and their predicament while they picked straw from their hair and clothing. Inwardly, they felt beaten and betrayed. In the span of a few short weeks, they'd been airborne, ice-bound, adrift, attacked, marooned, chased, hunted, and almost trampled to death. All in an effort to become... prisoners? And apparently with the approval of the one person that they had come to love and trust.

They had spent such a wonderful few weeks under the care, tutelage, and guidance of their newfound friend, Anya - - the wild and beautiful jungle-girl. They had put their very lives into her hands and she had never failed them. Now, back amongst her people, she seemed to have turned on them and offered them up as captives... curiosities from a faraway world! Buffalo, sensitive to the hurt and confusion he read on the faces of the disheveled teens, extended his huge arms around Max and Dexter who sat sullenly on either side of him. Over the past few weeks, he had come to realize a growing sense of responsibility for these kids, as the hopelessness of their situation impressed itself upon them. He knew he couldn't begin to replace the parents they'd lost, but he wanted to make an effort to sooth their worries and offer his personal strength to cling to. Simon understood and nodded from across the cart with a weak smile and put his arm around Jeep (who was always happy to receive the attention). Buffalo had come to admire and respect them all and he wanted so much to tell them that everything was going to be all right, but that particular phrase was beginning to wear thin. And since he was somewhat afraid that he might reveal the anger and doubts that were stirring within him, he opted for the gentle reassurance of silence instead.

Unfortunately, he found little comfort in his own thoughts. As the creaking wooden sledge bumped uneasily over the rough stones of the road, flanked by the heavily armed workers who had captured them, he seethed with the bitterness and irritation he felt at being so easily fooled and taken. This shouldn't have happened, he told himself. He'd trusted Anya implicitly and, since he felt himself to be an excellent judge of character, he was very annoyed by the turn of events and his apparent misplaced loyalties. He had become very fond of her during their travels, (though he was reluctant to admit it), and he wondered now how he could have been so wrong about her. Had her exotic beauty, seductive dark eyes, and trim sleek figure clouded his judgment? Was he the victim of feminine wiles? He had known many women in his life, especially during the war when everyone's lives were topsy-turvy and the constant threat of danger threw people together in a frantic search for comfort and companionship. But none of them had ever really impressed him or stirred the deep heartfelt emotions he now felt beating in his breast. He felt betrayed.

They had followed Anya in the hopes of finding help, or a way to get home. But it had become clear over the past several weeks that not only was the existence of this Antediluvian inner-world completely unknown and unsuspected by the explorers and scientists back home, but Anya's people apparently had no knowledge of any other world beyond their own either. Or so it seemed. Their behavior and attitude toward them indicated that they were unaware of life outside their cavern and had experienced no previous contact with surface-dwellers of Earth. If so, where had these people come from? Why did they seem at once familiar.... and not? And more importantly, what was to be their fate at the hands of this primitive and savage-looking tribe? Buffalo, the big man, the veteran hero, master of his destiny, felt frustratingly helpless... again.

He cursed the fates that seemed to keep the situation always teasingly out of his control! It seemed they had been doomed the moment they fell down that blasted hole! They had barely survived the trip through the tunnels and without Anya's help, he knew they never would have survived the jungles. Undoubtedly, without her guidance they would all be insect-chow by now! But where had he gone wrong? Had they ever really had a choice other than to follow the barbarian girl? Could it be that she had been just pretending friendship in order to lure them unchallenged to… imprisonment? Enslavement?

Perhaps even *sacrifice?* The Incas and Aztecs made ritual sacrifices of their captives and enemies and Anya's people bore more than a passing resemblance to those ancient tribes!

No... that couldn't be. Deep inside, he was certain that he wasn't *that* wrong about her. Yet, as he gazed at the stern faces of the encircling escort of grim peasants, the reality of the situation suppressed his intuition and he became increasingly uneasy about their future. After all, they were definitely trapped and being treated somewhat like cattle. Oddly, they hadn't bothered to disarm him though... that was a point in their favor. Wasn't it?

Max was the first to counter the silence and raised many of the same questions that Buffalo had already been turning over in his mind. Dexter chimed in and added his "scientific" spin on the issues at hand, but it was Simon's confidence and enthusiasm that eventually broke the spell of despair. Soon the seemingly boundless energy of the three friends had them chattering nervously and even cracking jokes. Buffalo, thankful for their eternal optimism, a welcome distraction from their plight, rose to move forwards to the "high" end of the sloped platform... and the kids, eager to take in the passing view, soon joined him. They hung on to the tall rickety sides of the wooden sledge as it dragged and bumped along the well-worn ruts of the road and looked through the holes between the "basket-weave" of saplings. Buffalo estimated the sides to be about eight feet high and simple enough to climb, but the surrounding troop of guardians would be upon him in an instant if he tried.

The mist-enshrouded fortress city of Konton was still more than a few miles away even though their "draught-ant" pulled along at a fair pace, so the wayfarers resigned themselves to sightseeing. As it was, there wasn't a whole lot to see though. Now that they were off the higher knoll, and down amongst the crops, it was rather like traveling through the seemingly endless cornfields of Kansas. The narrow road was entirely flanked on both sides by plants and trees tended by the native farmers and their worker ants. Now and then, some of the laborers in the fields and orchards would pause and crane their necks to catch a glimpse of the passing "alien" captives, while their insect partners labored on without taking note of their passing at all. Several times the caged castaways got a delightfully closer look at these marvelous worker-ants in action. They seemed to fulfill many of the same functions as a good plow-horse or mule of the surface-world, but performed their tasks with obvious intelligence. Many of them didn't even require a human to drive, guide, or otherwise encourage them! They seemed to execute their duties with complete competence and independence.

But most of what they observed, was just acres and acres of green! Large plants and trees, about a quarter of the size of the great fern-trees they'd seen in the jungle, were planted thickly in neat rows upon either side of the road. Smaller plants were grown in equally neat rows beneath the trees to take advantage of the unused ground space and together they combined into an unbroken expanse of green that extended for miles in either direction, until blending seamlessly with the all-encompassing ring of jungle beyond. Row upon row of meticulously kept fruits and vegetables passed by like an endless botanical review of Nature's bounty. Some of the produce was already familiar to the castaways since the farmers were cultivating many of the plants that Anya had already introduced them to in the jungle. They saw Amak trees and Tikquan plants and, unfortunately, more of the bland and pasty Dujong "melons" than they cared to see!

Periodically, there would be a low flyover of a plumed squad of soldiers similar to the troop that had spirited Anya away. (A recon patrol sent to check on their progress, Buffalo surmised). Twice, the accompanying farmer-guards stopped for a ten-minute rest and the "captives" were given some bready but tasty type of plant-leaves to eat and all the water they could drink. They really weren't being badly treated... they were being respectfully cared for... but mostly ignored.

The captive haul of castaways continued plodding along the worn wagon rut for several hours. The huge city of Konton, that had so awed them from the knoll, was probably yet six to eight miles away and they were only traveling at the pace of a brisk walk. So they expected to continue in this fashion for a few more hours at least. Buffalo, already tired of the unchanging landscape and frustrated by his inability to alter the situation, decided to sit and shut his eyes for a brief nap. But, just as he was beginning to settle himself into the straw for an afternoon snooze, the sledge came to an abrupt halt with a jarring lurch.

Startled from near slumber by the sudden stop, Buffalo sat bolt upright and looked warily through the spaces in the woven walls to either side. All the surrounding guards had dropped to one knee and remained motionless in that position with their heads bowed! He looked up at the kids who still stood facing front and saw them staring ahead with wide-eyed expressions of wonder. Jeep loosed a low growl and Buffalo leapt up to see what had focused everyone's attention.

There, in the middle of the road and blocking their passage, was a mounted army the likes of which the most learned-men and historians of the surface-world could never begin to imagine. Numbering at least a thousand strong, heavily armed warriors with plumes and battle standards sat astride great shiny black ants fitted with intricately carved and inlaid plates of iridescent armor! The smooth protective shielding glinted and flashed in brilliant hues of indigo-blue, purple, and magenta as the lively beasts shifted spiritedly in their line-up. They were splendidly adorned with battle trappings such as leather and bronze harnesses, silver chain mail, painted shields, and colorful banners with graphic images depicting the heraldry of the lineages they represented. Shiny metal spikes and long pointed horns protruded from helmets that were form-fitted to cover and protect the ant's heads while leaving a clear field of vision for the coal-black glossy bulbous eyes.

The warrior soldiers that rigidly sat astride these fearsome cavalry-ants were themselves a spectacle. Resembling some crazy blend of medieval knight, noble Aztec warrior, and savage Barbarian, they were bedecked head to toe in full-body armor of the utmost quality and craftsmanship. Even to the untrained eye of the castaways, it was apparent that the workmanship was of a very fine quality. The rider's armor was formed and detailed to resemble various fearsome insects and beasts that inhabited the cavern-world of Kontonqua! Some were fashioned into a serpentine motif with smooth-fitting scales that were inlaid with colorful and intricate geometric patterns; apparently designed to mimic a particular species of reptile that served as their totem - - a symbol representing their order or "clan". Others knights wore armor wrought in the shape of predatory insects such as wasps and beetles and even incorporated portions of the actual exoskeleton of their favorite beast in its manufacture. They skillfully adapted the insect's armor to be their own, but further augmented nature's design by adding colorful plumes, beaded leatherwork, and metal fittings wherever possible. There were even warriors suited in what appeared to be feathers of an unusual variety, although the castaways hadn't seen or heard a single bird of any type during their travels.

The mounted cavalry was well armed and carried a wide variety of effective weapons. Each soldier was a veritable arsenal unto himself. Most everyone had a long or short bow slung over one shoulder (with the necessary quiver and arrows to give it deadly purpose) and most sat with a razor-sharp sword of black obsidian in one hand and kept the other atop a sheathed dagger at their belt. (Buffalo was not at all surprised by the presence of obsidian... volcanic glass... and felt that it bolstered his ideas about the cavern's geothermal heating system). Many others had unique items such as wooden cudgels, large iron axes, spike-studded maces, flails, and barbed lances and pikes. Altogether a most formidable army!

Grouped in clans of armor-class determined by the particular totem they belonged to, the fierce-looking warriors sat quietly in formation on their spirited chargers with only the occasional creak of leather harness to break the stillness. With stolid but noble features, they stared somewhat arrogantly at the foreign captives held helplessly within the thatched walls of the farm sledge.

The initial shock of seeing this formidable barbarian cavalry, suddenly grouped before them and filling the road as far as the eye could see, stunned Buffalo and the kids to silence momentarily - - but they were tired of being treated like prisoners after all they'd been through. Max spoke up first, haltingly, and tried out some simple words like "friends" and "help" in the native Kontonquan tongue she and the others had partially learned from Anya. Simon and Dex joined in and Buffalo added a few choice words in his booming voice too, though with a note of seriousness; it was rather difficult for him to hide his displeasure with the entire situation. No one actually replied, but their entreaties did seem to trigger a reaction of sorts.

A lone highly-decorated warrior at the head of the column, urged his ant forward and barked a few short commands to the kneeling peasant-guards. As one, they quietly arose with heads bowed and paused in silence. Then, they suddenly lifted their heads and came to life as though released from a spell. The reanimated farmers moved quickly to gather around the sledge while Dexter, Max, and Simon, filled with uncertainty, huddled together around Buffalo at the center of the walled van. Two of the laborers attended to the "draught-ant" that pulled the sledge while two others released the tailgate that held Buffalo and the kids imprisoned. The rest formed a sort of gauntlet at the back of the sledge and awaited the emergence of the captives with their knives and staves at the ready. One of their guards, who had let down the back ramp, then motioned for them to step down out of the latticework cage. It looked, for all the world, as though they were to be executed on the spot!

Subdued by the grip of fear and with pained expressions evident upon their faces, Buffalo, Simon, Maxine, and Dexter proceeded very slowly down the ramp, practically frozen with terror. All eyes were on them as they nervously stepped off the back of the wooden tailgate and into the midst of the silent menacing throng. Expecting the worst, the harrowed captives fairly jumped when the two guards behind them suddenly sprang into the back of the sledge and pulled the tailgate up again after them! Then, just as unexpectedly, the other two guards that had been holding the harnessed ant steady, leaped upon its back, and in a flurry of movement and dust, rapidly brought the sledge full-circle - - turning it completely around within the confines of the narrow trail. The framework farm-sled carefully maneuvered around the castaways and began heading back up the trail they'd just traversed. Instantly, the remaining farmer-guards that surrounded Buffalo and the kids sheathed their knives and with a short sprint, leapt onto the thatched wooden sides of the sledge as it passed. As soon as the last of them had gotten safely aboard, clinging to its interlaced sapling sides, the draught-ant took off at a spirited trot and the whole rig sped into the distance leaving only a billowing dust trail behind.

Completely startled by the unexpected departure of their guards, Buffalo and the kids just stood for a moment, gawking wide-eyed at the receding sledge. Then, remembering the army that still blocked the road before them, they nervously turned as one to face the assembled barbarian ranks. The mounted warriors still sat stoically in formation, as silent and as rigid as their fidgeting "steeds" would allow. Plumes, feathers, banners, and battle standards added colorful splendor to the menacing host, but remained motionless in the windless atmosphere of the cavern. For a few nerve-wracking seconds, (that seemed an eternity), nothing transpired and the four wanderers felt terribly vulnerable and exposed in the face of the invincible savage legion that confronted them. Buffalo stared into the coldly confident eyes of the commanding officer, who was obviously sizing up Buffalo as well, trying vainly to discern what might be in store for them. Suddenly, the uncomfortable stillness was sliced by a single word... "Come!" uttered in English by the battalion's commander! The accent was thick, but the word was unmistakable. Four mounted soldiers then broke ranks and rode up alongside the castaways. They maneuvered their chargers in closely and then stopped and stretched out a hand towards the foreigners. Their faces were not unfriendly and their actions nonaggressive.

"He spoke English!" whispered Max to Buffalo.

"I think Anya may have had a hand in this," he whispered back, "Let's find out." Buffalo turned to address the commander and spoke up in a strong voice loud enough for all to hear and said, "Anya?"

There was no real response from the leader other than a somewhat puzzled expression and a slight look of disdain.

"Wait," spoke up Dexter Schornberg, "That's just what *we* called her! That's not her full name. It was longer than that. Remember?"

Buffalo paused to think back to what the patrol Captain had called her and then corrected himself. "Kwa-I-Anya?" he inquired in his most dignified tone. The commander smiled thinly and nodded his head curtly in assent. The four adventurers felt an instant sense of relief and their feelings of dread all but disappeared. They turned then to the waiting guardsmen at their flanks who still sat with proffered hands extended. It was now clear that they only wanted the castaway "prisoners" to join them and ride in tandem upon the backs of their battle-ants.

"Simon?" prompted Buffalo, "Howzabout you first?"

Simon looked just a little worried as he edged closer to step warily in front of the first nimble set of legs of the great black battle-ant. Its long antennae were flexing and he could see the rhythmic pulsing of its abdomen beneath the heavy plate-armor. The mounted soldier was one of the fierce-looking serpent clan with a helmet shaped to imitate the head of a striking snake. The helmet completely covered his head and he peered out of the open mouth while the large sharp fangs, protruding from both upper and lower jaws, acted as face-guards. No sooner had Simon gripped the offered hand than the ant swung its head around and ran its probing antennae over Simon's face! Max let out a little squeal and Simon instinctively recoiled, but the soldier held him firm. The ant's exploration of Simon's features was thorough but brief and it pulled its head back sharply when done. Without further delay, the armored rider whisked Simon from his feet and deposited him directly behind his saddle. Then the "Snake-soldier" urged his ant forward and with a smooth and gliding gait, the ant scurried off to meld seamlessly into the ranks of the assembled troop.

Max was standing sort of "next-in-line" but nervously announced, "I'm not ready yet!" and ran behind Dexter and gave him a little shove to persuade him to replace her. Dexter, no more certain about undergoing ant "imprinting" than Max was, loosed a deep sigh and stepped up to the next ant. Again, as soon as he made contact with the warrior, the ant swung its great head around to probe his features and Dexter shut his eyes tightly against the intrusive poking of the cold and slippery-looking antennae nubs that were thickly covered with tiny bristling hairs. Instinctively, remembering his glasses, Dexter quickly reached up to protect them... but so precise and gentle was the ant's inspection of Dexter's face that its examination was barely felt at all. In the next instant, it was over and he was hauled quickly and unceremoniously into position behind a "Wasp-soldier". The second burdened ant then moved off effortlessly into the throng. As they disappeared, they heard Dex holler, "Go on, Max! There's nothing to it!"

Maxine gave a nervous look of apprehension towards Buffalo, but she no longer cringed... and in fact, stepped forward quite bravely now that she had resolved to face her initial misgivings. She willingly held her hand aloft and squinted a bit as she approached the next ant in line. Knowing what she was about to endure, she courageously and unflinchingly accepted the ant's antennae-interrogation... and it wasn't until the brawny plate-covered "Beetle-guard" suddenly whisked her from her feet, while she still had her eyes closed, that she let slip another small girlish squeal of surprise.

Buffalo, (though no more eager than the rest to embrace this new insect experience), strode directly up to the fourth waiting guard, another

Serpent-clan member, and took the soldier's hand. He kept his eyes locked with those of the mounted-warrior while the ant surveyed his countenance and when the ant was through, he grabbed the saddle back with his free hand and vaulted onto the back of the armored steed by his own accord.

He'd no sooner done so than he heard a whine and two short barks. Jeep was watching nervously from the trail with his stump wagging... but he wasn't thrilled about Buffalo's new mode of transportation. "S'okay, Jeep!" Buffalo told the anxious pooch, "There's always room for one more, buddy... Jump! C'mon!" Jeep, uncertain about being so near one of these strange new insect-beasts, but unwilling to let Buffalo from his sight, made a couple of faltering attempts... and then, gaining confidence, made a huge leap into the air and landed squarely upon the large ebony ant's posterior, where he quickly made his way up its armor protected back to where Buffalo could grab him and settle him into his lap. The large warrior ant was none too pleased about this unknown mammal upon its back, but as Jeep settled down, the ant calmed as well and the guardsman skillfully maneuvered his steed to fall in behind the other warrior-ants as they carried the castaways into the heart of the mounted column.

To Buffalo's dismay, things were out of his direct control *again*; he was being whisked along like baggage and he was momentarily separated from the rest of his "crew". This was because each clan member rode only with the fellow warriors of his chosen battle-totem. They did catch glimpses of each other, through the tight screen of armored bodies and battle paraphernalia, and Buffalo was forced to calm his frustration by acknowledging that, by all indications, they seemed in good hands and safe from harm… for the moment.

The heavily armored battle-ants traveled at great speed and yet still managed to hold to tight formations. Buffalo estimated they were now moving at roughly twenty miles per hour and he was certain the ants were capable of much more if pressed. Despite their speed, the ride was as smooth as though they were floating on a cushion of air, no matter how rough or bumpy the road beneath them. Apparently, six legs were equivalent to the best shock absorbers ever invented! With every quick and well-placed step, the ant compensated perfectly to keep his back straight and level and they fairly glided over the rugged unevenness of the stone-paved artery that led to Konton.

The mountainous citadel now loomed close before them, with more and more of its secrets and details revealed as the miles melted away. The encircling mists and overall grayness of its ancient walls were ominous and foreboding, but there was no mistaking the exquisite beauty and craftsmanship of its bold and imposing architecture. It was almost cathedral-like in its enormous complexity. Like a Nôtre Dame gone wild and blended with medieval castles, its fanciful towers, spires, minarets, and domes were riotous in number, yet intricately engineered and assembled to interconnect and bridge support for the whole structure.

Just as they were getting really close, the battalion dipped down into a shallow valley of dense trees that completely overhung the roadway and they lost sight of the city for a mile or so. The trees were of an Amak variety, with hairy red fruits similar to the purple ones that Anya had amazed them with, and which had become a favorite delicacy for the castaways. Many workers and ants were here employed amongst the deep shadows of the thickly planted trees, industriously tending to the tender Jell-O-like treats. Buffalo wondered why the people of Konton would plant such a dense screen of trees so near to their city, but he was as yet unaware of the excellent perimeter defenses the orchard afforded, or the real need for it. It was also a practical arrangement, for the peasantry cultivated not only the sweet fruits of the trees, but also hunted the many insects and other beasts that were attracted to the sticky irresistible Amak.

All at once, they emerged from beneath the trees and found themselves being waved through enormous ornamented and fortified gates that were heavily guarded by keen well-armed troops. They were entering a huge open and busy esplanade surrounded by a tall outer ring of crenellated stone-block walls dotted with guard towers that completely encircled the massive fortress city of Konton... which itself dominated the center and shot skyward before them. Like first-time visitors to the "big city" that had never seen a skyscraper before, the surface-dwelling strangers gaped open-mouthed and craned their heads back to fully take in the marvelous complexity of the wondrous structure that towered upwards until nearly out of sight. Extending to either side for at least a mile, the colossal stronghold rose so magnificently into the sky and with such imaginative and intricate splendor that it easily bested any modern achievements of man's steel and concrete frameworks. From its immense buttresses to its catwalks and balconies to its ingenious domed skylights, this incredible man/insect earthwork was unrivaled and unmatched in human endeavor.

Now that they were at the foot of the edifice, the castaways could clearly see that the entire façade of the unique building was covered with wonderful glyphs and carvings of native Kontonquan life... human figures, gargantuan insects, flourishing jungles, and other imaginative scenes. Disturbingly, there were also many nightmarish images included. Strange human/insect mutations, horrific battle scenes, aberrations of nature, death struggles, and wailing tormented souls could be discerned amongst the carvings and gave the mystical city a diabolic aura that sent a chill into the hearts of the foreigners.

The lines of armored ants and their riders slowed to a walk as they threaded their way across the bustling esplanade filled with vendors and artisans and approached a huge portal entrance to the city itself. Most of the mounted troops peeled off to either side and arranged themselves into neat rows... standing at attention. A smaller squad carrying the castaways gathered behind the commander and approached the large archway, the western threshold to the inner maze of avenues. The aperture was framed with a complex grillwork, but they had little time to study it. Coming from the brightness of the cavern day, they had only a fleeting impression of its interior design and the inhabitants within, before the darkened gloom of its entryway dimmed the eyesight of the unprepared humans to near blackness.

Chapter 12
"Within the Walls"

Passing through the massive entry gates of Konton and into the enveloping shadows of the vestibule beyond proved to be an experience at once vexing and exhilarating for the newcomers. They were unexpectedly struck, and uncomfortably chilled, by the much cooler interior air and frustrated by the sudden obscuring shroud of darkness which robbed them of their first glimpse of this strange new "world-within-a-world". Anxiously waiting for their eyes to adjust to the interior gloom, the castaway's senses, mainly their hearing, could pick up only the echoing creak and clatter of the armor and armaments of their entourage.

As they glided smoothly along, curious passengers seated behind their guardian escorts, they became aware of an increasing tumult of voices and activity ahead. The narrow vestibule walls seemed to give way to a more "open" hollowness as they procccdcd, for thcy noticcd that thc surrounding noises began to echo and reverberate farther into the darkness. Then, thankfully, their vision was restored to them almost as quickly as it had been taken. It wasn't just the effects of their natural eyesight adjusting to the dark however, the passageway's interior was actually dimly lit from above and images began to slowly take shape. The illumination wasn't nearly the bright artificial "daylight" of the cavern outside, but it was more than adequate to reveal the details and splendor of the internal design and composition of the marvelous mound-city that now imprisoned them.

With their full vision returned, what met their gaze filled them with an awe and wonderment they would never forget. Their earlier first impressions of bustling activity within the tunnel had been only a hint of what was actually going on. It seemed as though everywhere they looked, they saw people and ants at work and on the move. They found themselves riding through a great earthen tunnel whose walls had been fortified with immense carved stonework columns and massive hand-hewn beams of wood. Carved upon them were more glyphs depicting strange ceremonies, weird human and animal faces, nightmarishly distorted figures, and epic battle scenes. The various reliefs were sculpted and chiseled into the superstructure as they had been on the outside... only here indoors, they were hand-painted in gloriously vivid colors as well. The immense tunnel, with its tall vaulted ceilings, was easily the size of any small-town Main Street, with its central thoroughfare and sidewalks, and organized in about the same way.

The center of the passage was reserved for two-way traffic and the ants, as large as they were, could comfortably walk two or three abreast in either direction. Unfortunately, they apparently had no concept of traffic "lanes", or keeping to one side, and the ants and natives traveling in *both* directions intermingled in a weaving, jostling, and constant "rush-hour" of confusion. Off to the sides of the passage was where commerce took place. The pace was a bit less hectic, but still somewhat chaotic as crowds of people and ants milled about thickly between the stalls and tables that were filled with produce, garments, and merchandise of all sorts. Merchants and craftsmen loudly hawked their wares to a meandering throng of soldiers, citizens, farmers, laborers, and what appeared to be... *slaves!*

Unmistakably, there were nervous and dejected looking men and women in the crowd - - ragged, chained, and tattooed - - that were trying to go about their business, but obviously in a subordinate position to everyone else around them. The sight of these miserable shackled unfortunates was extremely disturbing to the foreigners. Not only did the practice of slavery revile them, but they also couldn't help but wonder... was this how they themselves might end up? Surely Anya hadn't brought them all this way to suffer such a cruel fate! They stifled their concerns for the moment, for they were too caught up in the overall assault on their senses by the entire wondrous spectacle about them to ponder such dark implications.

Behind the rows of stalls and booths, many inviting and decorative doorways of what were presumably even more shops and businesses lined the walls of the gallery. The few that could be peered into seemed actively engaged in vigorous trade or the provision of services such as the serving of food and drink. It became obvious to the foreign travelers that they were catching their first glimpse of a Konton marketplace. The economic "hub" of a true civilization! Perhaps they weren't dealing with total barbarians after all?

Further evidence of the civic advancement of their hosts was found in their inventive ingenuity. While looking around and absorbing the scene and all its wonders, their attention was eventually drawn to the clever method for lighting the interior tunnels of the city. On the ceilings high above, were two wide rows of lichens that ran the length of the marketplace and branched off into every adjoining tunnel they saw. One row was a dark grayish green and the other glowed brightly as it emitted the soft yellowish light that pervaded the immense market chamber. They were the same glowing lichens that completely covered the ceiling of this incredible underworld cavern in such numbers that they actually simulated the bright daylight of the sun. Here, within the darkened interiors of this massive mountain of a city, the lichens had been carefully planted, cultivated, and arranged by the ingenuity of the humans and the labor of the industrious ants that attended them to form a lighting system for the city! They were neatly trimmed into separate and precise double rows and cared for by special and much smaller ants, (no larger than Jeep and probably bred for the purpose). These smaller industrious ant-farmers walked upside down on the ceiling along the parallel beds, meticulously attending their glowing crop.

One row was planted using the "daylight" variety of lichens - - which grew in the vast majority on the cavern ceiling and thereby provided the artificial fourteen-hour day. The other row had been selectively planted with the "starlight" variety - - which grew in weaker numbers in the outer cavern and created the illusion of starry streaks and constellations in the "nighttime" sky. Here, within the labyrinthine tunnels of Konton, and carefully grown in equal numbers side by side, the tiny plants provided a constant and efficient source of light. (In the private bedchambers, as the castaways were later to find out, only the "daylight" variety was encouraged to grow, so as to allow the occupants to rest in darkness. Small clear-sided pots with hinged doors had been cleverly devised to contain individual clusters of the "starlight" plants so that they could be used as lamps or carried about as lanterns at night).

171

No one in the group was sufficiently schooled in botany to explain exactly how the plants functioned. However, Dexter (who was sometimes akin to a walking encyclopedia) seemed to think the secret had something to do with the plant's respiration process. Most plants, like those on the cavern's floor, use light as energy to chemically convert carbon dioxide and water into carbohydrates - - in other words, photosynthesis. Dexter theorized that somehow the lichens sort of reversed that process to use carbohydrates and carbon dioxide to produce water... and *emit* light! He wasn't sure of the exact chemistry involved, but the whole ecosystem seemed to maintain a symbiotic balance between the green-leafed plants and the lichens that proved to be immensely successful... as the prolific nature of *both* plant forms firmly attested.

As the mounted troop passed through the plaza, the raucous tumult of voices subsided and heads began to turn in their direction. Buffalo and the kids realized they'd been noticed! The sudden awkward silence made them feel a bit uncomfortable as they looked about at the rigidly standing natives who were now gazing back with dour and suspicious expressions. Only the great ants that were moving freely about their business within the gallery seemed not to notice or care about the presence of the intruding "outerworlders". The marketplace was a large one, (it was actually the main trading center, though many smaller "marts" were scattered throughout the miles of tunnels that intertwined within the walls of Konton), and it took some time to cross it... a journey made longer by the discomfort of being warily scrutinized. As they were paraded by, the noise of commerce could be heard to resume again behind them as the merchants went back about their business, but the bustle of activity in their immediate surroundings would always abruptly cease as each newly encountered group of locals paused to witness their passing.

Despite this momentary interruption in buying and selling, the foreigners could see that business in the bazaar was brisk and that Konton seemed to be a city in its economic prime. The trading stalls were spotlessly clean and loaded to the brim with goods of all kinds. There was a bounty of produce, looking crisp and freshly picked, probably grown in the very fields they'd passed through earlier. There were vendors selling vegetables, fruits, grains, breads and baked goods, and even fancy pastries and other dessert sweets, (in fact, one confection stand was surrounded by several families that were expertly enjoying the pleasures of Amak!). There were stalls that served prepared foods too, and some of the delightful cooking aromas, wafting from smoky kitchens, were arousing pangs of hunger within the castaways. Sizzling pans were rattled over the grillwork of open braziers by busy and attentive chefs in one stall, while in another, great slabs of meat were turning on roasting spits over glowing coals that hissed and sparked in response to the drizzle of dripping fat.

Buffalo and the kids didn't know whether to be tempted or appalled, for this was their first glimpse of any substantial amount of meat on the Kontonquan menu and they had no idea what its source could be. The only animals they had seen in their travels that even remotely approached the size of the broiling meat were insects! And no matter how adventurous and open-minded they might feel to embrace Kontonquan culture, there wasn't one among them, (with the possible exception of Jeep!), that relished the thought of dining on bugmeat! Yet… the aroma of fresh barbecue was extremely enticing and their involuntary mouth-watering forewarned of a possible future conflict with their personal convictions!

It was during this unwanted wrestling match between taste buds and conscience, that Buffalo recognized the familiar odor of fish… and sure enough, they shortly passed a series of booths specializing in all sorts of fishes - - fresh, fried, baked, and smoked! Buffalo had long suspected the existence of abundant fish in the river, ever since their first day in the cavern, and here was proof. (This may seem like a matter of small consequence, but to a confirmed carnivore such as Buffalo Brewster, it meant relief from the weeks of mostly fruits and vegetables he'd had to endure in order to reach Konton, *and* a reprieve from possibly having to choose between veggies and insect meat later!)

In addition to foodstuffs, the market also featured many other wares of all description. Earthenware plates (both plain and decorative), platters, pots, cups, and jugs were sold in great profusion. Furnishings for the home, handy utensils, a variety of clothing, and personal items such as combs and brushes and various toiletries were also available. Craftsmen and artisans of many types worked intently in workshops behind their wares, both creating and selling the results of their labors. Their considerable skill, patience, and imagination was evident in the quality of what they offered - - in what had to be some of the most beautiful beadwork, jewelry, pottery, artwork, and sculpture to be found anywhere. Blacksmiths, leathercrafters, armorers, clothiers, masons, carpenters, coopers, basketweavers... almost every conceivable trade was represented in this Kontonquan commercial district.

Presently, they reached the far side of the market and the column of ant-mounted soldiers was obliged to slow down momentarily as they were forced to merge into single-file to accommodate the smaller dimensions of the tunnel that lay ahead. They did so with unparalleled precision, like an expert equestrian team, and it wasn't long before the foreigners were carried smoothly along into the broad shaft of the lesser tunnel. There were many such tunnels that joined with the main marketplace and this particular one, being a main artery, was heavy with traffic. But, they had no sooner entered it than they ducked into an even smaller branch that veered to the right and slanted distinctly upwards. This new tunnel was still plenty large enough to allow two-way traffic in single lanes and didn't seem to be very busy at all. Only occasionally did they pass others that were heading back down towards the trade-gallery. It was almost as brightly lit here as it had been in the larger tunnels for although the strips of glowing plants were, by rule of proportion, smaller and narrower than in the great market hall, the ceilings were much lower as well. In fact, the shaft's ceiling was low enough that, had Buffalo dared, he could have stood upon his ant's back and just about run his fingertips through the glowing plantlife.

Spaced at regular intervals along their route were dimly lit circular openings; entryways whose recesses averaged about twenty feet in depth. Each had a door set into its far end with a simple cloth or wooden covering. From the quick glimpses they had of the few doors that stood open, and from the fact that several of the hallways had young naked children playing in them, the castaways surmised that they were passing the entrances to some of the homes of the general citizenry of Konton. Scattered along the way too, were quite a few tunnel openings and intersections that branched off to either side. Most were more or less of equal size and identical to the one in which they traveled and the castaways couldn't help feeling that they could get quite easily lost in this labyrinth if not for their escort.

Presently, they came to a three-way split in their tunnel and the Captain of the Guard, the leader of the flying patrol that had earlier taken Anya, was awaiting them in the opening of the right-hand tunnel ahead. With but a slight motion of his hand, a signal was given to divide the squad and the mounted commander saluted and turned to lead his well-disciplined troops into the depths of the *other* two tunnels. As each of the newcomers reached the fork, fears of separation gripped them. However, at the last possible instant, their personal escorts turned into the right-hand tunnel and lined up directly behind the Captain. The remaining column, those without a foreign passenger, proceeded to follow their comrades into the two diverging tunnels until the last in line, a soldier bearing a standard, detached from the main body of the troop and turned to fall-in behind Buffalo and the kids. Only then, did the Captain signal to proceed and the small squad of six began their advance into the broad new passageway.

This new wider earthen tube inclined even more steeply than the one they had just quit, but more importantly, it also began a long slow gentle and consistent curve to the left. They traveled thus, in this enormous concentric upward spiral, for some time and realized that they must be climbing quite high above the cavern floor. After a while, they began to notice too that the entryways of the apartments they passed were spaced farther apart and seemed more fashionable and upscale. These entrances were larger and much more decorative then those of the homes they'd passed below. As they continued to ascend, the elegance of these portals improved dramatically with refinements such as intricately carved wooden doors, painted walls, thick fiber rugs, colorfully woven wall-hangings, and even objects d'art. There were no naked children playing in dusty doorways here, and the few inhabitants they saw were neatly clad in clean bright tunics. Obviously, the citizens that lived at these elevated levels were of a higher economic class than the "peasantry" dwelling below.

They continued on at a fair pace for the ants were capable of great speed and the Captain pushed on freely. The continual upward spiral seemed to transition into a tighter curve as they proceeded, though its actual diameter at this point must still have been a half mile or more. Glancing around, they were astonished to see that the home entranceways to either side were getting gradually even grander than those they had recently passed! Several had soldiers standing guard before magnificently carved and painted arches and gateways that framed openings to highly decorated hallways, many with splendid fountains, potted plants, and artful sculpture.

The travelers marveled at the finery and beauty of these "mansion" dwellings that they passed as they rode swiftly by. Great wealth was apparently demonstrated here, not by the display of gold or other precious metals, but by the intricacy and attention to detail in artistry and craftsmanship. The hand-wrought façades were quite extensive and exquisitely carved. They were boldly painted and beset with glistening iridescent beetle-shell cut into tiny fragments and arranged into wondrous inlaid mosaic patterns. Some were done merely as colorful designs, while others depicted figures and scenes from Kontonquan life... seemingly both mythical and historical. Spiritual ceremony and turbulent battles seemed to be popular subjects. A recurring theme in many of the battle murals recounted violent wars with horrifying insect-men... dark barbaric twisted figures that seemed to be half man, half fly! Buffalo shook his head critically. Where do they come up with this stuff? The legends and mythology of Konton appeared to even exceed those of the surface-world in being just plain weird!

The several people they saw throughout this vicinity were very well dressed and some were riding ants bedecked with elegant ornamental harnesses and trappings. Several men were seen riding the larger winged-ants that were fitted with richly crafted and armored bridles and saddles. Some were soldiers that would crisply salute with a closed fist across their chest as they passed the Captain, others appeared to be (judging by their fine garments and haughty carriage) noblemen... or perhaps even royalty!

Buffalo couldn't help but observe, with some sarcasm, that the layering of economic wealth within the city walls of Konton lent a whole new meaning to the term "upper class"! Evidently, the better off you were financially, the higher up you lived!

The castaways were greatly enjoying their personal tour of Kontonquan culture and society, especially the artful expression of Kontonquan extravagance! However, the view was soon to change once more for they were heading into a brightly lit and well-guarded tunnel just up ahead. It had a very ornate and sturdy gateway that stood open but was flanked by serious-looking warriors that blocked their path, stepping aside only after confirming the troop's identity and intentions. As the riders passed into the somewhat narrower corridor beyond, they were astounded by the magnificence of the wall murals. The walls here were decorated with a succession of very handsome and colorful mosaic portraits of rather stoic but regally dressed women! They were depicted in very elaborate headdresses and laden with jewels and gold. Their garments were of fine linen and belted with fanciful leather harnesses that, despite their finery, still managed to give their graceful feminine forms a barbaric warlike appearance. Various animal totems were cleverly and unobtrusively fitted into the design of their colorful costumes. But, what really set these murals apart, was the fact that here, the glowing plants were used not just for lighting, but as part of the artwork, to create glowing halos around the standing figures! This noble-looking succession of women apparently enjoyed some sort of divine status in Kontonquan culture!

The tunnel visibly grew brighter as they proceeded down its length and they knew it wasn't just due to the effect of the glowing lichens. In fact, they thought at first that they might once again emerge out into the open air of the cavern. Instead, the tunnel made an abrupt turn to the left and emptied into an imposing vaulted room of colossal proportions! The Captain brought his small squad to the very center of this great hall and halted them there. He then rode forward alone towards several sets of huge carved wooden doors at the far end of the colonnade, giving the foreigners an opportunity to pause and survey their new surroundings.

The enormous room was almost Medieval in its basic structure and design. Massive stone columns, carved with gargoyle-type faces, rose to a terrific height and lined the tapestry-covered walls to support the tremendous crisscrossed arches that hovered high overhead. The source of the brightness they had noted, emanated from huge frosted skylights that were situated between the intricate web-work of these archways, so as to allow the actual outside cavern light to filter into the room. The resulting shafts of light took on that "milky" appearance they'd seen in the jungles, as they caught the room's lazy swirl of airborne dust in their beams.

The floor was the next item to catch the interest of the waiting castaways. It appeared to be tiled in large tightly fit slabs of predominantly black marble, polished to a high luster so shiny that everything else in the room was mirrored in its surface. From their position in the center of the room, there extended a subtle golden pattern of inlaid thin radiating lines that formed a giant sunburst and stretched in all directions to the far reaches of the great hall. The hard cold marble floor encouraged otherwise quiet noises of far-off activity to echo hollowly around the chamber, giving the place a very solemn cathedral-like atmosphere. Though its architecture was alien to their realm of experience, the great hall nonetheless gave them a sense of comfort through familiarity, for its form and function was one quite commonly found in government buildings and other grandiose public places back home.

The guards that stood before various doorways around the room remained stolid and pretended not to notice them at all. However, upon closer inspection of the great hall, they realized that they were still being unobtrusively watched over. There were many small balconies above in the shadowy recesses between the tapestries and columns that harbored well-concealed bowmen at the ready. A few ants and people went quietly about their business at the fringes of the room, scooting in and out of darkened apertures, but most appeared to be trying nonchalantly to avoid the small mounted group. Max tried to whisper a comment about this to her brother, Simon, but was cut short by a curt hiss from her escort. Further examination of the Great Hall was then curtailed by the rapid return of the Captain. He once again took up his position at the head of the small squad and led them straight towards the massive and imposing doors at the end of the room.

There were three sets of center-opening wooden doors and the Captain unhesitatingly rode directly for the ones in the middle, unchallenged by the stolid guardsmen flanking each set. The huge doors opened soundlessly, as if by magic, when they drew near and shut behind them once again after they'd passed through. They proceeded now, gently upwards again, through a long spacious gallery lined on both sides by spear-toting guardsmen rigidly standing at attention. All of the guards they saw from this point onward seemed to be of the serpent-totem variety and were clad in scaly armor similar to those of the ranks of soldiers they'd first met. However, the headdresses of these particular troops were even more elaborate and their overall costume generally more ornate and colorful than any they'd yet encountered.

Presently, they reached another set of closed doors and they were challenged by two menacing-looking sentries that stood blocking their path. The verbal challenge was evidently a matter of formality though, because the guards and the Captain exchanged their phrases with rehearsed precision. Satisfied by the proper responses to the brief spoken ritual, the sentries bowed and stepped aside, only to snap to attention again back at their usual posts as the great doors slowly opened by some unseen hand. The Captain spoke a single quiet command to the soldiers of his entourage and they all dismounted. Each one then turned to assist his passenger from the back of his warrior ant, but the kids, with their usual exuberance and eagerness, had already slipped off to the floor before they could do so! Buffalo grinned, and still holding Jeep in his arms, swung his leg over to one side and similarly slid from the back of the armored ant, landing on the floor with a resounding thud of his heavy aviation boots. The Captain motioned them forward and led them on foot into the adjoining chamber. The sight they beheld took their breath away.

This new room was somewhat smaller than the Great Hall below, but its architecture was substantially more grand, even more fantastic, (almost bordering on the grotesque). Unlike the Great Hall, this room was evenly lit from *all* sides at once! As the little band moved out into the spacious room, they noticed the same style of ceiling with its milky colored skylights, but what *really* commanded their attention were the walls... or rather the seeming *absence* of them! Enormous plate windows spanned the spaces between a ring of evenly-spaced giant pillars that shaped the room into an almost perfect circular 360° panoramic view, interrupted only by the doors they had just walked through... and another area of darkened wall across the room directly opposite. The resulting view was incredible! They were perched at a terrific height, at the apex of the city, and all the surrounding landscape of Kontonqua stretched out before them. In three directions, the thick jungle they had traversed extended as far as the eye could see, until finally its detail was lost in the haze and mist of the distance. In the fourth direction, partially hidden by the doors they had just entered through, the immense cavern's bright ceiling descended to ground level just twenty or so miles away. They were looking eastward, over the bounty of agriculture that encircled the city, so they guessed that the base of the glowing cavern wall, in that particular direction at least, must be located just beyond the rings of cultivated fields.

They stood as if frozen for several minutes, transfixed by the beauty of it all, until Dexter broke the silence of the moment by calling their attention to a large multi-tiered platform that was slowly rising up from the floor in the very center of the room. It was built of smooth ivory-colored alabaster and rose, like a layer-cake, in five nested circular steps, each decreasing in size until topped by a solitary, elaborately-designed, golden chair carved with a serpent motif. As they stared in fascination at the highly polished glistening throne that had appeared from nowhere, it suddenly dawned on the castaways that they had been brought to the Royal Audience Chamber of a *palace*... situated at the very pinnacle of the great mound city that was Konton!

Dexter slowly edged forward to get a closer look at the magnificent golden throne which stood high upon the dais before them, but a deep grunt from the Captain beside him told him he'd best hold his position. The others prudently exercised patience and contented themselves to return to enjoying the wonderful panoramic views afforded by their position. The throne-room commanded an amazing overview of Konton's fields and the surrounding landscape; quite equal to that of the observation decks of any surface-world skyscraper. They gazed in wonder at the jungles they'd just recently trodden through... curiously now seen from high above the gargantuan fern trees that had served as their protective canopy... and which now looked very much like an endless and impenetrable green carpet.

Over the treetops, many tiny black dots darted across the expanse of sky and the castaways recognized them to be the distant forms of the winged insect-giants, plying the air above the jungles. Some soared singly, appearing to fly in randomly zigzagging patterns just above tree level or perhaps fluttering in lazy loops and twists, while yet others would streak past with unbelievable swiftness, careening from one end of the horizon to the other. Some species seemed to prefer to travel in groups of various sizes, but while some groups flew in careful graceful formations, yet others could be seen frantically hovering in tight clusters like gnats in a swamp. The scene in the air was quite entertaining and continually changing its patterns and performers. It was like watching a strange and mystical aerial ballet from a remote balcony. They fully realized however, that the seemingly innocent swirl of dots represented a multitude of menacing insect behemoths... including some of the most vicious of insect predators! When they would observe the occasional "dot" break from its intended path and suddenly go diving down into the trees, it rekindled the fear and anxiety they had lived with over the past few weeks… and renewed their appreciation for Anya's expert guidance and protection.

Closer at hand, they suddenly noticed a squad of perimeter guards come flying into view. They were evidently the same patrol that had earlier spotted their egress from the jungle for they bore the same insignia and colors. They seemed dangerously preoccupied with aerobatic maneuvers - - swooping, circling, and diving amongst the spires and turrets of the city as they conducted their rounds, keeping watch over both the city and its field workers. Every now and then, a gallant member of the troop, a fully armed air-patrol soldier mounted atop a sturdy ebony flyer, would zip closely past the immense plate windows that also doubled as sound dampeners, allowing just the faintest of buzzing sounds to penetrate and echo softly throughout the great chamber.

As they stood transfixed by this breathtaking display of aerial skill, they began to realize that the skies surrounding the city were becoming increasingly thick with mounted soldiers. Reinforcements in brightly glistening scale body-armor were pouring forth from somewhere below the throne-room. One after another, in rapid succession, valiant troops soared into view astride the huge black war-harnessed ants whose long transparent wings beat so quickly that they appeared to be only a rippling blur at the insect's sides. The strangers watched in curious fascination as the gathering horde sailed upwards and assembled into squad formations high above the city. Winged cavalry continued to stream forth from beneath them in a seemingly endless torrent and still the reason for the sudden spectacle was as yet unknown. Jeep suddenly barked sharply, as though sensing something was about to happen, and his unexpected outburst startled the Captain who now stared at him wide-eyed, apparently unaware that the canine was capable of such a noise. The Captain recovered quickly however and diverted everyone's attention back to the events that were unfolding in the skies around Konton by pointing off into the distance with a rigid finger. The fascinated group slowly approached the huge windows for a better view of the aerial ballet that was transpiring without.

Maxine was the first to spot the object of the Captain's focus; the one large "dot" in the distance that seemed to separate from all the others. It was of formidable size, even as far away as it was, and all the other insect "dots" gave it a wide berth, sometimes dodging madly beneath the safety of the trees just to escape its attention. It was apparent that somehow, the majority of insects seemed to be aware of the patrolled airspace surrounding the fortified city and purposely avoided flying too near its borders. Perhaps, over the years, the ever vigilant city-patrol had somehow "taught" the majority of insect behemoths to respect the boundaries of Konton. This one isolated brute however, showed no evident respect for guarded boundaries at all and simply continued the sidling path that would soon bring it into direct confrontation with the sentinels of the city - - ever watchful guardians who had been obviously called to arms in preparation for the beast's incursion. It was getting nearer now, close enough to make out some details of its shape and color. Black and yellow stripes. Dexter caught on first. "It's a wasp!" he softly exclaimed in dread.

"Kexl-huat," spoke the Captain as though instructing him.

Their attention was again drawn to the black storm of ants and warriors that now swirled in a tight circular formation high above them in such numbers as to look almost like a great tornado funnel. Yet, undeterred, the huge predatory gold and black wasp continued to weave its way unfalteringly towards the bristling collection of gleaming and grotesque spires and towers. When the watchful commanders of the legions overhead decided that the intruder's approach was a direct threat to the city, an imperceptible signal was given to break ranks and the winged cavalry began their attack! They started streaming outwards from the top of the swirl to intercept the enemy. The flight of menacing armored warriors split into three large squadrons, attempting to outflank the invading monster, and two groups looped off to the right and left while the third continued in a full frontal charge in a classic battle maneuver. The wasp however, was not to be so cooperative as to wait to be attacked from three sides at once! In a bold response to the stratagem, it suddenly altered its leisurely ambling flight into a direct and rapid strike at the heart of the onrushing center squad! Both flanking columns immediately turned tightly inwards to follow in its wake, but they lagged too far behind to stave off its formidable frontal assault.

If the ants could be compared in size, in surface-world terms, to large oxen, then this enormous predator wasp could easily be compared to a tractor-trailer... and about as unstoppable! Just before a collision with the charging army was inevitable, the behemoth dipped below, as if to fly beneath them. But, just as quickly, it changed direction again to a steep angle of ascent so as to bowl right up through their ranks from underneath! Its terrible stinger was rapidly brought up under and forward in a lethal thrust made possible by the folding of its striped abdomen under its thorax. The defending troopers however, were *not* taken by surprise! At the last possible second, the center squad darted and dispersed to either side and out of the path of the deadly poisonous weapon. In fact, the undaunted troops took advantage of the extreme close range to launch heavy spears at the marauder's exposed neck and underbelly, made more vulnerable by the bending of its body to deploy its stinger.

The Captain grinned and let loose a slight chuckle, beaming with pride at the expertly performed maneuver. In actuality, the entire attack strategy had been one of ambush all along, with the center squad being used as bait! Now the two flanking squads bore down upon the beast from behind to launch missiles of their own as they flew past. Arrows were mostly useless against the thick armor plating of the giant wasp. This method of lure and ambush, with stout spears at close quarters, had long ago been devised to deal with the monsters - - fortunately, wasps were blindly aggressive and somewhat predictable in their assault habits.

Several, but not all, of the spears stuck and held fast as the enraged black and yellow giant roared through the midst of the cavalry like an express train, attempting to escape the onslaught. The squadrons regrouped and chased after it so quickly however, that it was as if they had been sucked in by the vacuum of the creature's passing! They pursued the invader relentlessly as it circled the fields of Konton looking for easier prey that it could pounce on and quickly abduct. But each time it swooped down in an attempted raid on the farmers or their livestock, the courageous defenders intensified their attack to worry the beast and drive it from its intended victims. Twice more, the cunning troops executed their "bait and ambush" maneuver by sending a decoy squad to take up position in the path of the madly careening wasp. Like a bull in a bullfight, it couldn't seem to ignore the "easy" prey taunting it with such effrontery and each time it paid for its aggression with a neck full of bristling spears. The wasp looked exasperated by its inability to defend itself and began to shows signs of tiring.

The battle so far, had taken place fairly far out over the surrounding fields, but the commanding view from the throne-room, and the size of the combatants involved, made the action seem like "front row center" and the castaways watched in enthralled fascination, feeling quite safe from the dangers of the struggle.   Suddenly however, for whatever reasons, the creature turned and began flying directly for the towering throne room of the city... and it no longer seemed interested in the decoy squads... it was purposely avoiding them in fact! Nervousness crept over the foreign spectators as the approaching wasp loomed ever larger, bringing the battle-action closer than they had been prepared for! It had seemed so "remote", acted out in the distance, silenced by the thickness of the great windows... like watching a movie screen. Now, the huge windows made them feel conspicuous - - trapped and vulnerable... like a meal under glass!

They stood transfixed and watched in horror as the angry insect predator continued unwaveringly in its flight towards the glass-walled crown of Konton. Its speed was incredible and it threatened to crash directly through the thick transparent window-plating before anyone could even think to run for the safety of the tunnels! The castaways gasped and fell back in terrified surprise, Dexter and Maxine actually sprawled on the mirrored floor, covering their heads, as the giant beast with its glossy orange eyes and slavering jaws zoomed to within inches of the great windows and stopped short, hovering menacingly before them. Its long powerful wings beat the air with such force that a loud deep rumbling filled the room and set the huge panes of glass to shivering! Even the Captain was momentarily caught off guard by the sight of the huge bristly head and iridescent compound eyes whose many facets reflected a thousand pinpoints of light. Its crushing jaws dripped frothy saliva and worked the air fruitlessly in search of a victim while its club-shaped antennae probed the glass with audible thumping sounds. Apparently, the poor creature had caught sight of itself in the mirroring effect of the great windows, and despite the harassing attacks of the Konton guard had flown post-haste to investigate its perceived rival! Cruel spears protruded from behind its shiny black armored head, made glossy by the excretions of its free-flowing wounds. And its yellow abdomen pulsed rapidly… a clue to the extent of its pain and exhaustion. Then, just as suddenly as it had arrived, the huge animal wheeled in midair and dropped from sight!

The castaways leaped to their feet and ran closer to the glass, searching for the terrible behemoth in all directions for several tense moments, unsure of where it had disappeared. The loud vibration of its wings droned softer, louder, soft again, as though it was hovering somewhere nearby. Then, squads of winged flyers suddenly appeared, diving from above and the wasp was instantly in full view again as it rose up from beneath the throne-room to meet the charge of the ant warriors!

Its doom was certain. There were just too many soldiers for the wasp to defeat and it was plainly too tired to run. Two at a time, the mounted warriors sped past the beast from above, launching barbed spears at its neck and thorax, as they continually evaded the powerful mandibles and poisonous sting that sought to deal death among them. The wasp was hovering very erratically now and its end came quickly, without dramatic death-throes. The giant wasp, weakened by blood loss, just ceased to beat it wings and gravity took control instantly. It plummeted with unexpected rapidity, a victim of its own enormous bulk, and bounced and rolled along the steeply sloped sides of the great earthen-work mound until finally coming to rest with an explosive thud at the base of the city.

The excitement was over... the newcomers watched with spellbound admiration as the ferocious warriors of this amazingly disciplined cavalry gathered once more in the skies before them. For Buffalo and the kids, it was as though they had entirely forgotten all that they had been through, along with the current nature of their predicament, so enthralled were they by the spectacle of the proud triumphant warriors and the events they had just witnessed. The winged flyers circled hypnotically around the elevated throne-room and rose out of view of its magnificent panoramic windows to assemble in the air high over the vaulted milky dome that was its roof. Their vague shapes made wonderful swirling patterns on the opaque ivory glass of the rotunda ceiling and the group stared at the ballet of silhouettes in fascination. Muffled voices could be heard. A throng of voices arose as if in the distance. The sounds of a joyous chant began to echo throughout the halls and quite unexpectedly, even the Captain himself began to softly intone the words, joining in the victory song of the guard, for that is what it was. The chorus was brief and the squadrons soon dispersed to once again return to their previous stations... no doubt to also swap stories of courage and valor and to care for their valiant steeds.

It was at this point, that the Captain visibly stiffened and tightened his command over the foreigners. He physically began to herd them in the direction of the raised serpent throne. He was now stern and serious again as he pushed and pulled them into a neat row off to the side the base of the tiered platform, about twenty feet from its lowest alabaster step. His actions and demeanor as he muttered barely comprehensible instructions and commands emphasized his seriousness and they understood that polite compliance was in order. They didn't get a chance to dwell on the curt change in his behavior however, for their attention was soon attracted to their left… to a thin sliver of light that suddenly appeared in the darkened wall across the room. The bright thin line ran from floor to ceiling of the domed palace chamber and threw a radiant line across the polished black floor that slowly widened into a "V" shape. The light was being cast from behind great doors that were now soundlessly swinging open out of the tremendous wall behind the dais. A wall that just moments before had appeared to be completely seamless. As the aperture silently widened, the castaways could do nothing but stand awkwardly in the barren room and patiently stare into the increasingly blinding light, nervously suspicious of what manifestation might next befall them.   The tension mounted to near unbearable levels and if the sheer wonder of it all hadn't been so completely riveting, their first impulse might've been to make a dash for the exit!

Chapter 13
"Audience with a Queen"

Buffalo, with Jeep sitting rather well behaved by his side, stood closest to the slowly opening fissure, his neck craned to the left to witness this new spectacle. Each of the kids, Simon, Max, and Dexter, stood and waited in nervous anticipation in a rigid line to his right, similarly held spellbound by the agonizingly slow yawning of the previously concealed doors. The Captain maintained a posture of attention next to Dexter and cautioned them all to silence… a Kontonquan word they fully understood for they'd had it impressed upon them many times by Anya during their adventures in the jungle. The doors were quite thick and heavy and seemed to be moving of their own accord; there were no human "doormen" to be seen. Apparently, they were operated mechanically somehow from some remote location… with an ingenious design and power, for the massive doors swung as lightly and silently as though made of paper.

Their first glimpse through the ever-widening crack of the center-opening doors revealed a brilliant white staircase that wound upwards and out of sight into chambers that were above and off to the side of the throne-room itself. The stairwell was very brightly lit and the whiteness of the steps and walls within were so dazzling that it caused the anxiously awaiting group to have to squint against the brilliance. As the doors finally pivoted to their fullest extension, it could be seen that the staircase, about eight-feet wide, was flanked on either side by a short and narrow hallway. At the very back of each of these two hallways, stood a tall darkened archway that led further into darkened tunnels beyond.

No sooner had the doors halted their swing, than began a faint and even-measured thumping. As the muffled thumping grew somewhat louder, little flecks of light were noticed to be rhythmically bobbing up and down within the darkened confines of the two flanking passageways! The rapid thumping grew steadily louder and seemed to be drawing nearer. Buffalo and the kids had no idea what to expect next, and so they were completely taken by surprise when nightmarish figures suddenly and simultaneously burst forth into the brilliance of the stairwell... issuing in single file from both blackened archways to either side of the main stairs! The initial shock of seeing these horrific figures bounding into the dazzling light so startled the newcomers, that they momentarily recoiled - - until they realized that they were being advanced upon, not by monsters, but by humans! Fearsome warriors in full ceremonial regalia!

Demonic-looking Snake-men in darkly glistening scale-armor that mimicked their reptilian totem jogged forth into the throne-room, pouring in unison from both archways alongside the stairs. The bobbing flecks of light they'd seen had come from the pair of gleaming gems that occupied the eye-sockets of the silver Serpent helms that were fitted to the soldier's heads. The shining helmets were spotlessly polished as was the highly reflective blue-black metallic finish of the fine full-body armor in which they were all clad. The workmanship on the armor was remarkable, for the suits were almost skintight and custom fitted to each warrior head-to-toe. The overlapping scales were ingeniously crafted - - small and finely plated to give maximum protection while allowing a fully flexible range of movement. The thumping sound issued from the soft stamping of the leather-shod feet of the Serpent Knights as they jogged in ritual fashion through the tunnels and into the throne-room with perfect unified precision.

The hearts of the castaways had been set to thumping also... by the sudden jolt of seeing these fierce apparitions emerge out of the emptiness of those pitch-black tunnels. But, they quickly recovered their composure and watched in fascination as almost a hundred Royal Serpent Guards padded in to form a "V"-shaped wedge that emanated from the base of the throne. Once in formation, they stood at absolute attention, unflinching and almost totally silent. No small task considering the creaky metallic nature of their armor.

Once again, the attention of the foreigners was returned to the stairwell. They noticed movement upon the stairs and the spectral bobbing of shadows against the wall, cast by figures descending from above. Several petite pairs of naked brown feet with painted toes appeared on the topmost steps and continued the spiraling descent. Golden ankle bracelets that were softly chiming, shapely brown limbs, wispy flowing gowns in soft pastel colors... more and more details of the figures upon the stairs were revealed with each downward step taken... and still more followed behind! As they came fully into view, the foreigners were held spellbound by the mystical scene that unfolded itself before them. They were completely and instantly enthralled by this majestic pageant, tantalizingly revealed to them as a vanguard of raven-haired and bronze-skinned women so gracefully and ceremoniously descended the highly polished stairs. Each was exotically lovelier than the next!

Looking for all the world like ancient Egyptian queens, as if copied from painted hieroglyphs, they slowly advanced, rank after rank, with poise and regal posture, each carrying a small lit brazier that burned with a different colored flame. They were adorned with many types of precious jewels and metals fashioned into belts, bracelets, earrings, necklaces, and elaborate headdresses. Also like ancient Egyptians, they wore make-up of wonderfully vivid colors; finely applied and detailed, with particular attention paid to the eyes, some of which were painted in very elaborate and imaginative designs. Their glistening ebony hair was thickly braided and pinned into cascades of tresses at the back of the head. Many of the girls incorporated elaborate headbands or the aforementioned headdresses, wrought in both silver and gold and often inlaid with colorful stones. Fragrant perfumes filled the air as they entered the throne-room.

Though the features of the girls were of unparalleled beauty, the expressions on their faces were serious, solemn, and unsmiling. They kept their eyes averted and downcast and pretended not to notice the strangers standing in the throne-room. Promenading with quiet dignity and soundlessly measured step, they strode through the great doors and split into two groups as they approached the rear of the serpentine throne. They wound around the sides of the multi-tiered dais, with only the slightest hint of the rustle of sheer silky fabrics, to arrange themselves evenly along its alabaster steps from bottom to top. When each level had been filled, they all knelt gracefully, gently placing their smoking braziers before them. With a sudden and audible fizzle, the multi-colored wisps flared brightly all at once and went out, in the process sending a large swirling cloud toward the ceiling and leaving behind a delightful perfumed scent in the air.

The kids were captivated by the display and several errant "ooh's" and "ah's" escaped their lips. It was quite an effective performance and Buffalo had a suspicion that this spectacle was deliberately being staged primarily for their benefit, a little razzle-dazzle to impress the outer-world strangers. Then he heard a familiar sound. A soft tinkling chime, like tiny bells, that he had unwittingly come to recognize and cherish. How he could distinguish that one melodious sound from all the other soft metallic clinking and rustling of jewelry, arms, and armor in the room he did not know, but he recognized the sweet and delicate chiming of Anya's ankle bracelet. And, there she was… descending the stairs where the parade of maidens had been!

She was no longer dressed as the "barbarian warrioress" though she wore much of the same jewelry, keeping her adornments few and simple. (But again, Buffalo noted, those exquisite features needed no "extras" to enhance her natural beauty and radiance!) Instead of the rugged brown leather tunic they were accustomed to seeing her in, she now wore a white sheer gown of delicately flowing wraps, pinned and belted in just the right places to veil, but not conceal the lovely athletic figure underneath. Her long dusky ebony hair, carefully washed and combed, hung loose and flowing about her shoulders, held in check by an exquisitely crafted silver and gem-encrusted headband that encircled her brow. She alone of all the previous maidens flashed a broad white smile. Her large dark eyes sparkled teasingly from her fresh-scrubbed face and professed a mischievous glint that radiated her coltish spirit throughout the room. The chest of every man within the throne-room seemed to swell with renewed pride as she entered... and the room itself seemed to somehow brighten.

So fixed had Buffalo been upon Anya's presence, that he only now noticed the two slender figures in tow at Anya's side! Accompanying Anya, each linking a hand to hers, were two girls somewhat younger than she and almost equal to her in beauty, for their fine girlish features were strikingly similar to hers in every detail, only less mature. The girls appeared to be twins and were still in their young teens... probably about Max's age. Buffalo figured them to possibly be Anya's sisters for he knew she was far too young herself to have children of that age. She was practically still a child herself... although admittedly, and for the first time, he found himself rethinking the image of the proud and stubborn jungle-girl; replacing it with a new appreciation for this dazzling woman with the noble carriage and feminine mystique.

Despite Anya's change of clothing and appearance, the kids were not in the least bit fooled. They recognized her immediately and, in their delight in seeing her once again, forgot the Captain's instructions and started forward to greet her, speaking her name aloud. Anya stopped them in their tracks with a firm and serious glance followed by a quick and decisive shake of the head. Embarrassed by their unintended breach of protocol, the kids shuffled back into their assigned positions and Anya, favoring them with a nod and a smile, continued to proceed across the room and up the steps of the rostrum to the highest level, where she sat with her two sisters at the very base of the serpent throne.

The two young girls were extremely pretty, but quiet and shy looking. One of them cautiously leaned close to Anya and whispered something while glancing furtively at the strangers. Anya smiled even more broadly and seemed to blush somewhat before nodding almost imperceptibly in reply to her sister's question. She quickly regained her regal posture however and sat with great poise impassively overlooking the assembled military guard in the throne-room. Buffalo and the kids beheld her with pride and admiration, but longed for the kind of close companionship they'd enjoyed over the past few weeks while in her company.

Their reflection was soon interrupted however, by a soft raspy sound that was beginning to well up within the room. They looked towards the ranks of Serpent Knights and saw that each of them was shaking a painted bulbous object decorated with colored streamers. The rattle, possibly made of wood or some similar material, was very much like a maraca and the sound it made was obviously intended to mimic the warning alarm of a rattlesnake. The raspy din continued to swell in volume to a very loud level… and then abruptly stopped.

A loud fizzle from above caused them to turn their attention immediately back to the tiered dais where Anya sat… and behind her they were startled to see a figure suddenly seated upon the serpentine throne amongst dissipating tendrils of colored smoke! The figure was that of an older woman clad in an alluring combination of close-fitting shiny body-armor and flowing white silken wraps that somehow floated gently about her in little curling undulations, though no breeze could be felt within the chamber. The mail she wore was finely tooled and almost paper-thin, clinging tightly to her body beneath the veiling swirl of wraps. The glistening silver mail delineated her strong and still attractive figure, accentuating her narrow waist and broad shoulders, it was topped with a silvery mail hood that completely covered her head, neck, and hair. The sculpted hood closely framed her face and formed a sharply pointed widow's peak on her forehead. Circling the top of her head was a golden snake, fashioned as a crown, with its raised head and gleaming red ruby eyes poised as if to strike out... its gaping mouth was inset with wickedly curved ivory fangs.

None of the wayward travelers had seen her enter the room, yet she sat there in quiet repose as though she'd always been present. The visual eeriness of the smoke-enshrouded figure, with her calmly wielded regal dominance, was enough to send a quick chill through the castaways as they waited for her to speak or acknowledge them. But instead, the barbarian Serpent-Queen just sat stolidly, radiating her power and royalty, a magnificently impressive figure, transfixing her subjects with beautiful, but serious and calculating, coal-black eyes. "Smoke and mirrors..." thought Buffalo privately.

Although considerably older than Anya, the Queen's beauty and vitality had not faded in the least. However, years of difficult ruling and the struggle to maintain power, (as they were later to find out), had cast a certain hardness over her features, etching lines of wisdom and worry into her pale golden skin. Yet she maintained the strong confident look of a monarch in absolute control and the merest glance in one's general direction was enough to shake you to your foundations and command your immediate and unswerving attention. She was a determined woman of great power and influence. Someone that you definitely would not want to make an enemy of.

Despite her years, it was also quite evident from the resemblance that she was undoubtedly Anya's mother. Unfortunately, her serious demeanor seemed to allow no room for the kind of delightful lightness of spirit that surrounded Anya like an aura of joy. Curtly, she nodded to the Captain that had escorted Buffalo and the kids through the avenues of the city and he, in turn, immediately motioned for them to move forward in a line to the front of the raised dais, at the point of the "V" formed by the Knights. The Queen fixed her emotionless dark eyes upon them for several uncomfortable minutes and then, without averting her eyes, she leaned her head slowly towards Anya and summoned her in an almost whispered sultry lilting tone, "Kwa-I-Anya?"

Anya arose with a dramatic air and, facing the Queen, delivered an eloquent bow with her hands pressed together before her. She then moved to her mother's side and turned to address the assembled throng while gesturing towards Buffalo (and Jeep), Simon, Maxine, and Dexter.

"Mother of Kontonqua," she announced in a voice loud enough for all to hear, "I present to you... the strangers from the fountain of life..." There was a sudden general commotion in the ranks of the Knights, but one glance from the Queen brought the room to dead silence once again. Anya continued almost without interruption, "...the rescuers of the Queen's daughter from the jaws of the Clekweg...

our allies in the struggles against the Ikusk… lost wizards from a far-off land… fierce warriors… and the protectors of Konton's Royal Princess!"

"Wow! Are we all that?" whispered Dex.

"Shhh!" Max admonished.

The growing tension of the ensuing silence was almost unbearable as the Serpent-Queen just sat quietly, pondering Anya's declaration while she assessed the strangers before her. At last she spoke aloud, and in a firm commanding tone she coolly voiced her thoughts, seemingly directed more to Buffalo than any other. "If it were not for the oddity of your appearance… your obvious lack of familiarity with all things Kontonquan… and the gallantry you have exhibited in the protection of my daughter… I would have you immediately sent to the Temple of X'Poca. There to be judged by the High-Priests who would alone decide whether to release you, enslave you, or perhaps offer you as sacrifice to X'Poca himself." The kids went noticeably pale at this suggestion while the Queen continued, "As matters stand however, I will give you a chance to explain yourselves. I have taken into consideration my daughter's entreaties as well as the writings at Tuak-ah'nahi. The ancient legends have taught us… prepared us… to expect visitors for a long, long time. That has been foretold. We just didn't expect… the likes of *you*."

Not quite all of this was immediately understood by the newcomers, with their very basic smattering of the Kontonquan language, but Anya acted as a sort of interpreter and filled in the gaps with the little bit of English that she had managed to pick up. The Queen's mention of sacrifice particularly did not sit well with Buffalo… it rather riled him up. After all they had endured to come to this place, it did little to bolster his sense of security or make him feel "at home". Buffalo's pride obliged him to respond, and in a total breach of etiquette he spoke aloud, "Do you always welcome strangers with death threats? We came here seeking help…"

There was a sharp, "Hssst!" from the Captain of the Guards, who shot Buffalo a malevolent look and began to take steps towards him. The ranks of soldiers behind began to grumble menacingly. The kid's eyes went wide with the imminent threat...

"Stop!" interjected the Queen, "I will allow it. They seem not to know of our ways." Anya turned pale and looked as though she were about to faint. The Queen turned her attention back to Buffalo and addressed him directly, fixing him with her piercing dark eyes.

"There are no… **strangers**… in Kontonqua," she replied slowly and with chilling emphasis on the word, "strangers". The impact of her words sent shivers down the spines of the wayward out-worlders. It could very well be as they'd feared… the cavern was sealed off from the rest of mankind, a lost world, possibly with no way out at all! Their sudden pallor was not lost on the Queen who continued stoically, "One is either of Konton, Ikuskqua, or the Temple of X'Poca, and that is *all*. But this you will come to know in time. My daughter, Kwa-I-Anya, has informed me of all that has passed since her abduction and rescue. What I wish to learn concerns the supposed land of your origin… and how you found your way to Kontonqua. Speak."

Buffalo regained his composure and mumbled a few words by way of an apology... and then did his best to give an abbreviated version of the troubles and obstacles that the castaways had encountered and overcome in order to find their way to the cavern. The story of their travels drew many skeptical glances from the surrounding phalanx of warriors, many of which could no longer remain impassive upon hearing such an absurd yarn, though they never physically broke attention. Instead, they showed their disdain and disbelief with their poorly concealed smiles, rolling eyes, and the occasional groan or loosed chuckle.

The Queen, on the other hand, seemed genuinely interested in the tale. She at first had difficulty with the concept of an airplane, a *machine* that could fly... but Buffalo drew parallels to the giant wasp that had been defeated earlier and she nodded in acquiescence, still obviously unconvinced. She grew visibly curious at the mention of snow and ice as though recalling a memory, (or rather the *description* of it... as it had to be an unknown item here in the depths of this sweltering jungle), but seemed genuinely saddened and introspective when told of their entrapment in the ice-cave and their subsequent wild ride in the rapids of the underground tunnel. He had wanted to leave the next part out, certain it was "*too unbelievable*", but Dexter Kelly broke in anyway and related the encounter and narrow escape from the Plesiosaur in the black pool. Oddly, that part of the story actually seemed to be received with some acceptance from the cynical guardsmen. When Buffalo concluded his tale with their watery expulsion into the cavern and related their subsequent discovery and rescue of Anya, the Queen shut her eyes and nodded with gentle understanding.

Momentarily, she drew a long breath and spoke. "Your story is not unlike that of our ancestors. It is because of these similarities, that I tend to believe that you speak with truth... though much of what you say defies common sense and assails the basic religious beliefs of our people. However, I am willing to offer you my protection and the city as safe haven... provided you strive to learn our language, ways, and customs. Teachers will be provided, as will food and lodging... for a time. No one lives within the city without contributing to its survival. Eventually, you must become active *contributing* citizens. Laziness is not tolerated... and criminal acts lead to enslavement. If, at any time, you are called upon for services to be rendered, you will respond in kind or face ejection from the city.

Should you instead *choose* to leave us, I will provide safe passage to the borders of our domain... but, be warned: ours is a land of great dangers, its denizens thirst for blood, and there are others out there not nearly as beneficent as we... in fact, they rather thrive upon their brutality. The facts of your journey alone, as you have just related them in this room, would result in instant death at the hands of the Ikusks... or the Priests of the Temple of X'Poca. Certainly from *X'Poca*... God himself!"

Chapter 14
"Lessons to be Learned"

Those last stunning words were not delivered philosophically, but with cold conviction, and seemed to have a sobering effect on everyone in the room. As the kids stood slack-jawed and wide-eyed, waiting for some further explanation of the Queen's remark, the audience came to an abrupt end. The Queen's entourage of exotic beauties, who had sat quietly and almost without movement throughout the entire interview, suddenly arose and began flitting about. Some ascended the dais to attend the Queen while others went off to perform various tasks. The ranks of serpent guards stayed in formation but relaxed their stance and some even spoke quietly amongst themselves. Soft music of pipe, lute, and drum began to pervade the huge chamber from some hidden source. A pair of obviously wealthy high-ranking citizens strolled from the rear of the room and up to the base of the stairs, pausing momentarily to kneel reverently with heads bowed. At a soft command from the Queen, they climbed the stairs and began conferring with her in low tones accompanied by much gesticulating.

After all the initial hoopla and fanfare, the newcomers suddenly felt… *ignored*. It was just too great a let down after all they'd been through to get here! Indignation and anger welled up within Buffalo. He was usually a force to be reckoned with himself and was unaccustomed to such dismissals. So, he was about to step forward to address the Queen and give the lady a piece of his mind when he suddenly saw the frantic face of Anya perk up above the heads of her attending maids. She'd caught Buffalo's demeanor and intent and she now shook her head wildly, her wide

207

fear-filled eyes silently pleading with him to hold his ground. After their weeks together in the jungle, Buffalo had a keen respect for Anya's strength and ferocity… so it was only her expression of total panic that now stopped him and gave him pause. Anya was not a girl to be so easily flustered.

Buffalo's attitude had not gone unnoticed by the Captain either and he hurriedly stepped up behind, clapping a hand on Buffalo's shoulder to stop him. Buffalo's interruption would be considered an affront to the Queen and would not be tolerated, possibly leading to unfortunate and irreversible circumstances. Buffalo however, was unaware of his violation of protocol and he was feeling rankled and edgy. When he felt a firm grip clamp down on his shoulder, it set off his inner "aggressor alarm" (acquired from his years of service with the Army Air Corps... and numerous bar fights). Already angered by the Queen's perceived discourtesy and distracted by Anya's imploring signals, he forgot the situation at hand and acted on impulse. Instinctively, he spun to face his assailant and hunkered down as he did so... with his right hand balled up into a fist and his left hand up and open for defense. However, he straightened up immediately, somewhat sheepishly, when he saw that it was only the Captain of the Guards standing placidly before him. Nonetheless, Buffalo's reflexive action still caused quite a commotion in the nearby ranks of soldiers! Spears were instantly leveled at his chest in a lightning quick response to defend and protect their Captain.

Though the surrounding soldiers were menacingly serious, there was a thin smile of one-upmanship on each of their faces. For although at 6'3", Buffalo towered a good seven inches above the tallest of these mound-dwelling warriors - - and the gargantuan muscles that rippled beneath his strange garments gave rise to speculation that he might be one of the strongest men in all Kontonqua - - there was little concern that he could survive a battle with the best of the Queen's Guard, armed only with a puny knife. They had the advantage... and they knew it.

The music stopped and the throne room fell deathly quiet. The air was thick with tension as all eyes were once again trained upon the foreigners. Jeep leapt to Buffalo's side, faced the Captain, and bristled with a threatening growl until Buffalo called him off with a murmured command. The Queen leaned forward upon her throne and waved one of the bureaucrats aside to better witness the events transpiring below. There was a long uncomfortable pause as the Captain stood stoically glaring into Buffalo's eyes and then, just as the tension peaked, he smiled a broad grin and nodded approval while waving the flat of his hand towards his troops with an accompanying command. He looked upon Buffalo with a new respect and felt he could perhaps treat him with some professional courtesy, for he recognized and appreciated the warrior prowess he'd seen displayed. The troops fell back into their ranks and the music picked up again where it had left off. The chamber's occupants resumed their hubbub and went about their business now with something new to discuss. Buffalo let out a long slow breath and glanced back at Anya, only to see her roll her eyes to the ceiling and puff out her cheeks in a quick exhalation of relief.

The Captain extended a hand in friendship and spoke kindly in a low and powerful tone, "You have nothing to fear here, you are as one with us now. The Queen has just granted you full citizenship with privileges. You are, temporarily at least, under her protection and in Konton there are none who would dare question or defy her. You need only perform your duties as required and all will be well. You also seem to have the favor of the Kwa-Ia, a powerful ally... you are most fortunate. Follow me and I'll bring you to your lodgings and perhaps answer a few questions that you may have."

Thanks to Anya's teachings, between them they understood much of the Captain's speech, at least enough to place their trust in him, and the group surrendered their indignation to fall in behind the Captain as he turned to leave. Simon, Max, and Dexter looked quizzically at each other and whispered simultaneously, "What duties?"

The Captain of the Guard led them across the room and toward a doorway other than the one they'd entered through. He spoke a curt command to the two rigid Serpent Guards that stood watch on either side of it and they instantly moved to open the large wooden doors. The passageway revealed on the other side differed from what they'd expected to see. This time there were no rows of ceremonial guards or harnessed ants to ride, no grand hall or overt display of opulence. This simple passage was just a set of wide stone steps with an ornate balustrade that led down a brightly lit circular stairwell decorated with mosaics; not mosaics in the form of artworks or pictorials however, just colorful geometric designs. As they walked, the stone steps beneath their feet echoed their footfalls loudly and, curiously, even their whispers would bounce off the walls and ceilings and return almost as a shout.

The Captain spoke up as they were descending the long gently-curving staircase. His manner was more relaxed now and he spoke somewhat like a tour guide as he went. "This place is known as the "Hall of Unveiling", so named after the

210

traitor Va-Aktom whispered his plans to an accomplice at the *base* of these stairs and was overheard by one of the Queen's attendants at the *top* of the stairs. Needless to say, the Queen ordered him expelled from the city... by means of the throne room balcony. That was in the year 2862."

"2862?" interrupted Dex, "What year is it now?"

"Why, 3144 of course! Our people have been here much longer actually, but that is when we started counting the passing of the years by noting the phases of development in the ant larvae."

Max spoke up and asked, "Then it wasn't the same Queen we just... met...?" and let her question trail off as she suddenly realized the silliness of it. It would be impossible for the beautiful and robust woman they'd just met to be something over 280 years old!

"No... it was her great-great-grandmother," replied the Captain gently, aware of Max's embarrassment at the obvious answer. "We have been a society ruled by Queens for many many generations... since shortly after we arrived here in the underland we call Kontonqua. At least, that is what our historians tell us and... Oh, right here by the way, is the spot where Na'wa-Hanatay the Strong was assassinated, but that is another story."

The group paused to peruse the nondescript "spot" respectfully... and then filed past with as much reverence as they could muster for the fallen Na'wa-Hanatay. They continued to follow the Captain as he went on with his narrative about the history and deeds of past queens... until finally, they reached the base of the long spiraling stairway. They found themselves in a large stonework foyer with two more guards stoically guarding yet another large set of doors at its far end. They crossed the shining spotless floor in silence and the guards opened the doors before them without prompting or ceremony.

What struck them next, as the doors swung wide, was the sudden invasion of unexpected urban noise and cool moist air that assailed them through the open doorway. In direct contrast to the echoing hollowness of the stairwell and the relative silence of the foyer, their ears were suddenly assaulted by the murmuring sounds of many voices and laughter, the general clatter of busy people, and the liquid burbling of flowing torrents of water. They stepped forward, passing yet two more guards on the outside who shut the great doors behind them, and then paused to take in the sights that confronted them.

They were in an extremely large chamber that rose several stories above them and was brightly lit from clear skylights in the ceiling. Here too, were tiers of balconies that ringed the room, but these were all lavishly draped with the most exotically beautiful flowering plants they'd yet encountered. In fact, the entire room was thick with vegetation, ferns and flowers everywhere they looked, and with great fern trees lining the walls all around them. In the center of the great room was a large ornate fountain spewing gracefully arching streams of cool water into a dark bubbling pool noisily agitated by the constant cascade. The large central stone sculpture in the fountain, from which the water gushed, appeared to be a representation of the Queen-Mother surrounded by warrior ants and soldiers. At her feet, at the base of the work, cowered hideous demonic figures; much like fly-faced gargoyles with obviously pained expressions on their faces.

The room was fairly crowded, with well-dressed people and families of the upper classes milling about. There were older folks sitting by the fountain talking, lovers walking arm in arm, mothers with infants, and several children chasing each other in a tag-like game across the great hall. The scene was instantly rejuvenating… like a breath of fresh air. The unconfined feeling of space and light, combined with the coolness of the humidity from all the plants and water, brought smiles to the faces of the wanderers and a sensation of relief and well-being they probably hadn't felt since they left their homes, (in what seemed like *ages* ago). Even Jeep was leaping about like a puppy, running circles around them with his tail-stump wagging and a sparkle in his eye.

Witnessing the serenity of the scene before them also brought some feelings of longing for what they'd left behind. Both Simon and Max had often wondered if they'd ever see their scientist Dad again. He'd been expecting them for Christmas at the Arctic station and by now had probably assumed them to be dead. Even though Buffalo had radioed a proper "Mayday!" it was doubtful that the plane would ever be found, considering the pile of ice that had toppled down on top of it. And, in the event the plane *was* found, they were sure that all evidence of their own whereabouts had been completely erased by the ensuing avalanche. The crash would of course be investigated, and the disappearance of the passengers would most likely be ascribed to the explosion… or perhaps to the severe winter weather of northern Canada.

Simon and Max's mother had died when they were young and their father, possibly out of a grief he could not deal with, had devoted himself to his research, leaving Max and Simon in the care of various aunts, uncles, and eventually a governess throughout most of their childhood. This was not to say that he was cold or uncaring, it was just that he was happiest when he was working, and his work sometimes carried him to remote and harsh environs for months at a time. Places quite unsuitable for the raising of a family. The invitation to join him at the Arctic lab had been a surprise; a rare treat and a sign that their father was perhaps taking a renewed interest in them, now that they were teens. Too late, unfortunately.

All of this was probably hardest for Dexter, or at least it *should* have been. As an only-child, he was constantly clucked over by his adoring and doting parents, and he *should've* missed their attention. However, the same logical encyclopedic mind that, in an unquenchable thirst for knowledge, had begged to accompany Max and Simon on their Arctic trip in the first place, was now too involved in noting and cataloguing all their recent adventures and discoveries to dwell upon what had been left behind. Perhaps Dex had just never curbed his curiosity long enough to ponder the danger of their position or the impossibility of their eventual return to the civilization above. He seemed quite content to just immerse himself in analyzing the wonders of this new and hostile land. Had the hopelessness of their predicament not fully set in for him yet? Or was he just the eternal optimist?

Buffalo on the other hand was of a different attitude altogether and took everything in stride for a different reason. He had always been a loner and a drifter with no familial ties to speak of and no particular attachments to return to. His needs were simple and few. In essence, according to his basic philosophy, "Everybody has to be someplace, and this was just another place to be." As for Jeep, well, he was just happy to be any place that Buffalo was and content to get his occasional skritch behind the ears.

"Follow me..." The deeply intoned voice of the Captain brought them around from their nostalgic reveries, and they placidly strolled in his wake, taking in all the wonderful sights of the great bright hall as they went. Despite their feelings of homesickness, the grandeur of the place filled them with a warm inner peace that seemed to lend them some hope and security. There was a comfort and familiarity here in this urban park-like setting that soothed them... that provided a connection to the world they'd left behind. The Captain led them pretty much directly across the great mall, briefly skirting the massive center fountain which wafted a delightful cooling mist over them as they passed.

Ahead they saw a single soldier standing with a large ant that was decked out in finely tooled trappings and harnessed to a very ornate sledge. As they approached they saw that this sledge was not at all like the rough-hewn farm sledge that had delivered them up to the column of soldiers outside the city. This sledge was intricately carved and obviously built for comfort, with wide roomy seats in double rows that were cushioned and covered in some sort of soft fabric. The sides of the sledge were open and without doors reminding them of a winter sleigh as it might be depicted in an old Currier & Ives print.

The Captain spoke a few brief words to the waiting soldier who then nodded in return and handed over a lead much like a rein but without the attached bridle. The Captain stepped up into the sledge to take his seat on the front bench and beckoned for them to follow suit. Dexter jumped up eagerly and slid in next to the Captain. Jeep followed close on his heels and insisted on sitting directly between them where he quickly settled down and sat alertly facing forward as though it was his job to drive!

As Buffalo moved into the rear seat he took note of Jeep's behavior and considered his own feelings and measure of their escort... the "Captain of the Guard". The man was stocky, but obviously fast and strong... well muscled. His serious careworn face, set with piercing black eyes, belied a gentle and noble spirit. Buffalo guessed that he was not the sort to have been born to his position, but had probably earned it through his warrior prowess and hard work, rising through the ranks by his skills, courage and wisdom. He seemed an honorable man. Jeep was an excellent judge of character and he wouldn't have positioned himself in such close proximity if he didn't feel completely at ease. Buffalo decided at that moment to unconditionally trust the Captain... on Jeep's "recommendation".

Max and Simon trailed in last and sat comfortably next to Buffalo. Big as he was, there was still plenty of room in the wide sledge. No sooner had they settled in than the sledge jerked forward with a lurch and began to slide almost effortlessly along at a smooth and comfortable pace. They left the great hall by means of a large bright tunnel, as wide as a city avenue, and began to pass many wealthy-looking residences similar to the ones they had seen on the way to the throne room. As the Captain was later to explain, the city was, as they had earlier theorized, organized in a sort of caste system of wealth and power. But, what they hadn't realized was that this system involved both humans *and* ants collectively.

The pinnacle of the city was reserved exclusively for the Queen, the royal family, and their attendants. It contained the Throne Room, from where they had just come, the Royal residences, and many private and secret chambers. Just below the Throne Room, and off of the large columned hall through which they had originally arrived, were the administration centers which effectively ran the city's daily affairs and carried out the Queen's will. Farther down the mound, (the area through which they were now traveling), were the homes of the wealthy merchant-class who conducted their business on the lower levels but had access to the Queen's ear and so in many ways were directly responsible for the governing of the city. Immediately below the levels of the merchants were the many levels of the middle-class, that immense group of workers, soldiers, artisans, teachers, administrators, etc. which really comprised the backbone of the city. The lower levels of the mound, in addition to being the location of all the main market places and manufacturing sectors, also housed the lower-class laborers of the city. In crowded and dingy, but never squalid, tiny apartments dwelt the masses that toiled in the fields and performed the menial tasks of the city. Unfairly, they were the ones that had the least, but risked the most... for in conducting their labors they were often exposed to more danger than anyone else in the city. In the fields and orchards for example, it was entirely possible that an unsuspecting worker could get picked off by one of the many predatory insects, even under the watchful eye of the elite winged guard that patrolled the skies above.

Since the entire city was a cooperative environment with the ants, *their* rules were also to be obeyed and slackers were not tolerated, everyone had a duty. Anyone found to be negligent, criminal, or just lazy, could be enslaved to "work-off" their crime - - or be ejected from the colony... and that meant almost certain death. The ants themselves, were usually only found in the upper reaches of the city if they were performing some form of task for their human associates, such as pulling a sledge, doing repair work, or as mounts in the service of the aerial troops. They were much more common on the lower floors of the city where they came and went as they pleased in pursuit of their own business, which included tasks such as the maintenance of the tunnels and lighting and gathering harvest with the human farmers.

However, the ant's true lair lay far *beneath* the city itself. These ants, like termites, were actually subterranean dwellers, inhabiting seemingly endless interwoven tunnels that descended far down into the earth. In these sub-tunnels could be found the nurseries where the eggs of the colony were tended, the food storage chambers, the cultivated fungus "farms", and farther down, the "Throne Room" of the massive egg-laden Queen Ant herself. Beneath all of this was an engineering marvel devised solely by the ants themselves. A complex web of thin-walled membranes that had been constructed in sturdy concentric circles within a huge chamber, the width of the entire circumference of the city. Combined with the clever use of venting throughout the mound, this great "air-conditioning" chamber provided ducting for a form of natural heat exchange that aerated the entire colony and maintained a comfortably controlled climate of fresh air throughout.

Although humans were allowed in the subterranean ant tunnels to conduct business and assist the ants with certain tasks, generally, the farther down you went, the less likely you were to find evidence of human intervention. It was said that only the Queen Mother herself was ever allowed free passage all the way down to the Queen Ant's chambers and was the only human allowed to make personal contact with her. The symbiotic relationship between ants and humans that existed here had developed over thousands of years into an intricate one. What had originally begun as a simple attempt by a primitive tribe to domesticate the ants for draught-animal use had grown through time into a complex and completely cooperative relationship. The arrangement mutually benefited both species and guaranteed the survival of the vulnerable humans in this inhospitable cavern. It had allowed their combined talents to turn both their preyed-upon colonies into a strong, secure, and thriving fortress-city.

After a quick trip downward through the realms of the rich, the wide roadway branched off into several smaller ones, and the Captain veered off to the right to continue along the outermost path. He communicated with the ant that was pulling the sledge by slapping its hard carapace-covered thorax with the leather rein in his hand. The extremely hard and bony exoskeleton of the ant probably felt nothing more than a tapping sensation; nonetheless the ant responded to the signals smartly and without complaint. They began to pass more modest dwellings built into the sides of the tunnels, each one having a sort of portico that one entered through to reach the actual entry of the home itself. These were mostly rather austere in appearance and simply done; nothing like the elaborately sculpted and decorated spacious verandas of the wealthier homes above.

The middle-class levels were much busier and, somewhat embarrassingly, their passage attracted the attention of many curious onlookers as they traveled. The attitude of the citizenry didn't seem to be hostile in any way, but it did make the castaways a little self-conscious of their foreign appearance. They didn't have much farther to go however, for shortly the Captain directed the ant to pull up in front of the doorway of a very typical-looking home for this class level. It was neat and clean, as was all the others, but the front porch differed in that it didn't have the kinds of personal effects or touches that gave evidence of habitation. It appeared to be vacant. Evidently, this was the case, for the Captain suddenly extended a hand and said, "Welcome to your new home!"

With some apprehension, the group clustered into the small porch-like area before the door and made a quick inspection of their assigned abode. Simon found a thin rope hanging by the door and gave it a tentative tug. They heard a faint hollow chime intone from somewhere within and Max loosed a giggle of delight. A doorbell! The Captain again took the initiative as he pushed open the wooden door of the dwelling to reveal the tidy cluster of rooms within that could best be described as an "apartment".

They had barely stepped inside before all three kids and Jeep ran off wildly to explore their new home. In rapid succession, each one would pop their head back into the large central hallway and holler out their findings. "This one's a bedroom, an' it's got a closet!" "Yeah, this one, too, an' here's our stuff!" "This one looks like a kitchen, but there's no place to cook!" "Hey, *WOW!* …this one's got a *window*!" "Yeah…*Wowww…look at that*!" "Ummmm, there's no ummmm… *bathroom.*" Buffalo followed right behind and confirmed all their discoveries.

Indeed, there appeared to be three bedrooms, each with low wooden bunks covered with fuzzy-looking mattresses and blankets, (they were later to find out that the mattresses were made of caterpillar silk and wonderfully comfortable!). Their gear was neatly stowed in one of the bedroom closets and seemed to have been inspected but untouched. There was a sort of kitchen and tiny pantry stocked with "ready-to-eat" type foods and all the proper utensils and dishware they were likely to need in order to consume them. In a corner, there were some large casks of fresh water with ladles. However, as Max had noted, there was no apparent place to cook or even deal with the preparation of hot meals.

Moving on, Buffalo found all the kids gathered in the last room looking out a narrow open window that, for all its small size, still boasted a magnificent view of the surrounding countryside, as well as revealing the still astounding height at which they were situated! This final room appeared to be a kind of sitting room or living room and contained some low wooden chairs and tables. There were some other furnishings scattered throughout the apartment that still bore closer inspection... among them, the many basket-weave chests that the Captain explained were to be used for storage and which also contained many useful day-to-day items that they would need.

The ceilings of the apartment, like everywhere else in the tunnels of Konton, were covered with the strips of light-giving lichens, but here inside, there was to be found only the single "daylight" variety. The Captain explained that the private chambers of Konton usually contained only the single variety of "Lowa-tay", (the light-emitting lichens cultivated from the cavern's walls), that was known as "**A**lowa-tay" or daylight. The nighttime variety was known as "**Na**lowa-tay", and while useful in the tunnels and public places of the city for continual illumination, it would be somewhat of a nuisance in chambers that were meant for rest and sleep. He left the room for a moment and came back with a foot-tall canister made out of shell or carapace that had a handle on the top and a sliding door on the front. Pulling back on the door, he revealed a dark interior that contained a quantity of the nighttime lichen, or

Nalowa-tay, that he said would soon be glowing brightly as the night cycle began. This could be used to see in the dark of the apartment, or even outside if necessary, and was to be kept on the shelf next to the front door so that it could be tended by the small gardening ants that would come and go as they pleased. As with every lit room and abode in the city, there was a small aperture over their entryway that the ants could freely use to gain access, in and out of the apartment, to properly maintain the ceiling lichens. The Captain continued to explain that the Lowa-tay were also the reason that the kitchen space lacked cooking facilities. Cooking fumes or smoke of any kind weakened the plants and would eventually kill them.

For this reason, all cooking for each level was done on special balconies on the outside of the mound where it didn't interfere with the interior horticulture and air supply. Preparation of meals was a professional occupation and performed by skilled individuals for each class. The local citizens contributed to the overall stock of food for each community kitchen either by purchasing from the public markets below or by hunting and harvesting from the surrounding jungle, (a dangerous pastime but terrific sport!). Meals were then prepared twice daily and evenly distributed among all those of a given level. Non-contributors were dealt with harshly, but they really weren't an issue. They were, for the most part, nonexistent... for the better your contributions were, the better your meals were, and that was worth working for.

Now that their kitchen worries were explained, the next question that burned in the minds of the kids was "What about the ***bathroom?!***" For by now, they were all beginning to feel the need for a little personal relief. In the jungle, it had been relatively easy, if a bit discomfiting, to momentarily disappear behind a fern, but since coming to Konton early that morning, none of them had had the advantage of a proper facility! The Captain laughed and said, "You don't think we'd be a thriving city if we'd forgotten that little detail, do you? Come, follow me. There is more yet to see."

The Captain again took the lead as they exited through the front door. Buffalo noted that there was no form of lock upon the door. "Hmm," he thought, "very trusting of the citizenry... a side benefit of communal living; a crime-*free* society? And yet, hadn't 'what's-his-name', Nanook the Strong, been assassinated?" Silently, Buffalo wondered how many disgruntled or rebellious citizens disappeared in the night. The security arrangements seemed to work very much in the favor of the ruling Monarchy and her loyal military.

"Take note of your emblem," said the Captain, breaking in on Buffalo's morbid thoughts, "so you'll be able to recognize your dwelling." The group turned their attention towards the spot indicated by the Captain and noticed for the first time, a small symbol like an Egyptian cartouche, carved above the portico. It was a vertical rectangle with rounded corners and contained the likeness of a serpent encircling a quiver of arrows placed above a cluster of ferns. Looking around, they noticed that all the homes had similar emblems over their porches, but each one differed in its content.

"Cool!" said Dexter, "What's it mean?"

"Roughly translated," replied the Captain, "it's the symbol of a sly and cunning woodsman or hunter. It probably dates back to the original occupant of this dwelling... seldom are the emblems altered or changed once inscribed. New ones are sometimes added, but the older emblems are preserved out of respect. "Come..." He turned around and the gang followed dutifully behind. The Captain led them across the "street" and towards a narrow dim alleyway. They noticed for the first time that between every several homes on the "inside ring" of the avenue there was a similar opening. The passage was barely large enough to allow two adults to walk side-by-side, although the kids had no such difficulty. They walked the length of two back-to-back apartments and emerged onto another street very much like their own, another of the concentric circular avenues that led up and down the mound. After first checking for "traffic", they crossed directly over and into another alley. The alleys were arranged like the spokes of a wheel and allowed quick foot-travel between the outer and inner neighborhoods of the city. Twice more they traversed similar thoroughfares, sometimes eliciting the curious attention of the locals. But the group just smiled and waved as they passed through and the onlookers usually smiled back and went about their business. Word of the "other-landers", and directives about dealing with them, had apparently already spread throughout the colony.

After completing a distance of about four city-blocks, the noise of rushing water could be heard and continued to increase in volume as they traveled the last alleyway. When they reached its end, they emerged into a large brightly-lit plaza whose walls and floors were completely tiled in a white pearlescent material and decorated with wonderfully colorful inlaid borders. There was a thick tubular column of the same material, stretching from floor to ceiling in the very center of the room and from its several decorative spouts, torrents of crystal clear water gushed into a large circular pool. Several people were sitting on the bench-like edges of the pool, draped in robes or towels, but others, young and old alike, were unabashedly bathing naked in the sparkling cascade of water. This, after all, explained the Captain noticing the kids' shocked expressions, was a *public* bath. There were several more that serviced this level... and a great many more designed just like it, more or less, on every level throughout the mound. More opulent above... and more austere below.

The great column in the middle of the room was actually one of five large conduits that vertically connected the basically "cone-shaped" city and supplied water throughout the levels. The upper classes, had the benefit of sharing five convenient bathhouses on each level amongst less people, but the lower classes had to make due with the same five conduits, resulting in larger more crowded baths that were sometimes an irksome distance away for some of the populace unlucky enough not to dwell near one. Toilets were in small private rooms arranged around the outer walls of each public bath and were really nothing more than a seat over a trough that emptied into pipelines that joined a much larger drainage system that ran straight down through all the levels to the sub-caverns, where the waste was collected and recycled for use in the fields as fertilizer.

Maxine's brow was deeply furrowed in thought and the Captain paused his commentary on the baths to ask if she were troubled. She stumbled over her words at first, but then unleashed the torrent of thoughts that concerned her. "Umm... no, I guess... well, it's just that... this isn't at all like home. We have *plumbing* in our house! It's quite a trip to come all the way here if you really have to go, if you know what I mean. What about the middle of the night... or if you're sick... or..."

The Captain chuckled over her anxiety and set her mind to ease, "Don't worry young one... in the corner of your kitchen there are some clay pots for that purpose. Everyone has... "emergencies"... use the pots and bring them here to be emptied and cleaned when it's convenient."

Max looked visibly relieved and a flush spread across her cheeks. "Oh... well that different... " she said sheepishly.

The only other doorways along the walls of the circular room were alleys just like the one they had come through, giving access to the baths to all those who lived along the outer spiraling streets. "Again," spoke the Captain, "take note of the number beside the passageway through which you arrived so you don't leave by a wrong alley and get lost." The "number" the Captain had referred to was an inlaid character upon the wall that really meant nothing to the castaways, for they had precious little knowledge of the Kontonquan written language or its numerical system. However, its shape seemed singular enough when compared to the other numbers around the room, so that they felt confident they wouldn't have any difficulties finding their way "home".

"It's been a very long and interesting day," continued the Captain, "but it is soon to draw to a close and I still have many duties to perform. I will be taking my leave of you now, but I will see you again very soon. I suggest that you avail yourselves of the facilities here and return to your lodging for a much needed rest. I assure you, you will be completely safe. If you do get lost or have any difficulties, do not be afraid to approach any citizen and ask for help. They have been apprised of your status and position. If anything, they may be a bit frightened by your appearance, for strangers have been heretofore unknown in our land, but be patient, they *will* cooperate." And with that said, the Captain bid farewell, nodded curtly, spun on his heel, and left.

The Captain seemed to be a good man, thought Buffalo, but something about the way he said that last "They *will* cooperate" sounded a bit menacing... it left him unsettled and raised questions in his mind. Konton was a highly organized compartmentalized communal hive... but maybe it wasn't such a perfect society. Certainly, it was a tightly controlled monarchy. Was it a tyranny?

Chapter 15
"<u>Assimilation</u>"

      Getting back from the public baths took a bit longer than necessary. Not because they had any trouble finding their way, but because for the first time since arriving in this barbarian fortress-city, they were on their own, and they now had the opportunity to more closely inspect their surroundings. That's not to say that they weren't watched and observed however. The kids were too excited to notice, but Buffalo, being wary by nature, spied the shadows of hidden watchers and perceived the side-long glances of aimless citizens who "pretended" to give them little heed but were careful to keep them always in sight… from a respectful distance, of course.

      As they made their way back and witnessed first-hand the common-folk going about their daily business, it occurred to them that life in this underground bastion was not all that much different from the cities of the surface-world that they were already familiar with. Unquestionably, the insect-dependent relationship, bizarre architecture, and matriarchal/tribal government were uniquely extraordinary, almost to the point of incredulity, but it all worked together… it was alive and thriving. People and insects were living symbiotically and successfully in a tightly woven society with a history and culture that rivaled any civilization of the surface, past or present. Had the castaways landed in ancient Egypt, China, or Mexico, *those* civilizations would not have seemed any less peculiar to them at all. In fact, as each new corner was turned, and revealed more and more of everyday life in Konton, the more comfortable and at home they began to feel. The trappings, the objects and surroundings were different... but people were people the world over.

There were many quaint and pleasant-looking homes decorated with art and articles personal to those who inhabited them. Young children played in the wide avenues while grandparents looked on from the porticos, always busy with some domestic chore or intently manufacturing handmade crafts and goods. The streets were filled with people going about their business and the occasional ant or sledge that passed by was no more unusual than the passing of a horse and buggy in a Vermont village. The people themselves were shy, but friendly. Word of their arrival and position of Royal favor *had* been quickly spread, so instead of treating them with disdain or apprehension, the citizens smiled or nodded courteously, and several even spoke a few brief words.

Oddly, it was Jeep that seemed to elicit the most attention, a fascination almost akin to reverence, and it occurred to Buffalo that dogs could very well be an unknown species in this subterranean world. They'd not seen another like him yet... not so much as a mutt! Unintentionally, they also heard the giggles and gossip that tended to *follow* their passing, for clearly their features, clothing, and manners were absurd and out of place in this world where strangers were an assumed impossibility.

Eventually, they found their way back to their own residence and, once again, every nook and cranny was carefully and quickly inspected by the kids for details that they might've previously overlooked. Buffalo noticed from the window that the Captain hadn't been kidding... the cavern "sky" was beginning to darken, so he decided to assign sleeping quarters. Simon and Dexter wound up sharing a room as did Buffalo and Jeep, (who were quite accustomed to that arrangement and totally content with it). Max had a sizable room all to herself, for after all, she *was* a young lady… and it appeared that they might be here for quite some time. After quickly moving some beds around, the sleeping arrangements were settled to everyone's satisfaction.

The possibility of being stuck in this prehistoric and inhospitable cavern for the rest of their lives was a subject of distinct probability that Buffalo knew he would have to broach soon, for he knew that as delicate a subject as it was, it would have to be dealt with eventually. Buffalo saw Dexter begin to yawn and knew he didn't have much time before he'd lose them all to slumber, so he decided to get it over with. He grabbed the lantern filled with glowing lichens and called them all before him in the large room at the back, the one with the window and chairs, and began to pace while he gathered his thoughts.

He didn't know exactly how to begin. To say what he wanted to say; what *needed* to be said. This was definitely *not* his area of expertise. He stopped and stood awkwardly by the window scratching the back of his head. The kids sensed something weighty was coming, so they waited patiently and watched the big man struggle with his thoughts. After several false starts, Buffalo managed to say, "Look... we've all been caught up in this situation together... it's not what *any* of us ever expected to have to deal with. We've been going great-guns ever since the plane quit on us and it's been all we could do to just survive. In fact, I'm kinda surprised we *have*, considering the odds and the unbelievable... *stuff* we've had to face! Tunnels, rivers, jungles... *Bugs the size of buses!*" Buffalo pursed his lips and shook his head in silence while his mind raced over the events of the past several weeks.

"Don't forget the Plesiosaur!" added Dexter helpfully.

"Yeah....that too," muttered Buffalo, and he turned to look momentarily out the window at the dusky landscape. The jungles past the fields were now just a blackened silhouette against the diminishing light of the cavern ceiling. He could just barely make out the emerging brighter patterns of Nalowa-tay that defined the night sky. "Alright, look," he started again as he turned back to the three anxious faces shining in the light from the lantern. "I'm just a pilot. A pretty good one, though I guess it doesn't seem that way considerin' how I managed to crack up our transport to the pole. But this..." he faltered, searching for the right words, "this... *situation,* just isn't what I signed up for. I was only supposed to fly some kids and cargo off to the Arctic. A quick and easy buck over the holiday..." he trailed off as he noticed the hurt look in Max's eye. He stopped and drew in a long slow breath. Then with a surrendering sigh he went on, "Okay, let's be fair. You guys didn't ask for any of this either. It's just that I... um, I feel responsible... personally responsible."

"You couldn't have helped what happened to the plane!" interrupted Max.

"No. I don't mean that," he went on. "I mean a responsibility for what happens to us *now...* for what's to become of us. We're not through this yet, ya know." The kids were beginning to understand what Buffalo was driving at. They lowered their heads and stared solemnly at the floor. "You see," continued Buffalo, "I've always been a loner. I've never had to deal with taking care of nobody but myself. I've done my best to keep us all safe ever since the crash but, hey... it wasn't just a matter of *your* survival, it was mine as well! I was just doing my duty... as a pilot and as an adult... seeing through the delivery of my "cargo" until we were rescued. Well, this is the first chance we've really had to catch our breath... to stop and consider our options, our situation, and our... um... future."

Buffalo paused to let what he'd said sink in, and then went on, "From what we've learned so far about this underground world we're in, we know that the possibility of a rescue is out of the question. We've traveled too far without a trace for any hope on *that* score. But what's more, I'm also getting a sense that there's little chance of ever finding a way *out* of here... or that any of us will ever see the surface-world again. If there *were* a way out, these people, or even the bugs, would have found it by now. Of course, I'll do my best to keep looking for a way... but I think we may be here together for quite some time.... perhaps the rest of our lives..."

Sensing the negative tone his speech was taking, Buffalo drew a fresh breath and began again, hoping to sound more upbeat. "Anyway, what I wanted to say is that... you guys have been pretty good. Actually..." he nodded approvingly, "...great. Better than I would've expected from... well, *kids*. We've been through some scary and exhausting adventures. You've stuck it out and you've proven your stamina and resourcefulness through it all... you've got guts!. You guys have made me proud and you've held up better than some of the toughs I've known over the years!" This brought smiles to the faces of the three teens who then glanced beamingly at each other.

"Well, we've come this far and this may turn out to be as far as we get. I may have *been* a loner, but things are different now. We're all going to have to face a whole new way of life. It's been forced on us and there just isn't any alternative I'm aware of. We'll just to have to deal with it. A new culture, a new language, geography... heck, even a new *biology!* But, if you guys are willing, I'm of a mind to see all of this through... together... and to *stay* together."

"I don't know how much thought you've given to things since we arrived here, the consequences of our situation, but you may have... um... lost your families... forever. I've never *had* much of a family before... so it doesn't make a whole lot of difference to me. There's nothing I left behind that I can't do without. But *you* guys... well... I can't replace your moms and dads but I just wanted you to know that I'm here for you. Just about all we do have... is each other now. I'd like to keep it that way."

Buffalo almost didn't get to finish his last statement before the breath was practically knocked out of him as the three "orphans" jumped up and fell upon him in a massive hug. He was actually a bit shaken at first and didn't know quite how to react. Buffalo did not grow up in a happy family. He had been a product of mean urban streets and this show of emotion was something beyond his ken. But over the weeks together, seeing how these kids had bravely overcome all adversities, he'd unwittingly bonded with them. Strength was a trait that Buffalo had always admired and respected and these kids had plenty of it in their character. Gumption, he called it. Weeks of confusion, fear, and hardship had gone by without whining, complaining, or cowardice. These kids were tough as nails and Buffalo liked that a lot.

He relaxed and allowed his hugely muscled arms to gently enfold the three intrepid waifs. It was a sensation quite unlike anything he'd ever felt before. Somebody trembled, (was it him?), and he offered a comforting squeeze. "Come on guys," he said quietly.

"I think a good night's sleep will do us all a bit of good. We'll talk more in the morning, okay?" They nodded, red-eyed and emotionally spent but happy, and they shuffled off under their own steam to their respective rooms. Buffalo heard them sawing wood within minutes.

He sauntered off to his own room after making the rounds and found Jeep curled up on his bed. It was almost totally dark in the bedrooms by now, but by the light of the lantern, Buffalo managed to fix up a comfortable spot for Jeep, shoo him off the mattress, and get him resettled on his own little pallet by his bedside. Buffalo sat exhaustedly on the edge of the bed with the soft comfy mattress and it felt just about better than anything he could remember (though it could have been made of *thorns* and he probably wouldn't have cared at this point). He'd only intended to take off his boots but he didn't even get *that* far. He made the mistake of leaning back and was practically asleep before his head hit the pillow. He slept more soundly than he was usually accustomed to, yet at some point during the night he awoke briefly and thought he heard someone, one of the kids, quietly sobbing. He didn't know who and decided it didn't matter. The extreme intensity and danger of their adventures had earned them the right to a little emotional release. He rolled over in the darkness and drifted out again.

*   *   *   *   *   *   *   *

The comfort of the enveloping darkness was suddenly interrupted by a scream! Buffalo sat bolt upright and blinked his eyes. The room was actually bright again now, but his head was still in a groggy daze. Had he heard a scream, or was it just a part of a dream he'd been having? He wanted to get up to investigate but he suddenly realized that he couldn't move! His legs were numb and he couldn't get up!

"Brrr-ufff!" growled Jeep.

Buffalo looked down and saw Jeep sprawled across both his legs with his head cocked to one side and looking out the door. "What the... GET OFFA ME, YA FREELOADER!" Buffalo griped as he pushed the lazy hesitant mutt off his lower limbs... which were now numb and thick-feeling from the knees down. Jeep spilled from the bed and trotted to the center of the room. He then bowed low to the floor to stretch his forelimbs and bounded out the door.

"I'm coming!" shouted Buffalo to whoever had screamed, as he tried to spin his frame out of the bed. His feet hit the floor but he couldn't feel them. As he rose and tried to make his way across the room, he was assaulted by such an intense prickling and tingling sensation in his legs that he could have laughed and cried at the same time, if not for the seriousness of the situation. Half running and half hobbling, Buffalo stumbled down the hall to find the two boys and Jeep crowded into the doorway of Max's room. He peered over their shoulders and looked in.

Max was sitting up in bed with her head in her hands and trying to catch her breath. She giggled a bit and then looked up to see the whole gang gathered at her door. "I'm sorry," she said apologetically and then giggled again.   Her face was crimson with embarrassment. "It's just that... when I woke up... it was the first thing that I saw and I forgot where we were and it just... well, it startled me and I just... *screamed*?" she offered weakly.

"What - - ? Saw *what?"* asked Buffalo anxiously. In lieu of an answer, Max just sort of limply pointed a finger upwards. Looking up, they saw one of the small lichen-tending ants quietly going about its business while hanging upside-down on the ceiling. These specialized "horticulture" ants were roughly about two-feet long and of a more grayish coloration. The avidly gardening ant didn't seem to be the least bit disturbed by the commotion beneath it. "Well I'll be..." chuckled Buffalo. And the boys, (who were already on the verge of giggles), joined in heartily, especially when Jeep started fruitlessly leaping up at the innocent intruder and barking. The ant continued its work, undaunted, and Jeep was eventually content to just sit beneath it and watch, wagging his stump of a tail and letting out an occasional pitiful whimper as though he were waiting for a dog-treat to fall from the ceiling.

"Well... what do you say we find something that looks like breakfast," spoke up Buffalo, breaking through the giggles, "It appears to be light out again." They'd all been so tired the previous night that they'd all slept with their clothes on... it had become somewhat of a habit anyway, carried over from their weeks of travel in the jungle. Max was the only one who'd managed to at least remove her shoes and Dexter, to his credit, had remembered to take his glasses off. With a few yawns and stretches the group made their way down the adobe-plastered hallway and began foraging in the kitchen.

The pantry area of the kitchen was well stocked with mostly non-perishable items and some that were only slightly susceptible to attack from the many molds and fungi that flourished in the warm and humid clime. (Breakfast and snacks were not considered part of the communal dining arrangements as they generally required no cooking; therefore, every home boasted a well-stocked larder for "in-between" meals. Lunch and dinner could be partaken in the large cafeteria-style dining halls that were to be found on each level near the balcony cooking-fires. Prepared food could also be taken back to the home for consumption at leisure and at peace, for the great halls often became quite raucous if many large families gathered for their meals at once). The kids pored over the staples they found in the pantry and made several wondrous discoveries.

Although the items they found were commonplace to the Kontonquan natives, many were unknown taste sensations for the newcomers and they eagerly tried them all. Some were foods they recognized, such as nuts and grains, some of which Anya had introduced them to in the jungle. Others bore a *resemblance* to foods they'd once been familiar with - - cracker-like wafers, hard chewy biscuits, cereals, cookies, and preserves of fruits almost like jam. There were a few dried meats and fish, assorted vegetable chips, edible seeds, dried fruit, and even spices for seasoning their meals.

They also found many items that were totally new and different. Each had a unique and interesting flavor or texture and they found a few new favorite foods while also discovering others that had them pulling faces at the strange new taste sensations. They found curious pouches of sweet-smelling powders that provided no clue as to their purpose. Buffalo cautioned the kids against tasting them, suspecting that they might possibly be medicinal in purpose. However, much to their delight, they were later to find out that they were actually sweetened flavorings that could be added to water to make fruity or spicy drinks! (They would, in fact, later be told about some potent medicines that actually *were* kept in the apartment for treating simple ailments such as headache, cramps, and slight wounds for example. And they learned of the local "doctors" that ran apothecary shops, specializing in herbs and medicines that were used to treat the more severe complaints.)

They were so busy exploring all their inventory of snacks, that they didn't notice the cloaked figure standing in the doorway. They were startled from their rummaging by a delicate laugh and spun around to see a familiar shapely figure, (which even the roomy hooded-cloak could not effectively hide). Jeep lay at the intruder's feet, rolled over onto his back awaiting a scritch. Two slender and graceful hands emerged from the confines of the cloak to pull back the hood and just barely revealed the first glossy strands of raven hair and a flash of a winsome smile before the kids leapt forward shouting, *"Anya"!*

The kids engulfed her in a hug as she lowered the hood of her poncho-like cloak and tossed back her long flowing hair like a pony. She put her finger to her lips and made shushing sounds as she bent and embraced the kids with her strong but feminine arms which rippled slightly with just a hint of the athletic muscles that were scarcely hidden beneath the flawless bronzed skin. Buffalo stood still across the room, gazing wistfully, and for once was incapable of words or actions. He was completely taken by surprise by this sudden appearance... and the feelings which unexpectedly welled up inside him, feelings that were at once pleasant and comforting, yet confusing and unfamiliar. When Anya raised her soft dark eyes to look at him and again flashed that dazzling smile, even broader than before, he felt as though his very soul was being drawn forth from him and into the warmth and shadow of those ebony irises... and he welcomed the sensation. He felt a sudden dryness in his throat and when he tried to speak he blurted but just a raspy whisper, "Anya..."

Anya noticed this odd change in Buffalo's demeanor and her smile briefly faltered as she momentarily blushed with embarrassed confusion, her eyes darting away to break the connection while she attempted to sort her feelings. Then, with a sudden conviction, the full smile just as quickly returned, conveying a new sense of confidence as she once again focused her gaze on the towering handsome well-muscled figure she knew as Buff-a'loo. With a sigh, she turned her attention and shooed the excited kids back a bit so she could get down to business.

"Anya, where have you...?"

"Anya, what's going to...?"

"Anya, how did you...?" each of the three kids began.

"Wait... HUSH!" she cried, exasperated by the barrage of questions. "I've missed you all *so* much, but you must be quiet. No one must know that I'm here."

Buffalo was immediately smitten once again by the delicate lilt of Anya's soft melodic voice and some barrier of resistance inside him seemed to just melt away. He suddenly longed to be lost once more... traversing the perilous trails in the jungle depths of the cavern with this exotic beauty - - this warrior girl, confidently leading them on their way. "Why had it taken their separation for him to realize his feelings?" he mused, "Can you only truly appreciate something after it is missed?" He'd never felt this way before about anyone, but he knew the emotion for what it was, and it frustrated and annoyed him. He'd never let his guard down before... *ever*. Never let anyone get in too close. Not as a kid in the mean streets, not as a soldier in the field. It just invited trouble. He wasn't accustomed to being vulnerable and he considered his emerging feelings for Anya to be a vulnerable "chink" in his armor. As a conditioned defense, he did his best to suppress his feelings as Anya's words broke in upon his thoughts.

"The Queen Mother has expressly forbidden that I see you or speak with any of you. It is only with the aid of my closest handmaidens that I was able to conceal my whereabouts and sneak a visit with you at all."

"Why?" asked Max, "What have we done?"

"No... *no*," Anya quickly interjected, "You don't understand. It is nothing that you have done. You're just not supposed to *be* here. You see, for untold generations, we have lived within the confines of Kontonqua - - us, the Ikusks, and the Temple Priesthood. There just *isn't* anyone else. There's never been such thing as a... what you call a *'stranger'*. The closest thing to it is mentioned in the ancient tales of the scriptures; the holiest of texts kept by the Priesthood and passed down through the ages from our earliest ancestors. They were directly transcribed from the walls of The Gateway. The Gateway is one of our most holy sites and the foundation for many of our beliefs. Your very presence here is a sacrilege! It is a direct attack on the core principles of our religious beliefs. You have no idea what a time I have had convincing my Mother that you are neither Gods nor demons! She was quite angry that I led you here... that I didn't escape from you after you released me from the Konksihautl trap. She believes that I should have left you to your own devices in the jungle! She is very much afraid that your presence here will anger the Priesthood."

The kids looked at each other with worried apprehension. The audience with the Queen had gone fairly smoothly. They'd felt kind of... *welcomed*... and they had no idea that their presence had caused such a commotion... that it was *theologically* disturbing!

"W-what can we do?" asked Dexter weakly.

"Oh... nothing need be done for now," Anya smiled reassuringly, "Actually, your position is quite secure. Mother deliberated wisely before seeing you and chose her best option. She figured safely that whether God, demon, or mortal, the best path would be to treat you kindly. She concluded that if you were Godly, you would repay her kindness. If you were demonic, you might restrain from evil because of our graciousness. And... if you were mere mortal after all, she could always use extra hands in the labor force. She sensibly decided to watch over you closely and teach you in our ways first, so that she could better converse with and understand you."

"But why won't she let you see us?" asked Simon, "We've already spent weeks together in the jungle."

"That's just it," replied Anya, "Mother distrusts my *lack* of distrust. I've tried to explain your origins and what I know of your ways... and how you all befriended me throughout our journey. But, she's afraid that if you *are* spirits, you might be holding some sort of spell over me. Using me to infiltrate Konton. Listen... I cannot stay much longer. The best thing that you can do now is to cooperate with everyone. I'll keep working on Mother and you must stay out of trouble and mind those that come to teach you... they report directly to Mother. Remember - - you must do your *best* to conduct yourselves properly, for you are under her protection. She has boldly extended her power to protect and watch over you against the wishes of some of the high officials and merchant bosses ... and they would be only too happy to embarrass her and weaken her dominion. Most of our citizens are trustworthy, but be on your guard! Spies from both camps are everywhere!"

"What of the Captain," asked Buffalo, "I'm a pretty good judge of character and he seemed okay to me."

"Oh, yes," giggled Anya, "He is *most* trustworthy… an old family friend. It is he that is awaiting me outside now." This revelation brought a hot flush to Buffalo's skin and he envied the Captain's position of trust and confidence. To be able to escort this lovely warrior-princess about the city, to speak freely with her and be privy to her innermost secrets! Anya repeated, " I *must* be going. If you absolutely must speak with me, let the Captain know. I make no promises, but I will do my best to meet with you. Otherwise, I'll try to stop by whenever I can get away unnoticed. You are my good friends". And she shot a glance at Buffalo that spoke of more than just friendship behind her words. "I will look after you."

With that said, Anya bent to give a last hug to the children and took Buffalo's thick rough hands into her slender delicate ones to give him a reassuring grasp. The brief look in her eyes warmed him throughout for it seemed to bespeak of untold promises. She quickly lifted the hood once again, effectively hiding her features and turning, left with scarcely a rustle. But Buffalo smiled as he heard the familiar faint tinkling echo of her ankle bracelet as she scurried down the hall.

*   *   *   *   *   *

The castaways sat closely, enjoying what they could of their impromptu breakfast, and spoke quietly about Anya's visit. This was the first knowledge they'd really acquired about the actual perception of their predicament by these primitive people. They'd been so caught up in the events that had brought them here, their immediate survival, and possible means of rescue… that they'd not stopped to consider their own impact on this concealed and isolated society. They knew that their situation was precarious and could potentially become dangerous if this society, through their politics or religion, couldn't come to accept their story or the explanation of their existence. Simon quipped that he'd seen enough old Republic jungle-serials to know how these kinds of situations were usually resolved - - with human *sacrifice!* "If you can't figure out the problem, *remove* the problem." They'd had an uncomfortable chuckle over the possibility.

Luckily, before their imaginations could run too far, there was a pull at the bell that indicated another visitor. The kids all looked inquiringly at Buffalo. "Uh, well… I guess I'll get it," he said, and jumped up with Jeep at his heels. The kids all raced to the corner of the kitchen entryway and peered anxiously after Buffalo. He cautiously grasped the door handle, looked back at the kids quizzically, and steeling himself for any eventuality, slowly opened the door. Without a word, several elderly women just marched right in and shuffled past Buffalo, nodding and smiling and carrying various bundles. No less than five had funneled in! The last one stopped momentarily to feel the fabric of Buffalo's shirt, giggled and shook her head, and proceeded after the others into the "sitting-room", the large room in the front of the apartment directly next to the door. Buffalo absently shut the door while he peered into the sitting-room, obviously curious about the proceedings within. An elderly but authoritative voice with a questioning lilt sounded from within the room and a sudden flicker of understanding spread over Buffalo's face. He turned to the anxious and puzzled kids, and with a huge knowing grin, he gestured into the room with the flat of his hand...

"Fellas," he announced, "school is in session!"

The first few days of "class" were of course, the most difficult... and seemed, at least to the kids, to last forever. But the five elderly tutors proved to be extremely patient. Through the use of word association and pictographs the castaways were able to expand upon the smattering of Kontonquan language they'd already picked up from Anya. And, by continuing to speak Kontonquan, rather than English, even on their own free time, they rapidly became fairly fluent in the primitive language. Their schooling didn't quite end there though as they continued on for the better part of two months, learning about Kontonquan society, customs, culture, and even history, (though some aspects of the origins of the Kontonquan peoples were yet to be filled in).

Once they'd finally become totally fluent in the language, and comfortable with the dealings of everyday life, the group felt much more at home in this strange and wonderful city. As they came to know their neighbors, for instance, they also realized that they really had nothing to fear from these hard-working generous people. Once the Kontonquan's suspicions were allayed, they were treated as guests and extended every courtesy. In fact, some of their favorite times were spent just visiting, dining, and chatting with the "locals" who now accepted them and welcomed them into their families.

They took to wandering around the city freely and after a while, even felt quite at ease splitting up and exploring on their own. Discoveries such as a scroll-filled library, a gym, and game-rooms were of particular interest for the kids. And it was on one of these separate excursions that Buffalo happened upon the main training camp of the mounted troops. He was fascinated by the close association of the soldiers and their flying-ant "steeds" and the military precision and seriousness with which they conducted their training and exercises. Their stature and bearing was admirably noble, their methods and tactics meticulous, and their warrior ferocity unrivaled. Buffalo found himself drawn to their way of life and from then on made an effort to visit the training facilities as often as possible. He too was a fighter and a flyer and he longed to once again be airborne, with the wind in his face, soaring over the landscape far below. His opportunity was not long in coming.

The training facility was much like a Roman Coliseum… it was a large dusty ring where the soldiers practiced their ground maneuvers surrounded by high ornamental earthen-work walls that separated the arena from the stables and barracks. It lacked a roof and was completely open to the vastness of the cavern, built on a balcony, so that it acted as a sort of aerodrome, capable of launching flights of trainees into the skies around the city. Buffalo had stopped by to observe often enough that he became familiar with the "regulars" - - troops that he came to know by likeness and appearance as he watched from the galleries ringing the amphitheater. He thoroughly enjoyed seeing the snap maneuvers of the troops as they responded to the brusque commands of the drill sergeant whose voice echoed across the "hippodrome". He was particularly fascinated by the routine procedures that each guardsman needed to follow to bond with the ant that they would be flying. As they had witnessed upon their first day in the fields of Konton, it was imperative that each soldier approach their steed head on to be inspected by the ant's rapidly probing antennae before proceeding to mount their flyer. This ritual was carefully followed in reverse upon dismounting as well, and Buffalo casually wondered what the consequences of ignoring the procedure might be.

One day, as Buffalo was making his rounds, he stopped by the training arena and saw some unfamiliar faces; young boys who were evidently new recruits receiving their first lessons in "equestrian-ship". Directly beneath where Buffalo was sitting, one youth annoyingly caught his attention because he was acting somewhat oafish, choosing to joke with his friends rather than listen to the instructions being bellowed by the instructor. "One in every crowd," thought Buffalo. The boy was even annoying his own peers with his antics and probably would've been severely chastised or dismissed by the sergeant if he hadn't been crafty enough to confine his foolery to moments that the sergeant's back was turned. His recklessness almost cost him his life.

An ebony flying ant was brought in by a seasoned trooper for each of the new trainees. The highly spirited flyers were moved into position and soon stood saddled and patiently waiting next to each recruit they were assigned to. The drill sergeant, having wrapped up his pre-flight instructions, suddenly barked the order to mount. Every cadet stepped forward and turned to be recognized by the winged-steed at their side... except for the buffoon that chose to be callously inattentive. He turned sharply and stepped between the ant's fore and middle set of legs to head directly to the saddle. The ant, reacting swiftly to this insolent approach, wheeled deftly on its six legs, knocking the boy sideways with its foreleg femur and sending him sprawling into the dust! The ant lunged forward and was about to close it's snapping jaws about the boy's throat when it suddenly felt a vice-like grip encircling its *own* throat!

Buffalo, witnessing the slaughter that was about to take place, had leapt from the gallery above and landed directly between the angry ant and the stricken boy, facing it's charge head-on! In an instant, his left arm had encircled the ant's neck in a headlock with his left shoulder propped beneath the ant's "chin" and his hands clasped together in a death grip. Buffalo's hold tightened and his strong legs struggled to find purchase as he fought against the ant's advance upon the insolent youth. The ant's mandibles were frothing white foam and futilely snapping at the air in a vain effort to reach either him or the boy. It was Buffalo's *two* legs versus the ant's *six*, but Buffalo was a giant of a man with tremendous untapped strength and determination. He managed to hold the ant at bay until some quick-thinking recruits rushed in to grab their dimwitted comrade... who *still* hadn't the presence of mind to even run for his life! Buffalo glanced sideways and saw that he was looking directly eye-to-eye into a great ebony glossy orb that was the ant's compound lens. He saw his own distorted reflection combined with a determination from the ant equal to his own... and realized that this situation wasn't going to be easy to get out of. In fact, it got much worse.

The ant, desperate now to dislodge this new attacker, began whipping from side to side and circling erratically. At times, Buffalo's feet were entirely lifted the ground as he was swung back and forth as if being shaken by a giant terrier. But the ant couldn't loosen the grip of the stalwart human. Experienced guardsmen were running in from every side to help subdue the violent beast while rattled recruits were trying to calm their own flyers and exit the stadium. Buffalo saw troopers closing in brandishing catch-poles and ropes, but so did the ant. It suddenly spread its mighty pairs of wings and Buffalo knew he had to take instant action... he hadn't a moment to lose! To let go now would mean injury or death at the mercy of the snapping jaws... to just hang on would mean to risk dropping to his death somewhere over the fields or jungles of Kontonqua... there was only one way out and Buffalo knew he had but one chance to make it happen.

Buffalo unleashed his mighty thews and bounded up, swinging his muscled legs up, over, and around into the saddle with the dexterity of a rodeo rider. The ant's wings vibrated to life and with a great flurry and swirl of dust the ant rocketed into the air, doing its best to dislodge its rider on takeoff. Buffalo, who'd had some small amount of horseback training in the Army Cavalry before joining the Army Air-Force, gripped the saddle with his sturdy legs as he'd been taught and managed to find both the stirrups and reins. He noticed a sudden blinding brightness and realized that his powerful flyer had already zoomed to just beneath the cavern's ceiling! Looking down, he saw the great mound city of Konton far below, surrounded by its miles-wide colorful and well-manicured fields of fruits and vegetables. A swarm of black dots - - scrambled flyers - - were beginning to emerge from the top of the city. He had a brief gut-wrenching inkling of what was to come, and had time to mutter but a few choice expletives before it started.

Without warning, the ant began spinning violently in circles, doing snap rolls and barrel rolls, trying to throw off its passenger, yet Buffalo managed to cling to its armored carapace. Then, from this dizzying height it suddenly went into a steep dive straight for the floor of the cavern! Buffalo's hair was blasted back in the rushing wind, he was forced to squint, and his cheeks rippled backwards into a determined skull-like grimace as the mounting G-forces exerted intense pressure to dislodge him. Still he clung for dear life. As the ant neared the tops of the neatly cultivated fruit trees, it bottomed out its descent and zoomed back to the ceiling again! Thankfully, Buffalo's training as a fighter pilot had him prepared for the effects of the negative-gravity forces and he successfully fought the tendency to black out during this daredevil aerial maneuver. Several more times, the ant tried this method to rid itself of its rider, but to no avail... so it switched tactics. On its next downward swing, instead of climbing again, the ant chose to leave the safety of the Konton environs by leveling off at canopy height and bursting through the encircling ring of jungle vegetation and into the denser foliage. The berserk ant took to flying dangerously close to the undersides of the great tree-fern leaves that sheltered the jungle floor while quickly sidling back and forth to avoid the great boles of the trees in its path. It was obvious to Buffalo that the ant hoped to brush him off its back with the unexpected swish of a passing giant leaf or tree limb.

The ant's flight was truly amazing, its precision astounding, as it zipped along at blinding speeds between the riotous tangle of jungle leaves, lianas, and creepers. It zoomed over and under and between branches and obstacles... and often turned sideways or upside-down to squeeze through narrow spaces in the dense vegetation, all the while staying as perilously close as possible to the vines and branches it hoped would soon sweep Buffalo from its back. But the ant was flying at its maximum speed and beginning to tire and Buffalo could sense a growing sloppiness in its twists and turns. It wouldn't be long before the ant killed them both! Up till now, Buffalo had been just holding on, hunkering down, hoping only to survive. But, he suddenly realized deep inside that *this* was the thrill he'd been missing for quite some time... to *fly!* To **really** fly! He knew that he was unconsciously smiling now, the way he used to smile while dog-fighting in the skies over Europe, and actually enjoying this harrowing trip despite its looming threat of imminent death. He looked down at the "reins" of the bridle in his hands and saw that it was much like a horse's bridle, only stiff and square-shaped. He gingerly moved it to one side and the ant responded somewhat! He'd felt it! It was unmistakable! He moved it upwards a bit and the ant began to descend ever so slightly! This was a system he understood! The flight controls were much like the joystick of a plane!

Buffalo began copying the ant's movements; timing his positioning of the reins to match the zigzagging path of the ant's wild flight. Gradually, as he got the hang of matching the movements precisely, he started exercising his right of control over the ant, craftily adding in his own alterations to the flight path. The tiring ant, realizing the futility of its attempt to displace the giant upon its back and sensing the strong confidant hand now controlling the reins, reluctantly gave itself entirely over to the will of the experienced flyer and began to fly at Buffalo's command rather than its own.

The reins were really similar to a flight yoke and Buffalo experimented with his newly acquired controls: left and right were obvious, the animal swerved to either side accordingly, but what was interesting was that up caused the ant to descend and pushing down on the yoke increased *altitude*, that was because of the way in which the reins were hinged. Pushing down, for instance, would force the ant's chin upward and his body would follow. But, what was even more unusual and clever was that pushing *forward* on the yoke signaled the ant to increase its speed and pulling backwards slowed it down! Twisting the reins slightly would cause the ant to spin! Every control necessary for guidance conveniently located at one's fingertips! And the ant, now that it had fully accepted Buffalo's expert handling, responded with amazing speed and agility.

Buffalo was thoroughly enjoying his ride, but he had no idea where he was or how long the winged-ant could remain airborne. So, when he saw a jagged opening above, in the treetop canopy, he aimed for it and the ant maneuvered deftly up through the narrow gap between the overlapping leaves. Once above the treetops, flying in the vast openness of the cavern sky, Buffalo turned his charge back towards the way he guessed they'd come and gained altitude to try and spot the distant spires and domes of the great mound city of Konton. But, it wasn't the city he first saw, it was the "dots"... the riders... troops from the city, quickly growing in size as they rapidly advanced closer. His "rescue party" had finally caught up with him!

As the squad of twenty or so warriors advanced upon him, Buffalo could see the stunned looks of astonishment on their faces. Certainly, they had expected to find him dead or at least horribly injured - - that he would be calmly cruising along in full control of the rogue flyer was inexplicable! Because they were flying head on towards each other, the entire troop passed to either side of Buffalo with incredible speed. But they then wheeled their flyers in a tight arc and momentarily drew up alongside him. Buffalo looked to his right and saw the Captain of the Guard flying at his side with a fixed grin and giving him an approving nod of the head. He had gained an enormous amount of respect this day, both for saving the foolhardy recruit and for taming a raging flyer while in flight, a feat that had never been done. His story would be told and embellished around Kontonquan cook-fires for months to come.

The Captain called to him with a broad smile, "I see you have mastered taming *and* flying the Akt'Ki-hautl all in one day! Why bother with simple lessons?" he quipped with a wink and a gleam of playfulness in his eye. Buffalo did a double-take at the Captain's unexpected sarcasm and they shared a hearty laugh together that the entire troop could hear, even over the tumultuous buzzing of the many sets of wings. The Captain indicated a slight course correction and then he and Buffalo exchanged information of the recent events. The Captain thanked Buffalo for saving the life of the boy, but allowed that a punishment for the impertinent youth would still be in order. Buffalo returned that he hoped the penalty wouldn't be too harsh, for he related that the stricken look on the fallen cadet's face was probably a good indicator that the boy had already had a severe reversal in attitude!

Buffalo could see that they were rapidly approaching the tall spires of Konton and he realized that although he'd seemingly mastered flying an Akt'Ki-hautl, he had no idea how to land one and he made it known to the Captain. The Captain led the squad in lazy circles around the massive towers of Konton while he instructed Buffalo on the landing technique. Then he commanded the rest of his detail to land in one of the military aerodromes first so that Buffalo could observe the procedure. Buffalo next attempted his own landing... and while it wasn't exactly textbook, (or pretty), he soon found himself in a settling swirl of dust while his exhausted flyer was tucking away its wings, neatly folding them along its back... its thorax was heaving greatly. A tumultuous cheer roared up amongst the gathered soldiers and citizens who had speedily arrived to witness the big man's triumph... or demise.

As Buffalo's eyes quickly searched the surrounding galleries, he noticed the kids grouped together at one level, and Anya and the Queen Mother at another, higher up. They all seemed to have smiles that beamed with pride for their gentle giant... but there seemed to be some sort of concern as well. Buffalo then suddenly noticed many armed troops running to surround his flyer with spears drawn and wondered why, until the Captain rode up alongside.

"This is the moment of truth, my friend," he called to Buffalo. "You have a choice to make. You must either dismount and be recognized by your flyer, or let us attempt to restrain or kill him while you try to get out of the way. He won't like any hostile attempt to subdue him and he won't submit without a fight. If you choose to be recognized and bonded, there is a chance he may not accept you. There is little we can do if he does not. His jaws will be about your throat in an instant."

Now Buffalo understood the true meaning of the crowds and the cheers and jeers. He looked and saw money changing hands between some of the gathered throng. They were betting on his survival! He knew he had but one choice... his honor allowed him but one choice. He slid from the back of the great black flyer whose sides heaved with its labored breaths and the murmuring crowd fell silent. Buffalo stepped around the ant's left foreleg and unfalteringly moved to stand face to face with the spirited beast. Its powerful jaws were dripping with bubbling foam and worked the air in sticky pulsations as its head bobbed sporadically. It suddenly cocked its head to one side, as if to focus more intently on the impertinent human standing unwaveringly before it, and an almost audible gasp arose from the audience. For a brief moment, Buffalo's eyes met with those of the great flyer and he saw within a certain nobleness and understanding. There seemed to be an intelligence and calculation behind those glossy-black lifeless orbs. Suddenly, the ant's twin antennae shot forward and lightly tapped and probed Buffalo's unflinching features. Despite their size and formidableness, the ant's movements and control were deft and gentle and the sensitive pads on the antennae-tips were like two feathers tickling his face. An even greater cheer arose from the galleries... and from the surrounding troops! Buffalo had won the ant's approval... and everyone else's respect!

The exhausted rogue-flyer, having capitulated and accepted Buffalo, was now saved from expulsion or extermination and led off quietly to the stables where he would be well cared for and attended to... as Buffalo's *personal* flyer! It wasn't always necessary for a rider & steed relationship to be exclusive, but it made for a much stronger bond and all the most famous soldiers and "equestrians" throughout Kontonquan history were known as inseparable teams with their personally-linked mounts.

Buffalo turned to the riotous cheers of the surrounding throng and waved. The crowd went wild, stamping and arm-waving, throwing things into the air. Yet he could still hear the happy yells of Simon, Max, and Dexter over it all. He distinctly heard Jeep barking. And way up in the higher gallery, he thought he could almost see a twinkle in Anya's eye. A hero was born this day.

Chapter 16
"Temples of the Sun and Moon"

Perhaps it was due to Buffalo's recent daring exploits as a flyer, or perhaps it was because of favorable reports from the wizened squad of teacher-spies that spent the better part of each morning trying to Kontonqua-tize them (as Simon had cleverly dubbed the process!), but one morning the troop of elderly tutors failed to show… and an emissary from the palace-dome arrived instead! He delivered a curt but officially scripted note into Buffalo's hands, requesting the presence of all the castaways for a royal excursion the following day! Buffalo tried to ply more information from the dour-faced messenger, but he really had little to offer. Instead, he asked for Buffalo's reply, stipulated the time of departure, and warned against the discourtesy of being late. Buffalo assented to the arrangements and the envoy turned upon his heel and left.

The moment the door was shut, the kids were all over Buffalo with questions! "What's it all about?" "Where are we going?" "Do you think we'll see Anya?" "What should we…" Buffalo held up his huge paws to stave off the barrage of questions and after some time, managed to convince them that he knew nothing more about the matter than what was contained in the note! Little got done that day, and most of the marooned foreigner's time was spent in conjecture and speculation about the nature of the following day's events… and perhaps thankfully, for if they hadn't worn themselves out wracking their brains over possible scenarios, not one of them would have slept a wink that night!

Everyone was up bright and early in anticipation of the day's expedition... freshly scrubbed, breakfasted, and dressed in what had by now become a rather odd mix of Kontonquan fashion-sense and the castaway's leftover clothes from the surface-world. Over the months, despite careful cleaning and mending, the jungle soil, heat, and humidity had taken its toll on the cotton fibers of the displaced travelers clothing and they'd been obliged to incorporate the native barbarian trappings of the Kontonquan people into their own wardrobe.

Maxine proved to be the most readily adaptable and took to the new garments with enthusiasm... and actually rather enjoyed the look and feel of the shimmering leather-like cloth that formed her abbreviated tunic. She'd chosen an outfit that was very similar in style to the one that Anya had been wearing when first they'd met. Though she didn't mind the short skirt so much, she did feel somewhat uncomfortable with the sleeveless style of the bodice, so by way of compromise she continued to wear the white Tee she'd been marooned in, tied in the front.

Her favorite part of Kontonquan fashion couture however, was in the accessorizing! She loved the various leather belts and beadwork straps, whether they were functional - - like the handy shoulder pouch she began carrying - - or decorative... like the beaded wristbands she fancied. She also took to wearing a leather & beadwork headband tied around her forehead while using a smaller matching one to hold her pony-tail in place. She enjoyed braiding the fine leather "rawhide" and incorporating jewelry items; trinkets she picked up in the Bazaar... semi-precious stones, glass-beads, metals, and colorful insect parts, and often crafted her own designs in her evening "off" hours. She was also the only one in the group to have given herself over to wearing traditional Kontonquan footwear - - light but sturdy sandals with straps that laced up the shin of the leg. Though constructed of some sort of insect parts, she found them to be remarkably comfortable and durable.

The boys however, were insistent on continuing to wear their dilapidated sneakers … and there was no way that Buffalo was ever going to part with his trusty Army boots! (In fact, when the time finally came when there was just no material left to hold their boots and sneakers together, Buffalo and the boys found an expert craftsman in the Bazaar that was able to copy them in every detail, substituting similar Kontonquan materials for the rubber, leather, and canvas. The craftsman actually later became quite famous and wealthy when he started manufacturing similar shoes for Konton's upper class!)

Simon and Dexter were much more conservative in their crossover to Kontonquan fashion and were content to just add whatever practical accouterments befit a couple of young warrior/explorers such as themselves… shoulder harnesses, some light armor, side-bags, even a knife in a belt-sheath. And they learned to carry with them many of the common necessities needed for survival in and around Konton: flint for fire-making, whetstones for knife sharpening, a whistle, thread and rope, thorn-needles, and the iridescent flakes of Scarab Beetle carapace, or Paxui, which all of them carried, for it was the currency of Konton. Though it was fairly worthless as a raw material, it was etched with likenesses of the Queen Mother and her ancestors and produced in several denominations, passing for money for barter in the markets of the city.

Of course, Dexter was never without a pencil and a sheaf of paper for note-taking, (pencils were fashioned from a type of carbon-chalk the natives devised and paper was harvested from wasp's nests), and he even found a convex piece of polished glass in the Bazaar that worked nicely as a magnifying glass. He spent much of his time studying the minutia of the Kontonquan ecosystem and keeping detailed journals of his discoveries.

Simon took to carrying a fine Kontonquan longbow with a full quiver of black River-Reed arrows. Arrows in Konton were manufactured in two varieties: the graceful long-distance River-Reed, renowned for its accuracy, and the stouter short-distance Jungle Bulrush, capable of *occasionally* actually piercing the carapace of some of the insects... on a lucky shot. Simon had once had "beginner" archery classes in high-school and decided to pursue the skill here in Konton. He picked up mastery in the warrior "art-of-the-bow" quickly under the expert tutelage of a few of Konton's most highly skilled archers, (hand-picked by the Captain). They'd been quite cooperative and eager to help him develop once they'd witnessed his almost uncanny natural ability to anticipate and lead a moving target. They were equally impressed with his agility, unsuspected strength for his youth, and ability to rapidly nock arrow after arrow and accurately pinpoint targets in blindingly rapid succession.

For their part, Dexter and Maxine felt a need to defend themselves in this hostile world too... but Dexter just wasn't the type for close combat and Maxine, being female, was not allowed to train in the soldierly arts. Dexter, realizing how ridiculous he would look in armor, swinging swords and pikes around, opted instead to train with a sling and employed his own "guerilla" hit-and-run tactics. He became fairly accurate with the sling and slingshot... and his slight build and speed were a distinct advantage amongst the trees and foliage of the jungle.

Maxine wasn't left to be totally helpless either... for the women of Konton were as fierce as the men! However, since they were not openly trained in weapons combat and were generally forbidden to fly... instead, over many years, they had developed a unique *weaponless* combat method for themselves, creating a sisterhood of fighters devoted to protect the city itself, should it ever be invaded. They were the last hope for Konton's survival should it ever be overrun... they were trained to defend their homes and families in hand-to-hand combat with deadly skills. Theirs was a Martial Art deeply rooted in their primeval ancestry - - somewhat similar to Judo and Karate of the surface-world and just as precise, stealthy, and fierce. Its style used an opponent's flaws against themselves, delivering lightning-fast throws, kicks, and punches to vital and delicate vulnerable spots. It was called Jin-Jin and a master of it's principles was extremely dangerous and perfectly suited for fighting against small groups in the narrow tunnels of the city. Maxine, having always been particularly athletic and agile, was able to apply her years of gymnastics training... she excelled in the sport.

Buffalo had become a regular flyer ever since his wild ride on the rogue ant and soon thereafter began incorporating the trappings of the mounted guard into his daily costume. It just made sense... much of the light armor and belts they wore were designed to work in conjunction with the demands of working comfortably with the Akt'Kihautl, the great ebony flyers, and the materials used were even somewhat aerodynamic. Buffalo had been forced to give up the blue cotton work-shirt he favored and took to wearing just his flight shoulder-harness with its chest-straps over his bare thickly-muscled torso. In the continual heat and humidity of the cavern, being shirtless added to his comfort, like being at the beach... and he certainly had the build for it; he turned the heads of men and women alike who marveled in awe at the bulging muscles of the lean and athletic giant. He did however, as previously mentioned, retain his sturdy boots and kept his pilot's cargo pants in fairly good repair and covered with a strong set of armor-padded leggings similar to chaps, but with more straps and buckles and a thick leather belt that hugged his hips and kept his prized Bowie knife close at his side. He kept the knife sharp and in pristine condition and it dangled at his hip in a brand new sheath designed to hold the knife fast even in inverted flight. His smaller hunting knife, the one he normally kept in his boot, had been given to Simon a few weeks back... when Dexter, adding up their time in the cavern, had figured that it was probably somewhere around Simon's birthday!

Though Buffalo practiced with many of the weapons the armies of Konton employed, and became fairly proficient with most of them, it was the long sword and cudgel that suited him best, probably because of his size and brute strength. Armed with a shield and bludgeon, or a great broadsword, there was no opponent that was even a match for him. It was not uncommon for him to splinter his opponent's shield to confetti with a single strike dealt by his massive arm and shoulder muscles. Buffalo sometimes took to carrying a long sword in a sturdy scabbard at his side, opposite his Bowie knife, but he didn't usually carry a Kontonquan club. It just wasn't convenient. It did reside in the pouch alongside his saddle whenever he flew however... a weighty truncheon with cruel obsidian shards of glass embedded in its length.

The anxiously preening castaways were interrupted by a sudden ring of the bell and Jeep's barking rush to the door to greet the new arrival. It was the Captain of the Guard, (right on time... and they were ready!), with a royal ant-driven sledge pulled up behind him, awaiting them at the end of their entryway. He greeted them in his usual warm friendly manner, but would otherwise divulge nothing about the purpose of the day's excursion. He said only that it was for the Queen Mother to explain and that they would be meeting with her shortly at the Eastern gates.

The downward spiraling trip to the gate was short and uneventful, but Buffalo and the kids never ceased to marvel at the many sights and wonders that the narrow bustling streets of Konton revealed. Jeep stood with his front paws on the rail of the sled and let his tongue loll in the breeze of their motion. They were expected and recognized by the vigilant guards who manned the entry and therefore passed through the massive arched gateway, with its raised portcullis and armored fortifications, with little ceremony. Outside the towering walls of the city, they spotted a large resplendent gathering in the center of the encircling esplanade. A Royal *pageant* of colorful mounted troops was assembled (the Captain's finest), a veritable parade of magnificently decorated ant-drawn sledges, the Queen's Serpent Warriors, attendants and slaves, and even entertainers... amusing musicians and dancers that meandered around the outskirts of the procession.

The Captain pulled their sledge alongside the centerpiece of the spectacle - - an enormous hand-carved and intricately painted "barge" of a sled, studded with jewels and strung with golden ornaments and fitted with a fancy tented cover from which hung sheer lace drapes in soft pastel colors... successfully veiling the occupants within. This huge coach, with its many colorful flags and banners and emblazoned with the Queen's serpent crest, was easily large enough to accommodate her entire retinue of hand-maidens and personal bodyguards. It was pulled along by a harnessed team of no less than sixteen spirited draught-ants sporting colorful ceremonial armor and adorned with huge fluffy plumes.

As they drew to a halt, ceremonial horns blared forth a Royal fanfare and a hush fell over the gathered throng. The Captain arose and turned to face the Queen's carriage and Buffalo and the kids followed his lead to do the same. The veiled curtains parted to either side and they were delighted to see Anya framed within the aperture and looking radiant in a gauzy white floor-length ceremonial gown that was draped from one shoulder, belted with a bejeweled sash, and slit at its sides. The gathered crowd barely contained a shared gasp of awe. She was covered from head to toe in beautifully worked gold and lapis lazuli ornaments; a headpiece, necklaces, armbands, bracelets, rings... she was stunningly beautiful without makeup and jewelry, *with* them she looked like a goddess. Behind her, seated upon a throne, was her mother, the Queen, equally resplendent and surrounded by her attendants. Anya's eyes glinted as she smiled and looked upon the castaways, but she drew a breath and spoke to the crowd in general.

"Good people of Konton," she began, "This year marks a special anniversary as we celebrate the annual commemoration of Tuak-ah'nahi, for we have with us four honored guests… strangers to our land. In all our recorded history, there have been no strangers in Kontonqua… only those that originally "arrived". Yet the word stranger is not unknown to us. It is written upon the walls of Tuak-ah'nahi and explained in the scriptures. We initially welcomed our strangers with fear and suspicion for we were rigid in our beliefs, forgetting our own origins and our prehistory. But, the Queen Mother has satisfied herself that these strangers are not spies or demons… or Gods for that matter, but rather none other than fresh *arrivals*… humans thrust into this land as we once were. They have proven themselves worthy of our respect and admiration time and again, and now we accept these strangers as our friends… and take them today to visit the birthplace of our nation - - **Tuak-ah'nahi!**"

A loud cheer welled up from the surrounding guards and citizens and Anya glanced down to once again smile broadly upon the bewildered castaways. The Queen nodded her head in their direction also and smiled with warmth and understanding… and the veiled curtains drew closed. There was a sharp command from the front of the Queen's sledge and the entire procession lurched forward to begin the day's journey. The Captain pulled into line behind the Queen's carriage and the whole convoy moved east across the wide esplanade towards the fortified gate at the great wall.

The procession moved smoothly and with great festive gaiety; the musicians played a lively march, the dancers whirled and tumbled, jugglers performed, and food and drink were delivered to all by the Queen's servants upon worker-ants that carried a well-stocked larder upon their backs. They passed through the Eastern gates and continued on through the encircling cultivated-fields for several miles.

Konton had been built near the eastern wall of the great cavern and after leaving the fields they were fast approaching its side... where the "sky" curved downward to meet the ground. Buffalo and the kids recalled *their* first exploration of the cavern's wall, with Buffalo stepping up to the blinding light of the Lowa-tay, the light-emitting lichens, with his eyes tightly shut and then running his fingers through the coarse leafy vegetation. They all laughed as they recalled how the glowing dust had creepily clung to his hands and pants! That had been roughly around the *northern* extent of the cavern, the source of Tonqua, the river that basically divided Kontonqua from north to south. Anya had led them from that point through many miles of dense jungle, but they never once crossed the river... and their travels had been confined to the northeastern quadrant of the cavern, between Konton and the river's mouth. They knew so little of the rest of this land.

Buffalo had only dared to fly his Akt'Ki-hautl within the guarded confines of the local Konton environs. The Captain had warned him severely of flying south or west... especially of crossing the river. He wouldn't explain why. What secrets were being kept from the castaways? Their tutors had carefully sidestepped questions concerning Kontonquan geography and certain aspects of its history. What could they possibly be heading for so near the cavern's blinding walls? Buffalo remembered the searing light and wished he had kept sunglasses in that old flight bag he'd hauled along.

The road was well maintained and well traveled and the revelries of the entourage continued. As they drew closer to the cavern's edge, Buffalo and the kids noticed that there was an aperture ahead, a large gap in the cavern's wall that was carefully managed by the hand of man. A gateway! The Lowa-tay had been cut back to comfortably illuminate a hidden inner chamber beyond the opening and the ensuing landscape took on a "park-like" feel.

They soon passed through the natural rock archway of this new smaller chamber and the procession slowed and quieted. This seemed to be a place of reverence and was kept somewhat darker and subdued. The previously light-hearted music was now replaced by a more somber melody, almost canon-like in its composition. As the road continued, the smaller cavern diminished in size but began to show more of the intervention of man. Its sides were carved into recognizable forms and figures… and as they advanced, the natural walls began to become more of a man-made architectural structure with spires, balconies, doors, and windows.

The Queen's procession finally halted in a small open area at the edge of a large still black pool that effectively blocked their progress. There were two smaller lanes that split to circumnavigate the glassy-surfaced pond and they seemed to converge again on the far side of the pool. Buffalo and the kids could discern, in a niche of the apparent end-wall of the enclosure, a huge pile of boulders situated between two huge imposing structures... twin buildings facing each other and constructed in the same impressive and massive architectural design as Konton's finest towers. The building on the right was radiantly glowing yellow; apparently its entire carved surface was covered in gold! Its twin, on the left, was glowing more softly in white; it seemed to be constructed entirely of alabaster! The awe-inspiring view was spectacular... and the whole wondrous scene was flawlessly reflected in the calm waters of the pool that stood before it.

The diaphanous draperies of the Queen's "barge" once again parted and the Queen Mother, along with her train of ministers, maidens, warriors, and servants, stepped down from the carriage and proceeded to leisurely walk down the path to the left of the pool. Anya appeared from the side of the great sledge, all smiles, and beckoned for them to follow. They all exited their ant-drawn sled and the Captain stood decorously to one side as Anya approached and greeted them personally, giving each of the kids (and Jeep!) a warm hug while they briefly exchanged a few whispered words of affection. She stopped before Buffalo, (who was looking suddenly sheepish), as if uncertain what to do... and then she lunged forward to embrace the big man as well. Buffalo felt as if he'd melted... or was it just his heart? He suddenly realized how much he had longed for a moment such as this! He returned the sweet embrace, wrapping his muscular arms around the slender athletic figure of this proud barbarian princess, and gently enfolded her to him. Their caress lasted a few moments longer than just a casual "hug" and Buffalo was grateful to enjoy the soft warmth of Anya's form and to smell the sweet aroma of the perfume in her flowing hair. He felt her give a final squeeze as she broke free from his grasp, blushing a bit but looking serene; happy, as though she had settled her mind about something. The kids looked at each other with stifled, (though not very well stifled), grins… the significance of the awkward moment having not gone unnoticed!

Anya quickly regained her composure and led the way to the circular path, speaking to her cherished friends softly as they strolled along behind the Queen's Royal cortege. Jeep trailed the group and sniffed about; his nose told him everything *he* needed to know. "This is one of our most holy sites… Tuak-ah'nahi," she began and then nodded towards the building to the right of the rock pile, "That golden building is Su-ah'nahi, the guardian of the day. And that white one is Mu-ah'nahi, watcher of the night."

Buffalo and the kids recognized the word "ah-nahi" as meaning "temple". "Tuak" meant gateway, but the other prefixes were unknown to them.

Anya continued, "The walls of this temple record our history and year-round it is used by our priests, educators, and historians for meditation and research. However, once a year we celebrate Tuak-ah'nahi as the birthplace of our nation, the point of our arrival so many years ago… some *twelve-thousand* years ago! It is difficult to state exactly when… for as you have learned, we count every combined single period of light and dark as one *day* and four hundred of them make one full Kontonquan *year*, but it wasn't always like that… oh, no! When our people first arrived, they were *barbarians!* (Buffalo and the kids were quite startled by this remark and shot each other a quick side-long glance, feeling somewhat ashamed for having labeled "modern-day" Kontonquans as such!) It took many many years for our people to become civilized; to build Konton, and develop to be the learned people we are today! We didn't start recording our history and defining the days and years until almost five-thousand years ago." Anya knitted her eyebrows together and nodded in focused seriousness to emphasize the enormity of her people's achievement.

"The scriptures tell us," she went on in her lilting tone, "that our primitive ancestors once walked in a land without *walls,* where the days were bright and warm and the nights were dark and cold. There were rivers so vast that one could not see the other bank and mounds so high that no one had ever seen the top. Water fell from the sky and sometimes it grew so cold that this water fell as white puffs, like floating seeds from the Nu-akka plant! My ancestors fished the waters and hunted great furred beasts... but the fish and the beasts began to dwindle... other tribes were settling in the same land and *stealing* their food! Fighting soon erupted, brave warriors were murdered, innocent women and children were slaughtered or stolen and enslaved! The elders of my ancestor's tribe decided that they should look for a better place in which to live. There were rumors of a fresh land with abundant game across the waters. A land with almost no tribes at all... and a path to that paradise had just newly been discovered!

Most of the village made the journey, old and young, warrior and artisan... they traveled for many days into the wild lands, while the air grew more and more chill. The direction they had to travel somehow caused the days to grow colder and the nights to be almost unbearable. Water in its cold puffy form was always present in this new inhospitable place, piled so deep that they had to wade through it while the very air around them howled and blew like the gust from a bee's wings! Many died on that journey... and just as they thought that they might be getting nearer to their sought-after paradise, there was a sudden terrible tragedy that descended on them! The sky grew dark when it should have been light... and a blinding tumult of cold water-puffs fell angrily from above while a great wind blew and threatened to scatter the tribe! Just as their doom seemed inevitable, a refuge... a safe haven... a cave was found by a brave warrior-scout.

The cave was narrow, but it was dry, uninhabited, and out of the wind. The tunnel of the cave was very long and the tribe moved deep into it to build fires and escape the bitter cold. For several days they stayed, gathering their strength and waiting for conditions to improve, when suddenly there was a tremendous earth-rumble! The ground shook and rock fell from the ceiling! We have felt these earth-rumbles here in Kontonqua... we know what our ancestors must have gone through! They were courageous people! Anyway, when the rumbling stopped they found that they had been sealed within the cave! Thousands of stones had crashed to the ground over the mouth of the cave... the cave that had saved them was going to be their *tomb!* However, the same wise warrior-scout, Muh-ko-Natak, revealed that he had been secretly exploring the depths of the cave and found that it descended deep into the ground. Furthermore, the cave got warmer and the air smelled sweeter the deeper he went! It was his belief that the cave opened again into the paradise-land that the tribe was seeking.

Following Muh-ko-Natak's advice, the tribe traveled beneath the ground for many days, descending steadily into the depths of the cave, even farther than his explorations, until finally they reached its end… a blind passage! Or so they *thought,* until they saw a sliver of light! They discovered a narrow opening, just large enough for a man to squeeze through… and entered Kontonqua for the first time! They had *found* their paradise!" The pride in Anya's voice was readily apparent as she concluded her tale.

Dexter spoke up and remarked, "I think Anya's story is referring to Beringia…"

"Berin…whaaa?" interposed Simon.

"Beringia," continued Dexter, unflustered by Simon's query, "was the land bridge that connected Asia with North America during the last ice-age. The water table was lower then and the ocean's floor between Alaska and Siberia was exposed, allowing animals and prehistoric man to cross over and populate the New World. According to Anya's tale, her ancestors were most likely forced into a cave somewhere in what is now Alaska. And unless I'm mistaken, that huge pile of stones ahead marks the spot where they entered this jungle cavern!"

Anya spoke up again, "Dex-toor… I don't know much of what you are saying, but yes… this is where my ancestors stepped forth… sort of. You see, after the tribe settled in Kontonqua, they quickly understood that it was not the original paradise they had been seeking. It was too different from the world they had left. Life here was far more perilous than they had expected. The Ixtl, the insects, were unknown to them in this form; frighteningly large…

and the dangerous ones preyed upon them! They had made up their minds to send back workers to begin digging their way out of the cave that had led them here. But there was yet another tremendous ground-rumble! The cave collapsed entirely! They tried for many years to dig their way back out, but finally gave up. That pile of rocks between the temples is where they *stopped* digging after decades of labor. Hundreds of years later, our ancestors built Tuak-ah'nahi to commemorate the spot.

But all was for the best… life began to improve for them here as they discovered how to survive and benefit from what Kontonqua had to offer. And it was mainly due to the Aktz… the ants that we are bonded with. They didn't prey upon us, they *helped* us… as if they understood us. They are the reason for our survival. Without them, we would have perished. They watched over us, protected us, and eventually accepted us into their great mound nest. In return, we have fashioned a system to work and live together. They benefited from our woodcraft and agricultural knowledge to guarantee a continual food and water supply for their colony. And now that we have grown strong through the ages, it is we who protect *them* with our technologies, vast armies and beneficent governance. Our ancestors would be very pleased… life is good in Kontonqua. Ah… we are here!"

Anya's announcement was correct… they had just been too enthralled in the relating of her tale to notice… they had indeed reached the terminus of their pathway and arrived before the huge pile of rubble that marked the collapsed entrance of the tunnel that had so long ago brought the Asian ancestors of modern-day Kontonquans to this savage "paradise". The Queen Mother and her group had already arrived of course, and looked to be making preparations for a feast; spreading a large linen cloth upon the ground "picnic" style.

Looking up to their right, the castaways gasped as one. The edifice of the temple Su-ah'nahi would have been spectacularly breathtaking to behold just because of its detailed carvings alone. Carvings that were brilliantly sparkling in gold-covered radiance... but, what actually startled the surface-worlders was the enormous spherical image that occupied the entire upper portion of the temple's façade. It was unmistakably familiar, even in its stylized artistically-rendered form... the *Sun!*

"Of course... *Su-ah'nahi!*" murmured Dexter, "then *Mu-ah'nahi* must be..." They all turned as one... and there it was, carved into the face of the opposite temple in brilliant white alabaster... the *Moon!*

"So, it's true," whispered Max, putting their collective thoughts to words, "Anya's people once lived and walked upon the *surface* of the earth... *our* earth...under the sun and moon!"

"But their history, culture, and society probably have more in common with the early peoples that populated North America than with us," added Dexter, "Toltecs, Aztecs, Incans, Anasazi, Inuits... not to mention the Asians they descended from. It explains a lot about their lifestyle and appearance, the long straight dark hair for instance... and how they could have such a bronzed skin-tone without being exposed to the sun."

As they perused the carvings upon the sister-temples, the castaways noticed all sorts of now useless information recorded upon their surfaces: illustrations of star-charts, phases of the moon, seasonal changes, weather patterns, and even a total eclipse! They discovered pictographs of animals (including birds and reptiles) and how to hunt or care for them, plants and trees and their uses, maps, building plans, woodcraft, geography lessons, pictures of mountains and oceans, textile manufacturing, canoe-construction, weaving, and so much more! Instructions for survival back on the surface! Apparently, this was a kind of library, a repository for all the information that the Kontonquans would need if ever they were liberated from the confines of their "paradise" cavern and returned to the sunlit home of their ancestors.

They were startled from their contemplation of the temple's hieroglyphs by a voice behind them... the Queen! She had not spoken to them at all yet this day and barely acknowledged them, but now she stood and confronted them, with Anya at her side, while the rest of her entourage continued with their feast preparations. "I believe these images might look rather familiar to all of you," she began in her crisp stoic tone, as the castaways stood somewhat dumbfounded before her exalted personage and stared wide-eyed and nodded.

"I thought as much," she continued. "These walls recount the history of the events that brought my people to Kontonqua and provide all that is known about the world that was left behind. But that was ages ago and my people have endured and advanced much since then. Time has a way of erasing the truth and replacing it with what one would choose to remember. The stories told by our ancestors have long ago become legends... myths... no longer to be trusted as fact, but preserved as belief. What is written upon these walls has never been observed, directly experienced... or *proved* by my people. The scribes who chiseled these walls are long forgotten and my people know only of what they see... of what they experience in their daily lives. Tuak-ah'nahi is revered for its link to the ancients and its teachings have been incorporated into our faith, but it has not been taken *literally* for thousands of years. Perhaps you can now understand how your being here was such a jolt to our beliefs, to the accepted concept of the scope of our world."

"Had it not been for the rather persistent urgings of my daughter," here the Queen glanced at Anya with barely perceptible warmth, "I would have seen to it that your appearance did not *disturb* our way of life... or adversely affect our beliefs." A chill ran down the spines of the marooned foreigners as the Queen's revelations became understood. "But since your arrival, I have begun to look upon the teachings of Tuak-ah'nahi with renewed interest, and I have come to realize that your existence is explainable after all. The evidence is here," said the Queen Mother as she pointed directly at Jeep who sat by Buffalo's side with his head cocked questioningly, "and there..." The band of foreigners followed the Queen's gesturing finger towards a particular illustration upon the wall. They gasped in sudden comprehension as they looked upon a scene carved into the stone long ago... a scene of a primitive hunting party, accompanied by *dogs!*

"Well, I'll be..." mused Buffalo, "Jeep has saved our lives again and he didn't hafta do a thing."

"Once my ancestors," continued the Queen, "had loyal beasts such as the one you call 'Jeep'... four-legged friends that lived and worked among them. But the dangers of Kontonqua were unexpected and unknown. In their effort to protect their human pack-members from danger, these animals, our "wolf-friends", were all lost to the ferocity of the Ixtl.

So you see, the only explanation for 'Jeep's' existence is the truth of the history written upon these walls… and if *his* origins are documented with accuracy, then it stands to reason that your presence here is plausible as well. In any event, it is clear to me that we Kontonquans have nothing to fear. We need only accept as truth what has fallen into assertion. You are now as *we* once were… separated from your true home. So, I am happy to say, I welcome you… to ours." With this last statement, the Queen reached forward and clasped the hands of each of the castaways in turn and smiled quite warmly… the most emotion the little group had yet seen her display.

"Come," she bid as she motioned to the banquet spread upon the sward between the temples, "feast with us as we celebrate and tell us of the land our ancestors once knew."

And they did. At first, in their excitement, they offered too much to be comprehended; oceans populated with whales, fish, and octopus, monkeys swinging in the trees, elephants and giraffes, mountains and canyons, swamps and deserts, winter and summer. But they saw the incredulity on the faces of their hosts and realized just how absurd and alien the various complex ecosystems of their vast surface-world must seem to a people confined for eons to Kontonquan jungle life! It was just too much for anyone to believe and appreciate without first-hand experience. They quickly learned to curtail their enthusiasm and limit their information to the context of what the gathered revelers had come to celebrate and to explain the various pictographs upon the surrounding walls. Their audience was captivated and enlightened while several scribes feverishly recorded on paper tablets all that Buffalo and the kids had to offer.

The food and drink was excellent and the company grand. The former castaways were treated as "family" and in addition to the history lessons, jokes and stories volleyed back and forth for the remainder of the day while minstrels played, performers danced, and servants attended. The Captain of the Guard was seated next to Buffalo and the two of them got along famously, each relating their own particular favorite flying stories and battle tales. The Captain was most interested in Buffalo's attempt to describe the concept of an aircraft, a flying machine without a live component other than its pilot. Surprisingly, he didn't seem to find the notion ridiculous and Dexter surprised everyone and won instant admiration by folding together and demonstrating a simple paper airplane! But festivities inevitably draw to a close and by late afternoon, the party had wound down and the servants began packing up the provisions while the Queen and her guests made their leisurely way back around the pool to the waiting sledges.

Soon, all was ready for travel once more and the Queen and Anya bade farewell for the day as everyone climbed aboard their respective sledges. The Queen's "barge", surrounded by its armed-guard and drawn by its teams of sturdy draught-ants, lurched forward with the creak of wood, chain, and leather and the Captain pulled into position behind it once more as the caravan headed back over its previous track, this time to exit the temple grotto of Tuak-ah'nahi. Weary from the day's activities, full-bellied from a days worth of celebratory indulgence, gently rocked by the swaying of the sledge, the kids had dozed off in the rear seat almost immediately. Buffalo felt a bit drowsy himself and he hoped he wouldn't offend the Captain if he nodded off. They were just reentering the main cavern and Buffalo had briefly caught a glimpse of the distant spires of Konton through his fluttering eyelids when he suddenly snapped awake. Jeep had growled.

They came in fast… very fast and low along the base of the wall of the cavern. They knew precisely what their target was and they knew how to disrupt the procession in one pass - - they hit the Queen's sledge. It happened so fast that Buffalo could barely make them out, especially in the fast fading light of the cavern's dusk. *Flies!* They were *houseflies* almost the size of Konton's flying-ants… mounted by armed warriors the like of which Buffalo had never seen. In shape and form they seemed human, but they were horribly disfigured and twisted. They were clad in layers of grotesquely spiked black armor so deeply hued that it reflected almost no light. Thick cloth in deep colors of maroon, blue, and purple covered their extremities and fluttered from the joints between the armor, along with strapping belts of leather and chain-mail that bound the armor in place. The overall effect reminded Buffalo very much of ancient Samurai armor he'd once seen in a museum. But what really jolted him was their heads… what he at first took to be *masks*. Each of their black spiked and horned helmets was open-fronted to reveal a hideous half human, half fly-like face! Buffalo was momentarily taken aback. The heads of the attacking warriors were very dark in color, widely-shaped, and bristling with thick short hairs! Their eyes were deep red and compound like a fly's and set wide apart, almost to the sides of their faces! Their noses were flattened and almost indiscernible. Their fleshy grinning mouths which protruded slightly from their faces on a short stalky appendage dripped with frothy spittle and flashed human teeth!

All of this Buffalo perceived in an instant as he and the Captain, both men trained to action, dove from their sledge to either side. There were about two-dozen of the raiders split into groups of six and the high-pitched whine of the rapidly advancing fly's wings was a sound that Buffalo recognized from their travels with Anya! A sound that always caused her to draw them all to recoil in cover and hiding, but never once revealed its source with a visual sighting. Buffalo had always assumed it was just some predatory insect... not these gruesome-visaged warriors!

The first wave of attackers raced in directly for the Queen's carriage, ripping the tented roof from the great sledge. Screams erupted from the maidens and performers in the sudden confusion as many were knocked to the ground or injured by the falling tent-poles and framework that supported the colorful fabrics and ornamentation. Buffalo heard the sudden bewildered exclamations from the kids behind him as they were shocked from their slumber by the terrible rending sound, but he saw them react smartly... leaping from the sledge and taking refuge behind it until they could assess the situation. Jeep took up his position by Buffalo's side and bristled at the oncoming marauders, growling savagely as he did so.

The second wave hit the ant-teams in the front, wreaking havoc among the harnessed Akt'Juana who were unable to defend themselves while hitched to the barge. Several were killed and slumped lifeless in their tackle, thereby destroying any possibility of getting the Queen's sledge underway. A rallying cry next went up from the Queen's guard as they gathered their wits, readied their spears, and regrouped to encircle and defend their monarch.

The third and fourth waves came in almost simultaneously, each targeted for a specific objective. The third group of six came hurtling directly for the Captain's sledge and all those revelers that trailed behind the Queen's barge, obviously intent on preventing any support to the Queen and her defenders from that quarter. The fourth wave centered their attack directly on the Queen's sledge again, clearly looking to take full advantage of the chaos wreaked there. The Captain drew the long obsidian-edged sword that hung in its scabbard at his side and crouched cat-like, ready to face the rushing onslaught. He stood almost sideways to present as narrow a target as possible for the enemy spearmen while focusing his gaze intently on the onrushing charge, picking his mark with care.

Buffalo had only his Bowie knife and knew he would have little chance to use it in this type of warfare. He inwardly chided himself for not being prudent enough to have worn his broadsword for the day's excursion. He quickly scanned his surroundings for an impromptu weapon and spied one of the shattered wooden tent-poles lying not ten feet away. The pole was six-inches around and about eight feet long, rent at each end but otherwise sound. Buffalo wrapped his huge hands around the massive post and hefted it… yes, it would do nicely. With no time to lose, Buffalo turned to face the aerial assault team with the huge improvised club raised over his right shoulder in his best Yankee-slugger baseball stance.

The swooping raiders closed at a blinding pace, but the Captain was a true veteran, well versed in this type of battle. He nimbly avoided the anticipated hurled spear from the lead warrior, allowing it to imbed itself harmlessly as it shattered *through* the wall of the sledge they had all so recently occupied. He then followed with a spinning counterattack, swinging his razor-sharp sword in a wide arch that deftly sliced the wing from the marauder's fly as it zoomed past! The lopsided fly spun rapidly in corkscrew circles as it hurtled right past Buffalo, its doomed rider shrieking in fright and unable to free himself from the saddle-trappings... but Buffalo didn't flinch or allow his gaze to lose its lock on the next attacker in line. He only vaguely heard the muffled thud some distance behind him that abruptly ended the fly-warrior's horrid wailing. Instead, he renewed his grip on the tent-pole and smiled grimly as the second raider charged in.

The fly-mounted ambusher obviously thought he had found an easy target in his chosen victim... poorly armored, apparently unarmed, and holding a stick in a most unsoldierly manner. He unwisely chose to impale the big man as he passed, rather than hurl his spear. He never got the opportunity. Buffalo swung the massive timber with all his considerable strength in a roundhouse sweep that would have made Babe Ruth proud! The end of the makeshift club connected solidly with the head of the raider's fly, directly between its red eyes, and impacted with such force as to completely obliterate the fly's hideous head in a burst of yellowish goo and broken fly-parts and even further, imbedded itself halfway into the fly's thorax before it shattered in two! Buffalo's hands stung from the vibrating shock of the tremendous blow, but he was gratified to see the body of the fly, and its repulsive rider, flip end-over-end and abruptly fall crashing to the ground with the unfortunate warrior caught underneath where he was inconsiderately smeared into the greensward as the dead fly slid to a halt.

The remaining four warriors had chosen targets further behind the Captain's sledge and were already retreating into the distance before Buffalo or the Captain could do anything about it. They'd done their damage and Buffalo could see two sledges tipped on their sides and a third racing off, its draught-ant running in blind panic with no one at the reins. Several bodies lay scattered upon the ground but Buffalo surmised them to be mostly injuries... from the groaning and hysteria he heard coming from that direction... rather than fatalities.

The high-pitched whine of wings drew his attention back to the Queen's carriage where the fourth wave of marauders were now harrying the Queen's bodyguard and her attendees. Buffalo and the Captain raced forward to assist in the Queen's defense but there was little they could do. Two of the attackers and one of the flies already lay writhing upon the ground, successfully repelled by the stout spears of the highly effective combat-hardened Serpent Warriors, while the other four had focused their assault on the Queen's handmaidens and rapidly departed after taking a couple of hostages.

The raid was over as quickly as it had started. The gruesome fly-faced assailants were already but specks in the distance, attempting no secondary assault... and Buffalo could see why. A legion of mounted troops from the city, having detected the ambuscade from their watch towers and spires now suddenly landed in full force all around them to protect their Queen. The roar of the mighty wings of the armored coursers was deafening and dust swirled up from the powerful wash produced by their rapid beating... but the presence of fresh troops *was* reassuring. They had reacted with lightning precision and efficiency to have gotten to the scene so quickly, and at least half of the heavily armed squad, having instantly assessed the situation, already gave chase after the retreating raiders. But, it was doubtful they would be caught... the speed of the flies had a slight edge over the Akt'Ki-hautl, the flying warrior ants.

Buffalo felt a sudden chill as a nagging anxiety pressed itself into his consciousness as his eyes rapidly scanned the faces of the Queen's recovering entourage...maids and attendants, performers and advisors, ... her closest confidants were wailing and crying, picking themselves up from the wreckage of the tenting or crawling from their hiding places on the sledge to seek protection with the newly-arrived reinforcements. Buffalo's worry mounted as he failed to find the *one* face he wished most to see safely before him. The kids raced up behind him and as if to give voice to his concern, Dexter asked in a quavering tone, "Where's... Anya?"

A scream sounded from the direction of the Queen and her bodyguards. It wasn't a scream of being terrified or a scream of frailty. That would have been unbefitting a woman of the Queen's stature and her stoic nature and her carefully controlled composure forbade it. It was a scream of frustration, sternly exclaimed in reaction to the report she'd just been given and followed by a declaration that barely contained her rage. "This is an outrage... I shall not negotiate this time!" the Queen Mother spat tersely from between gritted teeth, "Even if it means *war*... I want my daughter back!"

Buffalo felt as though a mule had kicked his gut. It was just what he'd feared most and he felt his face flush as a berserker rage welled up from deep within him. Those hideous black-clad fly-*monsters* had taken the woman he loved... Anya!

Chapter 17
"Ikusks – The Unclean"

The Queen Mother flew directly back to Konton, transported and protected by a contingent of her best aerial troops. She was visibly infuriated and wished to get back to her citadel with all possible haste in order to consider the consequences of the unexpected attack and to consult with her spies and ministers. Her faithful Serpent Warriors meanwhile, remained behind to help sort out the mess left in the wake of the villainous ambush.

Dusk had by now transitioned into night and torches and lanterns were lit to aid in the recovery of the caravan and its coterie. Buffalo borrowed a torch and stepped over to one of the bodies of the fallen raiders. The kids, equally curious about their newly encountered enemy, were right at his heels. Jeep, with the hair on his back bristling, advanced cautiously towards the corpse of the hideous misshapen marauder. He held his head low and, uncharacteristically, his teeth were bared and he was emitting a low menacing growl. Buffalo bent to inspect the face of the downed assailant and grimaced with disgust as the light revealed the truly horrific features of the nightmarish being that lay crumpled upon the ground. The kids gasped and recoiled in revulsion at the sight of the gruesome warrior whose lifeless compound-eyes still reflected the light of the torch in hundreds of specks of iridescent red. In death, a thick milky slime drooled from the creature's mouthparts. It was indeed, a half-man, half-fly, and Buffalo could not understand what forces of nature could possibly have created such a repulsive mutation in humankind. Apparently, the statues, glyphs, and murals of

Konton were not as fanciful as Buffalo had supposed.

His inspection was suddenly interrupted by a hail from the Captain. Having removed the embedded enemy spear from their carriage, he had managed to maneuver their sledge through the debris to pull up directly behind them. "We must be on our way, my friends. I have given my orders to the reinforcements and there is nothing more that we can do here. I have no doubt the Queen Mother will wish to speak further with you. Let us ride!"

The Captain of the Guard unleashed the full potential of the spirited draught-ant the moment they were once again onboard, jolting them back into their benches by the lurch of the sudden acceleration. For a single ant, pulling a fully-loaded cumbersome vehicle such as a sled, its seemingly effortless power and speed was quite impressive… easily thirty miles-per-hour! And without headlamps of any sort, the ant kept precisely to the trail, avoiding all obstacles in almost total darkness. About halfway through their journey back to Konton, it even expertly dodged an oncoming convoy of military sledges on the narrow roadway; "rescue" workers racing past on their way to the site of the attack to aid in the cleanup efforts.

The Captain was mostly stoic on the return trip, avoiding the many questions Buffalo and the kids had about the attack and the strange enemy that carried out the ambush. He would say only that it was a matter for the Queen to discuss. As a soldier, he did however seem to grimly enjoy discussing the details of the brief battle itself; the strategies, the skills of the combatants, and the heroism of his troops. He acknowledged Buffalo's "kill" in his efforts to defend the Queen and was obviously impressed by the big man's power and battle-prowess.

After a time, they arrived at the outer-wall Eastern Gates and were waved through to cross the wide encircling promenade that ringed the city. However, the watchmen at the colossal mound's gated portico signaled their sledge to halt and exchanged a few whispered words with the Captain before they were once again allowed on their way... maneuvering immediately into side-tunnels that would avoid the continual throng of the popular marketplaces and speed them upward directly towards their apartments. But the Captain had other orders, he momentarily relayed the message received from the gateman that would alter their route... and their destiny. "It is as I thought," he revealed, "The Queen wishes to have an immediate audience. She has been in counsel with her advisors and generals and we are going to war." The grim revelation numbed Buffalo and the kids into stunned silence as the import of the Captain's words sunk in. War was a terrible thing... so, why did Buffalo feel an almost irrepressible urge to smile?

Their ride through the narrow winding passages was uneventful and soon they arrived at the doorway of the same great arched-hall that they'd been brought to upon their very first day in Konton, only this time the hall was bustling and echoing with activity. The Queen's declaration of war had obviously caused quite a stir. Soldiers, ministers, and messengers were dutifully racing back and forth amidst a tumult of urgent voices and sternly issued commands. It wasn't chaotic, it was just extremely busy... like the ever-present ants that mingled between the assembled workforce; efficient and focused, performing their duties with precision and enthusiasm.

The Captain handed his reins over to an eager young attendant and exited the sledge. Buffalo, Jeep, and the kids followed his lead and he led them into the great hall, careful to stay off to one side and out of the way of the hectic battle preparations. They took seats and rested patiently on the stone benches that filled the spaces between the massive pillars, fully expecting to have to wait for a suitable gap in the Queen's schedule before being admitted. They were well aware that the word "immediately" often held a different meaning for royalty and bureaucrats than it did for the general populace. However, the Captain received a signal from across the room just moments later and they were off again, winding their way carefully through the tables, desks, and personnel of the improvised war-room and towards the massive doors that they knew led upwards to the Queen's throne-room.

The stationed guards allowed them to pass with only the briefest of formalities and they were once again ascending the spacious hallway, this time on foot. The magnificent hall was still flanked with elite Serpent-warriors in bright ceremonial armor, but they were professionally impassive and unflinching and gave no apparent notice of their passing. They soon reached the ornate doors which opened into the throne-room, and the Captain exchanged ritual phrases that seemed to satisfy the two heavily-armed and menacing-looking guards. The large doors opened silently, and the small band entered into the pinnacle throne-room whose panoramic glass walls overlooked the dominion of the Queen of Konton.

In stark contrast to their previous visit, the room was eerily dark and quiet, but the view was still breathtaking. The plate-glass windows framed the Kontonquan night, displaying the vast jungles in subtle strokes of Payne's-gray and indigo-blue, revealed by the light of the starry Nalowa-tay lichens that sprawled haphazardly across the cavern ceiling. Tiny sparkling pinpoints of yellow mapped the locations of cook-fires and lanterns in the fields below... and a soft yellow glow emanated from the walls of the city itself, generated by all the lit windows and domes of the unique architectural wonder. Max pointed out distant bursts of light that would hover above the jungle for a moment and then dissipate in an eerie glowing stream. Dexter pondered softly, "I think those might be fireflies..."

After the commotion in the great hall below, the castaways fairly believed they would find a similar hubbub around the Queen and, drawing their attention away from the windows, were surprised to find her sitting quite alone upon the golden throne atop the alabaster-tiered dais... and reservedly gazing down upon them. They were the only ones in the huge audience chamber with her, (trusted enough to be *alone* with the Queen Mother!), and she was now motioning for them to come forward. As they reverently moved towards her, she arose and descended the stairs to meet them. She was, as always, radiantly beautiful despite her age... but the recent harrowing events had etched a burden of sorrow into her features that had not been there before and she now looked a bit drained. However, her regal composure was still completely intact and she confronted them with quiet strength and bold character. Her intensely dark eyes, peering from beneath heavy lids painted in deep-turquoise shadow with thickly-applied black eyeliner, were like pools of ink... yet they still managed to sparkle as she beheld the castaways one by one and met their gaze by way of greeting. After a moment's reflection, she turned her focus to Buffalo and spoke firmly with very little display of emotion.

"I have been told of your efforts to protect the caravan... and I am grateful for them. I had considered asking you to ride in our company... perhaps things would have turned out a bit differently if you had... but my ministers counseled against it, still afraid that your presence might be a threat to our ways. They're a suspicious cowardly lot and I wouldn't pay them any heed at all but for the fact that they represent the merchant classes and thereby exert their... influence. But enough of useless hindsight. Our day of celebration has been turned into one of catastrophe and explanations and preparations need to be made.

They were the Ikusk... those who attacked us... no doubt you've heard the name in passing. *(The Queen paused dramatically here as though to let this information sink in before she continued.)* You have been instructed over the course of the last few months in our language, our culture, and our way of life. Today, in our celebration of Tuak-ah'nahi, you received insight into much of our history as well. But there have been gaps in your education, intentional gaps... mostly concerning the Ikusk, the unclean ones, for we no longer speak of them. Their history is written upon the walls of Tuak-ah'nahi also, but not where you would readily find it. We are shamed by them. Still... evidence of their existence, and our past association, clearly manifests itself in our art and architecture; upon the very walls of Konton itself. Being the only other empire within our land, interaction is sometimes necessary... sometimes inescapable... but no longer welcome. Once, we were one and the same. Once we even tolerated each other. But that is all in the past and can no longer be. *Especially* after this latest incident...

To understand fully, one must go back to the very beginning...

You see... when our ancestors first entered this cavern, they were faced with many astonishing wonders and previously unknown dangers; plants and animals completely unfamiliar to them and beyond their scope of knowledge. They were uncertain how to hunt and gather to find sustenance here... how to *survive.* They knew nothing of the plantlife that filled the lush jungles that surrounded them. How were they to know what was wholesome to eat... or what might be deadly? We take these things for granted now... every day we consume meats, fruits, and vegetables that we know are palatable and nourishing for us. But, how did we *come* to know this? To develop such knowledge?

Many of the plants and animals that inhabit the cavern are inedible, indigestible, or even poisonous. Can one tell just by looking at them? Someone must inevitably be the first to taste an unknown food... then determine its edibility and further discover its nutritional potential and uses. Our tribe was understandably suspicious and proceeded cautiously to evaluate all the strange plants and animals they found for possible food value... even the insects. Many of our people sickened or died searching for, and experimenting with, possible foodstuffs and how they might be prepared.

As you can see by the bounty of the fields that currently surround Konton, we indeed discovered in time how to take full advantage of what nature here has to offer... but, as you have no doubt observed, we depend heavily on a *vegetarian* diet.

Our ancestors, on the other hand, had traditionally relied more often on the hunting of various beasts for fresh meat to sustain the tribe. But no such food was readily available within the confines of the cavern. No herds of four-legged mammals to stalk and slaughter... just the enormous Ixtl, the insects. In times of need on the surface-world, our ancestors had been familiar with the inclusion of considerably *smaller* insects in their diet and so they tried Ixtl flesh, but they discovered the insects that dwelt here to be indigestible and considerably *dangerous* to partake of. Their meat caused illness and had certain... side-effects. As for the red meat that our ancestors craved, the predatory insects of the cavern allowed only the most inconspicuous of those types of creatures to coexist. We were left with snakes, lizards, small rodents, fish and a few other insignificant animals... most of which have since become our modern "delicacies". So it was, that in the early days of our founding tribe's survival, it turned out to be the most basic of *plants*, leafy vegetables and fibrous roots, that proved to be the least perilous... and the most edible resources in the cavern. Their abundance saved the tribe.

Due to the horrible side-effects of experimenting with the flesh of the giant insects... something in their meat seems to cause the victim's insides to slowly melt away... partaking of Ixtl-flesh became forbidden by the tribal elders. Yet, many young hunters in the tribe were unhappy with that ruling and over time, stubbornly chose to ignore it. They continued in their quest for a source of the quantities of meat they so hungered for. Eventually, they found... the maggots.

On the far west side of the cavern, directly opposite Konton, there lies a swamp... infested with the filthy vermin. It is the source of the flies you encountered earlier. The hunters slaughtered the larvae with ease and found them to be extremely meaty, nonpoisonous, and quite tasty... however, *intoxicatingly* so. The hunters were enthralled. They tried to convince the rest of the tribe to join them in their flesh-feasting, but the elders would have none of it. They no longer trusted the idea of insects as sustenance... and with good reason. Unfortunately, despite the warnings, many members of the tribe were nevertheless tempted to join with the hunters. Driven by their craving for meat, they indulged in the regular consumption of maggot-flesh, despite the vile nature of the beasts - - gorging themselves on the roasted fatty tissue in secret wanton orgies of dancing and feasting, unwittingly becoming enslaved by the unsuspected *addictive* properties of the foul maggot-pulp. They formed a powerful secret clan and continued their indulgent revelries for many years. Over time, they subtly began to change...

It was barely noticeable at first... but in their attitude, they became surly, crude, and irritable... and then they began to slowly change physically as well. The hair on their bodies began to thicken and their skin grew dark and gray... their saliva thickened and became sticky causing them to drool almost continually... and while their reflexes became perceptibly heightened, their movements became somewhat erratic. It wasn't until the first *abnormal* baby of their faction was born however, that the elders caught on to what was happening.

The child wasn't entirely… human. It was an abomination. It had perceptible elements of *insect* attributes woven into its human anatomy. Most evident were the irises of the eyes, which had become iridescent red and multifaceted like that of a fly. The elders were outraged, the balance of the tribe became frightened and confused, horror boiled into anger, fighting broke out, and the baby was put to death. An ultimatum was given to the flesh-craving rebels to cease their consumption of the noxious maggot-flesh, the cause of their affliction. Instead they withdrew from the tribe and splintered off to form their own clan, the Ikusk. Their name literally means "meat-eaters" or "carnivores" in our ancient tongue. They settled in the west, in the cliffs overlooking the swamps, near to their food supply; where their "domesticated" flies bred the much coveted maggots for their dinner tables.

With the passing of the centuries, they have become the vile creatures you saw today; more fly than human, each generation more depraved than the last. They reside in the cliffs still, a mighty colony once almost as great as our own, but dwindling with each passing year behind the crumbling walls of their bleak fortress city… Ikuskqua. Come… let me show you."

The Queen Mother turned on her heel and the stunned group of listeners followed silently in her wake. She led them to the north-western side of the room, up to one of the great side windows nearest the rear entrance. There she stopped and reached for a decorative sash that hung to one side. She gave it a gentle tug and drapes began to descend from the valances that adorned all the window-tops around the entire circumference of the room ... but they weren't just plain curtains, they were embroidered in full-color into a detailed map! A 360-degree panoramic map that indicated all the features, locations, and landmarks of Kontonqua... rendered in a flattened perspective that coincided with the views from each of the now curtained windows behind!

The awed group of castaways did a slow pirouette as they tried to absorb both the beauty and knowledge that this new-found source of information had to impart. Across the room, to the east, the map had little new to offer; depicting the surrounding structures of Konton and the temple cavern of Tuak-ah'nahi that they had just today become aware of. But elsewhere, it was a treasure trove of enlightenment. "Look!" exclaimed Dex, pointing to the north, very near to where they were standing, "There's where we came in!" And sure enough, there was the mouth of the river, rendered and labeled in silvery thread, "Tak'Tonqua". They followed the river Tonqua, that virtually divided the entire cavern in two from north to south, walking southwards along the draped windows as they studied the landmarks. They saw depicted many of the places in the jungle that they had visited on their journey with Anya, all located on the *east* side of the river, the Konton side. The western side of the cavern was a complete mystery to them. About halfway down the room, facing almost directly westward, they found at the top of the map the swamp of which the Queen had spoken. It was spread across a great plateau... and between it and the river Tonqua lay vast plains, hills, and ravines. She had been quietly following behind and now spoke up again as she pointed to the renderings of the cliffs near the swamp. A dark dreary walled-city, a sinister-looking bastion, had been embroidered there in black... with a single foreboding word, Ikuskqua, sewn next to it in deep red.

"That is the city of the Ikusk," she stated as she continued her history lesson. "Until recent times, we maintained our association with them... the initial feud didn't last terribly long... they were still our people and life in the cavern was too fragile for such a rift. Cooperation was vital in order to survive. So, we've dealt with each other from almost the beginning... sharing knowledge, exploring, trading... awkwardly related "partners" forced to work together while drifting farther apart with each passing generation. We have been always wary of each other, neither trusting the other completely. Communication, interaction, and understanding became ever more difficult. Eventually, the situation became impossible.

Over the last several hundred years, the Ikusk have started to lose their humanity entirely. Their mutations have grown out of control, fueled by their insatiable lust for maggot-flesh and enhanced through their inappropriate practice of inbreeding. They've slowly gone mad... and their civilization has begun to crumble. They no longer have the intelligence or skills to even maintain their city. Their population has gone into decline as the poor twisted unfortunates suffer beneath the accumulated effects of generations of bizarre and unrestrained mutation. Their life-spans are now greatly diminished, their health poor, and their ability to procreate... uncertain. Horribly disfigured infants are commonly born and rarely survive...and the availability of healthy parenting stock is ever dwindling. They need mates that are more *human* than they to counter the years of accumulated effects. Kontonquan inhabitants that can draw their lineage directly back to the original lost tribe are prized as "pure blood"... needed to bolster their procreative health. But their inability to attract healthy mates has made them... desperate. That's when the Ikusk began to *prey* upon *us!*"

The Queen's face grew stern and flushed visibly and her words were spoken tersely as she tried vainly to contain the anger that welled up within her at this point of the narrative, "... and it's all that damned Prince Bik-cu's doing... it was *his* idea, I *know* it! Vile *despicable* man."

The Queen looked off to one side and drew a slow breath to calm herself. Presently, once again composed, she continued her tale, "About twenty years ago... it went unnoticed at first... a few young girls, venturing too near the jungle would disappear. The Ixtl were blamed for it. But the occurrences became too frequent and eventually one of the captured girls escaped and described the horror of her ordeal. Ikusk raiders were *stealing* our women! A company of soldiers was hastily dispatched to rescue the other captive girls, but they were repulsed. The Ikusk's city is in disrepair, but it is very well defensively situated and heavily fortified.

Time and again, Konton has attempted to liberate the kidnapped girls both through battle and negotiation... we even offered to *buy* them back! Over the course of the years before my rule, my predecessor, my... *mother*, failed miserably to correct this offense and eventually became... complacent. The kidnappings continued. After all, she reasoned... was it really worth entering into all-out war for the loss of a few farm-girls each year? That was my *mother's* decision. *(The Queen halted and stared coldly at the throne for a moment and then continued.)* She may have been my mother... but that didn't make her right... *or* a good ruler." *(The icy coolness with which the Queen spoke of her own mother gave Buffalo a chill. How could Anya, with all her abundant warmth and friendliness, be related to this woman?)*

"Anyway, since mother graciously departed six years ago, I now rule and I have changed our policies since. To the outrage of the Ikusk, and to the irritation of much of our merchant-class, I have halted all discourse and contact between our tribes. There is still some black-marketeering going on surreptitiously of course... it's almost impossible to stop... but we do try. The misfortunes of the Ikusk have been our burden for far too long. We cannot continue to support them while they continually victimize us... and since we have been unsuccessful in beating them in battle, my intent has been to isolate them and allow them to wither and decline in isolation until they reach their inevitable extinction. To this end, our squads of aerial troops have performed amazingly... greatly reducing the number of kidnappings and keeping the Ikusk at bay. The Ikusk have learned the *hard* way to curtail their attempts at abduction... *(The Queen smiled knowingly here and nodded in the direction of the Captain who in turn curtly saluted and seemed to almost blush with pride.)* Unfortunately, desperation has made the Ikusk even more reckless and bold in their raiding of late and at great price to them some of our maidens have still been stolen. And to make matters worse, the ruling patriarch of the Ikusk, Prince Bik-cu', whether for lust or revenge, has become *obsessed* with desire... for my daughter... Anya." *(Buffalo's blood boiled within him and he visibly bristled at this revelation. His agitation did not go unobserved by the Queen).*

"In fact, it was because of a previous attempt to kidnap my daughter that you four stumbled upon her and subsequently aided in her return. The day before you arrived in Kontonqua, Bik-cu', aided by several spies who are no longer with us, staged a successful raid that managed to capture Anya. Pursued and harried by our vigilant troops, the raiding party was quickly hunted down in the Southlands and dealt with, but the brute that held Anya managed to slip away. Though mortally wounded, he followed the river to avoid capture and was able to guide his mount unseen to the extreme northern limits of the cavern. He intended to skirt the cavern's edge westward from there to return to Ikuskqua, but Anya, clever girl that she is, unraveled her bonds and dispatched him near Tak'Tonqua, the river-mouth. She jumped from the back of the fly and into the waters of Tak'Tonqua's pool and after resting the night, was about to begin her return journey to Konton when she became startled by your voices and the barking of your... wolf-friend, and in fleeing you, she let down her guard and became ensnared in the Konksihautl trap.

So, while our troops searched fruitlessly in the South for my daughter, eventually assuming that she had been somehow successfully abducted to Ikuskqua, you four were actually escorting her back to Konton through the jungle. We mounted assaults against Ikuskqua in retaliation for Anya's capture and attacked the Ikuskquan outposts and maggot-breeding grounds in an attempt to force Bik-cu' to release her. Imagine my elation, anger, and confusion… and immediate suspicion... when the five of you emerged at the edge of our city. Elation at being reunited with my daughter who was quite safe... anger at being embroiled in pointless attacks that would only further enrage a bitter enemy... and confusion at being presented with a new and blasphemous phenomenon… *strangers* in our land. Forgive me if I was less than hospitable.

And now Bik-cu' has done the unthinkable once more… and on one of our most holy of days. I thought he'd been sufficiently subdued and isolated, but this affront to my house and the citizens of Konton cannot go unpunished. I had hoped to quietly allow the Ikusk to slide into oblivion… but I can no longer exercise such patience. His boldness has driven me to declare war and a decisive battle he shall have!"

Buffalo could contain his anxiety no longer and forcefully interjected, "I want to be a part of this… war. I *must* be allowed. I need to go with the troops and do what I can to save Anya!"

The Queen looked intently at the big man through narrowed lids for a moment and a knowing smile spread stealthily across her face. She quietly purred, "Yes, your… *interest* in my daughter has not gone unnoticed. Very well. Captain? When we are through here, see that this man is equipped and ready to ride with you in the morning. We attack at first light!"

"W-what about *us?* " chimed in Simon, Max, and Dexter simultaneously, "We want to go too!"

"I'm afraid *that* is out of the question," replied the Queen, fixing them with a gaze that warned against trying any attempt to challenge her decision, "Warfare is best left to *seasoned* warriors. You will yet have your day."

In anger and annoyance, the kids turned away so as to not reveal the full extent of their emotion as their grim faces bloomed in reddening frustration. After an awkward silence, the Queen drew a breath and continued, "Well, I have done my best to fill the gaps in your knowledge concerning the history of Kontonqua and the events that have led to this particular moment. The Captain can fill you in on the details of our campaign and the tactics to be used. I still have many preparations to make… have you any questions?"

With arms folded in defiance, Dexter had been focusing on the map and following the path of the river to avert his thoughts from having to deal with his emotions. His eyes fell on another depiction of a small citadel at the river's end. "What's that at the end of the map?" he asked while pointing a finger southward.

Intrigued by not having noticed the drawing before, Buffalo and the kids strolled down to the south end of the throne room to gaze at this newly discovered feature. The drawing showed a massive and evil-looking structure with two mammoth towers and a huge central building topped with a multi-colored dome skylight. The building was actually situated so that it straddled the river Tonqua itself… near where it exited the cavern. The red letters written beside it were known to them. It was a common word used frequently by much of the citizenry and taught to them by their tutors… and yet, to see it written as a map location gave them pause… and a bit of a chill. X'Poca…it meant God.

"That is the Temple of X'Poca," explained the Queen, "Our deity." Buffalo and the kids turned to look at her quizzically as though she'd suddenly become a lunatic. Unfazed, she continued, "When the tribe was forced to split, there were those that remained outside the rift and could choose neither side to reside with. They were led by a devoutly spiritual shaman that had always looked to the heavens and counseled the tribe. Greatly disturbed by the tearing of the tribe, at odds with the tribal elders, beset by the horrible beasts of Kontonqua, and trapped beneath the earth in a world far away from the heavens that had always guided them, they turned inward to their faith. They departed from the conflict to set up their own conclave and devote themselves entirely to their religious beliefs... but over the years, it has become more of a fanaticism.

They were left to their own devices and formed a Priesthood... and no one really took them seriously... until they found X'Poca. Unable to consult with the heavens for leadership and guidance, they needed a new idol to worship, a new mouthpiece to the Almighty. They bestowed that honor upon X'Poca... a very ancient soul... the king of all the Ixtl... the only being that *everything* that moves in the cavern *fears*.

For some reason... perhaps faith? X'Poca allowed the Priesthood to approach him and care for him without consuming them as he did all else. They brought him offerings and he protected them. Over time, they deified him and built the temple you see here in his honor and he resides there still. The Priesthood normally remains in studious religious seclusion, but they are not above wielding X'Poca's power with great ferocity on any unbelievers or if their doctrine is questioned or disobeyed. Because of that "influence", both Konton and Ikuskqua respect their beliefs and make tribute several times each year to support them. The followers of X'Poca want for nothing. So it has always been."

Chapter 18
"The Charge of the Bug Brigade!"

It was perhaps the most difficult night they'd spent in Kontonqua so far... neither Buffalo or the kids got much sleep due to the anticipation of the battle to come. They'd used most of the evening to muse at length over the new history "lesson" they'd gotten from Anya's mother, the Queen... and to speculate on the nature of the war that was about to begin mere hours away. Buffalo talked softly with the kids into the night while he cleaned and inspected his warrior's trappings and weapons.

Finally satisfied with his preparedness, he decided it was time to broach a rather delicate subject. "Guys..." he began, "There's one last thing we have to cover before we hit the sack." All eyes had his attention as he continued. "No soldier has ever gone off into battle without first making his peace... tying up loose ends so to speak... in the event that, umm, well, it's always a possibility that a pilot, or soldier, might not..." Buffalo fidgeted around in his seat awkwardly.

"We've already talked about that," interjected Max, "between ourselves I mean."

"You have?" wondered Buffalo.

Max nodded wide-eyed but silently in the affirmative.

"Yes... but not one of us is willing to believe it's possible! After all we've *been* through?" added Dex.

"And you're like the biggest man in this cavern... and... and the *toughest*." said Simon.

"If *you* can't bring Anya back, no one can." Max stated and the other two agreed.

Buffalo stared blankly at the three kids whose faces were fixed in grim conviction... absolutely certain of his success and invulnerability. A broad smile spread across his face and he laughed heartily out loud. "All right," he chuckled, "Looks like the three of you will see me through this with just *your* determination alone! With support like that, I can't lose!"

But Buffalo still continued stubbornly with the words he just had to say, "Okay... it's not the speech I intended to give... but you guys know what you mean to me should anything go wrong, right? And promise you'll take care of ol' Jeep for me too?" Dexter and Max cut him off from any further morbid reflections by running up and giving Buffalo the hug of his life! Simon hesitated and held back, looking sheepish... becoming a young man had its downside. "C'mon, Simon... you too," ordered Buffalo, "You're never too old for a group hug!" Simon grinned happily and threw his arms around the gentle giant.

*   *   *   *   *   *   *

Buffalo's inner alarm awoke him at the first glow of Allowa-tay. He dressed in silence, carefully fitting and adjusting each strap and buckle of his warrior raiment over his usual cargo pants and boots, yanking on the harnesses until he was satisfied that all was sturdily in place. Lastly, he buckled on the scabbard belt that held his trusty Bowie knife to his right hip and his custom-made broadsword to his left. Being such a large man, Buffalo found the traditional short-swords of the Serpent Guard to be too light and ineffectual for his tastes... (even his favorite cudgel had started to feel inadequate), he preferred swinging a weapon with some serious heft to it, so some time ago he'd sought out the best blacksmiths in Konton to fabricate a sword proportional to his huge frame. He had described to them a sword he'd remembered seeing in a museum once, in the section on medieval arms and armor, only "heftier"... and the resulting weapon truly could be described as a "Bastard Sword" for it certainly was a conglomeration of many of the swords favored by the knights of the Middle Ages... and just as deadly. Long and solid, he wielded the 45-inch sword, with it's razor-sharp double edges, with frightening results. Buffalo wasn't interested in swordplay... he was more concerned with just separating the souls of his enemies from their earthly vessels. His heavily muscled frame swung the heavy iron sword more like a cleaver than a Claymore and many a wooden training post had been reduced to toothpicks by Buffalo's round-house swing!

Buffalo gave Jeep a parting scritch on the top of his head and walked into the central hallway of the apartment that had become home to the castaways. He heard the soft snoring of the kids and looked in on each of them to say a last "Goodbye" that he hoped would not actually *be* his last. Turning to the front door, he opened it just as the Captain, in full ceremonial battle dress, was about to knock. "Ah... my friend... it looks to be a fine day for a battle that will be glowingly recorded into Konton's history... are you ready?" Buffalo nodded that he was. But... in the unchanging controlled environment of the cavern, when was it *not* a "fine" day?

A short sledge-drive brought them to the main aerodrome balcony of the Serpent Guard and the air of the large arena was practically electric. Banners and flags were waving everywhere, not by wind but by enthusiastic spectators, squires were racing about trying to carry out last-minute orders at their master's bidding, craftsmen sharpened weapons and fine-tuned harnesses and trappings, and throngs of supportive citizens had gathered to witness the pride of the city being fielded into action. Buffalo knew that similar scenes were being played out at the three other military aerodromes that the city supported. Here, mounted troops in the hundreds were collectively gathered in neat rows on the arena floor, in brilliant battle attire, awaiting the orders to ascend and assemble in the skies above the city. War had gotten quickly into everyone's blood... and the adrenalin was running high.

A cheer went up as Buffalo and the Captain entered the stadium and proceeded to its center where two highly polished ants in spectacular harness awaited. Beaming squires that had saddled and buffed the carapaces of the personal flyers of Buffalo and the Captain stood by proudly as the two approached. Buffalo waived to the troops while the Captain chose to remain stoic as they drew near to their respective Akt'Ki-hautl. Each walked directly to the head of their battle-ant and stood confidently before it awaiting the bonding ritual. Both ants quickly but deftly tapped their probing antennae over the face of their rider and then withdrew to accept the pairing. Buffalo reached forward and gave his ant a pat on the head and whispered, "Ready to do some serious flying today, Silver?" ... his own little ritual that his personal ant didn't seem to mind, and a name borrowed from a popular radio show that Buffalo enjoyed.

"Silver", the very same ant that had previously tried to kill its originally assigned recruit and wound up being retrained by Buffalo in a nightmarish flight that should have meant certain death for the both of them, had proven to be a perfect match for the big man. Larger than most of its kind, it easily carried the weight of its huge rider, and being sharply intuitive, it quickly learned to become spiritedly responsive to Buffalo's unique piloting approach... a style he based more on his experience at the yoke of a WWII fighter plane than as an Aero-trooper of Konton! Silver barely budged under the bulk of the muscular giant that launched himself into the saddle upon its back... and the pair stood patiently waiting for the Captain to signal for the takeoff.

The Captain, for his part, took his time and ceremoniously mounted his flyer with much more decorum than Buffalo had. He paused to turn in his saddle and inspected the troops gathered behind him once more. The arena fell silent and everyone waited... Buffalo wondered what they were waiting for? There. They heard it. A lone horn sounded deeply and mournfully from high above... coming from the pinnacle of the city! Other horns from up and down the great mound city's walls took up the call and the air was suddenly filled with a resounding low bellow! The Captain made a pointed gesture to the skies above and his flyer's wings sprung from its sides to become a loud throbbing blur as ant and rider lifted in a cloud of dust from the arena floor. Within a heartbeat, Buffalo nudged his ant, and Silver too extended his powerful transparent pairs of wings and began to rise with exceeding speed as they beat the air too fast for the human eye to see, yet powerful enough to lift them both effortlessly into the air, "Hi ho, Silver... away!" shouted Buffalo to no one in particular. He couldn't resist, but it's doubtful anyone noticed his playful battle cry over the sudden deafening roar of wings as the hundreds of assembled and anxious troops lifted into the sky almost as one!

Up and up with incredible speed the Captain led the column of flyers to circle high above the mound city while he awaited the gathering of all his soldiers from the various aerodromes. Resplendent flyers, noble Serpent Guards, Beetle Guards, Wasp Guards... all heavily armed, could be seen streaming from the four aerodrome balconies below, each unit rising into the air from different sides of the great mound. Buffalo flew in his commander's wake and took in the sights as he waited for the mission to begin. Kontonqua was truly a gorgeous sight from this altitude... past the ring of brightly multicolored crops of carefully cultivated fields below, dense green jungle in many subtle shades extended in every direction as far as the eye could see. The dazzling "sky" of Allowa-tay lit the cavern brightly and evenly and made every day a "sunny" one. Buffalo looked to the city they circled and saw the great throne room windows at the apex of the mound. He could just about make out the shape of the Queen Mother standing behind the highly reflective panels of "glass" reviewing her armies... accompanied by three slightly shorter figures... and the shape of what could only be a dog! Buffalo grinned happily to himself and nodded towards the spectators with whom he'd shared so much adventure of late. Things were getting better, he was regaining control over his destiny at last... he was flying again, doing what he loved most... and going off to war. Nobody enjoyed a good scrap more than Buffalo! And now he knew that his buddies, his "kids" and his canine pal, would be well taken care of should anything befall him.

And then the real reason for this mission returned upon his thoughts and he flushed with renewed anger. Anya, the barbarian jungle girl, the fierce warrior, the delightful princess, the... what the heck!... *just admit it*... the love of his life... was being held captive, and who knows what, by some half-mutant deranged prince almost two hundred miles away! Buffalo seethed at the thought, so much so that he almost missed the Captain's signal to advance! The troops had rallied while he pondered Anya's peril and the Captain led the huge assembled army of flyers, with Buffalo at his side, in a straight line directly west from Konton. This was no sneak attack, it was all out war... and the spies of Ikuskqua had probably already forewarned Prince Bik-cu' anyway.

The squadron flew four abreast and at a comfortable sixty miles per hour, so as to not tire out their ebony ant-flyers prematurely. The steady hum of the combined ant's vibrating wings reminded Buffalo very much of the drone of engines when he flew with his WWII squadron over the skies of Europe. It was a fantastic feeling to once again have wind whipping at his face and blowing through his hair... a feeling he'd rather missed in this windless terrarium beneath the Earth, and Buffalo drew in a long slow breath of the sweet-smelling jungle aroma. The great fronds of the huge jungle fern-trees passed steadily below like an endless glistening carpet. In the air, flying insects of all types gave them a wide berth as they passed, forewarned by the noise of their approach and frightened off by the great numbers of aerial warriors aloft. After about an hour or so, the Captain gestured downward and Buffalo looked to see the river Tonqua flowing far below. It was wide and greenish from this height and he could make out the shadows of many creatures, large and small, plying it's cool deep waters. A flash of silver upon the river to his left caught his eye... a school of fish had broken the surface, leaping into the air to escape the shadow of a much larger predator chasing them from the depths, intent on a meal.

Buffalo and the column continued due west towards far off Ikuskqua, still roughly two hours flying time away. With the river now already about ten miles behind them, Buffalo noticed a distinct change in the surrounding landscape below. The large jungle fern-trees were given over to much lower scrub and the terrain had become rocky and hilly. There were vast plains ahead with various herds of herbivorous insects of many kind grazing upon the tall grasses. Some Buffalo recognized while others were a completely new discovery to him. A nearby herd of colorful leafhoppers became somewhat spooked by the passage of the troops overhead and raised a dust cloud as they raced away to the south, running and leaping into one another in their frenzy to escape.

This place is just chock full of wonders thought Buffalo as they proceeded... for a short while later, the terrain quickly changed again, becoming one of tall rocky ridges and chiseled valleys, some of which contained some *very* deep chasms and gorges. It was just past these mini-mountains, another fifteen miles or so, that Buffalo noticed the Captain becoming somewhat more tense and rigid, (if that were possible), and Buffalo figured they must be drawing close to the land of their enemies. A barren escarpment before them led to a plateau of misty swampland and Buffalo could smell the foulness of the rotting vegetation long before he got above it. It was a land of sphagnum moss, fungi, and mold enveloped in a vapor of stench... a land of endless grayness and bogs with bubbling hot springs that belched sulfur as well as other unpleasantness.

Creepy crawlies abounded here and Buffalo could see huge centipedes, sowbugs, and silverfish, among others, scurrying through the mud beneath the swirling mists. It was significantly warmer here as well and Buffalo realized that this region was very likely the source of thermal heating that kept the life-cycle of the plants within the cavern thriving. It was also much darker than the cavern should be, almost like continual twilight, for the light-emitting lichens, the Low-atay, also suffered from the foul odors here and didn't grow above this land as profusely as elsewhere. All in all, it was a bleak and desperate place befitting the wretched mutant fly-humans that called it home.

Buffalo's observations were cut short as a staccato horn blast sounded directly behind him. He looked to the Captain who returned his gaze with a grim smile and pointed ahead. Buffalo looked to the distance to see the barren western wall of the cavern some five miles distant, devoid of any Alloway-tay at all... but with a huge and grotesque walled fortress-city hewn into the rock wall itself! Ikuskqua! It was massive and very medieval looking with huge but crumbling towers and spires. It was heavily fortified with a foreboding wall of ramparts and crenellated parapets lined with hundreds of embrasures from which to rain arrows down upon any advancing army. Dark banners hung from chains atop the spires and giant spikes of iron jutted from the very walls themselves. The booming of a deep-sounding drum began to well up and could be heard coming from somewhere in the direction of the menacing walled bastion. Some sort of wavering fuzzy dark line seemed to hang in the air before the walls, stretching from horizon to horizon. It confused Buffalo at first... until he realized that what he was seeing was the circling ranks of Ikuskqua's aerial army, poised to meet them in battle to protect their city!

"Fight well, my friend!" shouted the Captain over the drone of wings to Buffalo, "This day we make history settling an old score and rescuing our Princess... all in one day! To rid our land of these vile abominations will ensure happiness and peace throughout Kontonqua for generations to come! Hit them fast and hard, but never fly between two at once!" With those parting words of advice, the Captain gave the signal for the charge to begin and with a roar of beating wings, the ranks behind them quickly fanned out to either side. When a single advancing line had formed to match that of the enemy awaiting them, the Captain pointed rigidly ahead and the avenging aero-troops of Konton urged their mounts to double their speed... while lowering their pikes and lances and drawing their swords, maces, and flails!

"For Konton... for Kwa-I-Anya... for the Queen!" yelled the Captain. An answering shout reverberated among the Serpent ranks echoing the commander's rallying cry. In defiance, a warbling yell rose up from the holding line of defenders that faced them - - and then they too advanced... at even *greater* speed in a direct frontal formation to repel the charging line of Konton's Aero-troopers. Their weapons and tactics may have been crude but it was an unfortunate fact that the *flies* had a slight edge on both maneuverability and speed over the larger ebony flying battle-ants. Had they been flown by more than brutish grunts they might have proved an unstoppable threat to Konton. Thankfully, the ants were intuitively smarter... and tougher, and easier to control; very responsive to a deft touch.

It took mere seconds to bridge the gap and the two aerial combatant front lines rushed at each other to close with terrific speed, cutting through each other's ranks with weapons flailing. Soldiers were bellowing, screaming, and cursing as riders of both armies were injured or unseated, cut from their mounts to fall to their deaths in the pits of ooze below. Several ants and flies fell too... spiraling to their deaths as the result of lopped wings or legs and carrying their helpless and horrified riders with them to certain doom. Buffalo had opted to draw his great broadsword and picked his first victim from the onrushing line. A large and particularly ugly fly-warrior that was dressed entirely in black leather with short iron spikes studding his harness. He was waving a great mace over his head and bellowing as he advanced. He's just asking for it, Buffalo decided.

As the two were about to clash, Buffalo nudged his flyer to suddenly perform a snap-spin of 180°, and flying upside down, he urged the ant rapidly upward to pass directly over the head of the gruesome-faced mutant! This maneuver took place in the space of an instant and took the Ikuskquan brute entirely by surprise! He tried vainly to raise his cruel mace in a blind swing to protect himself, but Buffalo's longer sword, swung by the unleashed power of his massive right arm, split the grotesque head of the fly-rider right down the middle, separating his large reflective red eyes from each other right down to his neck!

A grim satisfaction brought a smile to Buffalo's lips but he had no time to revel in his kill...

at such speeds, the battle landscape changed rapidly! After the initial forward clash, both forces broke through each other's lines and quickly wheeled or looped to rejoin the attack, hoping to catch a slow enemy from behind. Buffalo's ant was incredibly responsive to his touch and righted itself and then actually spun in midair, a yaw maneuver, traveling backwards for a brief moment before the powerfully vibrating wings reversed its course to once again fly forward... to charge any attackers foolish enough to try following in its wake. Buffalo, with Silver, was quicker than the Ikusks and caught a burly Ikuskquan hammer-wielder by surprise in mid-turn, separating his gruesome head from his rotund body.

After that, the aerial battle lost its discipline and became an out-and-out melee... with individual ant and fly troops racing in all directions to try to gain an advantage, either chasing someone to make a kill, or attempting to escape from someone with similar intent! Zipping rapidly to the cavern's ceiling or diving dangerously through the swirling swamp mist, soldiers of both camps were engaged in one-on-one dogfighting in an all-out deadly game of "Tag".

Buffalo was confused and shook his head in disbelief. Hadn't anyone here ever learned the value of squadron *formation* flying? As a veteran pilot, Buffalo knew full-well the worth of a wingman... and a backup team! This was madness! But fortunately for Buffalo, his knowledge of aerial combat and use of WWII tactics kept him safe, at least for a time,... and tallied an impressive list of victims caught by surprise by his unusual and unpredictable maneuvers! But that only worked for a while. Unfortunately... perhaps it was the adrenalin of the battle, or perhaps Buffalo got a bit cocky after racking up sixteen mutant souls that would never again threaten Anya or her people... but just after disemboweling the flying steed of his seventeen victim, Buffalo foolishly wheeled to charge two Ikusks bearing down on him side-by-side... flying opposite to each other about thirty feet apart.

"Eighteen and nineteen are gonna be a snap", thought Buffalo as he whirled his great sword in a circle of death over his head and aimed to fly directly between the two foolish attackers... "Maybe I can take out both of these uglies with one pass!"

The parting advice of the Captain came back to him too late, *"...never fly between two at once..."* and Buffalo got trapped by the oldest Ikuskquan trick in the book. He saw two prime targets flying directly at him for a tempting meeting with the swing of his deadly blade... what he didn't see was the almost invisible looped strand of spider silk they stretched between them! Still, to his credit he *did* manage to sever the wing of the flyer to his right as they passed... but that didn't stop the trick maneuver from working... it just didn't work as planned. Buffalo too *should* have been caught in the snare and cut in two if the Ikusquan trick had gone as calculated.

As it happened, the disabled fly he had maimed spiraled outward and downward... but the brave warrior upon it's back, though doomed, still held fast to his end of the silken line. As he fell and the line was drawn taught, it had encircled the head of Buffalo's bonded mount "Silver" and with a sudden and shocking popping noise, the snare closed tight and the head of Buffalo's charger-ant was instantly separated from its body, dropping away and tumbling downward, it's jaws snapping futilely at the air as it fell to the swamps below! Buffalo bellowed in sheer anger and horror at the loss of his trusty flyer... Silver! How could he have been so *stupid*! The ant's decapitated body, not yet realizing that it was dead, still beat it's wings but it was rapidly losing altitude. It soon spiraled out of control and Buffalo hung on for dear life... he had never thought for an instant that his life would end this way, but he was facing certain death as he watched the foul mists of the Ikuskquan swamp draw frighteningly closer at incredible speed!

It was a dead tree that saved him... at least partially... it broke his fall. The ant's headless body, barely functioning, careened haphazardly directly into a rotten old trunk with twisted branches and it slowed their descent but threw Buffalo from his saddle. He tumbled end-over-end for a brief moment and landed flat on his back, knocking the wind from the big man's lungs. Had it been just mud he'd landed in, Buffalo might have gotten up and rejoined the battle somehow... but there were rocks in abundance here as well, and Buffalo's head made neat contact with one of them. He was gazing upward, trying with difficulty to breathe, gasping, watching a multitude of black dots zooming through the air, chasing one after another, as his vision blurred and all went black.

Chapter 19
"The Prince of Mutants"

Buffalo was still having trouble breathing... though now it felt as though he were drowning! He was gasping and spluttering for air as a cold torrent of water suddenly hit him in the face! He became aware of a great weight pressing down upon him as he slowly regained consciousness and opened his eyes. As his blurred vision focused, the first thing he saw was the black rough-hewn stonework floor he was kneeling upon. The puddle around him made the stone shine like wet coal. Another deluge hit him and he coughed and shook the water from his face and beard and looked upward. He was in a large dark hall with heavy black stonework walls and large black support columns ringing the room. Before him was a burly fly-warrior in barbaric leather trappings with a bucket in his hands, laughing... which was actually something more like burbling. His faceted red eyes stared at Buffalo unblinkingly, but his tubular drooling mouth-parts were twisted in a grimace that could somewhat be described as a smile as he was openly quite amused with his soaking wake-up-call of the Kontonquan stranger. Having done his job, he shuffled off to the wings of the large hall, chuckling to himself as he went.

With the corpulent fly-mutant out of the way, Buffalo could see a large dark throne about thirty yards away against the far wall of the darkened gallery. It was a bulky block of black obsidian with spires and spikes that rose halfway up the wall. Seated in a diagonal slouch, and glaring angrily, was a lanky man in layered robes of silk. The garment had vivid images and intricate designs delicately embroidered all over it in muted colors of maroon and indigo... and was trimmed with cobalt-blue collar and sleeves.

The reclining figure had to be Prince Bik-cu', but not at all the gruesome "King-of-Mutants" that Buffalo had expected... he was taller than most and looked to be well muscled. His skin was not of the grayish-green pallor that the Ikuskquan warriors displayed, but rather bronzed more like the people of Konton. He had a long aquiline nose and cruel thin lips. A shock of glossy black hair covered his forehead and almost obscured the thick black unibrow that was knit in an angry "V" above his eyes. It was the eyes however that gave him away... while the lids were still shaped like a human's, the entire orb within had been replaced with the bright red iridescent facets of a housefly.

Buffalo heard the rattle of chain-links and noticed a figure in white, lying prone off to one side at the base of the throne. Anya! Somehow, even in her state of despair, totally disheveled and with her long dark hair covering half her elfin face, she still managed to look radiant and delectable despite being obviously miserable. Her normal raiment had been replaced with a simple white diaphanous slave's tunic. Her jewelry was gone, the wristlets and armbands gone, her sandals were gone and she was left barefoot... even the tinkling bells she wore around her slender ankle had been taken... and replaced with a heavy iron shackle. She looked at Buffalo longingly but with agonizing worry and shame. Shame that he should see her thus, brought so low. Worry because she knew what Bik-cu' was capable of, and what the valiant out-worlder would soon endure... if he could.

"Anya!" yelled Buffalo as renewed anger and frustration sent a surge of adrenalin to his mighty muscles and he tried to rise from the floor, fully intending to close his hands around Bik-cu's throat. But the weight he'd felt upon awakening was a huge wooden yoke across his shoulders that his arms and wrists were shackled to... and the yoke was chained to the floor. He grunted and stiffened with all his might against the bonds but even Buffalo's great strength could not budge those thick chains. Someone behind him kicked him savagely in the kidneys and laughed with a choking gurgling sound. Another joined in the fun. And another. Anya felt so helpless and horrified by Buffalo's torment that she hung her head and sobbed quietly to herself... not wanting Bik-cu' to have the satisfaction of seeing her inner pain.

"Enough!" commanded Bik-cu', "I wish to speak with the barbarian surface-dweller... Buffalo... Brewster." Buffalo had only told a select few his surname... which the Prince mangled entirely with his thick Ikuskquan accent... but how had he come by it?

Buffalo grunted through clenched teeth, subduing the pain of the recent beating, and shot an angry but questioning look towards Bik-cu'. His wet hair hung bedraggled across his stern face but it wasn't enough to hide the daggers that would've flown from his eyes if he could but will it.

"Surprised?" continued the Prince in a bored slimy voice, "My spies have kept me well informed of everything there is to know about you... *and* that sorry lot of younglings you've been dragging along behind you. Since the first day you arrived at Konton. So, excuse me for not being astonished by your appearance... or if I don't grovel, worried that

319

you're some kind of God... or honor you as a foreign *guest* here in this cavern prison we call Kontonqua. You see, unlike those fools across the river, I've never doubted the legends of our ancestors, in fact, I've always rather fancied the existence of a surface world... and here you are... living proof. Unfortunately, you are of little use to us... since you are obviously just as trapped as we.

And *still* those misguided idiots in Konton guard the only known exit and choose to worship it... when we should be *digging* our way through! They gave up ages ago and decided it was for the best to just remain here and try to prosper, turning the exit path into a temple! That was *their* decision... not *ours!* We would have persevered... kept at it for as long as it took to get through. They robbed us of a chance for a way out, back to the land of sun and moon and the hunt... and *forced* us to stay in this insect hell-hole by blocking and guarding the only known exit. But they didn't teach you about any of *that...* did they?"

Bik-cu' paused to wipe some froth from his lips with the corner of his silken sleeve. He glared at Buffalo for a while, then sighed and continued more calmly. "Did you really think that you could so brazenly attack my city? It was almost pitiful to witness such courageous but hopeless carnage. In the end, those misguided Serpent puppets were repulsed as always... our city may not be in the best of repair, but we are far from weak... and we have the numbers. My soldiers are loyal to *me...* because I give them what they seek.... plenty of meat for their bellies, honey wine for their troubles, and women as they want them... even the occasional Konton maiden. And we both know what a comfort *they* can be..." he trailed off and looked towards Anya with a malicious and depraved grin.   Buffalo fairly bellowed in anger and threw himself upwards once more.   The wooden yoke creaked against his onslaught and the chains were held rigid from the floor making little crackling noises.   Several Ikuskquan guards behind him gasped at his superhuman attempt to escape... but the bonds and shackles held firm.

Bik-cu' chuckled softly, "Spirited effort!" he applauded, "Most impressive... but useless just the same. However... *you* are not useless to me. You have a purpose. That is why you are not dead. You see, I not only know everything about you and your doings in Konton... but I also know how you feel about this precious jewel at my side... the Kwa-Ia. Despite what they have told you over in that hive of lies, Ikuskqua is not depraved, not decadently descending into ruin.   It's true, we have some *shortcomings* in our technological abilities... and at times, my men can be admittedly rather crude... but we are still very much a civilization, and therefore the concept of "civility" is still a part of our principles.

That is why I would much prefer that this maiden daughter of Konton at my feet would *willingly* accept my *generous* offer to be my... consort.   I don't wish to spend every night sleeplessly awaiting a dagger in my ribs. Yet my patience is wearing thin... she doesn't seem to truly appreciate me... yet. That's where your services are required. I'm well aware of how you two feel about each other... you may both live in naive denial, but it's been quite obvious to those around you, you don't hide it well. My spies have left out no details. So, I'm thinking that *you* might coerce the girl where I have failed... in fact, I believe you'll soon be screaming and begging her to offer her loyalty to me... to be my wife. And as long as you live... I don't think she'll ever betray me."

"You're mad... you're insane!" Buffalo spat through his clenched jaw.

"We'll see..." and Prince Bik-cu' nodded curtly to his gathered minions. The audience was over.

"No! Please!" pleaded Anya, crawling over and grabbing the Prince's robes, "I beg you... do not do this!"

"Do you *concede* already?" purred the Prince. Anya bowed her head and let go of the robes in hopelessness. After a moment she replied. "No..." she whispered quietly.

A veritable horde of Ikuskquan soldiers surrounded Buffalo, loosening his chains, but not the great wooden yoke. He struggled heroically against them but there were just too many of the brutes. "Don't do it, Anya!" he bellowed and received a punch to the ribs which he ignored, "Don't ever give in! They'll kill me anyway! Don't let that bastard have you!" and his booming voice became muffled as he was hustled to the back of the main throne chamber and into one of the adjoining side rooms.

A few tense moments later, that seemed like hours, Buffalo's imploring counsel was replaced with screams. Not the shrill screams of a man in fear or a coward... but rather the deep defiant grunting screams of a tortured man refusing to bow to his enemies, stubbornly defying their attempts to reduce him to a trembling wretch.

*   *   *   *   *   *   *

The exact methods of torture the Ikuskquan inquisitors employed are not important, suffice it to say that Buffalo held out against means most foul and well into the night... before he finally passed out beyond their abilities to reawaken him once more to extend their amusement.

Chapter 20
"Escape"

Buffalo felt cool water on his face once again... but not the torrent of a tossed bucket... someone was dabbing at his brow with a wet cloth. He opened his eyes and it was very dark. A dirty undernourished scraggly man with long unkempt dusky hair was patting at his face with an even dirtier rag that smelled faintly of urine. "How are you, my friend?" spoke the tattered soul. Buffalo stirred and attempted to rise... he was bone-achingly sore and very raw in places. Parts of him stung like the devil. "You have slept for more than three days..." offered the stranger, " I wasn't at all sure you would ever awaken..."

Buffalo tested his limbs... thankfully, nothing seemed broken. He sat up covered in moldy straw and took inventory of his body. He was hurt pretty badly, but nothing was done to him that time couldn't repair. He still wore his Konton warrior harness but with empty scabbards of course... and he smelled *terrible!* Obviously, one doesn't make use of facilities when one is in a coma... and the body doesn't stop functioning just because you're asleep... he stunk and he was very uncomfortable.

"Who... are you?" Buffalo muttered softly.

"I am Tsil-se-Ulkul... you can call me Tsil," said the bedraggled man. "So, it is *true.* I have heard rumors of strangers in our lands... even down here where all is forgotten."

Buffalo looked around to see where "here" was. The room had a very low ceiling, it was doubtful he could even stand fully upright in it. It was dark stone block everywhere he looked but for a heavy wooden door set at one end and a tiny rounded slit of a window near the ceiling at the other. The floor was covered in the same moldy straw that clung to his body and he could hear the rush of water coming from somewhere. "Let me guess...dungeon?" theorized Buffalo. The dirty prisoner, for that is what he was, nodded in affirmation.

"Call me Buffalo. How long have you been... here?" asked the big man.

"Ah, well... let's see... four years, roughly." said Tsil counting on his fingers, "I was the Kontonquan Captain of the Flying Royal Dragon-Guard of the Queen you know... captured during the renowned Lake Chinotonk Campaign."

"*Dragon* Guard? The Queen is protected by the *Serpent* Guard... and has been since she took over from her mother six years ago," stated Buffalo.

Tsil looked confused and then a bit sad as he looked downcast at the floor, "Maybe it has been somewhat longer..." he mumbled. But then he suddenly brightened and said, "But we can *leave* now!"

"What?" queried Buffalo, somewhat skeptical, "How's that possible?"

"Come, follow me," beckoned Captain Tsil. And he led the grunting and groaning stranger, who at first had a bit of trouble standing, around a corner of the "L" shaped room. The sound of water grew louder and Buffalo saw where it was coming from. Against the wall, along the floor, there was a stone drain with a curved arch. It was comprised of a well deep enough for one person to stand and bathe in on the inside of the dungeon wall, separated by thick iron bars from a gushing torrent of water that flowed along in one of the city's sewer tunnels. "Most of those are already loose," said Tsil with pride, pointing to the heavy iron bars, "I've been working on them for years.... with *this*!" and he produced a feeble bit of scrap metal that may have once been a fork. "With your muscles, we shouldn't have any further trouble at all!" he added.

Buffalo achingly climbed down into the cool refreshing water of the bathing well... it felt wonderfully rejuvenating though it smelled rather foul... and he took the time to clean himself and soak his face and scrub his hair. It was sewer water, but the eddy formed in the cell was mostly clean as the torrent that rushed past a few feet away on the other side of the bars carried most of the city refuse rapidly downstream. When he'd sufficiently restored his humanity, Buffalo tossed the water from his hair and beard and turned to Captain Tsil. "So... what's the plan?"

Tsil explained that he'd intended to escape soon anyway by himself... until the huge foreigner had been placed in his cell. It was then that he realized that the two of them would have a better chance together... and that Buffalo's strength could save him weeks of work on the sewer bars... not to mention bettering his chances of crossing the great swamp beyond.

Buffalo shook his head, "No good... I came here to rescue Anya, the princess of Konton, and I'm not leaving without her."

Captain Tsil became visibly agitated and counseled against it... impossible he said; the odds were not in their favor, the Ikuskquan guardsmen were too powerful and too many, and chances were Buffalo would die to no avail. And where would that leave her? Better to sneak across the swamps, make their way back to Konton, and return with a guerilla force, entering the city back through the unprotected sewer system and surprising the Ikusks from within.

Buffalo could see the wisdom in Captain Tsil's advice... and he knew he needed to be rational and honest with himself. He needed *time* to heal. He wouldn't be the man he had been for weeks yet. The Ikuskquan interrogators were very talented at inflicting pain and exuberant in their work.

He turned to the five iron bars that stood in the way of freedom and grabbed the first one on the left... he pushed and it popped out easily. "See?" said Captain Tsil proudly and excitedly, "I have been very busy in my imprisonment!"

Buffalo grabbed the next bar and it hardly budged. He tried the rest and none of them even wiggled... they would have to remove at least three to escape! He turned to Tsil, "Six years and that's all you managed to do? *One* bar?" Tsil looked hurt.

Buffalo turned his attention back to the sewer bars and grabbed the second with both of his huge paws. Pushing his back against the well wall for support, he also brought up one knee to add leverage to the force he exerted against the thick iron bar of the old cistern barricade. Buffalo grunted and closed his eyes to concentrate as he applied as much pressure as he could possibly muster. The stone lintel block of the arch was rotted by years of disrepair and excessive moisture. He felt the bar begin to give and then with a snapping groan the great block which the bars were set into cracked and crumbled as half the block separated and fell into the rushing waters of the sewer culvert. All the bars were now loose and standing askew.

"I knew you could do it!" exclaimed Captain Tsil.

"You probably loosened 'em..." offered Buffalo in an effort to assuage the Captain's years of ineffectualness. "When do we go?" he asked.

"Now!" said the Captain with enthusiastic delight. "It's not like we have luggage!" Tsil took a moment to glance around the barren dank cell as though checking for belongings. Then his dark eyes widened slyly and he said, "Unless you'd like to wait for the next round of "negotiations" with our captors..."

"Uh... no," countered Buffalo, and glanced sideways at Tsil quizzically, "You're a strange one for a Konton Captain..." Captain Tsil looked him in the eye and smiled a broad impish grin.

Buffalo turned and pushed the remaining bars aside and stepped into the torrent of the city's sewer system. Captain Tsil followed, easing himself down into the bathing well and then through the aperture to join Buffalo, then taking point to lead the way to freedom. Carefully, the two liberated prisoners, in chest-high water, made their way along the sewer tunnel towards a distant light... wary of losing their footing in the fast rushing stream.

"Well, this is certainly a welcome change from my past six years of captivity!" said the delightfully emancipated Captain.

"I dunno..." returned Buffalo. "Seems like I've done this tunnel thing before...."

But with arms extended to the slimy culvert walls to steady themselves against the current, they progressed steadfastly, and it wasn't really that long before they reached the end of the tunnel and Buffalo saw that they had a *real* chance of escape after all. The conduit had led to an opening in the fortress wall where the city's sewage discharge poured into a polluted pool maybe twenty feet below. There had once been bars here too, but the continual rush of waste water had rusted them through long ago. Looking outward, he could see the vast mist-enshrouded swamps that completely encircled Ikuskqua. If they could but avoid the multitude of unpleasant insect monsters that dwelled there, the mist would effectively hide their escape. How long it would take to make their way back home, almost two hundred miles - - over the plateau, across the hills and ravines, across the vast plains, swimming the river Tonqua, through the jungles surrounding Konton again - - Buffalo had no idea. Without weapons, Buffalo sort of doubted it could be done at all. But, to stay here was madness, out there at least was opportunity.

Captain Tsil looked at Buffalo with that grin again and counted, "One, two, *three...*" and on three he leaped from the sill of the effluvial vent to ride the waterfall of sewage into the pool below... with Buffalo close behind.

They broke the surface spluttering and swam to the shore of the open cesspool. Dragging themselves out upon the bank of dead grass, they chuckled quietly for a moment at each other's brownish muck-covered appearance and unusual aroma... then they got quickly serious again and looked stealthily around. No alarms, no shouts, no one in sight. It looked as though they were, so far, successfully "on the lam". Tsil arose and while hunched over began heading east, padding silently away from the horrible walled city of Ikusks. Buffalo followed in his footsteps and the two hurried along taking full advantage of the swirling mists and pausing to take cover wherever cover could be found. They passed another pool and Buffalo hissed to Tsil to get his attention. He motioned that he wished to stop momentarily... and he lowered himself into the pool of reasonably fresh water to clean the drying accumulated sewer muck from his body and clothes. Captain Tsil wasted no time to do the same. The risk of water predators was great, but the humane comfort achieved was significant.

Presently, soaked but much cleaner, Buffalo and Captain Tsil resumed their escape and threaded their way carefully through the foul swamp, skirting sulfuric hot-springs and avoiding many dangerous creepy crawlies by hiding behind dead trees and rocks until they'd passed. They had traveled about a mile from the city's walls when they heard voices ahead in the fog. Sneaking carefully, they drew closer and hid behind a large fallen log to reconnoiter the situation before them.

Two brawny Ikusks, with a fly-drawn sledge, were gathering weapons and the fallen bodies of warriors that littered the ground from the recent aerial battle. "I don't see why I always have to draw this detail..." muttered one of the workers gutturally, "Damned gruesome work this is... what'd I ever do to deserve this..."

"Aww, shut it, will you?" griped the other, "You never stop complaining. But it's not going to change anything, is it? At least we're not mucking out the stables or the hatchery..."

The second brute was referring to the "farm"... just to the north of Ikuskqua. Located there was a heavily-guarded niche in the cavern wall where the Ikuskquans raised their flies and maggots for meat, draught use, and for mounts. Long ago, the flies had bred indiscriminately throughout the swamps, but the Ikusk had managed to domesticate and control the fly population to serve their needs.

Buffalo and Tsil watched as the two thugs scavenged the area, collecting only loot and their own fallen comrades. Konton soldiers were routinely stripped of any valuables and rolled into the nearest pool or bog. Buffalo and Tsil looked at one another and at the fly attached to the wooden sledge. They both had the same idea. Creeping stealthily around unseen and unheard to the far side of the sledge, Tsil kept vigil while Buffalo quickly selected a set of daggers and swords for the pair to wield. Silently they waited behind a nearby stump for the two unfortunate Ikuskquans to return with another body. The pair were taken entirely by surprise as the huge foreign giant and the scraggly Kontonquan Captain leapt before them brandishing swords! They dropped the body they were lugging between them and tried in vain to draw their own weapons, but their efforts culminated in nothing more than a choked gurgle as Buffalo's mighty swing separated one's head from his body and Tsil's rapid lunge drove a sword point deep into the neck of the other. They both fell twitching to the ground and Buffalo checked around, looking and listening, to assure himself that their ambush had not drawn attention. Working together in silence, Buffalo and Tsil crept to the front of the sledge and took opposite sides of the gruesomely hairy draught insect and quickly undid the harnesses that tethered the fly to the sledge.

Unlike the ants, which came in different varieties and were assigned different tasks depending on their size and ability to fly or work as draught animals, the Ikuskquan flies only came in one form. Large brownish-iridescent hairy brutes with wings... and being winged, they were *all* capable of flight. And smelled terrible. As they led

331

the large insect from it's tack, Buffalo stepped in front of the beast and looked it right in the face. It was pretty horrible. It's lifeless red-faceted eyes reflected hundreds of Buffalo heads, it's short pulpy antennae jerked spasmodically, and it's fleshy proboscis writhed and drooled while making soft slobbering noises.

"What are you doing?" asked Captain Tsil while he was gathering up several lengths of leather bridle from the sledge's harness.

"Waiting for the fly to imprint me with it's antennae, so it'll let me ride it." returned Buffalo.

Captain Tsil stifled a howl of laughter that would have otherwise given them away and had to pause, holding onto the side of the sledge for support, as he looked down at the mud and waited for his impulse to subside. He took a deep breath and with tears in his eyes turned to Buffalo again... and almost started giggling again as soon as he looked into the confused big man's eyes.

"I... I haven't laughed... like that... in years," Tsil managed haltingly. "Buffalo... my friend... only the Aktz, the ants, imprint! These flies are stupid and will let *anyone* ride them... if you can coax them into the air that is."

Buffalo felt suddenly foolish and annoyed. Grumpily he asked, "What's with the leather straps?"

"Well... we have ourselves a fly, but no saddle or bridle. I think we can make do with these... but it will be tricky. Flies are difficult to control even with the proper tack. They're very erratic fliers." Tsil busied himself rigging up a crude harness around the head of the skittish beast. When he'd finished, he hopped atop the fly and settled himself directly behind it's head, gripping firmly with his legs and knees. He patted the hairy brown carapace behind him and nodded to Buffalo who soon joined him. He handed Buffalo a set of reins that he had passed around the belly of the fly. "Hang on tight to these," he advised, "this flight might be very unpredictable... but with any luck, we could be in Konton in hours instead of weeks!"

Captain Tsil nudged the fly... he rocked forward... he slapped the crude reins he held against the sides of the fly's head... the fly just flitted about jerkily on the ground. Finally, he just balled up his fist and bonked the fly atop the head between the glossy red eyes. Success! The fly, irritated by these unknown and clumsy passengers, spread it's wings and lifted, with some difficulty under the combined weight of the two riders, into the mists.

Tsil successfully turned the fly *away* from the walls of Ikuskqua and headed somewhat eastward. They both knew the added risks involved by flying and hoped desperately that they hadn't been spotted from the walls or towers. To be set upon now, by a company of Ikusks bent on recapturing them, would be a crushing defeat... as they would be nearly impossible to outrun. But if nothing else, the Ikuskquan fly was fairly fast and stayed low, and they left the swamps behind them shortly and dipped down over the edge of the plateau where they knew that they were finally out of view of the fortress *city* at least... they now had to pray they didn't stumble across a random raiding or hunting party!

Buffalo was used to the sturdy flying ants and their strong deliberate flight... the grotesque fly they were riding was inconsistent and irregular in its handling and changed paths unpredictably. Tsil was obviously having much difficulty in controlling it. "I cannot get him to rise much," he shouted back to

Buffalo over the high-pitched whine of the fly's thrumming wings. "I cannot get altitude... we may be too heavy riding together. If we do not climb, we will not make it over the hills just ahead... but at least we will have escaped our Ikuskquan captors with enough distance to make it extremely difficult for them to find us again! *And* we'll have cut at least five days walking time from our journey."

But, as they neared the craggy mountains and ravines that separated them from the plains and river, things got much worse quickly. Buffalo had earlier noted, on the flight to Ikuskqua, how desolate and rocky, jagged and barren, this precipitous topography was... with its bleak cliffs and bottomless canyons. They were frightfully close to impacting a rock or cliff as the fly they were riding was apparently tiring fast and getting sloppy in it's flight. It was painfully obvious that the laboring fly would be unable to make it over the high hills that loomed before them.

Captain Tsil informed Buffalo of his intent to attempt a landing with the fatigued insect before it killed them all. Instead, to both Buffalo's and Tsil's horror, it suddenly dipped into the nearest chasm and dropped like a stone, exhausted and spent!

Chapter 21
"In the Spider's Lair"

Captain Tsil did his utmost to goad the fly back to normal flight, but the fly was near death and its wings were flitting only occasionally... enough perhaps to prevent them from a *fatal* crash if they were lucky... but the chasm was very deep and they'd not seen the bottom yet! (What Tsil and Buffalo had not known was that the fly they'd hijacked for their escape was an aged fellow that was relegated to sledge duty because he was considered no longer *fit* to fly!). Buffalo looked around in desperation... there was nothing down here that looked to be of any use to save them... though there was, oddly, vegetation growing here whereas there hadn't been above. Mostly lianas and fungi. Huge mushrooms sprouted from the walls and the ravine abundantly flourished with them. The chasm was yet another mystery... another microcosm of life; different bugs, different plants... each eking out an existence hidden far from the predominant ecosystem of the cavern floor higher up.

Finally, they saw the bottom of the ravine and braced for impact... it was lushly covered in giant mushrooms that might just break their fall! But the fly they were riding to their doom had a sudden revival and pulled out of the dive and leveled off, zipping crazily along the length of the gorge about thirty feet above its base. It was weaving uncontrollably and threatened to unseat them by smacking one side of the narrow walls of the ravine or the other... Tsil had no control whatsoever. The fly was soon laboring again and they knew that its end was near... its flitting wings and strained breathing were more like death throes...involuntary spasms. Flying this way was madness and they desperately wished to land, but the dying fly's wild dash determined their fate for them. The careening fly flew blindly right into an immense spider's web that had been constructed to stretch across the bottom of the gorge!

Like flying into a great trampoline, the sticky web elastically bent to completely absorb and entrap the fly, nullifying its forward momentum, but Tsil and Buffalo were thrown to either side by the impact and bounced and rolled once or twice as the web oscillated back and forth sickeningly and then finally returned to it's static position. Buffalo had landed to the fly's lower right and was not really stuck... he was fortunate enough to have landed on his side and not enough of the web strands were in contact with his body to really hold him fast... they were designed for larger prey.

Captain Tsil, unfortunately, was on the other side of the fly and flat on his back, spread-eagled, and too weak from years of captivity to resist the sticky strands despite his struggles. "Whatever you do," he shouted, "move slowly and do not vibrate the web!" But their mount heeded no such advice... in its frantic attempt to cling to life, it kept flitting its wings and moving its legs. The resulting vibrations were plenty enough of a signal to bring the huge predatory owner of the web out from its hiding place among the rocks to see if its next meal had been snared!

It was a huge glossy black-and-yellow banded spider with legs that were more brownish than black nearest to its body... an Orb-Weaver! It moved incredibly quickly and headed directly for the dying fly, navigating the sticky thin strands of web like an expert tightrope walker. Each of its eight long thin legs were placed with amazing precision upon each nexus of web strand as it bore down on its helpless prey. It paused momentarily just before the dying fly, and then with a final leap, it pounced and sank its fangs deep into the softer tissues of the fly's neck...and then, without even waiting for the fly to expire, the monster spider doubled its abdomen under and forward and began spewing silk from the glands located there. Expertly, the gigantic spider began rolling the fly with its front legs while covering it with its silky secretions. In mere moments, the live fly they'd been riding was entombed in a silken cocoon which still shook occasionally with the last feeble spasms of the victim trapped inside!

Buffalo had no idea what to do... he *could* manage to make his way upon the web... but to do what? Their fly-mount was doomed and not worth the effort to save it. To try and free Captain Tsil might alert the behemoth spider to attack *them!* Buffalo, man of action, remained still instead... and hoped the great spider would soon return to its hiding place and allow him to quietly free the Captain. But though he calmly waited for the spider to leave, the spider had no such intention. As soon as it was done with spinning the fly's cocoon, it made its way haltingly to investigate Captain Tsil! With a curse, Buffalo started picking his way sideways across the web to aid Tsil... he had to move carefully and deliberately, with focused precision... the web was too sticky to allow more than three points of contact; his boot soles and one hand... he held his stolen iron sword at the ready in the other. If he slipped, he could become hopelessly entangled in the spider silk and both of them would become spider snacks!

Pull up one foot and feel the sticky strand release with a "twang", step to the next open space to the left and balance upright, so the right hand can be pulled free of the web. Then, quickly grab the next strand over to the left before you either fall backwards to the ravine floor or forwards back into the web! Repeat as quickly as humanly possible!

Agonizingly slowly, Buffalo used this method to cover the distance between himself and Tsil... but it was a losing race. The giant Orb-Weaver was deftly maneuvering the strands and before Buffalo could intervene, it pounced upon Captain Tsil, just the same as it had the fly, and sank it's sharp fangs into the Captain's chest, pumping its venom into Tsil's quivering body... venom that would very soon begin turning his insides into suckable goo! To his credit, Captain Tsil never once screamed or cried out. Buffalo loosed a primal yell, enraged at the loss of his friend and liberator... he was so close to saving him! Within three more strands, he was close enough to the spider's backside to make an attack... too late to save Captain Tsil... but the Orb-Weaver would pay.

Once more the powerful shoulders heaved and Buffalo's Ikuskquan sword swung through the air with an audible "swoosh"! The iron blade clove into the spider's abdomen and released a torrent of greenish ooze, but the spider wasn't defeated that easyily... it squealed a horrible high-pitched whine and turned to face this new challenge! It wheeled quickly and Buffalo was suddenly facing a furious foe that fixed its eight eyes upon him with deadly intent! The Orb-Weaver lunged forward with its glossy pointed fangs aimed at Buffalo's throat and Buffalo parried with his sword held upright between them. Holding on to the web for dear life with his right hand, his back almost pressed into the sticky strands, Buffalo struggled to hold the dripping fangs from piercing him. With the sword held rigidly aloft between them, it was force against force, will against will, like a deadly arm-wrestling tournament... but ever so slowly Buffalo managed to force the angry brute back until he had him almost at arm's length. Buffalo then suddenly ducked and pulled his arm down quickly, slicing the spider's face between it's drooling fangs as he did so. The spider was caught off guard and its relentless force against the blade caused it to lunge forward when resistance from the sword was suddenly removed...but Buffalo was no longer in its target path. His feint maneuver had left him crouching below the spider's head! Buffalo wasted no time, this was his advantage, and balancing in a squatting position upon the spider's web, he used both hands to drive his sword upwards into the spider's unprotected chin... and kept pushing the sharp blade upwards until he met with what he hoped was the spider's brain! The giant Orb-Weaver thrashed about with a blood-curdling death scream and then rolled over and bounced along the web to fall lifeless with a great thud to the chasm's floor... landing in a cluster of large dirty-white mushrooms that released a cloud of spores.

Buffalo, shook himself... had he really managed to kill a giant *spider*... single-handedly? A man hard pressed can rise to the most amazing challenges, he thought. But he quickly turned his attention back to Captain Tsil... even though he knew there was nothing he could do for the man. He made his way across the web to where the Captain was lying... but Tsil was barely alive. He was frothing at the mouth and as Buffalo drew close he managed to whisper, "Thank you for getting me out... freedom is... grand." and his eyes glazed over and his fitful breathing stopped. Buffalo suddenly felt like all hope and energy had just spilled from his body. He was totally sapped by the unexpected unfair loss of his new-found rescued friend. He placed his hand on the Captain's chest and bowed his head in a moment of deep respect... he would make certain that this man and his accomplishments would not be forgotten in Kontonquan history.

But inwardly, he felt as though he was now totally doomed to oblivion... how could he get out of this situation alone? Without assistance, how was he going to get back to Konton? How could he rescue Anya? He was stuck at the bottom of a precipitous gorge with no ride, no guide, no food or water... and at the mercy of untold giant insect predators... with nothing more than a couple of swords and daggers. All his efforts... and those of Captain Tsil... had been for naught.

The web he was perched upon vibrated a bit. He glanced over at their mummified mount and saw no movement. Buffalo stood balancing upon the strands of web, beside Tsil, and looked about... up and down the narrow endless chasm in both directions. It looked bleak. However, as observed earlier, there *was* at least vegetation down here... maybe he could find something to eat, and perhaps a spring, or a rivulet of water leaking down the sides of the ravine. The web vibrated again and he looked towards the wrapped body of their kidnapped fly... nothing twitched... but then flies are so... spastic.

After relieving Captain Tsil of the weapons he would no longer need, Buffalo made his way stickily downward to the floor of the chasm... he felt that vibration again before he got there. "What the heck *is* that..." Buffalo wondered. He stopped and looked around. There... at the base of the web, far to the side, was a great big ball of spider silk... about the size of a school bus! It wiggled and buzzed and then stopped. It was apparently another fresh meal for the giant Orb-Weaver, but it wasn't quite dead. It was getting steadily darker in the ravine and Buffalo realized that the cavern's lichens high above were changing over to nighttime. It was just as well... Buffalo was exhausted anyway. Still pained by the injuries inflicted by the Ikuskquan interrogators, and the expenditure of energy just holding on to the giant housefly's erratic and wild flight, not to mention going one-on-one with a gigantic spider... Buffalo was ready to sleep the sleep of ages. He crawled behind a barricade of rocks hidden by some tall toadstools and was asleep in an instant.

Chapter 22
"Black Beauty"

When Buffalo awoke, it was light again... if you could call it that, for being deep down within the crevasse, it was almost perpetually dim down there. His great worn-out muscles fairly screamed against movement of any sort, but he eventually managed to rouse himself. He looked about and realized how lucky he'd been to have made it through the night without being eaten by one of the denizens of this ravine. There were various huge ugly beasts, like millipedes and giant sow bugs meandering about the place... shuffling along the floor and adhering to the walls of the canyon. They were really disinterested detritus-feeders foraging amongst the various fungi for dead vegetation and were no threat to Buffalo whatsoever... but he didn't know it at the time.

Buffalo heard a welcome drip of water nearby and found a steady stream of droplets cascading down the rocks from above... he hovered his tongue beneath the irregular flow and tasted it... it was sweet and clean to the palette. He heard that vibration again and looked to see that bus-sized cocoon still palpitating with movement. Buffalo explored the immediate area and found some odd Amak-looking fruits nearby on a scrubby bush, seemingly of a very different variety. He considered at first that they might not be as edible as the ones with which he was already familiar, but he decided to try a bite... and then eat more later if he didn't expire in the meantime. By now an expert, he deftly handled the gelatinous meal with precision and derived a welcome burst of energy from its high fructose content. That giant cocoon started throbbing again.

Maybe it was because Buffalo himself had so recently been a prisoner... maybe it was because he felt so lonely at the bottom of the chasm... maybe he just felt charitable... but the entombment of a living entity, even a stupid bug, encased in an inescapable cocoon of suffocating death at the bottom of this God-forsaken ravine, bothered him. He knew it was madness. He knew it could end very badly... for him! But despite the risks, Buffalo felt a compassion that could not let him ignore the plight of the trapped insect within the cocoon.

Very carefully, Buffalo climbed back onto the Orb-Weaver's web and made his way over the top of the gigantic silk-wrapped behemoth. He drew the stolen dagger he'd acquired from the magnanimous Ikuskquan corpse-detail and plunged it into the silk strands at one end. The cords were elastic and strong, but they were no match for a good sharp iron-bladed knife. Buffalo continued to cut, separating the cocoon in two until he reached about midpoint... he realized then that he should probably have a contingency plan in case the insect trapped within should not be at all pleased with its release by its savior. There was a rock ledge in the cliff-wall off to his left, near the butt-end of the cocoon, that he felt he could successfully defend... if he could get to it before the ungrateful beast turned upon him!

Satisfied by "Plan B", Buffalo renewed his efforts to free the monster contained within the confining silken tomb. When his blade had cut through the final strands at the end of the pill-shaped vault, Buffalo prepared to leap to the safety of the rock ledge. But as the halves of the great cocoon began to separate with a cottony rending sound, Buffalo realized that the poor creature inside was in no shape to be a threat. The cocoon split open slowly and out spilled a giant all-black Bumble Bee which tumbled to the ground and remained where it landed, exhausted and near death.

Buffalo carefully picked his way back down the web and slowly walked in what he felt was a safe enough circle around the enormous bee lying upon its side. Moving from the back end foreword, he noted the large cruel stinger at the tip of the slowly throbbing abdomen, the heavily fuzzy thorax that should have been yellow but was all dusky black, (at least as compared to the surface-world variety...), the long gray glassy wings folded neatly upon its back, the sturdy legs, and the thick antennae atop the large head with its huge dense black eyes. The combination of glossy-black and soft dusky matte-black was extremely appealing to Buffalo... menacing and at the same time very sleek, like the new all-black '52 Mercury automobile Buffalo had seen and longed for in Life magazine... in another world.

Buffalo walked to the front of the great Bee and stood silently gazing into the large black orbs that were its compound eyes. Shark's eyes seem lifeless, devoid of understanding and emotion... the Aktz, or ants here in Kontonqua, as cooperative as they were, had a similar quality... eyes that hinted at intelligence but were seemingly barren of feeling or passion. This gigantic Bee, brought so low in its existence, seemed not to share that lifeless *distant* feature... there seemed somehow to be a life force behind them, a comprehension... a compassion. Buffalo extended his hand and placed it upon the side of the large Bumble Bee's head... he felt a brief sense of communion and then realized the insanity of his act. He was well within reach of the massive mandibles and if the bee had chosen to, he would be minced Buffalo right now.

But the great bee made no such aggressive move... and Buffalo backed away and returned to the tiny rivulet of water he'd earlier discovered. Using a small mushroom cap as a bowl, Buffalo gathered an inch or so of water and carefully brought it to the mouth of the almost lifeless Bee. It's mouthparts extended into the tiny pool and sucked up the welcome moisture with an audible slurp and an almost visible relief. Buffalo repeated the gesture... and since he hadn't doubled over and died a horribly painful death from the possible poisoning of the unknown variety of Amak, he ate heartily of the magenta/purplish hairy fruit and brought some to the huge Bee as well. The great beast ate slowly, but didn't miss a drop of the succulent treat.

Buffalo looked over the great Bumble Bee and checked all its appendages... everything seemed to be in order. He next checked the body of the immense brute and soon found the entry wounds of the Orb-Weaver's fangs. The twin piercings were located at the top of the bushy thorax but didn't seem deep... maybe the giant spider had not gotten a good solid hit upon its victim. As to why the venom wasn't completely debilitating the Bee, by turning its insides to mush, Buffalo couldn't be sure. Maybe the Bee had a natural defense against the spider's toxin, maybe the spider just failed miserably in its attack, in any event, the Bee seemed to be somewhat on the mend and Buffalo helped by gathering some mud he mixed with water drops and applying it like a salve upon the huge Bee's wounds.

After attending the fallen Bee, Buffalo decided it was time to scout the ravine and find a means of exit. He gathered his weapons and marched north, back along the route their late fly had flown. After a four hour march, picking his way between the gigantic mushrooms, Buffalo discovered absolutely nothing of interest... and the gorge was beginning to thin to its end. He'd scouted every niche and nook he'd found, but he saw no way to ascend the steep sides of the ravine. Not without proper equipment. At one point, he attempted to climb some dangling lianas... but they pulled free of the delicate perch they'd managed to obtain in the cliff-face and he fell backwards, back into the crevasse... luckily from not too great a height. Some Puffballs broke his fall, expelling a great green cloud of spores into the air that created such a fog that Buffalo had to wait for it to dispel before he could see again and proceed!

He'd circumvented many more spider webs along the way, for this fissure was evidently a favored home to spiders of several deadly varieties. And though he'd encountered many other unusual insects on the trip, he chose to skirt them and move forward with deliberate haste, he really had no time to squander. He felt so totally helpless and lost. Anya was most likely suffering at the whim of that evil, and quite insane, Prince Bik-cu', and he could do nothing about it, stuck at the bottom of a "bottomless" pit with no hope of rescue... and little hope of escape. (Why did that seem to be a running theme in his life lately?) His frustration boiled over and he unleashed a string of invective and physically took it out on some nearby innocent flat-topped stalky mushrooms, reducing them to confetti with his borrowed sword.

There was no way out at *this* end...nothing to do but make his way back and try the other direction. Another four wasted hours and he finally returned to the spot where he and Tsil had been ensnared. The enormous black bee was upright! It was lying upon its belly, it's six legs tucked under itself... it had managed the strength to roll upright! Perhaps it would survive after all.

Buffalo gathered some more water and warily approached the huge Bee... it didn't seem to take particular notice of his advance. Buffalo thrust the makeshift bowl of water under the Bee's mouthparts and it readily slurped at the refreshment with no aggressive act towards Buffalo. In fact, Buffalo made several more trips to try to satisfy the Bee's thirst, but it seemed to be almost insatiable. Buffalo decided to switch to the abundant Amak fruits for some nourishment. He brought one and peeled it and crouched before the giant beast's mouth... it accepted the treat with eagerness. While it slurped at the gelatin delicacy, Buffalo patted and rubbed the side of its face and spoke softly to the titanic insect... nothing particularly meaningful, the sort of kind words one might speak to a beloved pet recuperating from an illness.

The great Bee was just polishing off its fifth Amak fruit and Buffalo was about to get up and go. There was still enough daylight left to explore the southern part of the chasm. This time, he would not need to return to this spot, it was vital to find a way out of the ravine to the south... or die trying! The venom-crippled Bee would have to fend for its own. Buffalo was wise enough to realize that if the giant Bee recovered further, it might actually become a threat to his survival... it might very well wish to graduate from Amak fruit to "Buffalo" meat!

As Buffalo stood to leave, the huge Bee did something that was completely unexpected, so completely startling to the big man. Its twin antennae suddenly thrust forward and tapped themselves rapidly all over Buffalo's astonished face! Buffalo was so taken by surprise he fairly burst out laughing! An inerasable broad smile spread across his face for he had not felt such elation as this for a long while! This monster, this gigantic black Bumble Bee had just imprinted with him! Like the ebony flying ants of Konton, the huge Bee had just bonded with him... accepted him to be as one... he was *sure* of it!

He stepped forward with his arms held wide and embraced the huge head of the Bee and nearly wept as he softly spoke sincere words of gratitude. He had, moments before been at his lowest point with little hope of survival... and now this great Bee had given him *hope!* This beautiful black Bumble Bee was his ticket out of the ravine, his ride home... his chance to save the woman he loved.

Buffalo no longer felt any trepidation about being around the gigantic Bee... it was now "his" bee after all, just as much as *he* belonged to the bee. He knew there had been a mutual bond of trust created that he could depend upon. He wasted little time, even though the Bee was far from well, to get better acquainted with his "steed". He crawled up to its thorax, just behind the head and sat for hours, talking to his new-found friend and getting it used to the feeling of a human upon its back. He groomed the beast as well as he could and did his best to keep him fed and watered.

After a while, Buffalo had an idea and he climbed the spider's web again and used his iron knife to part the cocoon of the Ikuskquan fly... it was quite dead... and smelled like it. But Buffalo was only interested in the makeshift harness that Captain Tsil had improvised. He deftly removed it and gathered up all the strands of leather and tack that had been entombed with the doomed housefly... and brought them back down the web to the side of the great Bee. He let the bee sniff and taste the leather trappings and it prodded at them with it antennae too, then Buffalo went about fitting the harness to the much larger form of the bee. It was a tight fit, but Buffalo felt that he would have enough tack to actually control the bee *IF* he could get the bee used to responding to commands... and *IF* the great Bee recovered enough to fly!

Darkness was beginning to descend on the cavern once again and after tending to the Bee's needs one last time, Buffalo retreated to his "nest" behind the toadstools and dozed off fairly quickly. Nightmares of Anya's fate... and the torture he'd recently endured... thrust themselves into his dreams, at first causing him to sleep fitfully. But as bone weary as he was, he soon slipped into a deeper sleep that provided much needed rest and healed the wounds that troubled him.

Chapter 23
"Return to Konton"

Something wet was dabbing at Buffalo's face again.... "Oh, my God," thought Buffalo, "have I dreamt it all? A result of the torture I endured? Is this Captain Tsil, awakening me within the Ikuskquan dungeon all over again?!" Buffalo opened his eyes in dread that the events of the past few days were nothing more than a grotesque dream! Instead, he saw a huge black head with great glossy eyes hovering above him, awakening him with probing "kisses" from its mandible mouthparts, the way Jeep would often do with his tongue! Buffalo guffawed in his relief, "Hey, cut it out... will ya?!" He sat up and marveled at the change in the enormous Bumble Bee that now looked even larger than before, now that it was free standing and behaving with renewed vigor. The Bee shook its head like a terrier and backed off with a glint in its eye that Buffalo was sure was more than just a reflection. It walked with a bit of a limp on shaky legs and its great gray wings were somewhat curled along the edges, not rigid and ready for flight.

Buffalo used the water trickle to freshen up and then he and his new pal, which seemed to follow him everywhere like a puppy, shared breakfast... Amak fruits and water... "Wow, what variety on this menu," thought Buffalo sarcastically. And then they got down to business. Again, Buffalo climbed the sides of the Bee and spent time just sitting atop the huge thorax, directly behind the Bee's head, hoping to acclimatize the Bee to Buffalo's presence. Slowly, he introduced the use of the straps and reins he'd rigged up to acquaint the beast with the feel of a harness. He borrowed Tsil's clever improvised harness design, slightly different from the actual ones used by the Ikusk or Kontons, and added a few innovations of his own. Buffalo employed the techniques he'd learned in the Konton training arenas, and a bit of what he knew about horseback riding... and a lot of loving care. It took all day, but finally Buffalo got to the point where he could guide the great Bee around the ravine floor... lefts, rights, forward, circles, figure eights... even a "back-up" command were learned... the giant Bumble Bee was smart and caught on quickly.

After two more days of this routine, the great Bee was becoming incredibly responsive to Buffalo's command. They were both healing nicely too... the Bee's wings were full, strong, and rigid... it no longer limped and exuded an enthusiasm that lifted Buffalo's spirits. Buffalo was recuperating as well... the nightmares had subsided and his wounds had mostly healed. Something about the strict Amak diet did wonders for their healing and metabolism. He couldn't guess why. He practiced daily, holding both swords at once, for the added weight, and performed all the sword-play maneuvers he knew. He ran... and did calisthenics too... and though it took a week, he'd brought his mind and body back to where it had been before the "interrogations" began... perhaps even further. Buffalo was probably in the best shape he'd ever been... his huge frame bulged with muscles *he* didn't even know he had!

The giant Bumble Bee was getting restless... it kept shifting about and flitting its wings, testing them in anticipation of flight. The next day, it actually tried them out several times as it buzzed to life and lifted off, hovering in the air over the floor of the ravine... a trait the flies of Ikuskqua and the ebony flyers of the Serpent Guard were not capable of! The great Bee raised a lot of dust and pollen, but it didn't make any attempt to leave, yet... and Buffalo wondered if the Bee might actually abandon him down here. But the faithful Bee, that Buffalo had nick-named "Murk"... a play on words between the '52 Mercury he'd likened it to, and the darkness of its mantle... had no such intention.

It had been a little over a week now and Buffalo knew the time had come. Both he and the Bee were strong and ready, fully healed and eager to leave this barren declivity and venture into the skies of the cavern far above. Selecting the best member from each of the pairs of swords and daggers he'd collected, Buffalo filled his scabbards. He then approached the colossal Bumble Bee and stood before it to imprint in preparation for mounting and flight. The Bee didn't hesitate at all... it seemed to really enjoy Buffalo's company and was eager to serve as his steed and warhorse. And today, it seemed to anticipate Buffalo's intentions to actually fly... and seemed particularly enthusiastic and joyful because of it!

Buffalo climbed to his perch behind the huge Bee's head and grasped the reins firmly... he felt a burst of exuberance in anticipation of his first flight atop the great Bee and he grasped the Bee tightly with his knees. "Ready, Murk?" his voice barely contained his excitement. He pulled back and up upon the reins while also goading with his legs, a command he'd avoided while doing the "floor" exercises of the previous week... so as to avoid a premature flight! But this time he did it with purpose, and the gigantic Bee fully understood Buffalo's new intent and spread its mighty wings and tested them. Then with a deafening buzzing roar that reverberated against the sides of the narrow fissure, the Bee vibrated its powerful wings to a blur and easily lifted from the floor of the "bottomless" pit. It hovered for but a moment and then rapidly ascended between the steep cliffs that had entrapped both he and Buffalo in their depths. The Bee was exceptionally strong and a speedy flier, faster than the ants of Konton! Up and up they rose past a myriad of spider's webs, wildly sprouting mushrooms, and crisscrossed lianas... and soon the full brightness of the cavern revealed itself! They burst forth from the fathomless ravine in a rush of fresh air and excitement! It felt so good to be awash in bright light again and out of that dank dark pit! The air smelled sweet and clean again. After flying a few victory rounds, Buffalo directed Murk to land. Buffalo slid down the bushy thorax of the great Bee and hugged his head with his right arm and patted his snout with his left. "Attaboy, Murk! You did it! We're practically home!" and Buffalo offered an Amak fruit he'd stowed in his pocket to the big Bee who slurped at it greedily and seemed genuinely as happy as Buffalo!

He was reasonably certain that everything was okay... but the giant Bee had so recently been near death that Buffalo wanted to make sure that Murk was not overtaxed by the effort to clear the canyon. So, he took the time to inspect the Bee thoroughly with a careful walk-around. The huge beast's side's fairly heaved as it regained its breath, but it was ready... it was healed and raring to go. Buffalo knew the ravine ran north to south and the skies were gloomy to the west.... so it was the immediate mountains to the east they had to surmount, where the skies looked clearer. The weak fly they had stolen wasn't capable of clearing those hills and Buffalo knew it might yet be a challenge for his Bee because of its recent run-in with the Orb-Weaver. He needn't have worried though, Murk was not only fully recovered but *eager* to fly, eager to test its abilities and eager to impress Buffalo with its skills!

Satisfied by his inspection, Buffalo climbed back on board the willing Bee and Murk needed little prodding to once again fairly bound into the air. Murk reveled in flying and flew with snap precision to Buffalo's instructions... delivered subtly with only the slightest movements of the reins necessary. Buffalo was utterly delighted by Murk's size and power... a proper mount in proportion to the big man riding it! Flying atop Murk reminded Buffalo of flying the P-47 Thunderbolt in WWII... a massive U.S. fighter plane that, despite its size, was extremely tough and fast. He leaned forward and gave Murk a pat on the head just because. Murk sailed upward with ease and gained altitude rapidly. Within minutes, the two were heading due east and clearing the imposing ridges with plenty of room to spare. Buffalo settled Murk into a "cruising" speed he felt the big Bee would be comfortable with and the pair were soon crossing the expanse of plains.

Buffalo didn't know enough about Kontonqua to guide himself by the passing topography below, there were no visible landmarks he remembered seeing before. He recognized the river Tonqua of course, when they reached it, its greenish ribbon slithering across the expanse of the cavern... but he didn't know if he was flying directly east towards Konton or not. He could very well likely be too far to the north or south of the great mound-city. Of course, one method would be to follow the river north to the falls... and then fly south along the cavern wall until he ran into the city! But

Buffalo was too eager to get "home" and didn't want to take such a circuitous route if he didn't have to. He was certain he could spot the tall mound from a distance, if he had enough altitude.... and he was right. At great altitude and after only about twenty more minutes flying, (for Murk was very comfortable flying at a faster cruising pace than the ants of Konton), Buffalo spotted the spires of the city rising up from the jungle off to the southeast... like seeing a tall gray skyscraper encompassed by a sea of green fronds. He corrected his course and aimed Murk directly for the pinnacle of the city.

Buffalo was just about in sight of the city's surrounding cultivated fields when he realized that he had been seen too! A sudden swarm of dots were gathering above the apex of the city and then began streaming in his direction! The ever-watchful Serpent Guard of the city had noticed his approach and were moving to intercept! Buffalo knew he had to exercise caution... at this distance, the Serpent Guard would see him only as an intruding Bumble Bee and probably would not notice him atop the giant Bee at all... especially because they were considered untrainable and unfriendly to humans!

So, rather than continue barging towards the great mound, Buffalo signaled Murk to hover in place while he waved his arms in the air. The advancing Guard grew obviously suspicious as they approached, for this Bee was not behaving like a rogue insect intent on raiding their fields. When the Captain noticed a figure sitting astride the huge black Bee waving to him his eyes grew twice their normal size and his jaw fairly dropped in amazement! What bedevilment was *this?* And then when he drew close enough to recognize *Buffalo* he began whooping and hallooing with happiness while he fought back tears of joy that threatened to blind him as he directed his charger to fly in circles around this unprecedented but welcome apparition! The entire squadron was now flying in circles and whooping and Buffalo felt like he was in an old western; the wagon-train surrounded by a whooping ring of Indians on ponies! But inside, he couldn't be happier... he was pleased to see his friend the Captain, and that he was still in charge or hadn't fallen at the battle at Ikuskqua.

"Buffalo! You ingenious immortal giant! You are *alive!* And well I hope?" hollered the Captain. "We thought you *dead!* And what *madness* is this? Riding a *Great Bee?* That's not supposed to be possible! They are deadly rogues! How did you manage it?"

Buffalo laughed heartily. "To know me, is to love me!" he quipped. "I'll tell you everything back at the arena, my friend... in fact, I'll *race* you there!" shouted Buffalo with a gleam in his eye. Now he could get a chance to see what Murk could *really* do! Before the Captain could shout a perplexed reply, Murk, at Buffalo's command, suddenly dropped from the center of the encircling warriors and flew directly underneath them and made for the city's spires. Murk was obviously delighted to be given full rein and dashed effortlessly at incredible speed low over the miles of crops below. Buffalo could see the farmers and laborers pointing and scattering as he passed!

Such a lead did Buffalo have over the pursuing troops, that when he topped the outer crenellated barricade wall of the city, he pulled back on Murk's reins and flew straight up the side of the great mound! He did a quick loop around the throne room at the pinnacle, noticing many surprised and anxious faces pressed up against the tall "glass" windows as he passed, and then zipped straight back down the steep sides of the city... to land in a cloud of dust in the center of the main training arena. All before the Captain and his squad even arrived!

Buffalo slid from the back of the giant Bee and patted his head while offering another Amak from his pocket. In the brighter light of the cavern, Buffalo noticed how oddly magenta-colored these Amaks were, as opposed to the purplish coloration he was so familiar with. Soldiers and squires gathered with wide-eyed wonder, never having seen a great Bee close up, and then had to scurry out of the way again as the Captain and the main part of his troop landed adjacent to Buffalo.

The large ebony fliers were dwarfed by the size of Buffalo's mount and the ants were rather skittish at having this behemoth flyer in their arena. But they were well trained and trusted their human symbionts implicitly, they didn't panic. The Captain, after dismounting, approached Buffalo and said, "Ha, Ha... very funny.... I guess you win!" And he then embraced Buffalo with a bear hug Buffalo had not expected... the Captain had always been such a stoic man. The Captain released Buffalo and stepped back to look at the Great Bee. "Unbelievable..." he mused wonderingly, looking Murk up and down with obvious envy. "You must tell me all about this.... the great Bees have always been enemies and considered untrainable... you *must* explain how you did this!" And then the Captain narrowed his eyes and asked suspiciously, "And what was that bright reddish morsel I saw you treat your flyer to? Is that the trick?"

Buffalo laughed heartily and brought forth the last of the strange Amak fruits he'd hidden in his pockets. "It's no trick Captain... Murk here bonded to me because I saved him from certain death "by cocoon"... these Amaks just happened to be the one bit of sustenance I could find that helped us both out of a jam... and I think they helped *heal* us too. They make ya feel mighty good... I know that!" Buffalo answered.

The Captain looked at the fruit in Buffalo's hand with no less amazement than at the giant Bee! "Mother of God," he exclaimed, "these Amaks are of a rare medicinal property long thought lost in Kontonqua! Once these were sacred and used exclusively by the shamans for their healing properties... but the plants were over-harvested and we lost the ability to grow them before we learned how really valuable they were! Do you not understand? These fruits do *heal!* It's been said they might even have the ability to reverse the years of damage done to the Ikusks, if we could but grow them in abundance. Old wives' tales probably..."

"Well, I know where I got 'em... but I'm not crazy about going back there any time soon..." interrupted Buffalo, "But you've got *this* one... and it's got seeds inside, don't it?" Buffalo offered.

"Yes... indeed..." trailed off the Captain as he turned to leave the arena holding the precious fruit like it was a time-bomb.

Buffalo didn't get the chance to converse further with the Captain... he was suddenly attacked from all sides by flailing arms searching for a hug! "Buffalo! You're back!" Simon, Maxine, and Dexter were embracing him tearfully, clambering for attention all at once, and Jeep was barking up a storm!

"We missed you SO much!" said Max.
"I *knew* you weren't dead!" added Dex.

"Don't you ever leave us behind like that again!" scolded Max.

"*Wow...* where'd you get a *Bumble Bee* from?!" inquired Simon excitedly.

Jeep just leaped and barked, but he had a lot to say in his own way as well.

Buffalo could have played tough guy and shook off their embrace, but after all he'd been through, it felt really good. It felt like home. Without making remarks of remonstrance, he returned their hug mightily instead and said softly, "I missed you, too!"

The kids had a million questions about all that had occurred... but Buffalo noticed the advance of a Royal Sledge across the arena and so he told them, "Ya know what guys? I think there's someone *else* that wants answers too. And I don't wanna hafta repeat everything twice... so just hold your horses." The kids turned to see the royal seal upon the side of the sledge that drew up before them and they understood. Before boarding, Buffalo wanted to take a moment to introduce them all to Murk. The Great Bee, as they were known to the Kontons, was quite at ease and not at all exhausted by his recent flight to the city... he *was* somewhat uncomfortable around all these strange ants and humans, but Buffalo was at his side, so he was contented. Buffalo introduced each of the kids, and Jeep, to his magnificent new flyer... and Murk seemed to understand the association... he seemed to almost "welcome" the kids, though Jeep fairly confused him.

"You wait here, Murk..." instructed Buffalo to the Great Bee, "I'll be back before ya know it. I've gotta see a Queen Bee of a different kind!" And Buffalo entered the Royal sledge followed by the kids and Jeep... it was his first chance to really give his loyal hound a big hug and Jeep really lapped up the attention. The Queen's sledge lurched forward and looped around to exit the arena... and a gasp went up from the surrounding soldiers and citizenry that had gathered to marvel at the Great Bee in their midst. The sledge suddenly stopped and Buffalo looked around to see what the trouble might be. Murk was right behind the sledge... following Buffalo! This was going to be a problem. Buffalo and Murk had bonded and had been inseparable since he nursed him back to health. He had no way of teaching the Bee to get along without his company and there were no squires or other attendees that knew how to handle Murk, or would be allowed by Murk to interact with him!

"Well..." sighed Buffalo, "If the Queen wants to speak with me, she'll have to speak with Murk in attendance... there's just no other way! Excuse me guys..." and Buffalo exited the Royal sledge and walked around it to Murk. The big Bee moved his head to one side questioningly, like a dog might do and it made Buffalo chuckle. "I guess we're in this together, pal" he said as he rubbed the snout of the gigantic faithful flyer. With a quick bound, Buffalo leaped up and climbed his way through the thick hair of the thorax to his "saddle", his usual perch just behind the Bee's head.

With a couple of yelping barks, Jeep, unwilling to part from his recently returned master, leaped from the sledge and raced to the side of the Bee. Without breaking stride, like he'd done it a million times before, he bounded up to the top of one of the Bee's thick black legs and then leaped directly for the top of the thorax... and he almost made it too! Buffalo managed to hook his collar with his huge hand and assisted him the rest of the way up, so he could sit contentedly right behind Buffalo! Murk was rather upset at first by having this new strange being upon his back without bonding... but Buffalo was there... and the hound didn't seem to be much of a threat. If Buffalo accepted him, Murk accepted him.

That day brought a parade of unique sights that the people of Konton talked about for years... the passing through the streets and marketplace of the Queen's Royal Sledge filled with the children of a long forgotten world, followed by a Great Bee upon who's back rode a giant of a warrior (risen from the *dead!*), and accompanied by one of the extinct Ancient Wolf-Friends! The thickening crowd cheered and waved as the strange procession plied its way through the common areas of the great hive.

As they passed the stalls of the artisans, Buffalo heard a shout and saw T'mil the Blacksmith run up to Murk's side, "A truly great warrior needs a truly great weapon... I've been working on this for you!" he yelled up at Buffalo, and tossed up a huge gleaming broadsword he'd fashioned especially for the big man. It glinted brightly in the light as it tumbled and Buffalo caught it by the haft. It was a huge Bastard Sword of the type that Buffalo had commissioned! "I was hoping you would return... for if *you* don't wield it, I don't know who else could!" shouted T'mil who was already being swallowed by the tumult of the seething throng. Buffalo raised the razor sharp blade above his head and a rousing cheer welled up from the surrounding crowd. He drew the Ikuskquan iron sword from its sheath and tossed it towards one of the huge wooden support pillars of the marketplace where it stuck fast with a ringing sound and stayed there for years... many legends grew around it, mostly rather fanciful tales. Buffalo sheathed the new broadsword and he felt almost... complete. If only he had his trusty *Bowie* knife...

The odd procession made its way quickly upward through the passages towards the Queen's throne room. Buffalo was very happy that the tunnels of Konton were large enough to allow enough head-room for him, atop Murk, to maneuver through! The kids were obviously tickled by the recent events... they kept looking back at Buffalo and waving and giggling. Jeep was really content too... and had lain down pressed up against Buffalo's back, panting with his eyes squinting and his long pink tongue loosely flapping. Murk was handling the passageways with expert precision and remained directly behind the sledge with little guidance from Buffalo. When they reached the large outer hall, they caused quite a commotion however. The large room, full of government minions, was alive with the buzz of procedures and protocol. This was unprecedented! No one had ever ridden a beast of any kind into the Queen's chambers.... let alone a *Great Bee!*

Bureaucratic clerks were trying desperately to dissuade Buffalo from riding his Bee any further... entry into the Queen's throne room by Ixtl was strictly *forbidden!* Buffalo largely ignored them and continued to ride Murk right up to the huge wooden doors that led to the Queen's reception hall above. The ruffled clerks had the good sense to keep their distance. But, someone must have been savvy enough to alert the Queen Mother as to what was going on... for when they drew up to the huge wooden doors leading to the Queen's entryway, a servant ran up to the sentries on duty, (who looked quite flustered confronted by this strange spectacle!), and whispered something to them.

They presently opened the great doors without further questioning the new arrivals, obviously relieved that a decision had been made *for* them. The Royal Sledge advanced... so too, did Buffalo atop Murk. They climbed the passageways to the last set of doors and found them open in advance of their arrival. These guards too had been given instructions not to impede the progress of the surface-worlders... they marched unopposed directly into the Queen's throne room at the pinnacle of the great mound-city. Anya's mother, the Queen, stood alone in the room, calmly awaiting them.

Chapter 24
"Rescue Party"

The kids exited the sledge and kind of stood off to one side, uncertain as to whether this audience with the Queen was just to welcome Buffalo back, or whether there was another purpose to it. They weren't always particularly aware of recent political dealings, but they surmised enough to know that this face-to-face with the supreme leader of Konton wasn't about *them*. Buffalo rode Murk straight up to the Queen herself and she remained calm and unfazed. The Captain of the Serpent guard, having transferred the "rediscovered" medicinal Amak into the proper hands, entered the room from the Hall of Unveiling and stepped from the shadows to join his Queen. Buffalo slid from his perch atop the Giant Bee to approach the Queen and when he did so, he knelt upon one knee and took her hand to kiss it. It was a proper gesture... perhaps more medieval European than Kontonquan... but its effect was not unwelcome.

"So... you *live,*" noted the Queen unemotionally, "...of course you realize this will *spoil* our plans to honor your memory. The celebrations were to become an annual holiday for our people." Buffalo looked up in shock... was this to be the extent of his "heroic welcome return"? The Queen returned his gaze and suddenly raised a slender brown hand to cover her mouth, vainly trying to stifle her laughter...

"Welcome *home,* Buffalo Brewster!" she spoke loudly curtailing a chuckle and the Queen mother had a sincere smile and glint in her eye that Buffalo had not imagined her capable of... and he saw for the first time, the image of Anya reflected in her mother's face. She bid Buffalo to rise and then, to the shock of everyone, especially Buffalo, she gave the big man a hug and lingered there in his huge strong arms for a warm embrace. "We have a lot of ground to cover," recovered the Queen, pulling away from the foreign giant. "Please... let us compare notes and fill in the details of what has transpired... yours must be a particularly singular tale of wonder!"

Buffalo, for his part, relayed all the events as they happened on his end... the snare trap that beheaded his mount (which brought a grimace from the Captain...), the audience with Prince Bik-cu'... with Anya shackled to his throne (which caused everyone great pain...), the long hours of torture, and the dungeon meeting of his savior, Captain Tsil-se-Ulkul. The mention of the Dragon Captain's name brought forth quite some excitement from both the Serpent Captain and the Queen. Apparently, they had no idea he'd been alive all this time... and confined. Buffalo related the events of their escape and subsequent entrapment in the Orb-Weaver's web. The kids were absolutely enthralled by Buffalo's tale... like campers listening to a ghost story around a campfire. The Captain and the Queen were quite saddened at hearing of the passing of Captain Tsil. Buffalo continued... he explained about the Great Bee and about his unusual training techniques, the use of the fortuitous Amak fruits, and their eventual flight to freedom.

The Captain and the Queen seemed satisfied that all the related events tied in with their knowledge of all that had transpired since Buffalo and the Captain led their army of fliers into battle. But Buffalo now wanted to know *their* side of the story as well. The Captain took charge and began his discourse on the recent history of the past two weeks.

"The great battle before the walls of Ikuskqua started off well... but though we fought valiantly, we were eventually outnumbered." The Captain lowered his head and spoke dejectedly, this was obviously emotionally difficult for him, "My Guardsmen fought well, *you* fought well... each of us took down a multitude of foes. When you were lost, it hit the men hard, their morale suffered. The Ikusks came at us time and time again. Our Akt'Ki-hautl were tiring... after crossing Kontonqua to get to Ikuskqua... and then *three* hours of steady battle... there was little I could do. I decided to regroup at the base of the big escarpment leading up to the plateau of swamps. I thought we might catch a moment's respite... but that was when they hit us again, hard... hit us at our weakest. They must have had fresh troops waiting to join the battle... my guess is they held back a whole division of warriors at the "farm", where they raise their flies for food and burden.

They battered us mercilessly and all we could do eventually, was limp back to Konton. You, my friend, are not the *only* wounded warrior to have come wandering back to Konton from the great battle over the past two weeks... just the most spectacular. We have since been regrouping our units and preparing to attack again... before they bolster their forces anew. They lost many warriors last time... it had to be a four-to-one loss for them at least... they cannot endure such attrition again!"

"Sign me up!" announced Buffalo. "Murk and I are ready for battle again and we'll give those Ikusks a fair thrashing *this* time! Prince Bik-cu' is soon to breathe his last and Anya will be home before you know it!"

"Anya is... gone," interjected the Queen Mother quietly, sadly.

"W-what?!" stammered the shaken man. "What are you saying?" The kids echoed his disbelief.

The Queen elaborated distantly, visibly hurting "My spies tell me that Anya was most difficult... that Prince Bik-cu' could not seduce her, entice her, entreat her, nor corrupt her. At last, he grew weary of trying and... being an infantile deranged *selfish* man, he decided that if he could not have her, no one would. She has been given to the Priesthood of X'Poca for... sacrifice."

"What?! *When?!*" asked Buffalo, stunned.

"She's probably there now..." answered the Queen.

"Are you *kidding* me?" returned Buffalo anxiously, "Then why aren't you and your armies there to *save* her!?!" he fairly shouted.

"Beware your impertinence, surface-worlder!" scolded an angry Queen, "What do you truly know of our ways? The Priesthood is ancient... the Priesthood is all-knowing... the Priesthood of X'Poca *cannot* be challenged... that is the way in all Kontonqua, respected by Kontons and Ikusks alike! They do as they please and their word is law. Virgins are *regularly* sacrificed. This time, it just happens to be my... daughter..." and she trailed off despondently, visibly shaken, turning to look away out over the expanse of distant jungle to hide the bitter emotion she felt.

"Not if I can help it!" announced the big man. Buffalo turned and grasped the mantle "fur" of Murk's thorax and hauled himself up. "Sorry,

Jeep..." he apologized to his canine buddy, who was still nestled in Murk's fleece, "This time you've gotta stay." And Buffalo nudged Jeep to leap down from the Great Bee's back.

"And what about *us?!*" urged Simon, "Are we supposed to just "stay" again too?"

Buffalo shot Simon a look of concern and grim determination, "You don't know what you're up against. This is my fight. I *return* with Anya this time... or I *don't* return!" Grabbing the reins, he spun Murk about and exited the throne room the way he'd arrived. He heard the imploring voices of the kids, calling out to him from behind... but this was his mission, his job to finish... he hadn't a minute to lose! Navigating the narrow passage back down to the great hall was not difficult, there was nobody there... but when Buffalo entered the "bureaucratic" hall, there was a veritable throng of joyous Konton citizens to greet him! News of his survival and arrival had spread throughout the colony! This was total frustration for Buffalo! Not *now!* He had to get to a flight-balcony quickly so he could lift off and get to the Temple of X'Poca in time to hopefully rescue his beloved, the princess... the Kwa-I-Anya. But the citizenry of Konton, who revered their princess, were preventing him, in their untimely enthusiasm, from leaving in time to save her from certain death!

Relentlessly, Buffalo drove Murk through the gathered throng, waving and nodding, trying to be as polite as possible, while all the time egging Murk to move forward through the crowds as quickly as possible, without hurting anyone. Buffalo finally made it into the downward tunnels, but then went through the same scenario when he reached the marketplaces! Everyone was curious, everyone wanted to glimpse the Great Bee that was parading through the tunnels of their hive, everyone wanted to see the returned "ghost" warrior, they vied for a chance to just touch the Great Bee's legs or bushy thorax as he passed... this day was one that would be recorded in history, an event not to be missed! But it all added to Buffalo's dismay... he needed to go... *now!*

Finally, after a trip that took twice as long as it should have, Buffalo arrived at the outskirts of the main aerodrome... the Serpent Guard arena... and passed beneath its huge stone archway into the coliseum staging area that was an open balcony to the immense cavern. The Captain and the kids were waiting patiently there for him in the center, all astride large restless ebony flyers of the Serpent Guard. They were fully armed and prepared for battle.

Buffalo brought Murk to a halt before the little war-party "*What?* What are you doing here... *how* did you...?" Buffalo said through gritted teeth, still displaying the anger and frustration that had built up within him on his aggravating trip through the multitudes of cheering citizenry.

Simon spoke up, "Did you really think we were going to let you leave us behind... *again?* While you were held up making your way back through the crowds of onlookers, the Captain took us down the back way. We knew you'd make for the main arena, we just had to get here first!"

"But the *fliers...?*" inquired Buffalo.

Max took the question, "How is it that we are astride *fliers?* What did you think we would do if you didn't come back? Work in the Konton *kitchens?*" she teased. "As soon as we were told that you were missing... and presumed dead... the three of us decided that we'd follow in your footsteps and train to fly... so that we could scout the cavern for you. Not one of us believed you were *actually* dead... just missing or in trouble. We badgered the Captain... and well... we're all qualified fliers now. With a bonded winged-ant of our own!"

"And she's the first girl to ever do it!" added Dex, obviously proud of his friend. Maxine shot him an impish smile, but you could see that she was just as pleased with her accomplishment.

"Impressive enough..." noted Buffalo as he observed that the kids seemed also well *prepared* for battle. Simon had his longbow on his shoulder and a full quiver of arrows, and was dressed in more traditional Kontonquan warrior harness. Maxine carried a bone-handled dagger and was dressed in a sleek dark-brown leather Jin-Jin catsuit that hinted at the combat prowess she had been secretly training in... oddly, she was barefoot. And Dexter was equipped with a sling and a pouch of projectiles of some sort. "And I suppose you think you're prepared and ready to take on this X'Pocan *God* they speak of? To go toe-to-toe with Ikusks... or this Priesthood? To aid and rescue Anya?"

"Buffalo..." spoke up Max with quiet sincerity, "we're no longer the "kids" that began this adventure with you... as unprepared innocent naive castaways... we *are* ready. We've changed. We have no false hopes about rescue... or ever getting out of here. So, we are *Kontonquans* now. We're fine with that. We've studied hard to hone our skills and war-craft... we've hardened our minds and bodies... and we mean to get our friend and princess back!"

Buffalo squinted a bit and looked them over once more... after a brief pause, he winked and said, "Well, let's go get her then!"

"I am going *too*," interrupted the Captain, "I am here because I can save you precious time if I lead you to the Temple. Because of what I feel inside, I will fight at your side... but my warriors cannot assist us in any way. They are under strict orders to obey the ways of our laws and not interfere with the dealings of the Priesthood. I will deal with the consequences upon my return... if I return."

"You don't have to do this, my friend..." advised Buffalo.

The Captain just stared back at Buffalo with his famous stoic glare and said, "I've known the Kwa-Ia since she was born... I've practically raised her. She is my responsibility as much as she is yours. We're wasting time..."

"Then lead the way, Captain!" and Buffalo urged Murk to lift into the air! Just in time too, as joyous Konton revelers were suddenly starting to spill through the archway and into the arena, still hoping to partake in the merriment of the day and see the wonder of the Great Bee.

Murk hovered effortlessly, like a huge helicopter, raising considerable dust... while the eager ebony warrior-ants vibrated their glassy wings to life and lifted off, single file, with the Captain in the lead. Once they were all airborne, they formed a sort of wedge formation with The Captain flying point and leading the way low and quick over the surrounding promenade. Throngs of natives cheered their "fly-over" as they buzzed over the crenulated walls of the encircling barrier and made their way over the ring of fields. Buffalo had to hold Murk back a bit for he could easily outdistance the flying ants, being capable of generating a good 40mph or so faster in an all-out race. But direction was as important as speed, and the Captain knew the terrain they were flying over, so he saved them all a good bit of time by flying directly to the Temple. Buffalo would have had to fly west towards the river Tonqua first and then follow its southerly winding course until he ventured upon the Temple of X'Poca... of which the only thing he knew was that it was erected upon the spot where the river flowed *out* of the cavern. Why it was erected upon that spot, he didn't know... and right now, he didn't particularly care.

The rescue party of five soared quickly over the jungle treetops... the Captain was not holding back, he pushed the flying ants to their top speed. He didn't need to "save" their energy in anticipation of an aerial battle this time, he just needed to get to the temple with all possible haste. His knowledge of the terrain below was uncanny... he picked out subtle landmarks that were completely obscure to Buffalo and brought them to the Temple in just under two hours.

The jungle gave way to plains as they neared the Holy place and they dipped down to fly low over the savannah, hoping not to be spotted too soon before their unwelcome arrival. As they approached, Buffalo looked upon the Temple and took note of it as the wonder of architecture it was. It was built of brown stone and was partially embedded into the wall of rock that was the southern extremity of the cavern. It was a large elaborate building of spires and buttresses, but it had three main features that were quite unique - - huge square towers, that rose up upon either side of the river, (somewhat reminiscent of the towers of Notre Dame Cathedral). A huge decorative arch that spanned the river and connected the two towers. And a coliseum-sized room *behind* the arch topped by a giant circular skylight of ornamental glass. The river Tonqua flowed directly through a low wall that surrounded the entire complex, went under the main decorative arch, and disappeared beneath the large shallow-domed building!

The Captain was secretly hoping to at least *land* unnoticed, but as they drew close to the Temple of X'Poca, a squad of Ikuskquan warriors on battle-flies took to the air to intercept them! This was quite unexpected. He had believed they would face only the Priesthood... on the ground... which would have been bad enough. Ikuskquan aerial-troops were another matter. He hoped he hadn't made a critical error by driving his ants at top speed, thereby tiring them out! It was obvious now that an mid-air battle was inevitable!

It was twenty-five Ikusks to their five... but the rescuers had one advantage - - the bewildered Ikusks had never anticipated seeing, or dealing with, anything such as an enraged warrior the likes of Buffalo atop a Great Bee! Buffalo spurred Murk forward to meet the Ikusks head on... and even at a distance, he could see the fear in their horrid twisted faces! An arrow whizzed by Buffalo and lodged itself in the throat of the leading Ikuskquan flier. "Thank you, Simon!" shouted Buffalo as he drew his massive new broadsword and charged forward.

Murk was an absolutely amazing battle mount! He seemed to instinctively know exactly what Buffalo intended. As Buffalo was just about to clash with the "newly promoted" leader of the Ikuskquan guard, Murk responded deftly to Buffalo's guidance to suddenly fly *beneath* the charging group of brutes. As Buffalo was busy disemboweling the fly to his right, from underneath with a mighty roundhouse swing of his Bastard Sword, Murk had folded his abdomen under and brought forth his deadly stinger, to pierce and poison the fly to his left! Together, they rolled in midair to come up hovering directly behind the two they'd just "killed"... (they were still *technically* alive, for the moment, but in the process of falling to their deaths below). Changing direction instantly, they flew lengthwise from behind, along the Ikuskquan line so that Buffalo could behead three more before the dimwitted Ikusks even realized they'd been outflanked!

The battle was swift and brutal, but the Ikusks never stood a chance... the Captain and the kids were magnificent. Simon managed to take out *three* Ikusks with arrows... a rare feat because mounted archers were generally used against *fixed* targets... trying to hit a moving target *from* a moving target was generally thought unfeasible at best. But Simon had a steady hand and a keen eye... and an uncanny ability to judge speed and angle to hit targets with unerring precision.

Yet it was Murk that ruled the skies that day! He was an exceptionally strong flier and his ability to hover and/or instantly change direction was an unexpected challenge the Ikusks were unprepared for... not to mention his sting! Murk's deadly stinger accounted for the deaths of four Ikuskquan mounts, currently writhing in pain somewhere on the grasslands below, suffering the final fatal effects of his toxin.

The Konton rescue squad of five regrouped and made for the Temple once more. This time they managed to land unchallenged in a small park-like space just outside the main entrance. Several nervous Ikuskquan battle-flies were tethered there but no one else was to be seen. As soon as the Captain and the kids dismounted, their battle-hardened Akt'Ki-hautl pounced upon and tore apart the helpless flies, for the ants have formidable jaws, the flies had only sucking mouthparts... and the ants *hated* the flies. Besides, they were due a rewarding snack for their wonderful aerial performance against the Ikusks.

Buffalo slid from his perch atop his Great Bee and tried again to tell Murk to stay... but that was a command Murk was not comfortable with. Murk tried desperately to follow Buffalo through the courtyard, but when he and the Captain and kids opened the narrow doors to the Temple, he had no choice but to remain outside the cathedral... a situation he was clearly unhappy with. "Don't worry, Murk... I won't be long," soothed Buffalo, patting Murk's forehead. But Murk was still *very* agitated.

The ornate carved wooden doors snapped shut behind them with an audible click and Buffalo and his gang paused and squinted in the darkness of a long hall while waiting for their eyes to adjust from the brightness of the cavern without. It was decidedly darker and cooler in the Temple and water was loudly rushing somewhere nearby. A sinister laugh echoed throughout the large columned hall.

"What's this?" spoke a slimy voice familiar to Buffalo, echoing in the vast hall, "Has my fallen God... my misguided outer-world tourist... my *squealing* dungeon-fodder... returned with his children and an old man to pester me once again? Or was it my personal *bodyguard* that you wanted to see?" Twelve burly and brutish Ikuskquan fly-headed abominations, in full battle armor, stepped out from behind the massive pillars that lined the great hall ahead. The largest of them, a mean-looking hairy thug on the left seemed to be their leader. Prince Bik-cu', like most cowards, was not to be seen... probably hiding towards the rear, Buffalo thought.

Without issuing a command, each of Buffalo's followers drew their weapons and began spreading out and forward. In response, the Ikuskquan guardsmen drew their weapons. Their leader was just in the process of commanding them forward when he fell to his knees... clutching at an arrow that had pierced his throat. The Ikusks were stunned at first and then with a roar, raised their weapons and made to charge towards Buffalo and his followers. Buffalo was about to do the same and meet them head on, when a hand on his arm restrained him...

"Wait." said Dexter. He was deftly spinning his sling at his side. He suddenly released it and something shiny was lobbed through the air to land just in front of the attacking line of Ikusks. A glass vial hit the stone floor and shattered, exuding a bluish vapor that soon had the entire Ikuskquan troop coughing and wheezing and swiping at their eyes. "I've been waiting to try that..." said Dex, obviously happy with the results. "Something I cooked up back at the Konton kitchens. Count to fifteen for the air to clear and then close to attack!"

While Dexter was counting down, he took out a choking guard with his sling and a hefty stone and Simon got two more with arrows. Then the whole group charged to engage, but the mostly blinded Ikusks were no longer much of a threat. The Captain and Buffalo easily accounted for five between them and Maxine took out two with very cleverly placed pirouetting stun-kicks... and used her dagger for the "coup de grâce". Simon took out the last with his short sword in close combat. Before the brief battle was over, Buffalo saw a dark cloaked figure separate itself from one of the pillars at the rear and run for the safety of the doors at the far end of the hall. As soon as the last Ikuskquan bodyguard was dispatched, Buffalo lit off after him.

He reached the large wooden doors, a matched set to the ones through which they'd entered, and pushed them open boldly. The sound of rushing water was now a deafening roar and the darkened "room" ahead was actually a giant spillway with only a wide indoor stone bridge spanning the river Tonqua! At least it was a river on the *right* side of the bridge, where it entered the huge damp chamber from the jungles... to the *left* it was a raging waterfall that fell away into the darkness of a bottomless hole! Buffalo had just enough time to take in his surroundings when he was suddenly bashed by the door to his right. The old bridge was slippery and moss-covered and Buffalo lost his footing and went down. The sinister black-cloaked figure of Bik-cu' took off again, running away over the bridge... but he only got halfway across before he was felled by one of Dexter's well-placed stones! Buffalo regained his feet and narrowed the distance between himself and Bik-cu' in half a dozen leaps. Bik-cu' jumped up and turned to face the onrushing surface-dwelling giant with his jewel-encrusted sword drawn before him.

Much to his shock, Bik-cu' was almost felled by the first swing of Buffalo's sword, such was the power that the huge man dealt with one swing of his mighty broadsword! But Bik-cu' was an expert swordsman and managed to deflect the majority of the force to one side, though it caused him to stagger significantly. The Captain halted the kids at the doors and they watched, nervously. They had the utmost confidence in their hero and leader, Buffalo... but the Prince was a nasty piece of work and even a huge mountain of a man like Buffalo could be brought down by a single fatal mistake. Still, each suspected that this was a battle that Buffalo had to fight on his own, without their help or interference.

The Prince drew off his cape and used it on his left hand as a sort of tantalizing decoy while he taunted the big man with the scimitar-style bejeweled sword in his right. The two men circled each other like fighting roosters, each looking for an opening and feinting with jabs, trying to goad the other into a hasty move. Bik-cu' lunged and tried to blind Buffalo with the black cape, so as to mask the true intent of his attack,... but Buffalo anticipated the ruse and successfully parried the deadly sword-blade where he suspected it *would* be, not where Bik-cu' *wished* him to think it was. Round and round they went, the shrill clang of their swords echoing in the dank hall, heard sharply even over the din of the falls.

The Prince had managed to land several shallow cuts on Buffalo's arm, and Buffalo gave the Prince a deep slice to his cheek, but in the end, it was the big man's strength and endurance that persevered and won the duel. Bik-cu' was tiring and his overconfidence and sureness of his superiority was making him sloppy. So, when he once again tried his decoy cape-trick to blind Buffalo, the big man grabbed the cape in his mighty paw and yanked it so hard that it threw the Prince completely off balance on the slimy bridge... and his sword thrust went wide of the mark as a result. Buffalo's custom-made Bastard Sword came down like a lightning bolt in retaliation and shattered Bik-cu's blade in half! The resulting vibration of the blow stung Bik-cu's hand and arm so badly he dropped the useless hilt with a shrill scream.

The shriek was cut short however as Buffalo's enormous hand closed around his throat and drove the Prince backward until his spine hit the stone railings of the bridge with an audible thud. He then bent the lanky figure backwards to threateningly dangle his evil red-eyed skull over the falls. Buffalo put his sword to the Prince's throat as he glowered and demanded through gritted teeth, "Where... *is* she, Bik-cu'? Where is Anya?"

Like many self-absorbed men... suffering from years of having their way, no one ever telling them "No"... Prince Bik-cu' either failed to read, or chose to ignore, the deadly glint in Buffalo's eye... or the graveness in his voice. He chose unwisely to taunt him instead.

"She... is a *pretty* one, is she not, surface-man?" spluttered the Prince in his slimiest sneer, "She would not bend to be my... mate. She would not break even after listening to your pitiful screams. Heartless woman, isn't she? But she still serves a purpose... in the end. Now she can be... a meal fit for a God! Is that not an *esteemed* honor?"

"Wrong answer, Bik-cu'!" Buffalo spat contemptuously, and his blade drew blood as it bore down harder on the Prince's leathery throat. Suddenly, Bik-cu's right hand shot upward from between them... holding Buffalo's Bowie knife!

"Buffalo, look out!" shouted Max.

But Buffalo was quicker. He saw the hand go up with the flash of a blade and his left hand grabbed the sinewy wrist almost instinctively... bar fights are great training. Buffalo glared coldly into Bik-cu's face as the razor-sharp blade of his broadsword dug deeper still. Too late Prince Bik-cu' realized the serious intent in Buffalo's glaring eyes and panicked for the first time in his life.

"You..." Buffalo spoke slowly as the Prince tried desperately to plead for his pathetic life, "...disgust me." He finalized his words by cutting that vile life short as the great broadsword completely sliced through the neck in which it had been pressed. Prince Bik-cu's head tumbled into the abyss of the falls, his red eyes flashing each time the head spun upwards. The chilling effect was rhythmically repeated as it receded into the distance, until finally disappearing into the dark watery mist far below.

"And... I'll have my knife back if you please," stated Buffalo coldly as he plied the ex-Prince's dead fingers from his prized Bowie knife and let the lifeless corpse drop over the bridge to follow its head into oblivion.

Chapter 25
"Upon the Sacrificial Altar"

Now that the Prince and his unpleasant associates had been dispensed with, Buffalo and his companions proceeded to cross the moss-covered stone bridge over the river Tonqua and towards the set of doors at the other end of the dark dank room. Upon opening them, they saw a more brightly lit immense hallway that curved around what had to be a huge round coliseum or arena. The wide stone path was lined with enormous columns on the right... and a massive solid stone wall on the left. The huge wall rose up many stories, but the hallway level of the wall had evenly-spaced small windows carved into it for the Priests to observe what transpired within... for there they *were*... standing at the windows peering inwards! Bald-headed men in yellow robes tied with crimson sashes stood at each window gazing so intently on the happenings within, that they didn't notice the newcomers at all... until the roar of the falls alerted those nearby that the doors to the bridge-room had suddenly been opened!

Several turned and spotted Buffalo and his squad and instantly changed from curious devout religious-followers to fierce defenders! They hissed and crouched and drew cruel-looking daggers from beneath their flowing yellow robes... they grouped together and began to form a line of defense. Buffalo and his crew charged and attacked immediately, not wanting the Priests that stood in their way to gather their forces before they confronted them. Arrows and stones flew from Simon and Dex, finding their marks with deadly accuracy. Maxine performed amazing Jin-Jin acrobatic stunts to counter the similar fighting style of the Priests themselves and bested several of them. Buffalo had heard of a fighting style like this when he was in the war... the Japanese called it Jiu-Jutsu, a form of hand-to-hand combat that used the enemy's leverage against them. It took him by surprise initially, with an attacking Priest landing several kicks and blows that might have felled an ox... but not Buffalo. He tired of the little man's bobbing and weaving and eventually just grabbed him by the neck and twisted the life from him.

Buffalo and his crew forced the Priesthood contingent back... back through a large set of thick ancient-looking wooden doors that now stood open and led into the arena itself. They were carrying the day! The Priesthood was obviously no match for the skills and weapons of the Konton rescuers for they were beating them back mercilessly.

Then they heard a girl scream! They all looked to the center of the arena. A quick assessment of their environs told them they were in a huge stone coliseum set with small windows all around the ground level, shadowed by several balconies that hung over the pit as upper terraces. The balconies were filled with *hundreds* of taciturn members of the Priesthood, patiently observing the proceedings below... and protected behind a weave of heavy iron bars! The huge arena was easily six stories high and topped with the same glass shallow dome, (actually made of translucent obsidian... volcanic glass), that Buffalo had noted upon their first distant view of the Temple.

Directly across the amphitheater, a giant set of wooden doors, five stories high, were set into the back wall of the cavern itself. The vast dirt floor of the arena was littered with the skeletons of insects and humans alike. But the scream they'd heard had drawn their attention to the *middle* of the arena. In the center of the ring was a stone dais with two huge pillars with thick ropes and wooden bindings. The sylphlike figure of a lovely girl with dusky hair, dressed in a simple diaphanous white slave's garment, was tethered between the columns with her back to Buffalo and his followers... facing the huge set of ancient rough-hewn wooden doors. She screamed again, but it was more of a lament of despair and frustration, and she let herself dangle despondently from the loops of rough hemp that held her slender wrists... stretching her between the twin pillars. Anya!

Buffalo and the Captain and kids looked to quickly finish their battle with the group of Priests... but they were no longer there! They spun to see the remaining Priests backing away hurriedly, assisting their wounded from the great room, and then the huge wooden doors through which they'd entered were closed with a resounding boom... leaving them all *trapped* within the confines of the coliseum! A happy tumult in the form of hoots, jibes, laughter, and applause was elicited from the watchers in the mesh-protected galleries above.

"Anya!" called Buffalo turning his attention back towards the helpless captive.

"Buff... *Buffalo?!*" replied Anya uncertainly, and the dejected figure on the altar suddenly straightened up with renewed vigor as she twisted in her restraints and tried to crane her neck around to get a look at the man who spoke her name aloud. "Is it... *really* you? He... he told me... you were *dead!* And Simon... and Max... and..." and she broke off choking back a sob, unable to speak the rest of the names. As the little band of rescuers ran to her side, Anya recovered her composure and spoke nervously, fervidly, "What are you *doing* here?" a tremble of horror in her voice, "This *cannot* be! It is enough that I am to be given to X'Poca! You needn't sacrifice yourselves as well! You... all of you... will be killed for certain! You must go! The Priesthood will never..." She was talking a mile a minute, but she didn't get to finish her excited rant for Buffalo gently placed his huge paw over her mouth...

"Shhh... calm down," reassured the big man, gazing lovingly into the jungle-princess's startled wide dark eyes. "We're here to take you home. This is a mistake they'll pay for dearly. It's that monster Bik-cu's doing... but *he's* the one that's dead, not me! We'll figure out how to assuage the Priesthood later. Right now, we're leaving here... all of us *together*, one way or another!"

While Buffalo was offering solace to the barbarian princess upon the sacrificial altar, the Captain and Simon were busy with their daggers cutting through the thick twists of hemp that held her fast. As soon as her wrists were freed, Anya threw her arms around the surface-world giant that she had come to love. Buffalo basked in the feel of the lithesome jungle-girl's warm and feminine form pressed into his... but the moment of happiness was not to last. Booming drums sounded from somewhere over head... and a strained mechanical grinding began to fill the vast arena. It was like ancient gears were agonizingly meshing, being asked to move against their will. The whole building vibrated with the effort of their engagement... but the great wooden doors, the ones that stood five stories tall, did slowly begin to creak and move.

Buffalo pushed Anya and the others to the rear as the giant doors parted. The drums beat louder. This was X'Poca's temple, this was the center of a religion for the people of this forgotten cavern under the Earth... a religion revered and feared alike...this was the home of their *God*. The doors were swinging wide and they were about to meet their "maker"... the *God of Kontonqua*... X'Poca himself!

The doors were wide open now and halted with a shuddering thud. The drums stopped. The hum of the ancient mechanism stopped. All was silent. Yet something big, very big, was stirring in the darkness beyond the doors... in the confines of an adjoining cavern chamber. Steadily, with the confidence of expected reverence and supremacy, an enormous gray-green form began to ponderously emerge from the newly revealed room... It was a Praying Mantis! A gigantic and very old Praying Mantis... five stories tall, moss-covered, and greenish-gray with age, but formidable nonetheless!

Of course... a *Praying Mantis!* The "God" of the cavern... the one insect that all others feared! Amazingly stealthy and lethal, it was the top of the insect food chain. Enigmatically "perceptive" by human standards, they seem to have a consciousness and wisdom we can barely seem to understand or appreciate. And yet these cultured colonies of Indian ancestors, *civilized* people of the cavern, were offering human sacrifices, innocent victims, to this X'Poca... this... *insect*. All in the hopes of gaining almighty favor to thrive within the confines of the otherwise inhospitable cavern. Barbarians after all, thought Buffalo.

X'Poca entered the great coliseum and paused to size up it's meal. *Several* morsels this time cowered near the central dais... delightful! X'Poca moved his head from side to side sporadically, much like a parrot does, as he attempted to focus each glistening green eye on the proceedings before him. The morsels were dispersing! Must be quick!

Buffalo and his group drew weapons and fanned out across the dirt floor of the arena. "Remember the battle at the Konksihuatl trap!" advised Buffalo, "Spread out and harry the beast from all sides, stay out of its reach, worry it from each side so it doesn't focus on any single one of us!" Buffalo heard a faint buzzing from somewhere but his mind and focus was on the enormous deadly Mantis confronting them!

"And *then* what?" wondered Dex.

"Ummm... not sure," answered Buffalo, "Gotta figure out something as we go... look for a weakness... just don't get eaten!"

The behemoth Praying Mantis, having chosen it first victim, suddenly lunged for Maxine, using its malicious raptorial forelegs to try to ensnare her in the vice-like grip of its spiked arms. But as the deadly limbs shot forward to seize her, Max catapulted sideways to evade the strike!

The giant Mantid was ancient, but it was still very nimble... having missed its target with Max, it scuttled around to turn its attention to Dexter. Dexter leaped behind the skeletonized carcass of a huge beetle just in time... and though the Mantis reduced the beetle remains to mere shell fragments with a blow from it's forelimb, Dexter was unharmed. X'Poca received an arrow in its neck from Simon for its efforts and Dexter was able to crawl to safety unnoticed by the raging "God".

Buffalo ran up and delivered several blows with his broadsword to the rear legs of the deadly

Mantis... the Captain did pretty much the same on the other side... but the creature's exoskeleton was tough as nails. The swords did little more than scar the chitin. Anya, weaponless, hurled stones she picked off the arena floor. Buffalo heard the strange buzzing again over the cheers and jeers of the gathered Priesthood... what *was* that?

X'Poca spun and faced Buffalo... the ancient deity was very fast on its six slender legs. But when it lunged, Buffalo didn't try to evade the striking forelimbs, he hacked at them with his sturdy broadsword. The parry prevented Buffalo from being caught but only sliced off a few choice barbs... minimal damage, he'd have to do better! His efforts did however completely enrage the gigantic beast! X'Poca was used to benign *helpless* victims tied to an altar, not flitting morsels fighting back with stinging weapons! Dexter landed a missile right between the creature's big green eyes and it let out a squeal of frustration and redoubled its efforts to end their miserable mortal lives. It went after the Captain next, but he was successful in repelling its attack as well... and Buffalo took the opportunity to sprint forward and hack at one of the beast's joints on a rear leg! That *worked!* The softer ligaments of the joint parted to the razor-sharp blade in Buffalo's hands and the creature howled with pain and irritation. The incessant buzzing noise was becoming quite noticeable and the others heard it too.

X'Poca next turned his attention to Anya, the hapless girl in white that was to be his sacrificial sustenance for the day! It was Buffalo's turn to become enraged, to decoy the beast from his intended victim, and he lit into the giant Mantis with both his broadsword and Bowie knife, attempting to strike the soft underbelly of the behemoth. But the ancient Mantis was wary and wise and managed to evade Buffalo's strikes and kicked him to the wall of the arena where he landed with a resounding thump! Buffalo shook his head to avoid passing out and scrambled to his knees... just in time to avoid another stab by the giant spike-lined forearms of the humongous foe. The buzzing was so much *louder* than before.

Another of Simon's arrows ineffectually bounced off the hard carapace of the monster and several stones from Dexter's sling did the same. The Captain managed to land a significant blow, but almost lost his life doing it! Buffalo was getting apprehensive... there was not a single person in this room that he was prepared to lose... but the giant Mantis was massive, wise, and skilled. It was just a matter of time before it managed to seize one of them in its formidable forepaws to make an instant meal of them! One by one, they would fall, for there was no way out of the arena and they would eventually tire or make a fatal mistake. That continual buzzing was becoming really intense... where was it *coming* from?

Buffalo looked up to the lofty ceiling, which was indeed the source of the buzzing sound... its centerpiece was the huge shallow dark-glass obsidian dome that covered the coliseum below. It was at least fifty yards across and craftily manufactured by skilled artisans utilizing thin translucent shards of volcanic glass in an intricate geometric design of many shades of gray, brown, and black. But right now, more importantly, were the vague shadows of many many darker forms, dozens of them, milling about *atop* the dome... with a significantly larger black one at the center! A wild idea suddenly struck Buffalo and he hollered for the group to all harry the Kontonquan God at once... and to be ready to take immediate refuge under the balconies on his command!

The Konton "rescue squad" began shouting and worrying the great Mantid from all sides, distracting it from Buffalo's unseen rear attack. Using a fallen bug skeleton as a vaulting-point, Buffalo managed to leap to the back of the giant Mantis's wings that covered its elongated abdomen. The folded wings were slippery and a Praying Mantis holds its body at a steep angle, so Buffalo used both his broadsword and Bowie knife like climber's axes, to prevent himself from sliding off, digging their points into the softer leather-like wings to gain purchase. Moving quickly, he managed to find his footing and climbed the back of the Mantis rapidly, making his way upward and forward to the moss-covered thorax. The big bug knew that something was going on upon its backside, but its attention was focused on the annoying group of crumbs that were busy evading its efforts to eat them! The buzzing was louder now that Buffalo was about half-way up the back of the giant Mantid... and the jeering of the Priesthood was too! Buffalo was on an even keel with the first large iron-protected balcony and the seated spectators were not at all happy with the turn of events within the coliseum! Many Priests were throwing stones and refuse, hoping to dislodge the surface-world offender.

Buffalo had to be quick to pull off his plan... if X'Poca's focus were turned on him for a moment and the behemoth decided to shake him off... or worse, reach back with it's formidable forelimbs and brush Buffalo from his feet... he most likely would not survive the fall. The huge head of the beast was now looming near... almost there. Buffalo was at mid-thorax, about four stories above the floor of the arena and level with the second tier of balconies. He just needed to get to the very top of the thorax, just behind the great green head.

Fortunately, with his crew harrying the Mantis from all sides, X'Poca stayed roughly in the middle of the arena, just where Buffalo wanted him. Three more steps to go and Buffalo got to the position he planned to, the top of the thorax's back panel, a small level spot where he was able to balance on the lip of the carapace directly behind the creature's head. Buffalo was now roughly five stories above the coliseum floor and about as high as he dared go. But from here, the great obsidian dome was only about twenty feet higher... and buzzing with activity!

"Good Lord..." thought Buffalo, "There must be hundreds of them!" The combined weight of the bodies on the other side of that antique dome were already making the bits of glass in their delicate framework creak and wobble. Buffalo just needed to add a catalyst to advance the situation.

Suddenly, the mammoth head of the Mantis swiveled around and Buffalo was startled to find himself staring directly into one huge glossy green eye of X'Poca! Buffalo could see his own reflection in the highly polished curved surface of the eye which fairly glowed with a lime-green essence contained within the orb. At the center of the eye was a fuzzy black mass that was the pupil, the point of cognizance that hinted at the intelligence of the brain behind the beast... and it suddenly narrowed as it focused on Buffalo's human form and became instantly suspicious of his intentions!

Buffalo knew he had to act before X'Poca did! "I win this round old fella!" he smirked... and Buffalo hurled his heavy broadsword up at the weakening obsidian skylight! The haft of the heavy sword smacked into the center of the ancient glass dome and chunks of obsidian flew from the strike... not a large amount of damage initially, but it was enough to begin the chain reaction Buffalo was hoping for. The great glass dome was crackling loudly and shards of obsidian glass were starting to pop and chip away from its underside!

X'Poca reached back with a lightning jab of its left pincher to grab the intruder perched behind its head, but Buffalo was no longer there. He was sliding down the Mantis's mossy back, using his Bowie knife like a rudder to try and stay in the middle and not slide off to either side! As he fell, he hollered, "Anya... Captain... everyone! Take cover under the balconies! Get behind some shelter... Quick!" Buffalo made it all the way down the Mantis's back and slid right off the tail-end of the giant predator's abdomen! The momentum of his descent actually made him soar through the air for several yards as he cleared the rear of the beast's body... and he hit the dirt of the arena floor hard and rolled to a position of safety, well under the overhang of the balcony above. Anya was hiding nearby and ran to be at Buffalo's side, making certain that he was not hurt and helping him to seek refuge behind a large bony carcass.

A great rending sound suddenly filled the coliseum and the ear-splitting shrill shriek of shattering glass was almost deafening! At the apex of the coliseum's roof, the huge ancient glass dome was buckling under the weight of the gathered insects on top if it. They were searching for entry into the room and Buffalo gave it to them. Almost as if in slow motion, the entire structure suddenly collapsed and came crashing down upon the head of the great God X'Poca! Obsidian is one of the sharpest natural materials known to man and it very easily fragments into razor-sharp slivers! Deadly jagged shards of volcanic glass were flying everywhere, bouncing from the bony carapace of the great Mantid's back and flying into the galleries above where screaming Priests were desperately making for the doorways, trying to flee the room!

Buffalo and his followers took refuge behind the rubble of old insect carcasses scattered about the walls as the ruins of the circular glass-frame cascaded to the floor of the coliseum in a tremendously loud shattering crash! The falling glass had done some serious damage to X'Poca on its way down... one eye was torn open and a glob of green goo was oozing from it. Obsidian shards were deeply embedded all over its exoskeleton and it had lost the use of two of its legs. Both of the great God's antennae were uselessly twitching in the dirt of the arena floor amongst the remains of the twisted dome and a rising cloud of dust. But the ancient God wasn't finished yet... or didn't realize it. The great God X'Poca bellowed in defiance, but its end was sealed by the even deadlier threat that now hovered in the air where the glass dome had recently been.

Bees... hundreds of very large Bumble Bees were effortlessly hovering in the newly opened hole in the great ceiling, awaiting their call to action after the collapse of the great dome. Waiting for the anticipated signal to attack from their even larger black leader hovering in the center of the swarm... Buffalo's bonded mount... Murk!

The loyal black Bee suddenly dropped from the center of the swarm and the rest of his horde followed in his wake. X'Poca, the Mantis God, as ancient and injured as he was, was still considerably dangerous... but his attempts to protect himself and defeat the Bumble Bee attack was futile. The room rapidly filled with hundreds of Bees and even though X'Poca lashed out many times, trying in vain to capture even one of them, the Bee's ability to hover and instantly shift position allowed them to easily avoid the Mantis's strikes and out maneuver the old insect deity.

Suddenly realizing that he had no hope of defending himself, the wily old Mantis attempted to retreat back through the huge wooden doors and into the safety of his lair... but the Bees were quick to act. Murk led the attack, flying under the Mantid's soft underbelly and rolling over in mid-flight to strike upwards with his stinger, injecting his lethal venom into the unprotected abdomen. Numerous Bees followed his example and soon the great Mantis started showing signs of defeat. The repeated injections of toxin were too much for the ancient beast and it stumbled as its remaining legs collapsed under it. Fatally poisoned, it fell flat to the floor of the coliseum, where it twitched in agony for a time, trying without success to right itself. Soon, the large head of the primeval God slumped to the ground... and the light of consciousness faded from its one remaining eye. X'Poca was no more.

Murk's army of Bees closed in and swarmed all over the fallen "God"... the spoils of war, while Murk, the enormous and singular black Bee, landed in the center of the arena and seemed to be frantically searching for something, scuttling back and forth in his efforts. When Buffalo and Anya

393

stood up from behind the shelter of the big skeleton carapace they were hiding behind, Murk zeroed in on Buffalo and ran over to him like a faithful pup!

Murk ran right up to Buffalo, face-to-face, and tapped his countenance with its deft antennae. "Yes... it's me, Murk!" laughed Buffalo. And Murk sidled up to the big man and received his just reward... a mighty hug from the human who had saved his life.

Anya stood wide-eyed and amazed. Her hero was *bonded* with one of the untamables? A giant black Bumble Bee? After a moments reflection she thought, "Why not? This brave intrepid warrior had continually made the impossible *possible* from the moment he arrived in Kontonqua. He even bested the great God X'Poca! What *couldn't* he do?"

"Buffalo?" said Anya softly, innocently, her admiring eyes as wide as they could be, "I... I could use a... hug... as well."

Buffalo turned to look into the dark gentle eyes of the jungle princess, the lithe barbarian savage that had been his mentor and traveling companion... the abducted daughter of a Queen he'd risked his life for... the lovely sweet and exotic *girl* he would *forever* risk his life for! She was reaching out to him... her inquisitive eyes were searching his. Buffalo uneasily managed to put his feelings into words, "I... I am yours, Anya... always, if you'll have me. I... I *love* you!" confessed the giant surface-world castaway.

Relief washed across the face of the recent captive and she smiled that winsome smile that had won Buffalo's heart from the beginning, "Men of the surface-world must be terribly shy or very oblivious," she playfully teased, "What took you so long?"

When the others... Simon, Max, Dexter, and the Captain... left the safety of their respective hiding places, they saw Anya in the arms of their friend and protector, Buffalo, standing by a huge black Bee and exchanging a most passionate kiss. When Buffalo heard their excited giggling, he withdrew somewhat and blushed... but Anya would have none of that, she put her hand upon his rugged jaw and guided his lips back to hers.

Chapter 26
"The Heroes Return"

A short while later, Buffalo guided Murk to a gentle landing outside the Temple where the little Konton rescue party had left their ebony ant-flyers. Anya sat astride Murk directly behind the big bearded pilot... and the Captain had been right behind her, but he was now sliding from his perch and through the black fuzz of Murk's hairy thorax to the ground. Max, Simon, and Dexter were already there. Murk was such a strong flyer that Buffalo had been able to fly all three at once up and out of the coliseum, back through the hole where the obsidian dome had been. He hated to leave Anya even for the few brief minutes it took to fly the kids out of the temple, but he knew the Captain would not allow anything further to happen to her. And with the multitude of the Bee swarm still in attendance, making short work of the Mantis's remains, Buffalo was pretty sure that the Priesthood minions wouldn't dare to enter the arena until they'd all gone!

Without delay, they were all presently astride their respective warrior steeds and airborne once again and heading home to Konton. Buffalo felt a warm thrill of happiness... mostly because of their great success, winning the day... but also because Anya, the girl who had won his heart, was nuzzling her face into his back while hugging him tightly with her strong slender brown arms. The Captain expertly led them directly back the way they had come and Buffalo again marveled at his ability to pick out the smallest landmarks by which to navigate. Buffalo intended that he too would soon have the opportunity to explore the vastness of the cavern and become familiar with the minutiae of

Kontonquan terrain just as well. For he planned to fly with Murk a lot, he loved it so... and he had little doubt he would soon know his way around as though he'd always been here.

Upon arriving back at Konton, the rescuers did several "victory" laps around the throne room and esplanade of the city to show off their "prize"... Anya. She waved to the gathering throngs of citizens that were pouring into the promenade, turning out in great numbers to see the return of their beloved Kwa-Ia! When at last they landed their mounts in the main training arena of the Serpent Guard, the Queen Mother was already there awaiting them. As was a very happy hound... Jeep!

The Queen was obviously struggling with her feelings. She was at once happy with the return of her daughter... but quite concerned with Buffalo's interference in the affairs of the Priesthood. The Priesthood exerted considerable influence on her and her people. To anger them might make for difficult, if not devastating, times ahead. Despite her love for her daughter, she had been quite prepared to sacrifice her for the benefit of her colony... her people.

However, when she was informed of the particular events of the rescue... and found out that Prince Bik-cu' and his guard were actually *there*...in force, she became furious. Bik-cu'... within the temple itself! That was a presence that would *never* have been allowed by the former Priesthood Elders under any circumstances. It was a development that was both suspicious and malicious... she realized for the first time that Bik-cu' and the Priesthood had to have been working in secret against her! Entrance into the Temple by other than the Priests was not tolerated. For *Bik-cu'* to be allowed within the walls smacked of collusion and subterfuge, a devious partnership that could only suggest ill tidings towards Konton!

The Queen Mother bristled with anger at learning of this deceitful affiliation going on behind her back. She was subsequently relieved to hear of the death of Prince Bik-cu'... but still decided that perhaps it was time she and her army of Serpent Guards paid a visit to the Temple of X'Poca. The Exalted Leader of the Priesthood had some explaining to do.

There was a grand celebration for the return of Kwa-I-Anya that lasted a full week! During the merriment, Buffalo and the kids settled back into life within their pleasant little apartment... but with the addition of Murk, who now pretty much slept upon their doorstep, never at ease to be too far distant from his friend and savior, Buffalo. It had certain advantages in that it kept all but the most serious visitors from approaching their door!

Buffalo courted Anya in earnest and spent six months following the proper protocols of a fitting Kontonquan suitor to win her hand in marriage. Although it was all just a formality, since Buffalo and Anya had professed their love that day in the Temple coliseum - - and knew in their hearts that they belonged together... forever. Marriage was just a legal convenience, a matter of ceremony. Still, the ensuing wedding and celebration was one that the populace of Konton would never forget. It lasted weeks and was so lavish it became a lively entry into the history books of the Kontonquan chronicle.

Each of the kids, Max, Simon, and Dexter continued their education and even more importantly to them, their combat proficiencies. They became quite the talk of the mound-city and their assistance in matters dealing with the Ikusks, who were now leaderless and became an unpredictable tribe of ruthless marauders, was greatly needed and appreciated. Buffalo and the kids often flew with the Serpent Guard on missions of importance and had several harrowing adventures... but those will be left for another telling.

Dexter took it upon himself to write a memoir of all the events that led to their present situation - - from the crash of their Christmas transport, to the rescue of Anya from the grasp of the deadly Mantis, the "God" of the cavern... X'Poca. He interviewed each of his fellow "castaways" for their remembrances and personal stories, their opinions and point-of-view of events. He painstakingly recorded it all in a large insect-"leather" bound volume and procured a large glass jug from the marketplace.

Buffalo and his friends were a bit confused at first by what Dexter intended to do with the large tome he had compiled. Not to mention the jug. But when he explained his plan, they stood and just stared for a moment as the possibilities raced through their minds and then grinning with joy, they hooted and congratulated him on his most excellent idea! They *could* be rescued... it *was* possible! Dexter had found a way that just might work! Buffalo... Simon... Max... all of them... and especially, the lost tribes of Kontonqua might yet see the light of day!

There you have it. The entire sequence of events... at least, as best as everyone can remember them! I realize that it's almost too difficult to comprehend and believe all that has befallen us, but that is why I have written this book. And as proof, you hold it in your hands before you, do you not?

We will place the book within a large jug sealed with bees' wax, courtesy of Murk's hive, and tie it onto a raft of some sort, and set it adrift in the River Tonqua, near the south wall. If my theory is correct, the jug and raft will be dragged over the falls within the Temple of X'Poca and sucked into another underground stream, and hopefully emerge somewhere soon at the earth's surface.

It is now, by my rough calculations, May 16th, 1954… almost three-and-a-half years since we arrived in this strange and wonderful paradise that imprisons us. Please let our relatives and the world know of our fate. Do not forget us. And, if at all possible, try to arrange for our rescue. In the meantime, we will await within…

Epilogue

As Steven's eyes reached the end of that last sentence, his mind froze in its focus and he sat stock-still, as though time itself had stopped. His brain was racing - - trying to comprehend the enormity of the saga he'd just experienced. A chill ran through him and he suddenly realized that his jaw was hanging slack, his mouth agape. He blinked and took a slow deep breath as he gazed up to see the setting sun hovering on the horizon. Darkness was beginning to creep upon the still lagoon and the ever-present gulls and seabirds were settling into secluded roosts for the night. Evening crabs were scuttling about in the fringes of the surf.

"They're still *down* there...?" Steven muttered, somewhat unsure of what to believe. What had he just read? The factual account of four hopelessly lost people, trapped far below the Earth's crust in an antediluvian cavern populated with beasts and terrors beyond the comprehension of modern man? Or just the ramblings of some lunatic writer raving on about a fabricated fantasy-world populated only by his own fictitious and wild imaginings? Could it all be a crazy hoax? But then why the leather bound book? The jug and the raft? How to explain *their* existence? The pieces didn't fit in any way other than to confirm, in Steven's mind, the total authenticity of the tale contained within the pages of the long-submerged tome that had occupied his afternoon.

He gazed down upon the large handcrafted journal and thought about the events it had just narrated to him. "They *are* down there!" Steven whispered to himself with total conviction. He looked again at Dexter's last few lines. Sure... it made sense. Dexter had just forgotten to factor in the added weight of the water once the logs of the raft absorbed enough seawater to counter the buoyancy of the air-filled jug. He was correct in his basic assumptions at least. The jug *had* traveled through an underground waterway, probably much like the one that had brought the four castaways to the lost cavern of Kontonqua in the first place.

Somewhere, that tunnel had emptied into the sea... very likely from the seafloor itself. After bobbing to the surface, the raft-bound jug probably floated along, following the ocean's currents until it *almost* made landfall, right here in the Bahamas. Unfortunately, just as the jug cleared the reef, its waterlogged vessel, instead of delivering it to safety, most likely dragged it to the bottom of the lagoon where it stuck fast between the fingerlike branches of coral and eventually became encrusted and glued to the bottom with each year's growth of living reef.

Steven gently closed the covers of the delicately bound leather volume that resided in his lap. What to do now? He heard the familiar drone of his grandfather's car as it pulled into the driveway on the far side of the bungalow. He was both excited and uncertain about revealing his find to them... about sharing the fantastic adventure that had enthralled and engulfed him. *He* was certain of the book's authenticity and the artifacts themselves: the leathery book, the jug, the remnants of rope and beeswax were proof positive of the plight of the four lost souls in the cavern beneath the world.

But... what would his grandparents have to say about it all? How would they react to the evidence and cry for help that had washed to their shore? People always seem to greet extraordinary events with skepticism and disbelief. If his grandparents were to dismiss the facts as fantasy, would he be dooming Dexter and the others to a life of isolation far below?

Steven rose with the book under his arm as he heard the muffled double-thuds of car doors being shut. He turned to head for the quiet bungalow that would soon brighten with light at the flick of a switch and come alive with the return of its owners, laughing, talking, and preparing their evening meal. Already, he heard his grandmother calling out his name.

He would show them the book after dinner. And he and his grandparents would pore over the story once more. And he would trust them to believe... and then help him to get the story out and take action; to gain succor for all the trapped peoples of Kontonqua. Not alone for Buffalo, Anya, and the rest of the castaways, but for Anya's people of Konton... and the Ikusks as well, despite their depravity. This book had fallen into his hands for a reason. It was now his responsibility, his quest, to make certain that all those entombed within the cavern be brought back home... to once again experience the light and warmth of the sun.

This morning, Steven was a bored teenager vaguely wishing for the return of his school-year routine... this evening, he was a man with a mission: *They must be saved!*

STORY GLOSSARY

Alowa-tay: Daytime.

Akt'Ju-ana: Worker ants.

Akt'Ki-hautl: Warrior flying ants.

Akt'Lowatay: Small ants that attend the light-emitting lichens.

Akt'TakKwa: The ant Queen.

Aktz: General name for the ants.

Amak: Hairy purple gelatinous fruits.

Bik-cu': Prince and leader of the Ikusk tribe.

Chinotonk: Large lake along the river Tonqua situated almost in the middle of Kontonqua.

Clekweg: Native name for Tiger Beetle.

Dujong: Green leathery "cantaloupe-sized" edible starchy pods.

Ikusk: "The Unclean Ones" -- Splinter tribe of Kontonqua... sworn enemies of Konton. Name literally means "carnivores".

Ikuskqua: Crumbling fortress cliff-side city of the Ikusk.

Ixtl: Native name for insects.

Jin-Jin: Kontonquan Martial Art practiced by the women of Konton as a last measure to defend themselves and the city from invasion. Also, the sisterhood of those trained and accepted.

Kexl-huat: Native name for Ground Wasp.

Konksihautl: Native name for Earwig.

Kontonqua: Native name for huge underground cavern land, their tribe, and their language.

Konton: Fortress mound-city of original inhabitants of cavern.

Kwa-Ia: A Royal Daughter, princess... also: Kwa-I (as in Kwa-I-Anya).

Lowa-tay: The light-emitting lichens of the Kontonquan cavern. (**Alowa-tay** for daylight, **Nalowa-tay** for night).

Muh-ko-Natak: The warrior scout that saved the tribe from doom within the cave of Beringia.

Mu-ah'nahi: Temple of the Moon.

Na: No.

Nalowa-tay: Nightime.

Nu-akka: A large plant that distributes thousands of floating seed-pods, similar to dandelions.

Paxui: Iridescent Scarab Beetle carapace flakes used as money.

Qua: Home.

Su-ah'nahi: Temple of the Sun.

Tak-Ia: A Royal Son, prince… also: Tak-I (as in Tak-I-Tsuji).

Takka: Jungle (informal).

TakKwa: Mother, Queen, and Jungle (formal).

Tak'Tonqua: The mouth of the river Tonqua.

Tay: Light.

Tikquan: Plant with bulbous root used for cleansing.

Tonqua: The river that runs through the cavern.

Tsil-se-Ulkul: Konton Dragon Captain held prisoner by the Ikusk.

Tuak-ah'nahi: The combined Temples of the Sun and Moon at the collapsed fissure. Also the name of the yearly holiday.

Va-Aktom: Traitor overheard in "The Hall of Unveiling" in 2862.

X'Poca: Kontonquan name for God and the temple city of the Priesthood. Specifically, the "Ancient One" that resides in the Temple of X'Poca.

X'Poca-tay: The Priesthood of Kontonqua. Literally: Light of God.

Yiei: Yes.

Children's Books published by Ron Zalme

What Did Toby See?
Written and illustrated by Ron Zalme
An online book available free at www.ronzalme.com

Where Did Toby Go?
Written and illustrated by Ron Zalme
A print-on-demand book available at
www.Amazon.com

The Cardboard King & The Sparkle Queen
Written by Letty Case and illustrated by Ron Zalme
A print-on-demand book available at
www.Amazon.com

Over 50 other titles, illustrated by Ron Zalme,
but published by other major publishing houses
are currently available at www.Amazon.com,
www.BN.com and most major book stores.

11048482R00244